Praise for M.J. Ford

'Superb, gritty and realistic.'
Mel Sherratt, million-copy bestseller

'Well written and sizzling with tension. A cracking debut.'
James Nally, author of *Games With the Dead*

'A fabulous, page-turning thriller.'
Jacqui Rose, author of *Toxic*

'I absolutely loved this well written, riveting debut mystery and would have happily given it far more than five stars. I really hope this is the first book in a new series and look forward to reading more books by this author in the future.'
Goodreads reviewer

'*Hold My Hand* is an absolutely brilliant debut novel from a very talented author. It has an elaborate plot which is both convincing and exciting, with twists and turns, an unbelievably scary and thrilling conclusion. . . in fact, everything I want from a crime thriller.'
NetGalley reviewer

'A unique plot and storyline – I enjoyed the book immensely. It really makes you think.'
Goodreads reviewer

'Spectacularly assured.'
Amazon reviewer

'Excellent, and incredibly compelling.
I didn't want to put it down!'
Amazon reviewer

'A belter of a crime novel!'
Amazon reviewer

'Very atmospheric, with acute observations,
and full of twists and turns. Great characterisation.'
Amazon reviewer

ABOUT THE AUTHOR

M.J. Ford lives with his wife and family on the edge of the Peak District in the north of England. He has worked as an editor and writer of children's fiction for many years. His debut novel, *Hold My Hand*, was published in 2018. *Keep Her Close* is his second crime book. You can follow Michael @MJFordBooks.

By the same author:

Hold My Hand

Keep Her Close

M.J. FORD

avon.

Published by AVON
A division of HarperCollins*Publishers* Ltd
1 London Bridge Street
London SE1 9GF

www.harpercollins.co.uk

A Paperback Original 2019

1

A catalogue copy of this book is available from the British Library.

ISBN: 978-0-00-829377-2

Set in Bembo Std 11.5/13.5 pt by Palimpsest Book Production Limited,
Falkirk, Stirlingshire

Printed and bound in UK by CPI Group (UK) Ltd, Croydon CR0 4YY

This book is produced from independently certified FSC™ paper
to ensure responsible forest management.

For more information visit: www.harpercollins.co.uk/green

For Mum and Dad.

Chapter 1

WEDNESDAY

Dr Forster kept a box of tissues on the table, and for the last five weeks Detective Jo Masters had managed not to reach for a single one. It had become a point of principle during their sessions, a way of telling herself she was above all this. So she'd remained stubbornly dry-eyed through all five sixty-minute meetings, even though they'd touched on plenty of painful subjects, personal and professional – her relationships with her parents, her brother, her colleagues, her aspirations, and her fears. And Ben, of course. Lots of Ben. The psychologist was surgical at times, probing with questions that slipped almost unfelt, like a scalpel blade into the deepest recesses of her past, exposing places, incidents, and people she hadn't thought about for years.

People like Frank Tyndle. It was just another anecdote, an incident early in her relationship with Ben – and she'd managed to deflect the conversation the first time he'd come up. She wasn't sure why Dr Forster was returning to it now, so near the end of their allotted time together. It was almost like she knew there was a weakness there, something to be excised.

'I thought we'd covered Tyndle already,' said Jo, nonchalantly.

'Not really,' said Dr Forster. She checked back through the pad of notes on her lap. 'You mentioned him, in our first session, when we were discussing your miscarriage. You said something about karma, but we ran out of time. Do you believe in karma?'

The counsellor looked up, her expression quizzical. Jo was ninety per cent sure Dr Forster's brown frizzy hair was a wig, maybe as a result of cancer treatment. What was certain was that she'd drawn her eyebrows on a fraction too high, making her look perpetually curious.

'It's just something people say, isn't it?'

'I don't know,' replied Dr Forster. 'Is it?'

Jo sneaked a look at the minimalist clock-face on the wall. Twelve-forty. They had twenty minutes left, and so far Dr Forster had shown herself to be assiduous with her time-keeping.

'Tyndle was a nasty piece of work,' she began. *A wrong'un from the start,* as her friend Harry Ferman would have said. 'He ran the largest drug gang in Kent, and he was untouchable. The investigating team had bugs on all his known locations, but he was careful. Mostly. Had a temper, though. We got a break when one of his lieutenants, a guy called Jon Ruffell, nicknamed Rusty, tried to take over and failed. Tyndle went ballistic, and the listening device picked up that he was going to shoot the kneecaps off Rusty's sister. We knew he had access to firearms, so it was credible.'

'Go on,' said Forster.

Jo took a sip of water. 'The problem was the investigating team didn't have an address for Jon Ruffell's sister. The tribunal later said that was a failure of intelligence, but that's easy with hindsight. Ben and I were just back-up, so the plan was for us to follow Tyndle and direct the firearms to come to us. We knew it was going to be a close call.' Christ, she'd been scared. She'd thought Ben was too, but he hadn't shown it and would never admit it. He could be like that in an argument too. Just switch off. 'Our orders from the co-ordinating officer were clear. We were observing and tracking only. Now there was a gun in the equation, anything more was deemed an unnecessary risk. Ben knew it too. He didn't believe in heroes.'

It came back to her in spikes of adrenalin that made her skin tingle. From the moment they'd been in pursuit, she'd been thinking about the end game. What would they do if the firearms didn't get there in time? If Tyndle reached Joanne Ruffell's address first? How could they stop him?

'Tyndle must've made us for police, even in plain clothes, because suddenly he detoured. Pulled a U-turn through traffic, and sped off the other way. We followed. I was all for calling it off, discontinuing pursuit, but Ben had that look in his eyes. He said Tyndle was armed and that now he knew he was busted, he was too dangerous to leave on the street.'

'And did you agree?' Dr Forster's interruption made Jo focus on her.

'Ben was my superior.'

'That isn't what I asked,' said Dr Forster. Jo had noticed the counsellor liked to have her questions answered. She could be steely like that.

'I tossed it up the chain,' said Jo. 'And it came back in the affirmative. We were to stay in pursuit, blues on, in the hope Tyndle would think again. They just didn't want that gun on the streets, in Tyndle's hands, under any circumstances. They'd found the sister's address, but the armed response was re-routing to us. Parameters hadn't changed. We weren't to engage directly with Tyndle.'

Jo wondered if the doctor actually had access to the hearing papers and this was some sort of test. It was all in there, in the transcripts and statements. They only told half the story though. Such operational tactics looked fine on paper, but on the ground it could get . . . complicated. There were split-second decisions to be made.

'I remember we were doing close to ninety on an urban A-road, cutting through traffic. I trusted Ben behind the wheel. That was part of the training. And he was *good*. Then the lights went red ahead. The junction wasn't busy. And Tyndle wasn't braking. I shouted for Ben to stop. I think I did. But I can't blame him for not listening. If I'd outranked him, maybe he would have. He was single-minded. Tyndle was armed, and we couldn't let an armed suspect escape.' She paused, her mouth dry, and drained the rest of the water from her glass. The next bit was the hardest part to relive, and she'd never spelled it out to anyone before. 'The ambulance was suddenly there, right in front of us. It apparently had its sirens on, but I didn't hear it. There was no way Tyndle could've swerved. His bonnet caught the rear end of the ambulance, spun it round and up onto two wheels. Then it went over. Metal ripping. Sparks everywhere. Like something out of an action film, but a lot more real. Horrible, really. It slid up a bank, hit a tree.'

She remembered Ben pulling over, looking at her, and asking if she was okay. She'd thought that was odd, because *she* was fine.

'Training took over. I called an ambulance – another one. We got out of the car. I saw Tyndle in the road. No seatbelt, it seemed, so he'd gone straight through the windscreen. Ben told me to leave him. To prioritise. While he went to secure the firearm, I made my way to the ambulance. The paramedic was climbing out through the driver's window.' He'd been bleeding, and obviously dazed, dragging a leg with the foot kinked up at the wrong angle, enough to make her retch. 'The poor guy just said, "In the back". I left Ben with him and circled to the rear doors. I couldn't hear anything inside. The mechanism must've got stuck in the collision, because I couldn't get the fucking thing open. In the end, a guy came out from the pub across the junction. He brought a fireman's axe – Christ knows where he got it – and together we managed to use the head to lever the doors.'

She tried to drink again, but there was nothing in the glass.

'Would you like some more water?' asked Dr Forster.

Jo shook her head. She wished she'd never started the story, but she knew she couldn't leave it hanging. In her mind, the images were fresh.

'The other paramedic must've been travelling with the patient,' she continued quietly. 'He was on the floor, unconscious. The patient – a woman – she was pressed against the wall, still strapped into the stretcher which had gone over.' Jo remembered her face. The utter disbelief. 'She was talking . . . well, mumbling really. She was in a night-dress, hitched up around her waist. I . . . I got inside, trying to work out what to do. Who to help first. There was so much blood. My shoes were slipping in it. I mean, fucking *pints* of it. More than you'd think a person could lose, you know? I went to her, and then I realised what it was she was saying, over and over again, gripping her stomach. She was saying "My baby . . . my baby . . . my baby", like her brain was stuck on some kind of short circuit.'

Jo fell silent, so lost in the memories of almost ten years before that she didn't even realise Dr Forster had stood up to offer her a tissue. Jo took it, and wiped her eyes.

'She miscarried the foetus?' asked the counsellor, sitting back once more.

In any other person, Jo would have deemed the tone insensitive, but she'd grown accustomed to the psychologist's sometimes blunt questioning and exact use of language. Indeed, when everyone else around Jo spoke in euphemisms and platitudes about her last case – *your ordeal, the incident, that night* – it was actually refreshing to have a dose of the psychiatrist's candour. She'd have made a good detective, Jo thought. No bullshit.

'Yes,' she said, screwing up the tissue. 'They rushed her to hospital and tried to deliver by emergency C-section, but nothing could be done.'

Dr Forster leant forward slightly. 'That must have been very upsetting.'

Jo glanced at the clock again. Officially there were seven minutes remaining of their designated hour together.

'Of course,' she said. For a long time, she'd blamed herself. Nightmares, insomnia, anxiety. It had been Ben who helped her heal.

'And what happened to Frank Tyndle?'

'He got eighteen years for the drugs and firearms offences.'

'And for the death of the foetus in utero?'

Jo shook her head. She hadn't been in court – by then she'd been moved on to Hertfordshire, for the start of her investigative training on the road to becoming a detective. 'The woman had been on the way to hospital because of breach complications anyway. Hence the dash with the blues on. The prosecution couldn't prove the baby would have survived in normal circumstances, so they couldn't pin the death on Tyndle.'

'What did Ben think of that?'

He'd been spitting feathers, she remembered, and it had kindled a long and almost personal hatred of defence barristers.

'With eighteen years, there was a chance Tyndle could be out in half the time,' said Jo. 'Not that he was in much of a state to enjoy life. Going through the windscreen took most of his face off. Severe lacerations to the bone.'

Dr Forster cocked her head, completely unfazed. *You wouldn't be if you'd seen him . . .*

'Karma, perhaps?' said the counsellor.

'Ben thought so,' muttered Jo. 'Said he deserved everything he got.'

Neither of them spoke for at least thirty seconds. Jo looked at the screwed-up tissue in her hands. *So much for holding it together . . .*

Dr Forster put aside her writing pad, and placed her hands on her knees, looking at Jo like she was a rare specimen.

'Do you blame yourself for what happened to Ben later?' she asked.

With four minutes until the session ended, the question took Jo by surprise, telescoping time from the earliest days of her relationship with Ben to the final, terrible day when he was killed. It wasn't like she hadn't asked herself the same thing, or a version of it, a thousand times though. What if they hadn't argued that night? What if she hadn't left him alone and headed upstairs? What if she'd made the connections and arrested a suspect more quickly? Any number of minor actions on her part and he would still be alive.

'No,' she said firmly. 'I blame Dylan Jones.'

With the words came the memories: Ben, collapsed on her brother's kitchen floor, eyes still open but pupils dilated; the jagged edge of a broken wine bottle buried in his neck.

'What about Dylan, then?' asked the psychologist. 'Did he deserve his fate?'

What sort of a question was that? Dylan was abducted as a shy little boy and turned into a monster through neglect. He'd committed terrible, terrible acts, but they all came as a consequence of his mistreatment. There was no karma there. No justice at all, cosmic, legal, or otherwise.

'I think he was better off dead, after everything that had happened to him,' said Jo.

'A mercy killing?' said Dr Forster. This time the surprise on her face looked real as well as painted on.

'Maybe,' said Jo, meeting her eye. In the end, there'd been no choice. Dylan had tried to kill Jo. It had been him or her.

One minute to go until she could leave. Dr Forster saw her glance at the clock.

'It must be hard in your job,' the psychologist said.

It was not a question but a comment, and such a vague one that Jo wondered if she was supposed to respond. What did it even mean, anyway? Being a woman in a predominantly man's world?

'Lots of jobs are hard. Isn't yours?'

Dr Forster gave a rare smile. 'It has challenges. Challenging patients. But you must see the worst in human nature. Awful things.'

'That's why we do it,' said Jo. 'To make awful things better. To deliver justice.'

'And when you can't – how does that make you feel?'

'Part of the role,' said Jo. 'You move on. Do better next time.'

'Sounds simple.' The tone wasn't exactly sarcastic, but there was a degree of challenge there that Jo didn't entirely like.

The clock chimed.

'I guess that's it, then,' said Jo, standing up.

Chapter 2

As Jo took her winter coat from the stand in the vestibule, Dr Forster emerged from the consulting room. She really was a tiny woman, little more than five feet tall, and away from her chair she looked quite fragile.

'Detective Masters,' she said, 'the Welfare Unit mandated six hours as a minimum, but I'd be keen for you to continue. I feel there's quite a lot more for us to talk about.'

Jo wasn't sure that she agreed. Really, she felt she'd spent plenty of time in the past.

'But it's my choice?'

'Thames Valley Police will ask me for a recommendation, but ultimately it is your decision,' She paused. 'But . . . Jo, don't play down what you went through. And don't underestimate the impact it could have on you psychologically.'

Jo started to put on her coat, trying to hold back the mental images from the previous case assailing her. Ben's dead body, his throat slashed. Her nephew William's terrified screams as he was snatched from his bed. The pale, distorted form of Dylan Jones as he tried to strangle her.

'I won't,' she said. 'This has been really helpful, but I just want to get back to work properly.'

'I understand that,' said Dr Forster. 'How are you faring with the anxiety medication?'

'I stopped taking it,' Jo said. There was no reason to lie.

'Fair enough,' said Forster. 'Are you doing anything nice for your birthday?'

Jo glanced up sharply. It wasn't for a few days, but she was sure she'd never mentioned it. 'How did you know?'

'On your file,' said Dr Forster. 'I've an eye for detail.'

'The answer is not much,' said Jo. 'Thirty-nine is hardly a big one, is it?'

'After the year you've had, that's a questionable assertion,' said Dr Forster. 'Goodbye, Detective Masters. Look after yourself.'

* * *

The grand Georgian house where Dr Forster had her practice rooms was in the leafiest part of north Oxford, between the Woodstock and Banbury roads. It didn't take much detective work to establish that the sleek Mercedes coupé parked outside belonged to her, as the number plate read **F0RST3R**. That level of narcissism seemed rather out of character for the diminutive psychologist, and Jo assumed therefore it had been an ill-conceived gift, perhaps from a partner.

As she wrapped her scarf around her neck against a freezing wind, Jo felt the vibration near her hip. She reached a gloved hand into her purse for her phone. The text was from her brother.

Would you mind heading to the house? Estate agent has lost key! Viewing at 1.30. P x

It was twenty to already.

No probs, she texted back. *How's the beach?*

Her brother had decided the family needed some time away, and Jo got that. For all the shit she'd been through that year, her nephew Will had suffered worse, and his school hadn't put up a great fight about the absence. Not that ten days of winter sun would go far to erase the mental scars of being taken from his bed by Dylan Jones, a man raised in isolation and depravity, who looked like something from a horror movie.

Her phone pinged as a picture message came through. It was a selfie of Paul, tanned and healthy, seated at some poolside bar with what looked like a strawberry daiquiri, ornately garnished with a pineapple slice and a Jamaican flag.

Not jealous, she replied, pocketing her phone and pulling on her gloves.

And really, she wasn't. Much. Though the thought of the sun on her face was appealing. It was quite some time since she'd had a proper break. In fact, the last prolonged period of annual leave had been Padua with Ben, about fifteen months ago. A top-floor apartment overlooking some piazza or other, a warm Mediterranean breeze tickling the blinds, the muffled chatter of the restaurant customers below. Afterwards, they'd calculated it was during the holiday that she'd conceived. Ben had even suggested that Padua would be an acceptable name if it turned out to be a girl.

'Enough, Josephine,' she muttered to herself.

She drove back out of Oxford towards Horton, the village where she'd grown up and where Paul, until recently, had occupied the family home with his wife and two children. Maybe she needed to talk to Lucas about going away. They'd been together almost six months, so a holiday wasn't moving too fast. Somewhere hot preferably. Sandy. Cocktails (virgin for teetotal Lucas, obviously). Somewhere free from the bloody footprints of the dead. Lucas preferred winter sports, but surely he could be coaxed onto a windsurfing board. The estate agents selling her brother's house – The Rookery – were under strict instructions to drive potential viewers in from the other end of the crescent. It seemed a rather pointless subterfuge to Jo – they'd find out soon enough what had happened nearby at Sally Carruthers' 'House of Horrors', as the papers had called it.

Jo pulled up outside to find the estate agent and a couple already waiting. She climbed out of her car and apologised, then scrambled for the key to let them in.

'It's a beautiful house,' said the young woman.

'Oh – it's not mine,' said Jo quickly, as they walked inside. 'My brother's on holiday.' She let the estate agent past as well, then turned to go. 'I'll leave you to it?'

'Do you have to rush off?' he said. 'I'm sure Mr and Mrs Daley might have some questions.'

'Oh . . . sure,' said Jo, with little enthusiasm. She followed them in. The house was immaculate inside – Amelia had hired professional cleaners to keep on top of things while they rented in central Oxford. Most of the furniture had been moved out already. There'd never really been any question of them staying here, not after what had happened just a stone's throw from the end of the back garden. The heating was on, but Jo resisted taking off her coat. The sooner she could be on her way again, the better.

'I'll take you upstairs first,' said the estate agent. 'Save the best parts until the end!'

Jo waited in the entrance hall while the estate agent led the Daleys to the first floor. She heard various exclamations of surprise and delight as they inspected the bedrooms, the family bathroom, and as they came downstairs, both were smiling. They checked the living room, the study, and the under-stairs cupboard before going to the kitchen.

'Oh wow!' said the woman.

Jo drifted in behind them. From the slight tension in the estate agent's face, Jo guessed he'd been fully briefed on the background to the marketing of The Rookery. The brutal murder of Detective Ben Coombs, not ten feet from where they all stood. The kidnapping of William Masters, her six-year-old nephew, from the upstairs bedroom by a psychopath. With a vague smile pasted across her features, Jo found her eyes drifting to the island, wondering if the cleaners had missed even the tiniest spot of blood. Dylan had plunged the broken bottle right through Ben's carotid. The coroner said he'd probably lost consciousness in a matter of seconds. He'd have known that was it, thought Jo, and it brought the sudden threat of tears to her eyes, which she surreptitiously blinked away.

The Daleys, though, were oblivious. 'The light in here is amazing!' said the man, gazing up at the glass panes of the orangerie-style extension.

'And those bi-folds open right onto the garden,' said the woman. She touched her stomach as she said it, and Jo wondered if she was pregnant, imagining her children gambolling in and out of the kitchen in a scene of domestic bliss. Or maybe they already had kids. A house this size didn't make sense for a couple.

Jo looked briefly out of the back herself. The branches of the trees at the bottom of the garden were bare, giving a view out towards the fields. Sally Carruthers' barn, where she and her husband had kept Dylan Jones for three decades, had been levelled, leaving a bare patch of earth. She looked at her watch. An hour until her shift started.

'I'm sorry,' she said. 'I really must be going.'

'That's all right,' said Mrs Daley. 'I think we might do another circuit.' She looked to her husband, who nodded happily.

'Shall I draw up the paperwork now then?' asked the agent, with a cocky smile. 'Only kidding . . . take some time to think about it.'

'Have you had many other viewings?' asked the young man.

The briefest pause. 'A few, yes. But I happen to know the vendors would entertain any offers, even if under the guide price.'

You bet they would, thought Jo. She wondered about the logic of not being completely honest with the potential buyers. These days, even though the survey wouldn't explicitly say 'Someone was murdered in the kitchen six months ago', a perfunctory search of the address online would bring up a host of news stories laying out the gory details. She even considered telling them herself. Imagine if they moved in, *then* found out . . .

The estate agent was giving her a wary look as if he could read her discomfort. Offloading The Rookery would probably garner some serious kudos in the sales office. Three per cent well earned.

'Nice to meet you both,' she said.

The woman frowned. 'Sorry, do I know you from somewhere?' she asked.

Maybe the front pages of the Oxford Times *and most of the national press?* She'd been variously described as a 'Hero Detective', 'Brave Policewoman', and in one of the tabloids, 'The Clown Killer'. Thames Valley Police had insisted on a photo shoot, much to Jo's dismay. Another attempt to polish her up for public consumption. To 'control the message', as the media officer had said repeatedly.

Jo shook her head. 'I don't think so.' She bid the Daleys goodbye, and breathed a sigh of relief to be back at the front door. She decided then and there that she'd never visit the house again.

'You can keep my key,' she called to the estate agent.

She drove away, taking the longer route to avoid Sally's bungalow.

* * *

She wondered about dropping in to see her mother at the nursing home. It had been only a couple of days since her last visit, and that hadn't gone brilliantly. Mrs Masters had made accusations that staff had helped themselves to some money she had squirrelled away at the back of a drawer. She had insisted that Jo find the culprit, which left her with the unenviable task of mediating between the staff and her mother. In the end a compromise had been reached. From then on, all of Jo's mum's petty cash would be documented, and stored in the home's safe.

Jo took the bypass out towards Wheatley. The issue with the money was a minor awkwardness, because otherwise, reconnection with her mum had been an unexpected joy. In her lucid moments, they talked about Dad and happier times. Madeleine Masters had no idea of the ordeal her family had undergone that year. It wasn't even a conscious decision not to tell her, more a tacit understanding that the news would unlikely penetrate the thick fog of dementia anyway. There'd been some worry that Will himself might bring it up – after all, he was only six, and could hardly be expected to maintain the family subterfuge – but so far he hadn't. Unsurprisingly, he wasn't keen to relive any of that night. Even with his trauma therapist, he was apparently silent on the subject, preferring to focus discussions on his latest passion: astronauts.

Jo reached the home – Evergreen Lodge – and pulled in along the tree-lined drive. She normally brought flowers or chocolates, but she didn't think her mum would care. Most the sweets went in a cupboard, to be dished out to staff anyway, and the flowers always wilted in the overheated atmosphere of the residents' rooms. At the door, she was about to press the buzzer when her phone rang. It was St Aldates station.

'What's up?' she answered.

'You busy?' said DI Andy Carrick.

Jo looked through the reinforced glass panel. Mrs Deekins was sitting in her normal spot in the corridor, staring at the opposite wall. She could almost smell the place already. Overcooked food, disinfectant, sadness. Radiators cranked to max.

'Not especially.'

'Head over to Oriel College,' said Carrick.

'What is it?' asked Jo.

'Missing person,' said Carrick. 'Signs of a struggle. A student called . . .' he paused, and Jo guessed he was checking his notes, 'Malin Sigurdsson.'

'You there already?'

'Division meeting,' sighed Carrick. 'Pryce is on his way though.'

'Course he is,' said Jo with a smile. 'I'll be about fifteen minutes.'

She returned to the car, wondering what awaited at Oriel. Missing people were reported several times a week. Most showed up within forty-eight hours, and unless it was a minor, the police rarely got involved. But indications of violence escalated the case to another level.

She appreciated Carrick giving her the call. Despite being the toast of the town in the summer, she'd sensed the Detective Chief Inspector, Phil Stratton, keeping her at arm's length for the last few months. There'd been a couple of murders, one a straightforward domestic, the second drug-related, but she'd been sidelined on both cases in favour of Dimitriou and the new kid taking over from the mother-to-be Heidi Tan, Detective Constable Jack Pryce. Sure, they were both competent investigators, but Jo knew she was being treated with kid gloves. Indeed, when she'd asked for a quiet word with Stratton, he'd said as much, though he'd used words like 'operational sensitivity' and 'workplace welfare'. The simple fact was, no one higher up seemed to understand what was going on in Jo's head. How had she been affected by what had happened? Was she a liability? Perhaps Dr Forster could give an answer in her report. What had she meant that she'd 'support' more sessions, anyway – that Jo was still fucked up in the head somehow?

Jo only had herself to blame. She'd rushed back to work a few days after Ben's funeral, too soon even by her own admission. It was before she'd started seeing Lucas properly, and she'd felt more alone and isolated than ever, drinking too much and missing sleep. She wasn't really sure what had happened, but Heidi had found her in the toilets at the St Aldates station, mirror smashed and knuckles bleeding. The scary thing was, Jo didn't really remember actually lashing out. Heidi had done her best to keep it a secret, but the lacerations had bled enough to need proper medical attention, and the mirror came out of the departmental budget. No one bought Jo's explanation that it was an accident.

She flexed her knuckles now across the steering wheel – there were still a few scars. After that, Jo had agreed to the counselling, and then to medication. She told herself it was just to keep Stratton of her back, but she knew she was scared too. She'd seen plenty of PTSD in her career already – officers attendant on scenes of terror attacks particularly, or disturbing child cases – and it wasn't a road she wanted to follow.

The problem was that even with Dylan dead, and Sally Carruthers in psychiatric care, the case hadn't gone away for the Thames Valley Police either. The standards committee had come down hard on Stratton because of the mistakes he'd made in command. Quite rightly, Heidi had said – his eagerness to close the case at any cost had led to poor conclusions. In turn, Jo suspected, he'd decided she was to blame. And she got that, to an extent. She'd been the nexus of the case. Dylan was *her* childhood acquaintance, the crimes had taken place within a hundred yards of *her* childhood bedroom. It hadn't helped either that the internal inquiry reported a day after she received her medal for bravery in the line of duty. Talk about a kick in the teeth for her DCI.

But maybe this misper was a way to put all that to bed. A couple of solid cases would show him and her colleagues that she was the same Jo Masters as before. Prove it to herself as well. Then she could really bury Dylan Jones for good.

Chapter 3

Oriel College was nestled in the cobbled streets between the High Street and Christ Church College. Not Jo's natural milieu by any means, though she couldn't help but admire the gothic architecture of the entranceway, and the resplendent, perfectly mown quadrangle of grass inside, still coated on the shaded side with the silvery remains of a lingering frost. A sign read 'Open to visitors' – term had ended a week or so before, so the majority of students would have left. The city itself was noticeably quieter, enjoying a brief lull before the panic of Christmas shopping really set in.

PC Andrea Williams was waiting just to one side of the quad. As ever, the constable's height made Jo give her a second glance. She was at least six-two, possibly the tallest woman Jo had ever met in the flesh, and her dreadlocks gave her the appearance of being a couple of inches taller still. Dimitriou called her Andre the Giant, which only he found funny, and which had earned him a verbal warning when Stratton heard him say it. Dimitriou protested that Heidi had once called him George Michael's less talented, uglier sibling, on the basis of their shared Greek heritage, and the fact that he had murdered a rendition of 'Club Tropicana' on a work karaoke night.

'And I dare you to say it to Andrea's face,' Heidi had added. Jo would have liked to see that, because she knew that Williams had been an accomplished judoka before joining the force, only missing out on the national team through injury. She could probably have tossed Dimitriou's gangly frame from one side of a holding cell to the other.

'Morning, Andrea,' said Jo.

'Ma'am,' said Williams. 'Follow me.'

They proceeded under a sort of covered walkway (Williams had to stoop), into another quad surrounded by nineteenth-century terraces, then down a set of stairs into a more modern section of housing. Jo had somewhat lost her bearings – these colleges had been reconstructed so many times over the centuries, to no obvious plan, that it was easy to get lost. A set of clipped heels fell into step beside them.

'You're the other detective?' said a slightly cadaverous-looking fifty-something woman in a plaid suit, holding out a hand. Jo shook it as she slowed.

'Jo Masters,' she said.

'Belinda Frampton-Keys. I'm the Vice Provost. I do hope you can get to the bottom of this. Malin is *such* a promising member of the MCR.'

'The MCR?'

Frampton-Keys looked confused for a moment, as if the abbreviation should be in common currency. 'Middle Common Room. It's how we refer to postgraduate students.'

'Was it you who reported the disappearance?'

'That's right. Malin's fellow student, a girl called Anna Mull, was supposed to meet Malin this morning for a coffee. When she didn't show up and didn't answer calls, Anna went to her room. Curtains were still drawn, which wasn't like Malin, so

Anna came to find a member of staff. We knocked several times, then entered using our own key. When we saw what was inside, I called the police.'

Williams led her towards a door behind police tape. Stationed beside it was Oliver Pinker. Squat, ginger-haired and affable, he was often paired with Williams, though the sight of the two together was strangely disconcerting, like a double act about to break into some mysterious dramatic display. He handed her polythene booties and gloves, and she stepped under the tape into a sterile linoleum corridor with several dorm rooms and a fire door at the end. The Vice Provost attempted to follow, but Williams placed a hand on her arm. 'Best if you stay off the crime scene, ma'am,' she said.

'Crime scene?' said Frampton-Keys. 'Has that been established?'

Jo smiled reassuringly. 'We'll let you know as soon as possible.'

The second internal door was open, and Pryce emerged, on the phone, wearing gloves too. Almost as tall as Andrea Williams, with doe-like dark eyes and floppy, black hair, he'd turned a few heads when he'd first arrived at St Aldates three months ago. Even Jo, normally immune to such things, hadn't failed to notice. The most disconcerting thing was the more than passing resemblance he bore to Ben. If you took away all the anger, passion, and the hint of danger from her former boyfriend, Pryce was a fair approximation of what might remain. His background was in computer forensics, and he'd been fast-tracked into investigative work from the private sector without ever serving time on the beat – a new kind of professional rather than vocational police officer. He remained essentially naïve, in an almost endearing way, but he proved himself more than able to pull his weight, arriving early and leaving late but without ever drawing attention to the fact. Indeed, Heidi had had to convince him to accurately record his overtime. His paperwork, as Stratton never ceased to extol, was exemplary. He nodded to Jo as he spoke.

'. . . very sorry I can't give you more specifics over the phone. If you could relay this to Mr Cranleigh as a matter of urgency. They can reach me on this number, or through the Thames Valley switchboard . . . Pryce. Jack Pryce . . . Of course . . . Goodbye.' He hung up, and flashed his gaze back to Jo. 'Boss,' he said, nodding. 'Just chatting to the father's office. He's in a meeting.'

'We can notify Mr Cranleigh,' called Frampton-Keys from outside. 'He's a close friend.'

'That's quite all right,' said Jo. 'Let us handle it, please.'

'Want to look?' said Pryce, gesturing to the door.

He let her enter first. Once over the threshold, Jo was immediately back at her own student digs in Brighton, twenty years before. The single bed, utility shelves loaded with books, 2-star hotel curtains, office chair, scuff-marks on the walls. The college might have looked glamorous on the post-cards, but student rooms were the same everywhere. Malin Sigurdsson had tried to improve it – there were pot-plants, and some rather fetching black-and-white photos of seascapes on the walls. A musical instrument case stood beside a music stand. Jo guessed a flute. But she was confused. 'Carrick said there were signs of a struggle.'

'In the bathroom,' said Pryce.

He moved aside, and Jo realised his body had been obscuring another door. She pushed it open.

Blood. Not a lot, but a patch on the wall above the bath, a smeared handprint across the sink, and a few drops on the floor. Like someone had hit their head, then stumbled around. There were several bottles of expensive cosmetics scattered around the sink, a few had rolled off.

'Anyone in the other rooms?'

Pryce shook his head. 'Not according to the Vice Provost. Most students have gone home, even the postgrads. Malin's the last resident in this dorm block.'

'Sorry, you said the father was called Cranleigh?'

'Sigurdsson is the mother's name.'

'So they're separated?

'Yep. Dad's in Parliament. MP for Witney. Using the mother's name could just be a security thing, I suppose.'

Jo's mind went automatically to *kidnap*, but she checked herself. Until a ransom demand came through, there was no point in jumping to conclusions.

'Been in touch with the hospitals?'

'Nothing yet,' said Pryce. 'Her description is circulating.'

'Vehicle?'

'She doesn't even hold a licence.'

They backed out again into the bedroom. Jo went to look at the photos above the desk. There were several of mixed-sex groups in various happy poses. But one picture in particular caught Jo's eye – a striking teenage girl with her arms around the neck of what must have been her mother – the resemblance was undeniable. They both had perfect high cheekbones, piercing green intelligent eyes with more than a hint of defiance, almost imperceptible cleft in the tip of the nose. The older woman's hair hung straight and tended to silver, though she still wore it long. The younger's was a natural blonde. If the Scandinavian surname didn't give their heritage away, the looks would. Perhaps the photographer was particularly talented, but to Jo the pair looked almost otherworldly – their beauty made her think of a race of elves. Jo's eyes passed back over the other pictures, and there was the same girl in most of them nestled among her friends. In some she looked slightly less ethereal, but in all she was quite stunning. One showed an orchestra, including Malin with a clarinet.

'That's our girl then,' said Jo. 'She's beautiful.'

'That she is,' said Pryce, his pale cheeks reddening as if he'd said something inappropriate.

Jo pretended not to notice. 'Have you called forensics?'

'Didn't want to until you got here, ma'am – strictly it's the lead investigator's role to designate and delegate resources.'

Always by the book, thought Jo. Dimitriou said he once saw Pryce raise his hand to go to the toilet, but she was sure it was a joke. Fact was, since Pryce had joined them, he had proved himself diligent and thorough – almost exactly the opposite of George Dimitriou.

'Well, let's designate,' said Jo. 'Initial thoughts?'

Pryce drew himself up and threw a glance around the room.

'I'd say it's someone known to Malin,' he said. 'There's no sign of a forced entry – door's self-locking on a spring mechanism, with a spy-hole. Implies she let him in. Maybe they argued in the bathroom, it got physical, and Malin got hurt. He panicked and removed her body.'

'You think she's dead?'

'Don't you? There's no shower curtain.'

Jo felt her own cheeks flush. She was surprised she'd missed that. It explained why there was no more blood outside the bathroom. Still, the way Pryce had said it, almost matter-of-factly, gave her pause. It was a feature of his personality she'd noticed before – the distance he could keep from things, almost a protective shell. In the brief few months they'd worked together, she'd never seen him lose his temper once. Given the sort of people they had to deal with, that showed some restraint.

'It's a good theory,' she admitted. 'Let's get forensics in then.'

'They're over in Didcot for the next few hours.'

'Course they are.' Since the pooling of resources in the name of cost savings, getting a forensics team in place in a timely manner was increasingly challenging. 'I'll draw up a brief back at the station.'

It would all take time to process anyway, and quite possibly be useless. If Frampton-Keys had entered, with goodness knew who else, the integrity of the scene was already compromised. Still, Jo sensed, she needed to do this one by every letter of the book if she was going to keep Stratton happy.

'And see if we can find out Malin's recent movements,' she added, opening the wardrobe. Inside were clothes, neatly sorted, a few nice dresses in dry-cleaning bags and a good collection of shoes. She tipped one over. Designer. Clearly Malin wasn't short of a few quid.

She went to the desk beside the bed and pulled open the top drawer, finding a box of condoms. She turned to Pryce.

'Anything on a boyfriend?'

'Vice Provost said she didn't know of one,' said Pryce.

The drawer below had stationery, a lighter, fag papers. A roll of extra-thick foil looked distinctly out of place. She took the drawer out, then the other two, crouching down. There was a plastic bag taped to the underside of the desktop. She detached it, opened it up and sniffed the dark putty-like substance inside. Just weed. She placed the bag on the desk. 'We should probably try and find her dealer. Small college like this, it shouldn't be too hard to squeeze it out of someone.'

Though with the holidays, finding someone to squeeze might be tricky.

'No sign of her phone,' said Pryce, 'but we've got a computer.' He tapped the laptop case from the desk with a gloved hand. 'I can take a look once it's logged as potential evidence.'

'See if we can find her phone number too, and talk to Stratton about accessing the phone records. The blood should be plenty enough to convince him.'

Pryce's own phone began to ring, and he looked at the screen. 'It's Cranleigh's office. You want to take it?'

'Thanks.' He handed her the phone. 'Detective Sergeant Jo Masters.'

'Something about my daughter?' The voice was brusque, a little impatient.

'Mr Cranleigh?'

'That's right. Look, if she's done something silly . . .'

'Do you know your daughter's whereabouts?'

A pause. 'What's happened?'

'Sir, Malin is missing. My colleague and I are at her college now.'

'Well, where's she gone?' He seemed almost belligerent, and Jo, despite herself, was already forming a mental image of him. Tall, balding, fleshy around the face and neck, no longer the man who'd first drawn Malin's stunning mother.

'Mr Cranleigh, I'm afraid there are indications Malin might have been hurt.'

'Okay, I'm coming over. Is Bel there?'

It took Jo a moment to register that he was talking about the Vice Provost.

'We can come to you, if it's easier. We'll need to ask some questions.'

'Right, fine. Call my secretary – she knows the diary.' Another pause. 'No one's blabbed to the press, have they?'

Jo bit her tongue. 'No one from my team,' she said.

'Let's keep it that way, eh?'

'Of course,' said Jo.

Cranleigh hung up.

'That was brief,' said Pryce.

'He didn't seem all that surprised,' said Jo. 'Has Malin been in trouble before?'

'Not that I know of. I can get Detective Tan to have a look for priors?'

'Good.'

Jo looked around the room again, trying to make sense of

the contradictions. The Oxford beauty, the weed, the blood, the musical talent. The sooner they really got to know Malin Sigurdsson, the sooner the circumstances of her disappearance would become clearer.

'Let's go and speak with the friend,' she said. On the way out of the room, she told Pinker to keep everything clean until forensics arrived. She walked to the end of the corridor, to the fire door. Pushing the bar at the ends only, so as not to smudge possible prints, she opened it onto a narrow street. On the far side was the tall wall of another college. *Not overlooked.* She retreated inside and the door closed on its sprung hinges. 'Maybe get this door processed for prints too. If she was carried out, this seems the obvious route.'

'But he didn't come in that way,' said Pryce. 'No handle on the street side.'

Well spotted, again. Frampton-Keys was on her phone a few metres from where they'd left her, saying, 'Don't worry, Nick. I'm sure the police will do their best . . . No, of course not. Of course.' She saw Jo approaching. 'I've got to go.'

She put the phone away. 'Mr Cranleigh's very worried,' she said.

Bel and Nick. Very cosy.

'He's a politician, I heard,' said Jo. 'Why was he calling you?'

'We're good friends,' said the Vice Provost. 'Nicholas was an alumnus of this very college.'

'Is that why Malin is a student here?' asked Pryce.

Frampton-Keys flinched. 'She's here on her own merit.'

'Oh, I wasn't suggesting nepotism,' said Pryce. 'I was just wondering if it was a family tradition of some sort.'

The Vice Provost pursed her lips, obviously still offended by the unintended slight. 'Not that I'm aware of.'

'Any idea why she doesn't use his surname?'

'Oh, Malin isn't Mr Cranleigh's biological daughter,' said Frampton-Keys.

'So who's her real father?' asked Jo. She foresaw a headache already. They really shouldn't have been involving anyone but close family about the disappearance.

Frampton-Keys looked bemused. 'I'm sorry – I don't feel it's my place to talk about other people's private affairs. Her mother lives in Sweden, I believe.'

'Can we follow up on that, Jack?' Jo said. She faced the Vice Provost again.

'We'd like to talk with the friend who came to see her, if that's all right?'

'Anna Mull?' said Frampton-Keys. 'She's in the buttery.'

'Which is what? And where?' asked Jo. She was trying her best not to dislike the Vice Provost, but every sentence the senior academic uttered seemed designed to confound her and present the clear subtext: *This is not your place.*

'This way,' said Frampton-Keys.

They walked back towards the main quad. As they did, Jo asked, 'Apart from the fire exit in the corridor, what are the other ways out of the college?'

'There's a door out onto Oriel Street,' said Frampton-Keys. 'You need a security card to access it – all the students at the college have one.'

'And staff?'

The Vice Provost nodded. 'Yes, but I'm not sure what you're getting at.'

'Not getting at anything,' said Jo. 'But if someone took Malin from her room, they had to get into the college and out again. Are there cameras on the security door?'

'I'm afraid not. We have a surveillance system at the front of the college, covering the porters' lodge, but that's it. Sorry, you think she's been kidnapped?'

'It's a possibility.'

They took a passage past an open door leading into

kitchens. A young man wearing whites, with heavily tattooed forearms was unloading pallets of bread and nodded a greeting as they passed, and there were catering staff at work inside.

'I thought the students had gone home,' said Pryce.

'We've got a three-day conference coming in later,' said Frampton-Keys. 'Ornithologists. We can't afford to let the college go empty out of term.'

She turned a sharp right angle, then pushed open a heavy, metal-studded door into a cosy wooden-clad room of benches and tables, with a small hatch counter. A young woman with a short, dark pixie-cut and delicate features to match was sitting next to an empty mug and several screwed-up tissues, hands toying with her phone. She stood up sharply. She was wearing jeans, a thick sweater, and what looked like trail shoes. Sensible, in the current weather.

'Have you found her?' she asked meekly.

'Not yet,' said the Vice Provost. 'Anna, these visitors are police officers. They need to talk to you.'

Anna looked scared. Her already large, almond-shaped eyes opened wider, and she gave a single nod.

Jo introduced herself and Pryce, then sat down opposite the student. Frampton-Keys was still standing off to one side.

'Perhaps we could have some privacy?' asked Jo.

The Vice Provost frowned. 'I really should be here,' she said. 'It's a student welfare issue.'

Jo smiled tightly. 'It's an active police investigation. Anna's an adult, and we're only asking a few questions.'

Frampton-Keys' mouth twitched. 'Very well. Is that all right with you, Anna? You don't have to talk to them if you don't want to.'

Jo was close to losing her temper, but Anna said, 'Yes,' quietly, and the Vice Provost turned on her heels and left.

'Thanks for your time, Anna,' she said. 'How long have you known Malin?'

Anna looked up. 'Over three years. We matriculated together, chose to do our MPhil's here too. We're the only two doing a History Master's at Oriel.'

Jo's ears pricked up. She studied History as an undergrad at Sussex, what seemed like a lifetime ago.

'So you're close?' asked Pryce.

'I'm probably her best friend,' said Anna. She didn't elaborate, so Jo decided to get straight to the point.

'It looks like she might have had a fight with someone in her room. Have you any idea who that might be?'

Anna didn't answer straight away. 'No.'

'No enemies?'

Anna smiled. 'Everyone loved Malin.'

'What about a boyfriend?'

'Nothing serious.'

'But she had relationships?'

'Yes.'

'And recently?'

Anna shot a look towards the door, as if she thought someone was on the other side. 'Ross,' she said. 'Ross Catskill.'

'Is he a student at the college?'

Anna laughed, a low chuckle. 'I doubt Ross even has any GCSEs. Sorry, that sounds awful, doesn't it? He runs an events company in Oxford – Calibre.'

'So Malin was seeing Catskill,' said Pryce. 'What was the relationship like?'

'Just an on-off thing,' said Anna. 'I don't know what she saw in him. I mean, I guess he's sort of good-looking, but that's about it.'

'You don't like him much, then?' said Pryce. 'Do you think he might have hurt Malin?' Anna stared down at her hands, and a few seconds of silence followed.

'Anna?' said Pryce. 'Did you hear the question?'

Anna looked up, at him, directly. 'You know when you just get a bad feeling about someone?'

Pryce nodded. 'All the time.' He turned to Jo. 'Sounds like we should pay Mr Catskill a visit. Anna, when did you last have contact with Malin?'

'Last night,' said Anna. 'We went for a drink. I left her about 9.50 pm.'

'That's very accurate,' said Pryce.

'I wanted to watch the ten o'clock news back in my room,' said Anna.

'Just the two of you met up?' asked Jo.

Anna nodded. 'The King's Arms. We'd been in the Bodleian Library all day working. We had a meal at the pub too.'

'Can you remember the top story on the news?' asked Jo's colleague.

He asked it in an innocent enough tone, but Anna clearly caught the shift of emphasis in the conversation, and Jo saw something flintier in her gaze as she addressed Pryce.

'The thing with the royal press secretary leak,' she said. 'Then interest rates. I'm afraid I can't remember much else. I was tired.'

'And nothing from Malin after 9.50?' said Jo.

'No. I went to sleep.'

'And where's your room?'

'I live out now. Shared house on Longwall Street.'

'But not with your best friend?' asked Pryce.

Anna blushed. 'Her mum wanted her in the college, actually. Funnily enough, she thought it was safer.'

Jo felt sorry for the girl. She seemed completely out of her depth. But there was still a difficult subject to broach. 'Anna, do you know if Malin had a drug problem?'

Anna looked down at her hands. 'I never saw her take anything.'

'But you know she did, right? It's okay. You're not in trouble.'

'I know she used to. She went to hospital once, in our second year.'

'Something she took?'

'I think so.'

'And what did the college do about it?'

Anna actually smiled. 'Nothing. I think Malin's step-dad might have handled it.'

Maybe I dismissed the nepotism a bit too quickly.

Jo relaxed in her chair, then fished out her card and slid it across the table. 'My number's on there if you think of anything else. Are you staying around in Oxford?'

'For another day,' said Anna. 'Then I'm going home for Christmas to my family.' She grabbed a tissue and blew her nose. 'What do you think happened to her?'

'Too early to say,' said Jo, standing up. Pryce did the same. 'But we'll get working on it. You've been very helpful, Anna.'

Malin's friend remained seated. 'She's a good person, you know.'

Jo wondered what that was supposed to mean.

'We have no doubt about it,' said Pryce. 'And we'll find her. I promise.'

Jo wished he hadn't said it. Though he hadn't specified 'dead' or 'alive', Jo was pretty sure Anna's take-away would be the latter. Maybe Pryce was regretting going a bit hard on her. Most missing person cases did get solved, because most of the time the missing didn't want to stay that way. But this already felt a little different. The bloody handprint in the almost empty college. The almost archetypical angelic face concealing what was looking like a complicated life beneath. They likely would find Malin Sigurdsson, but Jo already had a creeping feeling this wouldn't be a happy ending.

Chapter 4

They decided to pay Ross Catskill a surprise visit. Calibre Events was over in the new Castle Street development, just across the city centre.

Jo called Carrick on the way. He didn't answer, so she left a message telling him where they were going. As she was doing so, Pryce's phone rang, and from what she could gather it was Stratton on the other end. She waited until he came off.

'Cranleigh's been onto the gaffer already,' said Pryce. 'Wanted an update.'

'I only spoke to him an hour ago, and he was too busy to have a conversation.' Even without meeting the MP for Witney, Jo was already forming a positive dislike for the man.

A young woman in business attire walked past and smiled warmly at Pryce.

'Friend of yours?' asked Jo after a few seconds.

'Who?' he said.

Jo nodded at the woman, who was walking away.

'I don't think so,' he replied. 'Why?'

Jo grinned. For someone who specialised in digital forensics, going over evidence with a fine-tooth comb, Jo had noticed he often missed some of the more basic social cues. She wondered if he was somewhere on the spectrum. His desk at work was scrupulously neat and spotlessly clean, unlike her own, which was strewn with mugs and Post-it notes. Heidi called him 'the professor'.

'So what are your first impressions of Anna?' Jo asked him. 'She telling the truth?'

Pryce shrugged. 'Not all of it,' he said. 'She seemed nervous, but that's only natural. Plus, her friend's missing.'

'You think they're as close as she says? Hardly known each other long.'

Pryce shrugged. 'Three years? In a college like this, it's a long time I think.'

The Castle Street Hub, as it was called, was just a collection of the standard chain restaurants around a courtyard, with some business premises above, approached by metal steps. Calibre Events had a glass door and intercom to reception.

'Calibre Events. How can I help you?' said a female voice.

'We're looking for Ross Catskill,' said Jo. 'It's the police.'

'Mr Catskill is away on a premises visit at the moment,' came the reply.

'Whereabouts?' asked Jo.

'I'm afraid I can't give out that information.'

'What's your name please?' asked Jo.

'Selina,' said the receptionist.

Jo took out her warrant card, and held it to the camera. 'We're investigating a possible crime, Selina,' she said. 'Maybe you could let us in.'

A couple of seconds passed, then the buzzer went and Jo opened the door. They went up a set of backless stairs and into a small atrium where the receptionist sat behind a desk. Jo saw a small boardroom and another door with a WC sign, but that was it. The receptionist smiled, tapping at her keyboard. 'Mr Catskill will be busy until six-thirty,' she said. 'You could wait if you like. He might not come back at all though.'

Jo checked her watch. An hour.

'Is that his diary on screen?' asked Jo, leaning over the desk. 'You could help us actually. Where was Mr Catskill over the last, say, twenty-four hours?'

Selina shifted the monitor's angle. 'Is he in trouble?'

Jo wondered about her next move. Really, Selina was under no obligation to share anything.

'Quite possibly,' she said. 'More so if he doesn't help us in a timely manner.'

'Okay.' said the receptionist. 'Let me call Ross.'

She reached for the phone, but Jo leant across and got there first. 'Just tell us where he is,' she said. 'Pretty please.'

* * *

Jukebox was a nightclub above a supermarket on the edge of the shopping centre. Most people knew it by its nickname, Dirtbox, and Jo remembered it from her own time growing up. Sticky, worn carpets, plastic cups, themed nights that ranged from the cheesiest seventies pop to drum and bass. The sort of place that was dead at ten pm, by midnight was a meat-market of desperate youngsters, and by two boasted toilets like a warzone, awash with various forms of effluence. Though it ran student nights during term, it was more of a 'town' than 'gown' place – and provided a reliable stream of weekend calls to the emergency services related to post kicking-out time drunken altercations.

At six pm on a Wednesday, the scuffed double security door was closed. There was a letterbox, no signage, and no doorbell or other means of communication, so Jo closed her fist and pounded three times. A couple of shoppers heading back to their cars with full trolleys looked over curiously.

They'd told Selina not to call Catskill, but Jo hardly expected her to listen. If he'd gone already just to avoid them, that might make everything look a little clearer. Jo lifted her hand to bang again, when she heard footsteps from the other side of the door, then a bar mechanism being drawn.

It opened to reveal a man in a pale grey suit, and open-necked white shirt, brogues on his feet. His hair was moulded into tight waves that came just to his collar, and his skin carried the bronze tones of a natural tan. He was clean-shaven and his startling blue eyes latched onto Jo's.

'You must be Detectives Masters and Pryce,' he said. 'I was in a meeting, but my secretary told me to expect you. Want to come up?'

'Thank you,' said Jo. First impressions were that he was cool, affable, and confident. *Too suave, maybe?* He wore a lightly spiced scent that shouted quality. Jo and Pryce followed him up the stairs and into the empty nightclub. It had undergone some major changes since Jo's day, which was hardly surprising, and the layout was completely different to how she remembered. There were two bars and banquette seating. The dance floor remained in the same location, but looked less sticky. Maybe it was because it was illuminated by bright lights – it seemed a lot classier than she'd expected. There was another man behind the bar, holding an iPad and drinking a can of energy drink.

'Can I get you something?' asked Catskill. 'Tea? Coffee?' He waved at the optics. 'Something stronger?'

Jo shook her head. 'We need to talk to you about Malin Sigurdsson.'

He looked nonplussed. 'Mally? Sure. She's okay, right?'

'Probably not,' said Jo. She watched his face for any signs of guilt.

Catskill looked at the other man. 'Jav, we're pretty much done. I'll lock up if you want to go. Just forward the stocklist to my office.'

The man nodded, closed the case of the tablet, and left.

'This place yours, is it?' asked Pryce.

Ross sat down opposite them. 'I have a stake,' he said. 'Been supplying it for a few years, and the chance came up to buy out one of the previous owners. It's a bit of a dump, but it's kind of a cultural icon in Oxford. Has something happened to Malin?'

'We're not sure,' said Jo. 'When did you last see her?'

Catskill ran a hand through his locks. 'Wait, do I need a lawyer?' He was grinning as he said it.

'I don't know,' said Jo. 'Do you?'

Catskill steepled his hands, elbows on knees, all seriousness. 'I haven't seen her for at least a week.'

'Can you be more exact?' said Pryce, making notes in his copybook.

'Let me think.' Catskill lifted his hands, fingertips on forehead almost like he was praying. 'It would have been a couple of Fridays back. She came along to the opening night of a new cocktail place near the station. It's called Quench.'

'Anything since then?' said Jo. 'What about phone calls? Texts?'

Catskill shook his head. 'Nothing.'

'But you're her boyfriend?' asked Pryce.

Catskill smiled, a little coyly. 'I wouldn't say that. Malin's a sweet girl, but we're not that close.'

'Your relationship is sexual, though?' said Jo.

Catskill nodded. 'Er . . . it has been.'

'How old are you?' asked Jo.

Catskill crossed his legs and leant back. 'Is that relevant?'

Jo didn't reply. *Let him sweat.*

'I'm forty-two,' he said at last. 'How old are you, Detective?'

Jo would have guessed mid-thirties. 'Quite an age-gap. Must've been gratifying to have a young woman like Malin on your arm.'

Catskill looked unimpressed. 'Are you going to tell me what's happened?'

'Soon,' said Jo. 'Can you remember where you were last night, between say, ten pm and this morning?'

'I was in the office until about ten-thirty last night, then I drove home.'

'Which is where?' asked Pryce.

'Goring,' said Catskill.

Jo was familiar with it. A small village by the Thames, and a good forty minutes away. Stockbroker country. Well-to-do families.

'Strange place for a bachelor to live,' said Jo.

Catskill's right hand moved towards his left, as if fiddling with an imaginary ring. The top of his chest, in the V of his open shirt, flushed.

'You're not a bachelor?' said Jo.

'Sorry,' said Catskill. 'I think I've told you everything I can.'

He stood, but Jo remained seated. She was quite enjoying watching him squirm. 'So is there anyone who can confirm what time you got home last night?'

'My wife,' said Catskill quietly. 'No, wait – she was asleep. Maybe one of the neighbours would have seen me pull in?' He looked faintly desperate. 'Really, I don't want her to be involved in all this. She'll only worry. And the kids . . .'

'I think you need to be straight with us,' said Jo. 'Let's start with when you first met Malin . . .'

* * *

It had been two years ago, or thereabouts. Malin was looking for a job, which he'd found odd because he could tell from her clothing that she was well-off. He'd hooked her up working as a waitress at one of the college balls that year. Reports came back that she was a good worker, and soon she was a regular at more select bashes. She had a natural grace that let her fit into any sort of social milieu. When he found out later who her parents were, that made sense; step-dad a privately-educated English financier-then-MP, mum a Swedish socialite. She was beautiful, incredibly so, and he never thought she'd be interested in someone like him when she could have had any man she wanted. They first chatted properly after a party at Blenheim Palace. Some sheikh's kid or other had hired out the grounds, so Catskill was there to ensure things went off without a hitch. Everyone was stressed, so they'd had a drink afterwards to celebrate and one thing led to another. He assumed she'd see it as a mistake, but in the coming weeks they'd met several times. Always in hotels outside the city centre, occasionally at premises he knew would be empty and where they could get together under the pretext of work. He didn't tell her about his wife, because he assumed it would just fizzle out. But she was paranoid too, about her step-dad, mainly.

'Why was that?' asked Jo.

'His line of work. He was happy not to be involved in her life much, as long as there was no scandal. She used to think he was spying on her.'

Jo recalled Cranleigh's anxiety about the press. 'Do you think he was?'

'I never saw anyone, but like I said, we didn't see that much of each other.'

Catskill was flattered, he told them. Malin was a student at the university with her whole life ahead of her. A girl who could have done pretty much anything she put her mind to.

But eventually, he was the one who had called it off, about a month ago – he felt she was getting too attached.

'How did she take that?' Jo asked.

'Not great,' Catskill admitted. 'She said it didn't have to be serious. But I could see it was. She said she . . . she threatened to hurt herself.'

Jo thought about the blood in the room. *Self-harm?* Anna hadn't mentioned anything like that, but perhaps she had wanted to protect her friend's privacy.

'But you haven't had contact for twelve days?' asked Pryce.

Catskill shook his head. 'She'd been calling me at all hours,' he said. 'Begging to meet. You can check my phone records if you want. I told her to stay away. To be honest, I was scared she'd get to Emily – that's my wife. She could be determined, could Mally. Stubborn. She showed up at Quench and made a bit of a scene. I had to throw her out.'

'Sounds like you used her,' said Jo. 'She was a vulnerable girl half your age.'

Catskill looked angry, but it passed quickly. 'It might look like that, but it really wasn't. Malin's a clever girl. She looks like butter wouldn't melt, but that's part of her power.'

'She's missing,' said Jo. 'We think someone might have taken her against her will. Did she have any enemies that you know of?'

'When you're that beautiful, I think most women hate you, deep down,' said Catskill. 'But maybe she's just run away? She wasn't really very happy, I don't think.'

Jo thought of the pills she herself had stopped taking. Lots of people weren't happy.

'I'd like you to come to the station,' she said.

For the first time, Catskill looked alarmed. 'Am I under arrest?'

'No,' said Jo. 'But we'll need an official statement, and it would be helpful if we could confirm your alibi and cross-reference those phone records you mentioned.'

'I'm very busy,' he said. 'How long will all this take?'

Jo sensed they had him on the back foot already. *Just a little push needed*. 'Not long. If you're honest with us. We might not even have to involve your wife.'

Catskill seemed to realise he was hardly in a position to negotiate. 'Let me get my coat.'

* * *

The temperature in town seemed to have dropped another degree as they arrived back at the station. A biting wind whipped up St Aldates and everyone passing by had their heads down, extremities covered. Jo, chin tucked into her thick scarf, just wanted to get inside.

As they entered through the main doors, she could still see her breath. The front desk clerk was wearing gloves and a hat.

'It's bloody freezing in here,' she said.

'Boiler's gone,' said the clerk. 'They're saying it could be a couple of days waiting for parts this time of year.'

They booked Catskill in, then took him through to CID, where the air was just as chilly. A man in overalls stood by the door to the rec room, sipping from Dimitriou's Spurs mug, and inside another man on a small stepladder had the front off the boiler, and was tinkering with a screwdriver.

Pryce escorted Catskill to an interview room to get an official statement of what he'd told them at the club.

In his office, Stratton was talking animatedly to Detective Inspector Andy Carrick, who caught Jo's eye and waved. Stratton saw her too, then adjusted the blinds to make the glass partition of his office opaque. *Charming*. Heidi Tan emerged from the stairs, waddling slowly and holding her back. She was in a maternity top, a sheen of sweat on her forehead despite the cold.

'Dimitriou called. He'll be another twenty. Got a puncture on the way in.'

'How are you feeling?'

'Like a whale,' said Heidi. She eased herself into her desk chair.

'Only a week to go,' said Jo. 'Then you can swim away.' She sat opposite. 'We'll miss you.'

'Stop it,' said Heidi. 'You've got the professor now. I know Stratton prefers him.'

'Nonsense,' said Jo, though it was quite true. The Chief Inspector had made no secret of his admiration for Jack Pryce when they were looking for maternity cover. His application was apparently 'exceptional' and the team 'should be grateful to have him'. From what Jo had learned later, Stratton had a point. Pryce's aptitude scores were off the charts, and he had a proven track record in financial crime. Only Dimitriou failed to be impressed, muttering on several occasions variations of the same criticism, 'but what's he going to be like on the street?' The answer so far was, rather good.

'You don't have to lie for my benefit,' said Heidi. 'Did Stratton ever invite *me* to play golf?'

Jo laughed. 'Count your blessings.'

'Forensics are on their way to Oriel College now by the way. They had to finish up a scene over in Didcot. You got any paperclips?'

Jo fished in her drawer, pushing aside the gallantry medal, and tossed a box over. She sat down at the computer to put together a brief for the crime scene investigators, including prints from the desk, all of the bathroom, blood samples, hair and anything else from the bed. Catskill said they'd met in hotels, so if they found any traces of him in the room, that could be a break. So far though, Jo's instincts were cold on the director of Calibre Events.

'Would you mind contacting Belinda Frampton-Keys, the Vice Provost? We could do with a list of anyone who might have had access to the room.'

She heard the door to Stratton's office open, but kept her focus on the screen. 'Who've you got in the IR?' he asked.

She was typing her message to forensics as she spoke. 'It's the ex-boyfriend,' she said. 'Jack's checking out his story, but first impressions are that he's clean. The way he tells it, Malin was quite unstable.'

'Really?' Stratton sounded incredulous.

'Vulnerable, anyway. We've got her computer, and forensics are going in shortly to scrape up what they can. I think there may have been drugs involved.'

Stratton looked nervous. 'What sort of drugs?'

'We found weed, but heroin is my guess too.' She told him about the foil.

'Could've been to wrap her sandwiches.'

'I think students make their own sandwiches these days, sir,' said Heidi, with a barely concealed smile.

Stratton still seemed uncomfortable, scratching his eyebrow. 'It's very early still. Let's keep the drug stuff on the backburner for the moment.'

'It's the most obvious line of enquiry,' said Jo.

Stratton reddened. 'So, enquire,' he replied. 'Just don't put all our eggs in that basket.'

The phone in his office rang, and he went to get it.

'What's he so worried about?' asked Heidi.

A few moments later, the front desk clerk buzzed a man into the CID room. Stratton trotted forward to greet him.

'Nick!' he said. 'How are you holding up?'

Jo recognised MP Nicholas Cranleigh, but only vaguely – perhaps from pictures in the paper or something on TV. He wore a long black work coat over a suit. He was not quite as she'd envisaged, with his square, pugnacious face and neatly parted grey hair. She'd have guessed he was ex-military, rather than a banker.

'Not too bad, Phil,' he replied, his voice soft, almost unctuous. 'Have we got anything?'

Jo watched the two men shaking hands, gripping each other's elbows with a mixture of fondness and understanding. *Old mates . . .*

'We're making progress,' said Stratton. 'Forensics are over at the college, we're putting together a timeline of Malin's movements, and drawing up a network of associates. It won't be long. We've contacted Malin's mother.'

Cranleigh grimaced. 'I suppose that's sensible.' He released Stratton's arm and hand. 'So do you think she's all right?'

Stratton looked a little flummoxed, so Jo stepped in.

'Excuse me, Mr Cranleigh. I'm Detective Masters, and I'm the lead investigator. We hope so, sir. Maybe it's best to go somewhere private to discuss this?'

Cranleigh's eyes narrowed in recognition. 'Jill Masters, isn't it? From that awful case in the summer.'

'Jo,' she corrected him. 'I assume you're talking about the Niall McDonagh kidnap. Yes, it was unpleasant, but happily we got a result.'

'Stunning work by Jo here,' said Stratton, like a proud father. *Even though you didn't believe me any step of the way . . .*

'Team effort,' said Jo, acknowledging with a nod.

'You don't think that Malin's been kidnapped, do you?' asked Cranleigh.

'It's a possibility,' said Jo. 'Is there anyone who might hold a grudge against you?'

'Plenty,' said Cranleigh, with a wolfish smile. 'I'm a politician.' Jo couldn't believe he was able to joke at such a time, and maintained a serious expression. He caught on, and added, 'Honestly, no.'

'You weren't having Malin watched, then?'

'I beg your pardon?'

'In a private security capacity, I mean.'

Cranleigh shook his head with a bemused grin. 'Should I have been? I think you overestimate my means.' He turned to Stratton. 'Sorry, Phil, what's your detective getting at?'

'I'm not sure at all,' said Stratton, glaring. 'But we've got everyone working flat out.'

As soon as he'd said it, a voice came from the hallway. 'It is fucking freezing. Put the heating on before my balls vanish completely.'

Stratton stiffened.

DC George Dimitriou came striding into the CID room, legs clad in Lycra, top half in a windbreaker, plus gloves and a buff. He was carrying his cycle helmet in one hand, a small rucksack in the other. His sweaty face was specked with dirt. Everyone was silent, and Jo tried to catch his eye.

'What's up?' he asked. 'Colder than a morgue in here.'

Stratton grinned, teeth bared. 'Detective, this is Nicholas Cranleigh. *The Right Honourable* Nicholas Cranleigh. His daughter is missing.'

Dimitriou placed his helmet carefully on his desk, and wiped a streak of mud from his cheek. Sadly the ground didn't swallow him up. 'Ah, right. Nice to meet you, sir.' Jo almost expected him to bow, but he settled for straightening his shoulders.

Stratton, looking furious still, put a hand on Cranleigh's shoulder. 'Would you like to come into my office, Nick?' he said. 'Drink?'

'A coffee would be appreciated, if you've nothing stronger?'

Stratton looked from face to face in the CID room. 'Jo, make Mr Cranleigh a coffee would you?'

So I'm the tea girl now?

'Two sugars, please,' said Cranleigh. Jo nodded as the two men went into the office and closed the door.

'Fuck,' said Dimitriou under his breath. 'No one warned me.'

'I tried,' said Jo.

'I hope you weren't after a hot shower,' said Heidi. 'Boiler's kaput.'

Dimitriou groaned.

Jo fired off her email to forensics, then went to make the coffee. She stopped on the way at the interview room, knocked on the window panel and beckoned to Pryce.

'How's it going?' she asked, as he came to the door.

'Almost done. Catskill says he's got email records to show he was logged on in Goring at eleven-fifteen last night, so I can check that easily enough.'

'There's still a window,' said Jo. 'Think he'll give us prints and a DNA sample voluntarily?'

'He's just very worried we'll talk to his wife,' said Pryce. 'So shouldn't be a problem.'

'Malin's father is here,' said Jo. 'Probably best they don't cross paths.'

'Got it. Any news on forensics?'

'On their way. I'll go back to coordinate.'

'You need help?'

'I don't think so. I'll try and have another chat with the Vice Provost too.'

As he went back inside, Jo saw Ross Catskill sitting upright in the chair. 'Almost done now,' she said. 'You can leave soon.'

He smiled wanly.

Making the drinks, Jo pondered Cranleigh's reaction. He seemed worried, of course, but almost weary too. They'd have told him about the blood, surely. She tried to put herself in his shoes. If this were her daughter, her step-daughter even . . .

She placed the cups on the tray. She realised she was thinking like Ben, who always worked on the assumption that everyone was guilty until they could damn well prove themselves innocent to him. There was really no reason to think Cranleigh had anything to do with it, though she made a mental note to check his movements.

As she returned carrying the tray, Carrick was in the office too. She knocked at the door, and entered. She could tell at once that the room was frosty, and it wasn't just because the radiators weren't functioning. Carrick looked particularly sheepish, but carried on speaking:

'Seems she was still using a Swedish-registered phone. It's probably not going to be a problem, but a warrant takes longer to process.'

'Bloody EU red tape,' muttered Cranleigh.

'Thanks, Jo,' said Stratton, as she laid down the tray.

'I've been thinking, sir,' said Jo. 'Perhaps we should organise an appeal. Press conference. Get Malin's photo out there. She's very recognisable.'

'I'd rather not, actually,' said Cranleigh.

'Oh,' said Jo, placing a cup in front of him.

Cranleigh looked to Stratton. 'An appeal though – it's very . . . public.'

'That's rather the point,' said Jo. 'You're aware it's likely that Malin's injured? She might need medical attention.'

Cranleigh glanced at her briefly, eyes livid. 'I'm fully aware,' he said, 'that I didn't ask for your opinion. Whatever trouble my daughter has got herself into, I'd rather not have it splashed across the news. Can't we handle this discreetly, Phil?'

There it was again – the chumminess. Jo was sorely tempted to mention the drugs, but somehow kept the words in.

Stratton held up his hands to placate the situation. 'I'm sure we can, yes. Jo, would you excuse us a moment, please?'

She stood her ground, feeling like an idiot waitress. She'd never been great at holding her tongue, so it took an almighty effort of will not to club her boss over the head with the tray. 'Of course, sir. If you need me, I'll be back at the college coordinating the forensics team and speaking with the Vice Provost.'

As she turned, Cranleigh coughed.

'Actually, Detective,' said Stratton. 'I'm going to ask Andy Carrick to be the lead on this.' Jo turned slowly, fingers tight on the tray.

'May I ask why, sir?'

'He's the ranking detective,' said Stratton. 'He'll have Dimitriou as back-up. I hope you understand.' He stared at her, daring her to challenge his decision. Jo knew where the lines were with Stratton. Cross this one and she'd be in all sorts of trouble.

'Perfectly, sir,' she said. *So much for a chance to prove herself.*

'Excellent,' said Stratton, beaming. 'Besides, your shift's up. Type up what you've got then go home a get some rest. And good work today, Detective.'

With a bob of her head, Jo left his office.

Dimitriou was emerging from downstairs, dressed in work clothes, hair still slightly damp. 'Well, that was an unpleasant experience,' he said.

Jo realised he was probably talking about his cold shower.

'I need to bring you up to speed on this disappearance,' she said. 'Stratton wants you and Andy on it.' She pushed the picture of Malin Sigurdsson across the desk.

'Wow!' He glanced towards Stratton's office, and lowered his voice. 'She's a ten, huh?'

Ignoring him, Jo began to type, her fingers stabbing at the keys.

Chapter 5

Jo was thorough, losing herself in the details of the report, and not even looking up as Stratton, Carrick, and Cranleigh emerged from the office and picked up Dimitriou. She knew Carrick would feel terrible, but she was in too much of a foul mood even to give him the chance to show contrition for whipping the case from under her. Afterwards she texted Lucas and told him she'd be over at his place at eight, and could pick up a takeaway if there was anything he fancied. He answered almost immediately that he didn't mind.

Pryce came through. 'I've told Catskill we don't need him anymore. I thought you were going back to the college?' Jo rubbed her cold hands together, and explained she was being sidelined in favour of the boys' club. 'It's just you, Stratton, Carrick and Dimitriou. Think of it like a four-ball.'

Pryce looked bewildered. 'I don't think DI Carrick plays golf,' he replied.

'It was a joke,' said Jo. 'To break the tension and prevent me killing someone.'

She stood up, grabbed her coat, and left. Andy Carrick had texted with a single word, '*Sorry*', and an unhappy emoticon.

She appreciated the gesture and wrote back '*No hard feelings*,' with a face gritting its teeth in rage. If the last six months had taught her anything, it was that life was too short. She hoped they found Malin quickly, in good health.

Security lights illuminated the car park as she trailed over to her navy Peugeot. It was a dry day, but there was a thin layer of ice on the inside of the windscreen. She got in, started the engine and cranked the heaters. As she grabbed the de-icer, she wondered about getting a new car. Her brother had kindly offered her some money from the sale of the family house, *if* it ever happened, and her promotion had more than covered the costs of the fertility treatment back in the clinic in Bath. Compared to sixth months ago, in the aftermath of the break-up with Ben, she was comparatively well-off. At the moment, she was still paying for a one-bed flat in Oxford, though spending almost every night at Lucas's. She'd been meaning to talk with him about it, about moving in properly, but it seemed to be just the opening of a much bigger conversation they needed to have about the future. About family, particularly. When she thought about it, it brought her out in a sweat. Somehow Dr Forster had coaxed it all out of her, like the forensic interviewer she was in just their second session. Lucas was twenty-eight, and there was really no reason at all he should be thinking about kids, but Jo didn't have that luxury. She'd wasted her best years with Ben, only to be betrayed, and now – just shy of thirty-nine – she felt time slipping between her fingers at accelerated speed. The eggs she'd frozen with the Bright Futures clinic in the autumn would practically keep forever, but she was under no illusions that her chances of being a mother were anything but shrinking. If Lucas wasn't 'The One' – and how she hated that term – then she had to make some difficult decisions soon. Maybe tonight was the night to do it.

She cleared the ice, reversed carefully and drove out onto St Aldates.

There was a Korean place on the route back to Lucas's flat that they both liked, and she pulled up outside. She ordered a Bulgogi for herself, and veggie Bibimbap for him, and was waiting for the food to come when her phone rang.

'Hello?'

'Detective Masters, it's Anna Mull, Malin's friend. Have you found her?'

'Not yet,' said Jo. Anna didn't answer but let out a sigh, so Jo asked, 'Is there something else you want to tell me?'

'I don't know if I should say anything,' said Anna.

'Then you probably should,' said Jo. 'Even if it doesn't seem important, it might assist us.'

'You asked me earlier, about enemies . . .' Anna was speaking quietly, and Jo wondered if she was with someone else.

'And you said not,' Jo replied.

'Something happened,' she said. 'Last term. I don't know if it's important . . .'

She's really nervous.

'Why don't you tell me, and we'll see.'

'There's a tutor here – Professor Ronald Myers. Malin made a complaint about him . . . being inappropriate. Anyway, he's retired now. I just thought you should know. It's probably nothing.'

'You mean sexually inappropriate?'

'He tried to kiss her,' said Anna. 'She told him she wasn't interested.'

'And Myers teaches at Oriel?'

'Not anymore,' said Anna. 'He left in the summer.'

'How old is he?'

'I don't know. Sixties, I suppose. I didn't want to say before – it's seems quite unlikely . . .'

Jo's heart quickened, her chest fluttering. 'Do you know where we can find Myers now?'

'I'm sorry, I don't,' said Anna. 'Ms Frampton-Keys will be able to tell you. I'd rather you didn't mention me, though.'

'No, of course not. Thanks, Anna. Oh, one more thing. We spoke to Ross, and he told us that Malin thought she was being followed recently. Did she ever mention anything like that to you?'

A pause. 'I'm sorry – I don't think she did.'

'It's something you'd remember, presumably?'

'Well, yes. I can't imagine why she'd keep anything like that from me.'

'Okay – thanks for your time.'

Jo waited by the counter. Maybe she wasn't being followed at all, and it genuinely was paranoia. It did seem strange that she'd only made the claim to Ross Catskill. *Unless he's lying, to throw us off . . .*

Jo thought about ringing Frampton-Keys for Myers' address, but thought better of it. She'd shown where her loyalties lay already, and would probably call Professor Myers right after getting off the phone. The college office might help, but the same issue applied. She called Heidi instead, and asked casually for an address check without mentioning the case it related to. In half a minute, she had it.

'Thanks, Heidi.'

With the Korean food losing heat and filling the car with its scent, Jo turned around and drove to the address in the north east of the city. Her toes still stubbornly refused to warm up. Ronald Myers' place was a quaint cottage in Marston that opened right onto the narrow pavement. Jo drove past once and, seeing lights on, parked around the corner. She walked between the pools of light from the streetlamps, her breath clouding on the air. She used the heavy brass knocker.

As he opened the door onto a narrow and cosy hallway, Jo's first impression was that Myers wasn't all that old. A swarthy black beard covered his lower face; he looked more like a sea captain than a tutor of history. The thick and slightly shapeless jumper he wore only added to that impression, and his broad forearms stuck out through the bottom of the shrunken sleeves. His nails, on his squared fingertips, were thick and yellowing.

Jo introduced herself. 'We're investigating the disappearance of a former student of yours – Malin Sigurdsson.'

Myers' brows contracted around a deep vertical cleft. 'Has something happened to her?'

'Maybe I could come in?' said Jo.

Myers moved aside. 'Go on through,' he said.

Jo squeezed past and found herself in a cosy lounge, lined on two sides by floor-to-ceiling shelves of books. A wood-burning stove was blazing and she was too hot at once. On a small table was a set of car keys with a branded Morris Garages keyring.

'Can I get you anything?' asked Myers, with his back to her. He crouched, opened the stove and placed on another log.

'No, thank you,' she said. 'I won't take up much of your time. When did you last see Malin Sigurdsson?'

Myers straightened, turned to face her and spread his shovel-like hands. Jo wondered how he'd feel about giving fingerprints. 'I haven't seen her for weeks,' he said. 'Months. Not since I retired. Before the summer break.'

'So you've had no contact since then?'

He sat on a sagging armchair and placed both hands on his knees. 'Perhaps you could explain what this is about?'

'Malin's missing,' said Jo. 'We're following a number of leads to ascertain what might have happened.'

'I assure you I know nothing of that,' said Myers.

‘Can you tell me exactly the nature of your relationship with Malin?’

‘I was her tutor.’

‘Until you . . . *retired*?’ He nodded. ‘You see, I heard you left under something of a cloud.’

‘Who told you that?’

‘That doesn’t matter,’ said Jo. ‘You were attracted to Malin, though?’

‘Is that a crime?’

‘You tried to kiss her and she didn’t like it.’

‘I went through all this with the college,’ he said. ‘I made a mistake, as foolish old men are wont to do.’

‘Sounds like sexual assault to me,’ said Jo.

‘All right – I’d like you to leave,’ said Myers.

‘We haven’t finished talking.’

Myers stood up. ‘Do I need to call your superiors?’ he said. ‘I’m quite aware of my rights.’

Jo stood as well. ‘Don’t worry – we’re on top of things,’ she said. ‘All right if I have a look around?’

She began to walk towards another door. It looked like there was a dining area on the other side, with a set of stairs running right to left. Myers blocked her path.

‘It isn’t,’ he said. ‘This is my home, and I’ve made my wishes clear.’

‘We can come back with a warrant,’ she said.

‘Then do so.’ He gestured towards the door, impatient and resolute. ‘Good evening, detective.’

She showed herself out into the cold street, looking up and down. He was probably watching her from inside. She walked back to her car, drove slowly back past his house, then pulled up in a layby a couple of streets away. The fact he hadn’t consented to a search didn’t mean much, in her experience.

The food would be stone cold. She texted Lucas to let him

know she'd been delayed. It wouldn't be the first time work had got in the way of sustenance.

After five minutes, the headlights of a car emerged from the side street beside Myers' house. They reflected in her mirrors. Jo pressed herself down in her seat. An MG sports car passed, indicated left and turned out of sight. Jo started her engine and followed.

'Where are you off to, Ron?' she muttered.

They hit the A40, joining traffic and heading south. Jo stayed a couple of cars back. After less than a mile, Myers drifted across to the exit for Barton. Jo copied his signals. Her stomach felt light with nerves. He'd looked surprisingly strong for his age. If it came to it, she had a police-issue telescopic baton in the car, and CS gas spray.

He slowed as he drove past a small parade of shops, pulling into the car park. There were a few people around, and he reversed into a space. Jo felt the tension dip as she stopped on the road opposite. Maybe he was just coming out for a pint of milk. Was this the closest shop? When he got out, he was carrying a plastic bag. He walked away from the shop though, down a path between an illuminated launderette and a closed chip shop. Jo tucked the baton into her inner coat pocket, got out and crossed the road in pursuit.

There was a sign saying 'Recreation ground' pointing up the alley.

Jo wondered for a moment if she'd lost him when she reached a set of traffic lights at a smaller road. Behind a low fence opposite was a large open space lined with trees. Netting suspended between several trunks told her it was probably a cricket ground in the summer months. She saw a movement further up the pavement, as Myers dipped in through a gate. He was walking more quickly. She went across herself, and vaulted the fence, staying under the trees. She was breathing hard, but it was only nervousness making her heart pump faster. Myers walked towards a bench with a bin beside it. She knew what he was going to do, before he did it. He peered into the bin, then placed the bag inside. Jo smiled grimly, waited for him to leave, then hurried across to the bench herself, taking her pocket-torch from her handbag. The bin was empty but for the bag. She used a tissue between her fingers to fish it out. It wasn't heavy, but several items jostled inside.

She crouched and carefully tipped them onto the frost-covered grass. Four objects. The first three – a toothbrush, a pot of expensive face cream, a hairbrush – might feasibly have belonged to Myers himself. The last – a flimsy silk camisole nightdress – sealed it.

Got you, you fucker.

Jo wanted nothing more than to apprehend Myers herself, but she fought the urge. *No rush.* She bagged up the things, and walked calmly back towards her car, dialling Andy Carrick on the way. She could feel the lightness of her breath as she filled him in and the adrenalin of the pursuit seeped from her veins. As ever, he listened patiently without interrupting until she'd finished.

'Where are you now?'

'Following on foot. My guess is he'll head straight home.'

'Good work, Jo. Stay back and observe. We're on our way.'

Jo hung up, thrilled with the triumph, trying to imagine the look on DCI Stratton's face when they brought Myers in. *There's no way you can keep me out now . . .*

* * *

In the end, Myers did stop at the shop, and Carrick was already at his house with two squad cars by the time he returned. The retired tutor didn't try to run, and Jo walked over to hear

Carrick asking him to come to the station to answer questions relating to the possible murder of Malin Sigurdsson.

'You think I *killed* her?'

'Did you?' asked Carrick.

'Of course I bloody didn't,' said Myers.

'Then you won't mind helping us with our enquiries.'

'I don't see how I can,' said Myers.

Jo watched as they took him across to the squad car.

'Mind if I join you inside?' she said. 'In a purely observational capacity, of course.'

'Be my guest,' said Carrick. 'And again, sorry about earlier.'

'It's academic now,' said Jo.

Dimitriou was organising uniforms laying out the cordon.

'You're making us look bad,' he said, as Jo entered the house again.

She walked straight through to the pantry-style kitchen. A washing machine was running, and she switched it off at the wall. Then she went up a set of spiral stairs with a wrought-iron balustrade. The house was a two-up, two-down, with a small extension at the rear over both storeys. The room at the front had more books, and was given over to stacked storage crates; the rear one was Myers' bedroom with an en-suite. The bed was stripped. The pictures on the walls were tasteful water-colours. She checked the wardrobe, the linen basket, and any cupboards she could find.

Carrick was out in the garden, looking in the shed.

They met back downstairs.

'Nothing,' she said.

Dimitriou joined them. 'The shopping bag is full of cleaning products – bleach, clothes, rubber gloves, brushes. He was trying to cover his tracks.'

'He's washed his bedsheets,' said Jo.

Carrick was frowning.

'You're wondering why he took the toothbrush and the face cream,' she said. 'Trophies?'

He shrugged. 'Maybe, but there was a toothbrush in her college room as well. I've just come from there.' Jo cast her mind back. She didn't remember seeing one, but Carrick's nickname was Nikon, because of his freakishly photographic memory.

One of the uniforms came in. 'Excuse me, sir. We've done a preliminary search. Pretty sure the girl isn't here.'

She was at one point though, thought Jo. *So where's he put her?*

'Thanks,' said Carrick. He looked at the books on the shelves, as if one of them might contain the answers they needed. 'Dimi, stay here and coordinate. Knock on the neighbours, see if they can give us anything. Comings and goings, noises, suspicious behaviours.'

'What about me?' asked Jo.

'You're off shift, aren't you?' said Carrick.

'Stop winding me up, Andy,' said Jo. 'Let me come with you and have a crack at Myers.'

'The Chief won't be happy. But, well . . .'

'Fuck him?' said Jo.

Carrick grimaced. In the seven months since Jo had first met him, she'd never heard him use a single expletive.

'I agree with the sentiment,' he said, 'if not the manner of expression.'

Chapter 6

They had to call him though, and DCI Stratton arrived back at the station just before nine pm, as Jo and Carrick were getting ready to speak to Ronald Myers in IR1. Carrick had obviously briefed him on Jo's involvement, because he didn't say anything other than a mumbled, 'Great work, Detective Masters.'

'What's the old bastard done with her?' he said next.

'Dimi's standing by at the property,' said Carrick. 'Let's talk to Myers first before we rip the place up.'

'I'll be watching on the monitor,' said Stratton. 'And hold fire on communicating with Nick Cranleigh until we've got something concrete.'

'Yes, boss,' said Carrick.

He and Jo entered the interview room, and Myers started talking at once. 'I hope you've seen sense.' His lawyer sat beside him, a man of about the same age, but plump and florid, with badly-dyed blond hair.

Carrick started the tape and introduced Myers, himself and Jo for the record, then asked the counsel to state his name.

'Freddie Allgreave,' said the man. 'For the record, my client denies having anything material to do with the disappearance of Malin Sigurdsson.'

'We're investigating her death, now,' said Carrick.

'That as well,' said Myers. 'For God's sake, this is preposterous. You have no evidence.'

'Care to tell us why you were disposing of Malin's property a mile from your home?' asked Jo.

Myers glanced briefly at his lawyer, who nodded.

'I panicked. You seemed to think I was guilty of something, wanting to snoop around. So I tried to get rid of her things.'

'Why did you have those things in the first place?' asked Jo.

'That's none of your business,' said Myers.

'Did you steal them from her, maybe?' asked Jo. 'We know you liked her. You told us that before. Wanted something to sniff?'

Myers looked horrified. 'I'm not a pervert.'

Jo fought back her laughter. *You're a lot worse than that.*

'If you tell us where she is, right now, it's going to reflect a lot better on you when it comes to sentencing. Mr Allgreave will confirm that.'

The brief leant across and whispered something in his client's ear.

'I don't know where she is,' said Myers. 'I want to help.'

Jo took a breath. She didn't think he'd hold out long. Her vague theory was that he'd done something in a fit of temper, and all she needed to do was play on the same short fuse in the IR and he'd crack again. She was almost looking forward to it. 'Tell us about Malin,' she said. 'What was she like as a student?'

Myers pouted, as if he expected a trick. 'She was gifted,' he said. 'Our tutorials were stimulating.'

'I bet,' said Jo. 'And the one where you tried to stick your tongue down her throat. Did she find that stimulating?'

'I said before – it was a misunderstanding.'

'And dealt with internally at the college,' said Allgreave.

'Swept under the carpet, more like,' said Jo. Carrick was sitting back and listening carefully, letting her take the lead. She wondered in the back of her mind how Stratton, watching from the AV suite, would take the line of questioning. Not that she cared. She'd always scored highly in interrogation test scenarios.

'It was the friend who sent you on this wild goose chase, wasn't it?' said Myers.

Jo folded her arms. 'I don't know what you're talking about,' she replied.

'You know why the complaint was dropped, don't you?' said Myers. 'Because she never wanted to make it in the first place. It was that little minx Anna Mull who put her up to it. She's hated me ever since I told her to buck up her game.'

Jo didn't let her face betray her surprise. It might not even be true, but now wasn't the time to start digging. Carrick's phone, on the table in front of them, beeped. He turned it over and looked at the message, before showing it to Jo. It was from Dimitriou. 'Neighbours opposite report seeing blonde girl arriving with Myers three days ago by car. Leaving next morning.'

What the hell did that mean?

'Time to be open with us, Ron,' said Jo. 'Because we're this close to turning your house upside down. When did you last see Malin Sigurdsson?'

Myers' lips were sealed.

'Come on, Mr Myers,' said Carrick. 'If you didn't take her, that means someone else did. The quickest way to eliminate yourself from our enquiries is to tell the truth. We can still charge you with obstruction of justice for the unauthorised disposal of her possessions.'

Allgreave put a hand on Myers' arm. 'I'm sure my client will do his best to help you. He's an innocent man.'

Myers nodded gratefully. 'I saw her on Monday,' he said.

Three days ago . . .

'For what?' said Carrick.

Myers folded his arms. 'What do you think?' he said.

'Extra tutoring?' said Carrick.

'We enjoyed each other's company,' said Myers.

'You had sexual intercourse?' said Jo.

'And it was entirely our private right to do so,' said the professor.

'*You* and Malin Sigurdsson?' said Jo.

Myers looked at her with utter disdain.

'So you say you haven't seen her since Monday,' asked Carrick. 'Any contact at all? An argument, perhaps?'

'No,' said Myers. 'We parted . . . amicably.'

'And you didn't visit her in college?'

'I think I've answered that.'

'Answer again.'

'No, I didn't visit her in college. I don't even have a security pass anymore, and you can check with the porter's lodge to see if I signed in.'

'We'll need to take your fingerprints.'

'Do I have a choice?'

'No.'

Jo suspended the interview, and was glad to be out of the room with Carrick.

'Are you buying it, guv?'

Stratton joined them.

'We'll need to confirm the visitor was her,' said Carrick, 'but the days matched. Maybe Anna Mull can clarify. Sounds like she wasn't particularly fond of Myers.'

'I hope I'm not being shallow,' said Jo, 'but can you really see Malin Sigurdsson going for a bloke like that?'

Stratton cut in. 'If there's one thing this job has taught me, it's not to make assumptions about women.'

Jo guessed from his smile that it was supposed to be a joke. 'She accused him of sexual harassment. He lost his job. In my experience, women don't run to shag their sex pests.'

'He said the complaint was dropped,' said Stratton.

'We'll check with Frampton-Keys,' said Carrick. 'I'm with Jo on this, sir. Even if she dropped the accusation, I'm not sure how it squares with voluntarily spending the night at his house.'

Maybe, thought Jo, *we're not looking at a square.*

★ ★ ★

They took the prints, and Heidi gave the files a cursory scan before sending them to the lab for a confirmation.

'I'm ninety-nine per cent sure they're not a match for Malin's room,' she said.

Stratton looked aggrieved. 'I'm not sure we can hold him.'

'Agreed,' said Carrick, though Jo saw it pained him to admit it. 'We checked the evidence manifest from Malin's room, and it included a toothbrush. Which makes it more likely that the one at Myers' house was indeed a spare, taken there voluntarily.'

'We've got him on obstruction, though.'

'Pretty sure his lawyer could argue that was simply panic,' said Carrick, 'and he's not an ongoing material threat.'

'Are we finished at his house?' asked the DCI.

'Almost,' said Carrick. 'There's nothing obvious yet. Certainly no blood.'

'If he killed her at the college, there wouldn't be,' said Jo. 'He looks strong enough to carry her.' She knew that didn't answer the access problem, though.

'Okay, I want every nook and cranny looked into,' said Stratton. 'Find Myers a hotel. Get him what he needs from his house. And advise he doesn't go on any sudden holidays.'

Carrick did as asked, signing Myers' belongings back to him. On seeing Myers' unbelievably smug face as he pocketed his things, Jo couldn't help herself.

'Not sure how Mr Cranleigh is going to react when he hears about you and his daughter.'

Myers coloured. 'I don't know what you've got against me, Detective. Did you fail your Oxford entrance exam?'

'I never fancied the place,' said Jo. 'Something about all those one-on-one tutorials made me feel uneasy. Maybe my gut instinct was right.'

She left him in reception.

Back in the CID room, Heidi had shouldered her bag, and switched off her computer. 'That's me done.'

'You should go home too, Jo,' said Carrick. 'Jack's finishing up at the college.'

'Anything new?'

He shook his head. 'Oh, apparently Hana Sigurdsson is landing in the morning.'

'You want me here to liaise?'

Carrick shot a glance towards Stratton's closed door. 'Better not, for now,' he said, and Jo got it. There were times to push the DCI, and times to give. This was the latter.

* * *

Her car stank of the Korean food, which would have cooled to the point of inedibility. She opened the window, despite the cold outside, and let the wintry wind blast the smell away.

Lucas's flat was in the Northcote area of Abingdon, a quarter-hour from the station. It wasn't much – a two-bed on the upper floor of a small nineties block – but it was well kept, with Lucas himself taking care of the communal gardens on behalf of the residents. Jo parked up beside his beat-up Land Rover. It was the only car not covered in a fine sheen of frost, and touching the bonnet there was still a hint of warmth. He must have nipped out. She dropped the takeaway into the outdoor bin, and as she approached the front door, the security light blinked on.

She took the stairs, and let herself into the dark apartment. Turning on the light, she saw his work boots by the door and his coat hanging on the peg. Jo made her way through to the open-plan kitchen-lounge. The bedroom door was closed. She opened the fridge, but it was scarce pickings. A pineapple, several condiments, some milk and cheese. Half a bottle of Picpoul de Pinet. So she settled for an impromptu midnight feast of pineapple chunks and a glass of cold wine while sitting at the small dining table. When she'd first learned Lucas didn't indulge in alcohol, she'd been reticent to drink at his flat, but he'd insisted it was okay. She knew already she'd have trouble sleeping without it tonight. There was a torn brown envelope on the floor by the table leg. HMRC. Probably another tax return reminder. Though he worked for the college, he was a freelance contractor.

'Hey, stranger,' said a voice.

Jo almost jumped out of her skin, dropping the piece of paper.

Lucas stood in the doorway of the bedroom, one arm resting on the frame, his blond surfer's hair tousled, squinting a little into the light. He wore just a pair of shorts, his muscular torso on display, and padded towards her on bare feet.

'You scared the shit out of me,' said Jo.

He folded his arms around her, and kissed the underside of her neck. 'Sorry. I thought you were a burglar.'

His stubble brushed her cheek, and though there was still a hint of the soap he used, his hair carried the scent of burned wood.

'You smell funny,' she said.

He leant past her and stabbed at a piece of pineapple, popping it in her mouth.

'Bonfire,' he said. 'You want me to shower?'

'We'll have to wash the sheets,' she said.

'Guess so.' He went to the fridge and took out a carton of milk. Tipping it back, he took several gulps. 'Busy day, huh?'

'Complicated,' she answered.

He replaced the milk. 'Want to talk about it?'

'Not really,' she said. 'Not much to talk about at the moment. You go out somewhere?'

'Huh?'

'Car's warm,' she said.

'Just the shops, Sherlock,' he said.

He took himself off to the bathroom. She heard the shower start up.

In the first weeks of their relationship, her work was all he'd wanted to ask about, but he'd cottoned on quickly that Jo would rather talk about anything else and now he was much better at gauging her mood. She found his own work much more fascinating. Gardening wasn't a topic she'd ever thought about much before, but Lucas had been working across the colleges for around eight years, and his tales of collegiate politics, student high jinks, and academic malfeasance were as rich as any case she'd worked on. It helped that he was a naturally gifted mimic. He had an eye for humour, an open disposition, and, compared with most people Jo came across, a sometimes charming innocence. She almost didn't want to share the things she came across day to day – the banality of deaths, the lies and desperation, the lives shattered and inconsequential in the fringes of society – for fear it would drain some of that positivity from him.

Of his own history, she knew little. He'd grown up in Somerset, and the accent remained. His parents, who had separated when he was seven, were both dead. He had a sister, in New Zealand now, with whom he spoke a handful of times a year. His friends in Oxford were mostly in the same line of work. He wanted, ultimately, to own his own landscaping company, but he was in no rush. At twenty-eight, Jo hadn't been either.

She wondered, in moments of self-doubt, what he thought of her. Over a decade older, weighed down by the pressures of work, one seriously failed romantic life behind her. She hadn't told him about the counselling, not because she was ashamed of it, but because it might have meant talking more about what had happened that night in Sally Carruthers' barn. Anyone with eyes and ears to take in the news was aware of the basics, of course. She and Lucas had met during the case – he'd been a helpful witness in the search for a suspect. But it hadn't been until four weeks after, and the bruises had faded, that he'd left a message through the front desk, that his offer of a drink was still open. Dimitriou had overheard, and found it hilarious. And though every instinct had screamed at Jo that it was a bad time, she had taken him up on it, having run a thorough criminal record check, of course. She couldn't help herself. Besides, Lucas was as clean as they came. The fact he looked like a Greek God cast away on a sun-kissed desert island helped.

She finished her wine and put the glass by the sink with the empty bowl of pineapple. Peeling off her clothes in the bedroom, which smelled faintly of smoke too, she walked naked to the bathroom door. It was thick with steam inside, but she could make out the shape of Lucas in the shower.

For a moment, she remembered Malin's bloody handprint across her mirror.

Pulling back the shower curtain, she climbed in behind him stealthily, then threaded a hand over his rib cage and taut stomach, making him jump.

'Now you're scaring *me*,' he said, turning and pulling her towards him, into the flow of hot water.

She ran her fingers through his hair, and kissed him tenderly, glad to be free of her thoughts – for a little while, at least.

Chapter 7

THURSDAY

The phone woke her from a deep and dreamless slumber. Lucas groaned slightly as she prised herself from under his arm, reaching into the darkness. She found the phone and answered. It was almost three am.

'Jo Masters.'

'Sorry it's late, Serge. Williams here.'

'Andrea.'

'We've got a body, ma'am,' said the PC.

The fog lifted in an instant and Jo sat up in bed. The room was cold, and the skin across her upper body broke into gooseflesh at once.

'Malin Sigurdsson?'

'Hard to tell, ma'am. It's submerged.'

'What's up?' asked Lucas sleepily.

'Nothing,' said Jo, swinging her legs out of bed. 'Just work.'

With one hand still on the phone, she manoeuvred her dressing gown off the hook. 'Location?'

'Near Little Baldon,' said Williams. 'Just down from where the main road crosses the river.'

Jo moved into the hall. 'Who called it in?'

'Truck driver. He's still here.'

'Keep him there. I'll be over in twenty minutes.'

She hung up and dressed quickly, feeling guilty for the excitement that quickened her heart, even though it might well be the young girl she was looking for.

Outside, the car was iced over again, and she gave it a cursory scrape before setting off into the deserted back roads that crisscross the farmland south of Oxford. The heaters took a while to get going and her hands were freezing as they clutched the wheel. Her headlights picked up a badger, the odd rabbit, their peaceful night's ramblings disturbed by her progress through small villages at close to the speed limit. A patch of black ice took her by surprise, and the car slid nauseatingly for a moment before traction took hold. *Slow down, Jo. She's not going anywhere.*

She phoned Pryce. It wasn't strictly necessary, but he'd always been clear he kept strange hours, and unlike Carrick, he wasn't a family man. Plus, there was something about the empty roads, with the grey spectres of sleeping houses, that made her long for his steady company. He answered almost right away, and after she'd filled him in, asked, 'Where's Little Baldon?'

'Nowhere near Myers' place,' said Jo, and gave him directions.

'On my way.'

⋆ ⋆ ⋆

It was a lonely place to die, if indeed the death had occurred here; empty farmland, weather-blasted hedgerows, with the occasional house set well back from the road. There was a dilapidated and disused petrol garage a couple of hundred metres from the bridge and the overhanging trees had been stripped back by the cross-country progress of lorries. Jo saw the spinning lights of a squad car pulled up in a layby by woodland, and a truck a few metres on bearing the name 'CoolFlo Logistics'.

The driver was sitting in his cab on his phone, smoking a roll-up. Constable Andrea Williams sat in the passenger seat, notebook in hand. Jo pulled up on the grass verge opposite, put on her hazards, climbed out and crossed the road. Williams climbed down to talk.

'Hi, boss,' she said. 'We're doing shifts.' She pointed to the bridge. 'Olly Pinker's down there now. You'd better be careful – there's no path and it's pretty slippery.'

'Got it. Trucker okay?'

'Just wants to get moving,' said Williams. 'He's on a three-day haul to Hungary. Got to get to Portsmouth by seven.'

'How did he find her?'

'Stopped to take a shit. Worked his way into the bushes to be clear of the road. Saw her. It sounds feasible. His English isn't great.'

'Speak to his employer if you can. Explain things. We'll need his details. Plus his movements over the last twenty-four hours,' she said. 'If it checks out, take a statement here and cut him loose.'

'Yes, boss.'

Jo looked towards the lorry. Killers coming back to the site of their crimes was a documented phenomenon. Sometimes they were even the ones to find the body, despite the inherent risk of being caught. But Williams was right – this didn't feel like that. The call of nature in a secluded area made more sense on the surface. And killers tended not to call in their own misdeeds.

The river was about twelve feet wide, with trees on each side. It was still flowing a little in the centre, but around the banks it had frozen solid after the days of zero or sub-zero temperatures. The bridge was stone on one side of the road, but the other was metal fencing. Jo saw the way down, a small cutting by the more modern side, through thick foliage. She peered over. Torchlight shone in her face then dipped away.

'Sorry, ma'am,' hollered Pinker. 'Careful how you come down.'

Jo tucked her own small torch into her pocket, gripped the uppermost stanchion of the bridge and placed her foot with care, supporting her weight as she lowered herself. She had to let go, and half walked, half scrambled on hands and feet to get to the bottom. There might have been a path down here once, but it was overgrown long ago. She picked her way through the scrubby grass and dotted bushes to where the PC was standing further down the bank.

The woman's body was face-down, lodged almost entirely in ice a foot from shore. She was clothed, in jeans, and some sort of pale puffer jacket. Straight away it felt wrong to Jo. The hair was hard to make out, but it looked too dark to be Malin Sigurdsson's.

'Crime scene are on their way,' said Pinker. 'Maybe thirty minutes.'

Jo crouched closer, looking up and down the bank, then back to the bridge. It seemed unlikely the woman could have fallen in by accident from the road. There was no pavement at the top, and it was hardly the place for a stroll.

Pryce arrived shortly after at the top of the slope. He made it a couple of steps, before his feet went from beneath him. With a cry he slid to the bottom, before exclaiming, 'Fuck's sake!'

Straightening his long grey coat, he walked over to them. 'Is it our missing person?'

'I don't think so,' said Jo. 'Can't be sure though.'

Pryce shone his torch at the body. 'How the hell did she end up here?'

'Suicide?' said Pinker.

Pryce moved the beam of his torch to the bridge. 'That's a ten-foot drop,' he said. 'I can think of more promising methods.'

Pinker blushed. 'Maybe she went in further upstream then, and drifted this far.'

'It's a theory,' said Jo. 'The river must have been freezing up for a couple of days at least, I think, and it's hardly fast-flowing. We'll know more if we can get an ID.'

She placed a hand on the ice, to test its thickness. There was no give.

'I've got a toolkit in the boot,' said Pryce. 'We can break her out if you want.'

Jo stood up. 'Let's wait for forensics to get a few pictures first,' she said. Pinker rubbed his hands together. 'Don't suppose I could wait in the car, guv? Been down here for forty minutes.'

'Sure,' said Jo. 'Go warm your cockles.'

The constable made his way back to the slope and Jo followed. Pryce delayed, taking a few paces further up the bank, shining his torch into the trees, then he came too. Near the slope he suddenly stopped and lifted a foot. 'Bugger! I think I stood in dog shit.'

Above, Pinker cackled. 'Not dog shit, boss. That's evidence.'

* * *

Pryce cleaned his shoe in the water and replaced his footwear with sports pumps from the boot of his car. They sat in Jo's vehicle for the next hour, sharing a thermos of tea, while he filled Jo in on his work that afternoon. Prints had come back from Malin's room at Oriel, and they'd found two sets primarily. One was Malin's, found on her clarinet and all over the room. The other was focused around the drawers in the bathroom and bedroom. 'Like someone was looking for something,' he said. 'Whoever left those is likely our prime suspect, don't you think?'

'Sounds plausible,' said Jo.

Frampton-Keys had given a full statement on the Myers affair. It seemed that the old tutor was telling the truth about one thing at least. Malin had dropped her complaint of harassment. The Vice Provost insisted that Myers had left the college voluntarily after that, and had returned his security pass. He'd come into college just once since, to meet with a former colleague on a committee. She claimed to know nothing about Malin's extra-curricular relationships.

'You think Anna Mull had some sort of axe to grind?' asked Jo.

'Could be,' said Pryce. 'There were some concerns, last academic year – an accusation of plagiarism against Anna, by one Ronald Myers. She got off with a warning.'

'You think she knows more about the disappearance than she's letting on?'

Pryce shrugged. 'Everyone knows more than they let on. She was leaving for the vac today, wasn't she?'

'The *vac*? You mean the holidays? You sound like one of their lot.'

Pryce smiled, and raised his eyebrows. 'Guilty as charged, ma'am.'

'You came to uni here?'

'Cambridge,' he said. 'Computer science, though. Proper subject, not like History.'

'Hey, I studied History!' Jo protested.

His demeanour shifted and he looked suddenly quite mortified. 'Oh. I didn't . . . Sorry, ma'am.'

She laughed, reached across without thinking, and touched his wrist. 'Don't worry – I might have been offended two decades ago, but it's all a distant memory now.'

He looked at her hand, and she pulled it away again. *That was stupid, Josephine. Change the subject . . .*

'So how'd you end up being a plod?'

Pryce lay his head back on the rest. 'My father was in the force. That almost convinced me not to – he wasn't a happy man. My folks broke up when I was thirteen, mostly because he was never around. He died when I was seventeen at the grand old age of forty-nine.'

'So what changed your mind?' asked Jo. 'Can't have been the money.'

He looked at her. 'Maybe I'll let you go first.'

'Oh, I often ask myself the same question,' she said. 'I suppose I wanted to make a difference. Fuck, that sounds naff.'

'A little,' said Pryce. 'But at least you succeeded. That Dylan Jones stuff was . . . out there.'

Silence fell for a few seconds. She realised they'd never spoken of the case at all until then. In fact, few of her colleagues ever mentioned it. They must have recognised it was tacitly off-limits, at least for the time being.

'Sorry, if you don't want to talk about it . . .' continued Pryce.

'It's not that,' said Jo. 'They've had me seeing a shrink, that's all. I'm all talked out. Anyway, what about you?'

Pryce sipped his tea, and looked at her, as if considering sharing some confidence. His gaze was slightly disconcerting, and the car seemed a fraction too small.

'I worked in IT for a few years, but I suppose I wanted to see what it was all about. On the thin blue line.'

'And has it lived up to expectations?'

His eyes lingered on hers. 'So far, yes.'

Jo was glad to see the lights of the forensics van approaching. 'Why don't you see how Williams and Pinker are doing with the driver? I'll chat to these guys.'

* * *

After taking pictures, and some initial measurements, the crime scene team set to the task of getting the body out of the river. No one had an ice-pick, but they made use of Pryce's crowbar to chip away at the thicker ice, until cracks began to appear. Williams and Jo hauled the body up onto the bank together.

The dead woman was quite stiff, and Jo didn't know if it was rigor mortis, or that the extreme cold had frozen her limbs. As they rolled her over, Jo saw her suspicions confirmed – it clearly wasn't Malin Sigurdsson. The woman's skin was a light shade of violet, and one eye was half open, the other glued shut, but the features were all wrong. Her face was teardrop-shaped, the eyes widely spaced, with a pointed chin and thin lips. She could only have weighed seven or eight stone when not waterlogged. The right sleeve of her jacket was torn open, and three of the fingers on her right hand were misshapen grotesquely, snapped like twigs. Her right leg around the knees was badly skinned, protruding through a hole in her jeans.

'Something bashed her around,' said Pryce.

Jo glanced back to the road, and a new theory came to her. 'You think it was a hit and run? She gets knocked down and stumbles down here somehow?'

Pryce shrugged. 'Maybe. Odd place to be walking, though.'

The lead CSO was Mel Cropper, a dour man in his late

forties with an air of perpetual disappointment, three failed marriages, and a sense of humour that made people uncomfortable. Rumour had it his family owned a funeral parlour, but his elder brother had taken it over, and he'd chosen forensics to get his kicks. He was also very, very thorough. He pulled up the woman's top lip and shone a torch inside. Jo saw straightaway the victim's teeth were in good condition.

'Anything in her pockets?' asked Pryce.

Jo patted the jeans, but found nothing. Reaching into the woman's jacket, she felt something in the inside pocket. She pulled out a lanyard with a plastic tag case. There was a passport photo and a name underneath. Natalie Palmer. Though slightly blurred, it was unmistakably the woman before them. At the top of the tag was a crest, and the words 'Jesus College – Staff'.

'Christ, I know this one,' said Pinker. 'She went missing last week. The mother reported it and I went to take details in Blackbird Leys. Place was a real shithole. Mum's a smackhead.'

'Daughter too, maybe,' said Pryce.

'Still doesn't explain what she was doing out here,' said Jo. 'Can't imagine she gets her fix in a layby two miles from the city centre.' She watched Cropper work. 'Any idea of the cause of death?'

'Too early to say for sure, but I'd lean towards hit and run too. She somehow fell in. If she was already disorientated and injured, the cold of the water could well have induced cardiac arrest. And if she was high, it would only compromise her further.'

'When will we know for sure?' asked Pryce.

'Failing her waking up and telling us, we'll look at her lungs as soon as she's on the slab,' said Cropper. 'Given it looks criminal, I'm sure it'll bump anything else. Vera's back from sabbatical, you know.'

'I heard,' said Jo.

Vera was Vera Coyne, Thames Valley's most experienced pathologist. She was also, according to some insider gossip, the object of Cropper's unrequited affections.

Cropper fished out a purse and a set of keys from Natalie Palmer's jacket, handing them to Jo. The purse contained a five-pound note, a library card, and bank card in the same name, and the two keys were a Yale and a Mortice. Jo bagged them. There was no phone.

Jo thanked him and headed back towards the road, where Andrea Williams had set up a tape. There was no traffic and the lorry had moved on. The sun wouldn't be up for another couple of hours. Jo walked along the road, shining her torch on the tarmac. Nothing on the near side. But as she followed the far side she saw it, about twenty yards up from the bridge. A long slew of rubber, crossing the centre line. Someone had skidded to a sudden, barely controlled stop. She went back to where the markings began.

'Found something?' called Pryce.

'I think so,' she said. Crouching down on the road, she examined a small patch of blood.

'We're going to need to close this section, and mark out the skids with cones,' she said. 'Get a team to come out and extract this rubber. The CSOs can take proper measurements when the light's improved. Tell Cropper to sample the blood too. Heidi can check any ANPR cameras out this way.' She looked along the road, trying to imagine what Natalie was doing when the car hit her. 'We need to inform the mother. You want to come and do the honours?'

Pryce didn't look particularly happy about that, but nodded.

* * *

Jo had a text from Lucas asking if she'd be back for breakfast and replied in the negative. If Natalie had been a minor they would have gone round to the next of kin straight away, but Jo made the call to give it until after sunrise. She and Pryce returned to the station instead, in order to check the missing persons file Pinker had mentioned. Dimitriou was the assigned investigator, but the case was low priority. When they spoke to him at home, he seemed shocked.

'Ms Palmer couldn't even tell us where her daughter worked – just said she did cleaning jobs,' he said. 'Dad's a Polish national – out of the picture. We tried to call the phone but it was switched off. I'll see what the DCI wants to do. Makes sense for me to follow up.'

He didn't sound enthused at the idea, and was probably already anticipating the struggle ahead. A possible user in a hit and run, with no witnesses, at an undetermined time. As her old friend Harry Ferman would say, it looked like 'a hiding to nothing'.

As is happened, Stratton made the opposite call. 'You take the Palmer case, Jo,' he said.

'Sir, Dimitriou . . .'

'. . . has got a couple of days of training coming up. You stick with it, Masters. I've every faith in you.'

Jo sighed inwardly. *Every faith that I'll come back empty-handed, you Machiavellian bastard.*

'And take Jack along,' Stratton added. 'It'll be good experience on a bread-and-butter case.'

She shouldn't have been surprised. The Myers hand that had seemed a winner was looking like a busted flush, and that had been Jo's call. This was payback – to keep her off the case, and put her back in her place.

They drove out to the Blackbird Leys estate off the Cowley Road. The car thermometer said it was zero degrees outside.

The address for Natalie's mother was a narrow modern terrace. The front garden was strewn with rubbish, and the house to the left was boarded up. A mattress leaned against the fence, springs protruding from what looked like a burned patch. A black bag, torn open by rodents maybe, was spilling its contents. Not a soul in sight.

Jo rang the bell, but there was no sound from within. She knocked instead. When no one answered after a minute, and with nothing stirring inside, she thumped harder, opened the letter box and called out, 'Susan?'

'I'll check the back,' said Pryce. He squeezed past the mattress.

Jo banged the door again.

Next door on the right, an upstairs window opened and a middle-aged man looked out. 'Can you keep the fucking noise down, love?'

Jo held up her warrant card. 'With apologies. Do you know if Susan's in?'

The man closed his window again.

Nothing like the neighbourly spirit, thought Jo. Then the front door opened. It was Pryce. 'Back was unlocked.'

Jo stepped into a hallway of bare underlay. Straightaway she covered her nose.

'Christ, what's that smell?'

'Looks like a cat has been using the kitchen as a toilet,' said Pryce. 'At least, I hope it's a cat.'

Jo called for Susan again, announced herself as police, and began to search. In the front room was a sofa, and a small coffee table. The attachments for a wall-mounted TV were there, but no screen. Several makeshift ashtrays and beer cans were scattered about. It was freezing cold.

The kitchen was similarly sparse. Curled turds were piled in an under-counter space where it looked like there might have once been a washing machine. A cereal box lay on its side on the floor.

Jo went first up the stairs. Three doors opened off the landing, the first into a filthy bathroom that smelled faintly of vomit. The next was closed. The end door was slightly ajar. A woman in a dressing gown was sitting up in bed, her eyes glassy and unfocused. One arm was exposed and covered in angry red marks. On the floor at her side, though Jo hardly needed it for proof, was a syringe. The bedside table was strewn with other drug paraphernalia.

'Who are you?' asked the woman, lighting a cigarette. She didn't seem particularly alarmed at strangers coming up her stairs.

'We knocked,' said Jo. 'We're the police. Susan, is it?'

The woman nodded, and took a long suck. 'I suppose this is about Natalie?'

Jo nodded. 'Would you like to get dressed? We could talk downstairs.'

Susan Palmer nodded, so she must have registered Jo's words. Though if she had any idea of the news to come, her face didn't betray it. 'Give me a minute,' she said.

Jo and Pryce retreated to the lower floor to wait. Jo had been in plenty of addicts' homes before – the chaos was familiar enough; the lack of basic sanitation, the items of value sold long ago in a vain effort to score. The shell of a life once lived but now losing its grip on humanity as it hollowed to a banal routine of addiction. Pryce looked vaguely sickened at it all. They heard the toilet flush and water running, then feet moving upstairs. Less than ten minutes later, Susan Palmer entered the room, looking transformed. She was dressed in clean clothes, her hair brushed and tied back, her eyes bright. Whether it was chemical or not, Jo was impressed. In Susan's face was a shadow of the woman she must have once been. The news she'd come to deliver suddenly weighed more heavily on her tongue.

'Can I get you a cup of tea?' asked Susan.

Jo appreciated the politeness but at the same time recalled the kitchen. 'We're fine, thanks. Ms Palmer, I'm afraid we've got some bad news.'

Natalie's mother wrung her hands. 'She's dead, is she?'

Jo nodded. 'I'm sorry.'

Susan was speechless for a moment, eyes downcast to the corner of the room, as if accessing a memory. 'Right,' she muttered.

'You don't seem surprised,' said Pryce. His tone was tinged with curiosity.

'Where?' asked Susan.

'We found Natalie about two miles from the city, near a village called Little Baldon,' said Jo. 'It's too early to tell for certain, but it looks like she may have been hit by a car.'

Susan sat on the arm of the sofa, hands in her lap.

'Do you know why she might have been out that way?' asked Jo. 'Did she have . . . friends there?'

The mother shook her head. 'I don't think so. I knew something was wrong. Normally she'd call me if she was going to be back late.'

Jo took out her pocket book. 'When did you last see your daughter?'

'I . . . don't know,' said Susan. 'Maybe last week.'

'Have a think. Today is Thursday.'

'She had a job somewhere.'

'We believe she worked at Jesus College,' said Jo.

Susan shrugged. 'Rings a bell.'

'So she kept in touch by phone?' asked Pryce.

'Sometimes,' said Susan. 'When she had credit. Where did this happen again?'

'Near Little Baldon,' Jo repeated. 'Did Natalie have a car of her own?'

Susan laughed bitterly.

Jo waited a moment, before asking, 'Is that Natalie's room upstairs?' Susan nodded. 'Would it be okay to have a look inside?'

'She keeps it locked.'

The Mortice key in evidence would likely fit. They could break the door down, but that seemed unnecessary without the pressing suspicion of evidence inside, and the house was dilapidated enough already. It could wait.

Pryce leant forward. 'Ms Palmer, did your daughter have any history of sex work?'

The insensitivity of the question took Jo by surprise, and Susan looked up sharply. 'Shame on you.'

'I apologise, we need to know,' said Pryce. 'It seems odd she was in a remote location, so understanding why and how she went there might help us work out what happened.'

'She wasn't a prostitute,' said Susan, and she lifted her hand to her face as she began to cry. 'She was my little girl.'

'I think we've got what we need here,' said Jo, putting her pad away and giving Pryce a hard look. 'We're sorry for your loss. There's one more thing, though. I know it will be very difficult, but do you think you'd be able to carry out a formal identification for us in the coming day or two?'

'See her, you mean?'

'Yes,' said Jo. 'An officer would take you to the morgue, and you'd have to look at Natalie's face to confirm it's her.'

Susan nodded. 'I can manage that.'

Jo glanced at Pryce. She wasn't sure about leaving Susan Palmer alone. 'Is there anyone who can come over?' she said. 'Family or friends nearby?'

Susan shook her head. 'No . . . it was just us.'

Chapter 8

With Susan unable to give them anything useful, the next obvious line of enquiry was her daughter's place of work. They drove down the narrow lanes to get to Broad Street, one of the main tourist thoroughfares, past the looming Bodleian Library and the grave stone heads atop the railings outside the Sheldonian Theatre. All the parking spaces were full, so Jo pulled up on the pavement, right outside the arched entrance to Jesus College on Turl Street. The front door was locked, but there was a buzzer.

'How can I help you?' said a man's voice.

'Thames Valley Police,' said Jo.

'Hold on a moment.'

They waited, heard footsteps on stone inside, then the door opened. A forty-something man with sandy hair and a lazy left eye, wearing a college sweater peered out. Jo showed her warrant card. 'I wonder if there's someone we could speak with about a member of staff – Natalie Palmer.'

The man paused, then moved aside. 'Come in. I'll see who I can find.'

They waited in a vaulted stone vestibule outside a small office as the porter retreated inside and made a phone call. Shortly another man arrived, fractionally younger, and suited, with a college tie. 'I'm Gavin Maxwell,' he said. 'Facilities manager. I'm afraid the majority of our staff are away this time of year. You're looking for someone?'

Jo showed him the picture of Natalie. 'We believe this young lady worked at the college,' she said. 'I'm sorry to say that she's been found dead, in suspicious circumstances. We're wondering if there's anyone we could talk to – a colleague perhaps?'

Maxwell's eyes widened. 'Goodness, that's terrible. I'm afraid I don't recognise her. Are you sure it was this college?'

'Her body was found with a lanyard indicating she worked here,' said Jo. 'Perhaps as a cleaner.'

'Oh, right,' said Maxwell. 'Well, that might explain things. There's often a quick turnover. One minute.' He went into the office with the sandy-haired doorman, spoke for a few moments. The other man went off around the quad.

'Porter's gone to find another of the cleaning staff,' he said. 'Shouldn't be long.'

It wasn't. Soon the doorman returned and with him, wearing blue cleaning overalls, was a nervous-looking young woman.

'This is Heather Braddock,' said Maxwell. 'A colleague of Natalie's.'

'Esther Braddock,' said the woman, without umbrage. 'Is it true? You found Natalie? She's . . . dead?'

'I'm afraid so,' said Jo.

Esther covered her mouth. 'How?'

'We're not certain, but it might have been a hit and run. I'll be honest, we've got very little to go on at the moment, so we're just trying to paint a picture of what Natalie might have been doing in her final hours. When did you last see her?'

'Tuesday,' Braddock said quickly. 'We had lunch together after our morning shift, in the back of the college kitchen. She didn't show up for work either yesterday or today.'

'Is that unusual?'

'Very. She was normally very punctual. This job was important to her.'

'Can I ask,' said Pryce, 'did Natalie have a narcotics problem?'

The facilities manager reeled back. 'Surely not! We have a very strict policy on hiring staff at—'

'I'm sure you do,' said Pryce, 'but sometimes these things aren't obvious. Functioning addicts can conceal their habits very effectively. Did you know her mother has a drug problem?'

'That's really not college business, is it?' said Maxwell.

Jo focused on Braddock. 'Can you shed any light for us, Esther? Anything that might help?'

Braddock looked a little frightened to be the centre of attention. 'I never saw her doing drugs,' she said. 'She seemed, well, normal I guess. But . . .' Her eyes shifted sideways towards the facilities manager briefly.

'Go on,' urged Jo.

'It's probably nothing, but there was someone here, about two weeks ago, looking for Natalie. A guy. She seemed scared of him.'

'How so?'

'He said he was her boyfriend, but I'm pretty sure that wasn't true.'

'You know this man's name?'

She shook her head. 'I'm sorry.'

'Can you describe him?'

'Not tall – maybe five foot six or seven. But really big, muscular. He was wearing a vest, even though it was cold. And sweating a bit too, like he'd just come from the gym. Spiky hair.'

'Ethnicity?'

'White. But, like, very tanned. I remember thinking he must spend a lot of time on sunbeds.'

'And what did they talk about?'

'I don't know. Natalie told me not to get involved, and afterwards she wouldn't talk about it. They were arguing, though. It was right outside the front gates, in the street.'

'Did he assault her?'

'Nothing like that. But . . . well, he looked like he would have, if they were alone. She left with him.'

'In a vehicle?'

'You can't park here, so I don't know. They walked off together, towards the High Street.'

'And this was about a fortnight ago?' said Pryce. Esther nodded. 'But when she didn't turn up yesterday, you weren't worried.'

'A little, I just didn't think . . .' Esther's lip trembled. 'If I'd known . . .'

'It's all right,' said Jo. 'You've been very helpful. Do you think you could come to the station and look through a few pictures for us?'

'I finish here at midday,' said Esther. 'Then I have work at a supermarket in the afternoon.'

'It shouldn't take long,' said Jo. 'Perhaps your boss could spare you for an hour?' Maxwell didn't look especially keen, so Jo added, 'The sooner we rule out any drug connections to the college the better, I think.'

'Of course,' said the facilities manager smarmily. 'Take all the time you need, Esther.'

* * *

Back at her desk, Jo brought up all known violent offenders in the area, with a maximum height of five foot eight, and with a muscular build. A collection of mugshots flicked across the screen. Esther gave them all diligent attention, but shook her head at each picture. 'I'm really sorry,' she said afterwards. 'He was *really* big. You know, like a body builder.'

'That's all right,' said Jo. She wondered about doing a trawl of the gyms in town, but there'd be so many, and the chances of stumbling across their man was tiny. If he even *was* their man. There were a couple of CCTV cameras on the High Street that might show their guy with Natalie, and though Esther was able to give them a pretty accurate time for the altercation, between ten and half past in the morning, she wasn't sure on the actual day. That didn't deter Pryce though, who set off alone to gather what he could from the most obvious cameras where Turl Street met the High Street.

Jo admired his optimism. To her, the row outside Jesus College was hardly conclusive of anything. It wasn't even on the day of Natalie's disappearance, and there didn't seem any obvious connection to Little Baldon either.

Jo thanked Esther for her time and led her out. As she was exchanging details, a taxi pulled up outside the front of the St Aldates station building. The woman who emerged looked like a movie star, in a long coat lined with fur, her grey hair expensively styled. She walked up the steps and inside the building. Jo followed, just in time to hear the front desk clerk speaking with DCI Stratton on the internal phone.

'He's coming right out, Ms Sigurdsson. If you'd like to take a seat.'

Jo walked over and introduced herself. 'I can take you through, if you'd like. I'm Detective Masters.'

'Are you working on my daughter's case?' asked the woman. She was older than she had been in the only picture Jo had seen, with obvious lines on her face, and a brittle demeanour like fine porcelain, though her posture was erect. On her fingers were several chunky gold rings. She was looking around the room in a curious way, and Jo guessed this might be her first time in the surroundings of a British police station, with its utilitarian furniture, and collection of grim, vaguely threatening posters pinned to the noticeboard.

'Sort of,' said Jo.

As they passed the security gate, Stratton came jogging the other way. He saw Jo, then held out a hand to Hana Sigurdsson. 'Philip Stratton. I'm the Detective Chief Inspector,' he said. 'We didn't realise you were coming by.'

'I didn't tell you,' said Hana. 'I hope it's not a problem.'

'Of course not!' said Stratton. 'I've been keeping Malin's step-father abreast of the situation. I don't know what he's told you.'

'We haven't spoken directly for two years,' said Hana. 'And he isn't her step-father anymore. We're divorced.'

Stratton blushed. 'Right.'

They reached the CID room, where Hana Sigurdsson looked utterly incongruous against the drab surroundings.

'Sorry it's so cold in here,' said Jo's boss. 'We're having the central heating looked at.'

'I was born in Tore,' said Hana. 'A fraction south of the Arctic Circle. We would call this mild.'

She didn't smile, so it wasn't clear if she was making a joke or a criticism. The confusion battled on Stratton's face as he tried to work out which.

Jo came to his rescue. 'Shall I give Ms Sigurdsson an update, sir?'

'That would be appreciated, thank you,' said Malin's mother.

'Detective Carrick is leading the case,' said Stratton. He turned around, and spoke in a tone of borderline panic. 'Does anyone know where Andy's got to?'

'He's following up at . . . the house,' said Jo. It didn't seem the right time to divulge the recent discoveries about Ronald Myers. 'But I know all the relevant details. I can take Ms Sigurdsson through things.'

'Really, we should call Detective Carrick,' said Stratton. 'I'm sure he'll—'

'I'm rather tired,' said Hana. 'It's been a troubling few hours. Detective Masters here can share the necessary details.' Jo was impressed she'd taken in her name. Perhaps she wasn't quite as disengaged as she appeared.

Silenced, Stratton nodded.

'Come this way, please,' said Jo. 'Can I get you a drink of something?'

'A martini would be wonderful,' said Hana.

'I'm afraid we can stretch to tea or coffee or water,' said Jo.

'Water, then, please.' For the first time since entering, Hana Sigurdsson appeared slightly meek, as if the aloofness until that point was a façade she could no longer maintain.

In the visitor suite, Jo took her through the basics of the case so far, including the blood found in the bathroom, but didn't mention Catskill or Myers. She left them out deliberately, not because she felt inclined to conceal Malin's sexual activity from her mother, but because she still wasn't sure of their relevance herself. Both relationships to her looked odd, then again it wasn't her role to judge the peccadilloes and sexual proclivities of other women. Hana, listening patiently, nodded as Jo covered the salient points, and then at the end, asked a simple question.

'Do you think she's alive, Detective?'

Jo took a moment. In truth, on the balance of probabilities, it seemed more likely than ever that Malin was dead. They'd not heard a word since the disappearance. And looking into her mother's startling green eyes, she thought Hana suspected the same. 'We're working on the assumption that she is,' said

Jo. 'You might still catch her friend Anna at the college. She's leaving today I think.'

'Anna?'

'Anna Mull,' said Jo. 'It was she who first realised Malin was missing.'

'Oh, I know who she is,' said Hana, 'but I thought they'd drifted apart some time ago. At least, that's the impression Malin gave.'

'An argument?' said Jo.

'Oh, no, nothing like that,' said Hana. 'Just the ebbs and flows of friendship, I'm sure.'

The door opened and Andy Carrick came in, with Stratton at his back. He apologised for his absence, then began to recap the same information.

Hana stood up. 'Forgive me, Detective – your colleague has already been very thorough. It sounds as though, at the moment, you really know very little. This is disappointing, but I don't want to take up any more of the time that could be employed actually looking for my daughter.' She held out her hand to Jo, who shook it. 'You have my details, Detective Masters. I'll be staying at the Randolph for the coming days. Do you know it?'

'Of course,' interrupted Stratton. It was the most prestigious hotel in Oxford. 'Let me show you out.' Jo half expected him to curtsey.

When he'd left, Jo turned to Carrick.

'I know it's none of my business, but I think it might be worth chatting to Anna Mull again.'

'Oh yes?' said Carrick. 'I never met the girl.'

'Something doesn't quite add up there. Did you ever check up on her story about she and Malin having dinner together Tuesday night?'

Carrick nodded. 'Landlord at the King's Arms remembered

them. Malin anyway. She was with one other friend – a girl. Do you think she's lying to us?'

'I think she might be smarter than she let on. She implicated Catskill. And then she pointed the finger towards Myers. She claims to be Malin's friend, but doesn't live with her, and her mum doesn't seem to think they're close.'

Carrick cocked his head. 'When you put it like that . . .'

⋆ ⋆ ⋆

Jo logged on just after midday. A brief email from Vera Coyne in the pathology lab had come through, with some appended images of Natalie Palmer's anatomy. Jo skimmed the list of findings. Severe contusions to right hip, right elbow. Fractures to the right fingers and hands and a broken left wrist. Fractured skull. The pictures showed close-ups. The cause of death wasn't listed, but in the email Coyne said she suspected drowning.

Jo called her, and she answered after two rings. 'Hello?'

'Jo Masters. Just wanted to thank you for the quick work.'

'No problem. I've got you on speaker, by the way. Hands full. Literally. Cirrhotic liver. Life advice: don't drink.'

Bit late for that . . .

'So could it still be a hit and run?' said Jo.

She heard the rattle of equipment. 'Possible,' said Coyne. 'I'd have expected some more blunt force trauma on the lower body from vehicle impact, but it might just have clipped her.'

'And then she fell into the water?'

'Not my call,' said Coyne. 'But looking back at the scene-of-death photos, I personally think it would have been very hard to fall over the side of the bridge, especially with her injuries. But there's water in the lungs so she was alive before she entered. Still a slight question mark over whether it's river water or not, but that seems the most obvious interpretation prior to more comprehensive analysis.'

'Time of death?' said Jo.

'Can't give you much there,' said Coyne. 'There was little indication of putrefaction, but the water temp would severely retard the process. Mel Cropper tested her body temp at the scene, and even with the accelerated cooling due to conditions, I think well over twenty-four hours, but really she could have gone in several days ago. Stomach contents included undigested pasta. It'll be a few hours before we get toxicology.'

'Sexual activity?'

'No obvious indications,' said Coyne.

'Thanks again,' said Jo. 'Are you releasing the body? We need the mum to formally ID.'

'That's fine,' said Coyne. 'Full report should be with you tomorrow. Call if you need more.'

Afterwards, Jo rang Natalie's cleaning colleague Esther Braddock and confirmed that Natalie had indeed eaten a home-made pasta salad when they shared lunch. That narrowed the window somewhat to Tuesday itself, but it didn't answer why or how Natalie had found her way out to Little Baldon.

Jo called across the desk to Tan. 'Heidi, can we put out an appeal to motorists and general witnesses. Social media channels, local radio, and boards on both sides of the Little Baldon road. Might get nothing, but it's worth a shot. Looks like Natalie was killed some time on Tuesday after two pm.'

'On it,' said Heidi.

Stratton came jogging over. 'What's all this?'

'Coroner agrees it was probably a hit and run,' she said.

'Probably?' said Stratton. 'She couldn't have hurt herself falling in?'

She knew where the DCI was coming from. The chances of solving a random hit and run were small, and would affect his stats, but if the death could be chalked up to an accident under the influence of narcotics, no one would care less. 'There were skid marks on the road too,' she said. 'I think we have to pursue it as a suspicious death at least.'

Stratton sighed. 'Bloody marvellous. Jack was saying the victim's bedroom was locked.'

'Key's in evidence, sir.'

'Probably worth a look, don't you think?'

'I doubt it. I'm guessing Natalie locked it to keep her mum from flogging her stuff.'

'Indeed. Still, cover all bases, eh?'

'Is that an order, sir?'

Stratton flashed his most unfriendly smile. 'Consider it a request from your commanding officer.'

* * *

Pryce arrived back after she'd signed the key out of evidence. After much wrangling with the manager of a restaurant to get CCTV, it had come back empty. It looked like Natalie and her mystery muscleman had taken one of the other warren of medieval streets near Jesus college. 'Stratton wants us to look at Natalie's room,' she explained.

'Sounds good,' said Pryce.

'It *sounds* like a waste of time,' said Jo, 'but your enthusiasm is noted for your next performance review.'

He left to warm up the car, and Jo found Carrick back at his desk, clicking through his emails.

'How'd it go at Myers' house?'

'Nothing,' he replied. 'Some pornography, hard copy, but very vanilla.'

'A computer?'

'Would you believe, he doesn't even own one?' He rubbed

his tired eyes. 'We went over his car. No blood in the boot or the backseat. A couple of hairs in the front that look probable, but he admitted they'd been for a drive together.'

Jo could imagine it. If she'd seen them out she'd have assumed they were father and daughter.

Carrick's eyes widened a fraction as he looked at his screen. 'Hello. This might be something.'

She scooted her chair across.

The screen showed bank records for Malin Sigurdsson, and the tabs went back several months. Jo scanned the figures. Money came in from two sources – a Coutts bank account of N. Cranleigh, and a Norwegian Nordea account in her mother's name. In total, about four grand every month between them.

'She was doing all right,' said Jo. The payments stopped in June though.

'Yeah, and check out the outgoings. Notice anything?'

At first it looked like the normal things. Regular debit payments for small amounts at bookshops, cafes, a stationer's, the college bar, mobile phone charges. Then Jo saw what Carrick was getting at. There were an awful lot of cash withdrawals. Large amounts, including several at the maximum of £250.

'Maybe she ate out a lot,' said Carrick.

'Perhaps,' said Jo, 'but who pays for meals out with cash these days?'

Her phone rang through from the front desk.

'Hello?'

'Got a call for you. Mrs Plumley.'

'Who?'

'Says she lives in the flat beneath you.'

Jo realised he was talking about Deidre the octogenarian on the first floor of Lucas's block. She was a sweet old thing, with a family who rarely visited. Jo felt suddenly cold. *Had something happened to Lucas?*

‘What’s the matter?’ she asked, once the call had been connected.

‘Oh, Josie, thank goodness!’ came the tremulous voice. ‘There’s water coming through the ceiling. I tried calling Luke, but he’s not answering. I’m sorry to bother you at work, but I didn’t know who to call.’

‘Have you tried the building manager?’

‘I’ve not got their number.’

Jo tried to think. She didn’t know it either. She wondered how much water there was. She wasn’t sure where the stopcock was for the block, but Lucas would. He was working at Gloucester College, as far as she knew.

‘Hold on, Mrs Plumley. I’ll call back in a minute.’

She dialled Lucas straight away, but he didn’t pick up, so she left a message asking him to call her, then began to gather her things.

‘Something up?’ asked Pryce, as she went outside.

She told him about the water leak. ‘It’s probably a burst pipe. Back soon. Do you think you could go to Susan Palmer’s place solo?’

He looked disappointed. ‘Er . . . yeah. Sure.’

‘And see if you can get anything else from her about Little Baldon. There must be a link somewhere.’

She called Lucas repeatedly as she drove, but he still wasn’t answering. It wasn’t unusual for him not to pick up – a lot of the time he had his hands full at work. She pulled up at the college, and as she was hurrying into the visitor’s lodge, her phone rang. It was him.

‘Where are you?’ she said.

‘I got your message. I’m on my way back to the flat now.’ He was breathing hard. The doorman in the lodge was waiting patiently. Jo held up a hand to apologise, and signalled two minutes with her fingers.

'Oh, good. Deidre's in a state. She couldn't get hold of you.'

'I was shifting logs with Bob,' he said. 'Hey, you okay? You left early this morning.'

'Just work,' she replied. 'I'll see you later, all right?'

Jo hung up after he said goodbye. 'Sorry false alarm,' she said to the porter. As she left, she saw Bob, the Head Gardener at the college, rolling a cigarette just by the edge of the quadrangle inside. She didn't know him well. They'd spent no more than an hour together at the pub, one time in the late summer when she'd got out of work at a reasonable time. He was a sweet guy.

'Hello, Josie,' he said. 'How's tricks?'

'Good thanks,' she said. 'You've had a hard morning, I hear.'

He shrugged. 'Not especially. Had to scoop half a dozen carp out of the Provost's pond. This bloody weather.'

'I meant the logs,' said Jo.

Bob put his hand behind his ear. 'Eh? What's that?'

'Never mind,' said Jo. 'Just don't let Lucas make you do all the heavy lifting.'

He still looked confused. 'Sorry, lass, I'm not following you. He's got the morning off, hasn't he?'

She almost pushed it, but something made her cast aside the uneasy feeling in her gut, say 'Don't worry', and wave farewell.

Chapter 9

She opted not to go straight back to the station, but instead walked the short distance to Oriel, and the street behind the college by which Malin was surely taken. Pryce was right about the fire exit. No one could have opened it from the street side, which meant that whoever took Malin from the room must have gained access either through the other entrances, or have been admitted through the fire exit. Her mind circled back to Ronald Myers. If Malin had let him in this way, for some sort of encounter that even now she struggled to envisage, it wouldn't matter that his security pass had been returned.

But his car hadn't shown the smallest drop of Malin's blood, and though she thought he could probably lift Malin, manhandling her body into the back of an MG seemed almost farcical.

But who else? This person Ross Catskill claimed was following Malin? Maybe observing her movements, getting an idea of her routine and that of the college? If someone had planned a kidnap for a long time, it was possible they might work out a way in. The Oxford colleges had a stream of visitors, staff and students, and were hardly renowned for their high-tech security systems. In most, the only door staff monitoring the places were the porters in the lodges at the main entrances. Though many were ex-services, they were mostly in their sixties or older.

Jo grabbed a sandwich from a stall in the covered market, and ate it outside the Radcliffe Camera, the Palladian style library that sat in the square between the Bodleian Library and St Mary's Church. Even in all her layers, she was cold, but the cold sharpened her thoughts.

She could tell herself that people lied every day, and the reasons weren't always terrible, so why did the fact that Lucas had done so trouble her as much as it did? Perhaps because of Ben. The lie her ex had told, or rather the chronic gambling problem he'd hidden, had shattered their lives into pieces. The stakes weren't as high with Lucas, but the feeling of being betrayed was a painful echo, like the ache of an old war wound. But the worst part – the thing that made her hate *herself* a little bit – was the gnawing sense of her own cowardice. Even though in an interrogation room, she'd never rest until she had smashed through the lies to get to the truth, in her own life it was different. Because sometimes the truth could hurt a great deal.

* * *

When she got back to St Aldates, she was so cold she couldn't feel her feet. Pryce was there already, loading images onto his computer from a small digital camera. On his screen, Jo saw several photos of a small but tidy bedroom, with lilac curtains and what looked like a child's bookshelf. Pryce had taken a close-up, and it appeared that Natalie Palmer had a tendency towards romantic fiction. A single bed was neatly made, with a small lamp and a jewellery box on the table beside it.

'Looks like she had her life pretty together,' said Jo. 'How was Susan doing?'

Pryce detached his camera. 'Oblivious, mostly. I called social services. I'm not sure she'd have been able to ID herself, let alone her daughter.'

'Can't blame her.'

Heidi called over across the bank of desks. 'Guys, we've got a potential witness for your hit and run,' she said. 'Said they saw a van parked up by that bridge Tuesday evening.'

'Go on,' said Jo, moving towards her colleague, while Pryce remained seated.

'I'll email over the details, but' – she read from her notepad – 'A mum going to pick her daughter up from dance. She said she saw a white transit-style van – no markings that she recalls – stopped in the middle of the road, hazards on. She went around it. She didn't stop because she was running late, and she didn't see anybody near the vehicle.'

'What time was this?'

'Between 18.20 and 18.25, she thinks.'

'She thinks?' said Jo. 'That's a narrow window.'

'Like I said, she picks the daughter up at 18.30, and she left the house at 18.15. It was going to be tight. Sounds promising, right?'

'Damn right,' said Jo. 'If we find that van, and match the tyres. We should check with the ANPR network.'

'I'll take care of it,' said Pryce. 'I'll isolate all regs coming south from Oxford on the A4074 between the hours of say, 18.00 and 18.20 and north between 18.30 and 18.50.'

'The bridge isn't on the A4074,' said Heidi.

'No, but they're logically the most likely cameras,' said Pryce. 'My bet is that van may have been coming in or going out of Oxford prior to the accident.'

'Yes, professor,' muttered Heidi, loud enough for Jo to hear. Pryce didn't notice.

'Good work,' said Jo, smiling. She wondered how many white

vans there could possibly be within the time-frame. A handful at most. But they'd probably be looking at one with some damage from the impact with Natalie. *We're getting somewhere.* Solving the case would be satisfying, of course. Justice for the victim and for Susan Palmer. But it couldn't fail to go down well with Stratton too.

Jo knew she was getting ahead of herself.

'Keep me posted,' she said.

* * *

While Pryce carried out the checks, Jo was pleased to see the full report from Vera Coyne had arrived, because it stopped her thinking about Lucas. Toxicology confirmed there was no alcohol in Natalie's system, but there were traces of ketamine hydrochloride. Seemed an odd choice of poison while holding down an active job like cleaning, but Coyne couldn't say when it had been ingested, and there were no symptoms of prolonged or frequent dosages of that or any other narcotics. The water was definitely consistent with that from the river. And though Coyne couldn't rule out recent sexual activity, there were no indications of sexual violence.

Tests from the road surface had matched the blood residue with the victim also. Coyne had helpfully flagged a few details. The first that caught Jo's eye was that there was significant bruising on the left upper arm and on the neck. Coyne said this was likely to have been caused prior to the accident, as it would have taken some time to develop pre-mortem.

Jo called Pryce over to ask what he made of it. 'You think it's this meathead she was seen with?'

'Could be. Didn't the colleague say he was rough with her?'

Stratton emerged from his office, face like thunder.

'Jo, I know you're busy, but can you go with Andy to the Randolph?'

'Sorry, sir?'

He smiled, his words clipped by almost gritted teeth. 'Seems you made an impression on Hana Sigurdsson. She's requested you personally. I tried to explain you weren't on the case . . .' *I bet you did,* '. . . but she's quite insistent.'

'I'll come too,' said Pryce, pushing his chair back.

Stratton shook his head. 'Two detectives is probably enough, Jack,' he said.

Pryce looked a little put out.

'Stay on the ANPR,' said Jo. 'I shouldn't be long.'

* * *

'I'm sorry about all this,' said Carrick, as they drove through town to the hotel.

'It's fine,' she said. 'This hit and run might actually be going somewhere.' She told him about the lead on the white van. 'Pryce is looking through the road camera data.'

'You like him, don't you?'

'Pryce? He's very thorough. No Heidi, though.'

'I bet she's already got the babygros arranged by age,' said Carrick.

Jo laughed. It was rare for Andy to make jokes. He wasn't much of a person for small talk, generally, and she'd never seen him out with the other officers based at St Aldates. He was in his mid-forties now, the sort who kept his nose clean, did his job quietly. A sure-fire replacement for Stratton one day.

'He likes you,' said Carrick.

'Don't,' she said. 'You sound like Dimi.'

'I didn't mean like that,' said Carrick. 'I mean, he looks up to you.'

'You reckon?'

'Definitely. I never told you before, but I caught him looking at your old case files. Looking for inspiration, no doubt. Oh, and he definitely fancies you, too. Pinker tried to get a book running on when he's going to ask you out.'

'I hope you didn't partake.'

Carrick focused on the road, blushing. 'Andy . . .' she warned.

'I may have put a fiver on it. But I said before the Christmas party, so you two will have to move fast.'

Jo growled. 'Anyway, how are the kids?'

Carrick had an eight-year-old and a five-year-old. She and Lucas had bumped into the family one Saturday in the park, and they'd been shockingly polite and precocious, the younger girl regaling Jo with her seven times table. Carrick's wife, Jasmilla, was quite stunning, though when she'd mentioned it to Lucas that evening, he'd said in a gentlemanly way that he hadn't noticed. Lying, until recently, had never been his strong suit.

'They're good, thanks. You know what kids are like.'

'Not first-hand,' she said lightly. He had no idea of her history, but he must have realised the comment was a little bit insensitive, because he quickly moved the subject on. 'By the way, we've had no luck getting in touch with Anna Mull. Her phone's going straight to voicemail. We got hold of the parents – down in Godalming in Surrey. They say she's gone to see some friends in London for a couple of days before heading home.'

'It was probably nothing anyway,' said Jo. 'She seemed pretty scared when we interviewed her, which isn't surprising really. If she knew Malin was doing a lot of whatever, she probably didn't want to drop her mate in it.'

They pulled up across the road from the hotel, outside the Ashmolean museum. Parking in Oxford was always at a premium, so Carrick switched on the hazards and left his warrant card on the dashboard. It would discourage all but the most determined of traffic wardens.

The Randolph Hotel had been a landmark in Oxford city centre for as long as Jo could remember. Five storeys of late Victorian grandeur, festooned with flags, it had a formidable if slightly faded glory, occupying the corner of Beaumont Street and St Giles. Jo imagined it was the stay of choice for wealthy parents visiting their gifted progeny at the colleges. A doorman in full regalia tipped his hat as she and Carrick stepped off the street and onto the red carpet leading through the front doors into a lobby.

At the front desk, a male, suited receptionist, dark-skinned and well-groomed, with a French accent, asked how he could help. Jo told him they were here to see Hana Sigurdsson. Having phoned through, they were asked to wait in the bar area off to one side. It was manned by a single ancient bartender who looked like he might have been there since the hotel's inauguration, and they took a seat in the corner looking back towards the door. There were only small circular tables, so to leave space for Hana Sigurdsson, they sat beside each other on the cushioned leather seats.

Malin's mother glided in a few minutes later. She wore a long pale cardigan. She said something fondly to the elderly barman, then spotted them, and walked over. Carrick stood smartly and shook her hand. 'Ms Sigurdsson.'

'Please, call me Hana.' She gestured to the table. 'Would you like a drink? Gustav is quite the magician. While the rest of this place declines, he at least remains constant.' She had a way of speaking as if quoting from a text Jo had never read. The effect was dramatic, and forced, and Jo wondered if the confidence was just a coping mechanism. As if summoned, Gustav carried over what looked like a gin and tonic, laying it down with a wrinkled hand. 'Thank you,' she said.

'For your guests?' he muttered.

'We're fine, thanks,' said Jo. As he hobbled off, she turned to Hana. 'Thank you for your time.'

'My *time*?' she said, bemused. 'Detective Masters, my daughter is missing.' Jo felt a flush of embarrassment, but seeing her reaction, Hana Sigurdsson reached out, and almost fondly, put her hand on Jo's. The touch was cool, and it surprised her. 'Has there been any news?' she asked.

'We're exploring several avenues,' said Jo. 'Is there anything you can tell us about Malin that might help?'

'Such as?'

Carrick cleared his throat. 'Ms Sigurdsson, Hana – our investigations indicate that Malin was spending quite a lot of money recently.'

'Really?'

'Money that was coming into her account from both you and your ex-husband.'

Hana Sigurdsson flinched.

'Approximately two thousand a month, from each of you, until it stopped last June.'

Hana sipped her drink then smiled distantly. 'My daughter had some . . . problems.'

Jo sensed the topic being danced around. 'You mean with narcotics?'

Hana didn't reply directly. 'I always told Nicholas it was a mistake to let her come here, to this place. I wanted her to study in Sweden, where we don't have the same temptations. But Nicholas insisted. He went to the same college, you see. So did his father. One of your curious British traditions, as if stepping in your parent's footsteps is something to be proud of. Malin was suspended from her first school, for drinking. We got on top of that, but then it was drugs. *Only pot,* Nicholas said, as if it was nothing to worry about. And he, the man who happily fulminates about the scourge of drugs to your newspapers. I think it got worse when we divorced. I wanted to keep her in Sweden, but she had friends here, a year into her course. She kept on asking for more money, and I knew. Nicholas knew as well. He was worried it might reflect badly on him. So we put a stop to it. Her allowance. That might seem drastic to you, but we came up with a solution. We arranged for a friend at the college to provide her with money - an old crow quite high up.' Jo guessed she was referring to Belinda Frampton-Keys. 'That way we could monitor what was happening. Malin didn't like it, of course. She accused us of trying to control her, which we were. But over the summer, she got clean. We thought she was still clean.' She finished her drink in a long gulp, nodded discreetly across towards the bar. 'What has Nicholas said?'

'Not much,' said Jo. When Hana rolled her eyes, she felt emboldened to probe further. 'You divorced a few years ago, you said?'

'Sometimes I ask if we were ever truly a couple,' replied Hana wearily. 'Nicholas was the primary investor in my first husband, Christoff's, business. Speculator, might be a more accurate description. He always had a fondness for a bet. It turned out dotcom was a good one in the mid-nineties. We moved production to the UK in 1998. When Christoff died a few years later, it was very hard, for me, and for Malin. But Nicholas was helpful. He took care of everything. He'd never been married before, and when he asked me, I said yes. It lasted five years. We divorced just after Malin's first year.'

Gustav drifted over with another G&T, deposited it and took away the empty glass.

'And how did Malin take that?' asked Jo.

'Oh, Malin never liked Nicholas. But I always put that down to losing her father so young. It seemed to get worse as the years went on, rather than better.'

'How did Christoff die, if you don't mind me asking?'

'Heart attack,' said Hana. 'He seemed such a strong man, but he worked too hard. It was Nicholas who found him, in his office.'

'I'm very sorry,' said Jo.

'Don't be,' said Hana. 'Both were selfish men, in their own way.'

Her coldness shook Jo.

'Is there a chance, do you think, that Malin might have got herself into trouble over drugs?'

Hana looked mournful. 'She lived a charmed life, for so long. Nicholas always said it wouldn't last forever. He said your mistakes always catch up with you.' She finished her drink. 'It's hard to see that when you're young, isn't it?'

Jo was taken back, momentarily, to the story she'd told Dr Forster.

'You're talking about karma?'

'Oh no,' said Hana, flashing her teeth (pristine, considering her age). 'I'm talking about . . . sorry, I don't know the English word. In Swedish, we say *hybris*.'

'It's the same,' said Carrick. 'Hubris.'

'Her father was similar. He thought he was untouchable.'

She looked desperately sad.

'You've been very helpful,' said Carrick. 'Will you be staying here the whole time, Ms Sigurdsson, if we need to reach you?'

'I won't be going anywhere,' replied Malin's mother. 'And one more thing, detectives.' Though she spoke to both of them, she looked at Jo. 'I've been completely open with you, and I would appreciate it if the courtesy was returned. If there are any developments, anything at all, please keep me informed.'

She reached out again to touch Jo's hand, her gaze steely.

Jo felt laden with guilt as they made their way back to the car. 'You think we should have told her about Myers?'

'Not yet,' said Carrick. 'We don't know if it's pertinent to the disappearance. Malin's entitled to a private life, even if it is unusual.'

'I think I know why she was seeing him,' said Jo. 'They cut off the money six months ago, and that's when Malin started seeing Catskill. Then he ends things, and she starts up with Ron Myers, a person she once accused of harassment. What's the through-line?'

'The drugs,' said Carrick.

'She needed money to feed a habit that was out of control. My guess is that Catskill realised that. Whether Myers did or not, I bet he was giving her money.'

'Only one way to find out,' said Carrick. 'We ask him.'

'Stratton won't be happy,' said Jo.

'What's new?' said Carrick.

Chapter 10

When he opened his front door, Ronald Myers didn't look at all pleased to see them again, and despite their assurances he wasn't under arrest, he insisted on having his lawyer present.

'I'm not talking to you.'

'We have some follow-up questions,' said Jo. 'Just a few things to clarify.'

'And if I refuse?' said Myers.

'We'd rather not go down that road,' said Jo. 'We can do it here. You're not under caution. You're just helping with our enquiries.'

'You people made a terrible mess,' said Myers plaintively.

'And that's unfortunate,' said Carrick, 'but you must understand, we're only interested in finding Malin. And if you'd come clean about your relationship earlier, all the mess could have been avoided.'

'So it's my fault?'

'It's no one's fault,' said Jo. She felt like she was talking to a child. 'The sooner we clear up a few points, the sooner you never have to see us again.'

'I really don't know what's happened to her,' said Myers. 'I cared about her deeply.'

'We believe you,' said Carrick, 'but it's important that you're honest with us. You said you had a sexual relationship with Malin.'

'Indeed. And last time I checked, that wasn't a crime.'

'Forgive me if this sounds insensitive, but what did Malin get out of this arrangement?'

Ronald's eyes narrowed, just a fraction, and for a split-second. 'Insulting me will get you nowhere.'

'Did any money change hands?' Jo asked.

'Money?'

'Yes. You know what money is, I assume? Did you pay Malin Sigurdsson for her . . . er, company?'

'Of course I didn't. What do you take me for? What do you take *her* for?'

'A vulnerable young woman with a drug addiction she'd go to any length to quench. *Any* length.'

Myers looked away, impatiently. 'I'm not saying *anything else* without a lawyer.'

'I don't think we need any more,' said Carrick, turning from the door. Jo followed suit.

'Hey, wait!' said Myers. 'What happens now?'

Carrick turned back. 'I think we get a warrant to look at your bank records. Establish what was leaving your account, and if we can match it with Malin's spending habits.'

Jo played along. 'Good thinking.'

'No,' said Myers. 'Look, I may have taken Malin out for dinner a few times.'

'Just dinner?' said Carrick. 'Whereabouts? In Oxford.'

Myers clammed up. 'A place in Thame,' he said. 'We . . . we didn't want to be seen. For obvious reasons.'

'And other than that, did Malin ask you for money?'

Myers ran a hand over his beard. 'You're making it sound tawdry, but why shouldn't I give her something? I have plenty, she was a student. She needed books, food, a bicycle . . . stationery.'

Jo couldn't stop the burst of laughter, to which Myers slammed a hand on the doorframe. 'Enough of this! They were gifts. Nothing more. I can give gifts to whom I please.'

'She wasn't spending the money on stationery,' said Jo. 'It was going on heroin.'

'Well, I know nothing about that. Nothing at all. And you can't prove I did.'

'Thank you,' said Carrick. 'You've been very helpful.'

When they were back in the car, Jo turned to her colleague. 'Can we swing by Oriel college?' Carrick looked at her quizzically. 'I have a feeling I know whose prints we might have found in Malin's room.'

* * *

'*My* fingerprints?' Belinda Frampton-Keys looked flustered. 'Why?'

'It's just a formality,' said Carrick. 'We'll have you back at the college in half an hour.'

'I'm really busy,' said Frampton-Keys. 'Shouldn't you be out looking for Malin?'

Jo was losing patience. 'Did you enter Malin's room between Anna telling you she was missing and the first police officer arriving on the scene?'

'Well, yes – I told you that. We used our spare key. We thought she might be in danger.'

'That's what I don't understand. Why wouldn't you assume she was just out?'

'She didn't answer her phone. It was Anna Mull who was worried.'

'And why would she be worried? People don't answer phones all the time.'

Frampton-Keys looked back and forth between them. 'Maybe

she . . . well . . . they're friends, aren't they? People worry about their friends.'

'If their friends have drug problems,' said Carrick.

The Vice Provost coloured. 'We have a zero-tolerance policy on drugs at the college.'

'That's the second time I've heard that in two days,' said Jo. 'They say the same about prisons, but the addiction rate is higher inside than out.'

'I hardly think you can compare the college to a prison,' said Frampton-Keys, with a toss of her head.

'Of course not,' said Carrick. 'And having established Malin wasn't in her room, what did you do next?'

'I phoned the police.'

'Straightaway?'

A pause. 'Pretty much, yes.'

'Pretty much?'

'Yes, right away then.'

'You didn't enter the room?'

'Only to establish she wasn't inside. What are you getting at?'

'Forensics found a set of prints in the room that wasn't Malin's,' said Jo. 'It appears on all the drawers, the wardrobe door, in the bathroom cabinet. We thought it must be someone intimate with Malin, maybe even the person who hurt her, but now we've got another theory. That it was someone going through her things. Looking for something.'

Frampton-Keys didn't say anything but her face was twitching a little around the mouth.

'I looked over the statement Anna Mull gave,' said Jo. 'She told you that she came to you at around noon. You phoned us just after one.'

'I phoned her father's office. I wanted to know if he knew where Malin was.'

'You didn't mention this before.'

'I didn't think I had to?'

'There was blood in the bathroom. Quite a lot. You didn't think to phone the police first?'

'I suppose I panicked.'

'Fair enough,' said Jo. 'If we were to take your fingerprints, do you think they'd be a match for those in Malin's room?'

The Vice Provost did not answer.

'I understand why,' said Jo. 'The family have a right to privacy. If there was something *embarrassing* in Malin's room, why not remove it? But you must understand, removing evidence from a crime scene, especially class A drugs, is obstructing the course of a police investigation – a serious offence.'

Frampton-Keys looked at her sharply. 'Am I in trouble?'

Jo shook her head casually. 'Not if you tell us the truth now.'

The Vice Provost nodded briskly. 'I'll need to talk to Nicholas – Mr Cranleigh, first.'

She made to stand, but Jo remained planted. 'Don't worry about that,' she said. 'We'll be speaking to Mr Cranleigh ourselves, very soon. How about you tell us where the drugs are now?'

'I . . . I didn't know what it was. It's not something I know about at all. I flushed it down the toilet, like they do in the TV shows.'

'Very enterprising,' said Jo.

Carrick opened his copy book. 'We need you to be a lot more honest with us,' he said. 'For Malin's sake. We're aware of the sensitivities, both with Malin's father and the colleges, but if you hide things, it will only make the outcome worse. Do you understand?'

The Vice Provost nodded.

'Tell us, then,' said Jo.

It spilled out of her, and it turned out the 'zero tolerance' policy on drugs at college depended, strictly, on who your parents were. In addition to the hospital admission in her second year, one of the scouts – the name given to the cleaning ladies at the college – had found Malin semi-conscious at the beginning of her very first term, a needle still protruding between her toes. Malin had fled, that time, before the college authorities had come to the room, and the Dean had been keen to make an example of her before Nicholas Cranleigh had stepped in with assurances that Malin was struggling because of what had happened to her father. Jo wondered if the news had even reached Hana Sigurdsson in Sweden before it was hushed up. Frampton-Keys told them that Malin had voluntarily entered a drug programme and was being prescribed methadone in diminishing doses. And for the most part, it seemed to be working. Certainly, Malin's tutors all seemed to have no idea about her habit, reporting her as one of their more gifted students. Frampton-Keys began to well up as she spoke.

'When I saw the blood, I was cross,' she said. 'I thought Malin had probably just had a stupid accident. If I'd known it was something else – something worse – I wouldn't have taken those things.'

Carrick looked genuinely sympathetic as he nodded, but Jo struggled to feel much at all for Frampton-Keys. People always lied to the police, to keep their secrets hidden, but the Vice Provost had acted like she was above the whole process from the start. 'I can't promise this will exonerate you,' she said. 'What you did was stupid, and illegal. And if there's anything – anything at all – that you're not telling us now, then so help me God I'll drag you to the station in cuffs myself.'

Carrick shot her a sideways glance as if trying to read how sincere she was being. 'We know you want to find Malin as much as us,' he muttered.

Frampton-Keys sniffed. 'I pray you do,' she said. 'I really do.'

* * *

Stratton summoned Carrick as soon as they were back in the station, and Jo knew at once it was a boys-only meeting. Andy wouldn't downplay her involvement, she knew, and indeed, she caught Stratton throwing slightly pained glances at her through the partition of his office as Carrick filled him in. *That's right, you vindictive sod – I* do *know how to do my job . . .*

Pryce was in front of his screen, staring intently, chewing on the end of a pencil.

'Any luck with the ANPR on the 4074?' she asked.

'We've got eight hundred and ninety vehicles southbound in the time-frame,' he said. 'And six hundred northbound.'

More than she'd thought. 'And cross-reffing with vehicle types, any white transit-style vans?'

Pryce tapped his notepad. 'Five.'

He showed her a collection of printed images of drivers behind the wheel. It was next to impossible to see any faces due to the fact the pictures were taken after dusk. Jo noticed that one of the vehicles on the list was flagged as untaxed.

'Let's start there,' said Jo.

The van was registered to a Mark Hannity, address in Basingstoke.

'Good thinking,' said Stratton, arriving at their side.

'Any chance we could get a couple of uniforms to share the load?' asked Jo, though she knew the answer before she finished the question.

Stratton shook his head looking pained. 'I think you two should handle it, Jo. I mean, we wouldn't want to miss anything by being sloppy.'

In a clenched fist, she drove her nails into her palm. 'Of course not, sir.'

Chapter 11

It was close to 10.30 pm when she dropped Pryce back at the windswept station, and hardly anyone was braving the streets of Oxford in the bitter cold. Despite the settling frost, her blood was boiling.

'What a waste of fucking time!' she said.

They'd spent an hour waiting for Mark Hannity to arrive home, laden with takeaway from a chip shop. He was a sorry state, contrite about his lack of up-to-date tax – simply an oversight, he said, because he'd been in hospital recently. He still had a fixed boot on his foot where two toes had been amputated due to complications arising from his diabetes, so they didn't go hard on him. He allowed them to search the van he used for his struggling house clearance business. There were no dents that they could see, and he denied using the Little Baldon bridge. Jo watched him eat greasy fish and chips from a tray, her stomach grumbling.

Of the four remaining vans, two were in the Oxford environs, one in Didcot, and one in Bicester. They'd spoken to three of the owners at home – a plumber, a painter, and a florist, but the fourth, a food wholesaler of artisan French cheeses, was apparently out of the country until the following morning. Of the three interviews, none had been in the slightest bit productive, and Jo felt she'd wound back time to her days on the beat, carrying out mind-numbing door-to-door enquiries that never went anywhere. The plumber and the florist had been heading home from jobs, the painter on his way to pick up stock. All said their routes hadn't taken in the Little Baldon bridge, and none of their vehicles had any obvious impact markings either. It didn't mean they were clean, but it meant there was zero evidence to link them with the hit and run. She knew Stratton would never sign off on sampling the rubber from each of their tyres. Departmental budgets were tight, and the hit and run of a potential drug addict wouldn't meet the public interest threshold.

Pryce unclipped his seatbelt and muttered, 'For every door that closes, another opens.'

She curled her lip. 'What on earth does that mean?'

'Something one of our lecturers used to say on the investigative programme. I think it means even a lead that goes nowhere at least tells you where not to look for answers.'

'He must have been a hit at parties.'

'A woman actually,' said Pryce, smiling warmly. 'So what's next?'

'A fucking Tarot reading, maybe? Seems as good an option as any.'

Pryce looked askance at her. 'Are you okay?'

She really wasn't. Lucas would be at home, and with all the driving she'd had plenty of time to dwell. Would Bob have told him she'd stopped by? And if so, would he have an excuse already for the lies? She hardly relished that particular interrogation.

'I suppose we have to hope someone else comes forward from the public appeal,' said Jo. 'Or the culprit has a religious awakening and hands themselves in, and gives a full statement of their wrongs.'

Pryce chuckled. 'That happen often?'

Jo laughed as well. 'Hey, Jack,' she said, as Pryce was getting out of the car. 'You don't fancy a drink, do you?'

'Oh!' He blinked, like she'd just asked him something utterly unfathomable. 'Now?'

'That's what I was thinking. Look, no pressure. I just thought, y'know, it's been a shit day . . .'

'I'd love to,' he said. 'But I can't. Not tonight anyway. I've got—'

'It's fine,' said Jo. She was already starting the engine. 'You don't have to give me an excuse.' To her horror, she was blushing, and in the car's internal light, it must be obvious. 'Catch up tomorrow, okay?'

'Sure.'

He saluted awkwardly as she drove away. As she did, she worried she'd put him on the spot, made him feel uncomfortable. Maybe it was a bit odd, just the two of them. She was his superior, and even if the relationship was completely platonic, it wasn't really on. And she could hardly claim ignorance of that. When she and Ben had got together, they'd kept it a secret from almost everyone, but especially their commanding officer.

'Fuck,' she cursed herself. Though she hadn't been thinking of anything romantic, she couldn't deny her pride was bruised at the blunt rejection. That look on his face at her simple offer had taken her by surprise. Shock, but something else too. Pity, perhaps. Contempt, even. Okay, she was older, but hardly past it. And they'd been getting on well; he was easy to talk to. She didn't think he had a partner. Maybe she'd misread it. Carrick too. Or maybe he was just aware of what others would say if it got out. He might have got wind of the bet Pinker was running . . .

She stopped at the lights, and a young couple, red-cheeked and wrapped up, skipped across arm in arm. She felt suddenly even older. The knot in her stomach grew.

Shifting logs with Bob? No you weren't.

He'd lied so easily, and if there was one person she'd never thought would lie to her, it was him. Had the experience with Ben not taught her anything, or was it just a feature of falling in love that your critical faculties went out of the window? No, it wasn't just her. Her sister-in-law Amelia had said it from the first time she met Lucas. 'He's great, Jo. No edges, you know?'

'You mean boring,' Jo had said. At that stage, they'd only been seeing each other a month, and most of the hours they spent together were horizontal.

'No!' Amelia had protested. 'I mean genuine.'

Jo had scoffed to make light of it, but inside she'd been glowing. Amelia's affirmation shouldn't have meant anything. Jo was a grown woman, and she didn't need the approval of her brother's wife. Of anyone. But knowing they liked Lucas, admired his qualities, saw he was a *good* person, signified more than just that. It meant, in a vicarious way, that because he had chosen her, she was good too.

Or, at least, it had.

She hadn't travelled beyond the city centre when she decided to pull over. Taking out her phone, she messaged Lucas.

Working late, so staying at my place tonight. Sleep well x.

Adding the kiss, a tiny subterfuge, felt like a betrayal to herself as much as him.

We're both telling lies now.

* * *

She drove instead across town to The Three Crowns on Canterbury Road, and the warm light through the glass door of what was still called the Public Bar welcomed her. Lucas's text came back. *Don't work too hard. Happy birthday for tomorrow xxx* The mention of the date made her stomach twist with dread, and she was even angrier with him for bringing it up. She pushed the door open into the slightly musty interior, stepping over the landlord's shaggy Welsh collie that seemed as much part of the tired décor as the stains on the carpet and the old framed *Punch* cartoons that hung on the walls. There were half a dozen in, all regulars. A couple in their eighties who sat opposite one another and never spoke; Fat Eddie at the bar, with his thin strands of artfully back-combed hair, and the barmaid herself.

Harry Ferman was playing darts with another old-timer, Malc, but from the chaser and short on the corner table, and the scarf neatly folded on the seat, it looked like he was occupying his normal spot for the evening. She'd first met him during the Dylan Jones investigation, a former detective himself, brought back in because he knew the case better than anyone. In his late sixties, white-haired, he had a slightly shambolic air and a sickly pallor. In the months after, they'd met a few times, always in his local. She wasn't sure why exactly, and he'd been kind enough never to say how odd it was.

He noticed her as his playing partner retrieved his darts from the board.

'Well, well – not expecting you.'

'Need a bloody appointment, do I?' she mock scolded him. 'It's my birthday tomorrow. That enough?'

'Say no more.' He called across to the bar. 'Connie, whatever the young lady's having please.'

'Usual, please.' Jo peeled off her outer layers, and hung them on a wall-peg, then went across to the bar to claim her vodka tonic. 'Cheers, Connie.' She went back to the table to watch Ferman finish his game, which he did with a perfectly placed double-top. It took her back to the times she'd played with her dad in their garage – where he used to smoke out of her mother's sight.

Ferman shook Malc's hand and they both wandered back to their table.

'I don't feel young, Harry.'

'It's all relative.' As if to illustrate his point, he sat down in two discrete, laboured movements – a slow bend from the waist, then a sort of heavy flop backwards onto the cushioned seat.

'Thanks for the drink,' said Jo.

Ferman took a swig of his pint. 'If you don't mind me saying, you seem in less than festive cheer. Work or love-life?'

'A perfect shit-storm of both.'

Harry might be a functioning alcoholic, but he was a good listener. Certain things about Thames Valley Police had changed a lot since his day. Computers for one. And the all-pervasive drug problems faced by every city. The gender and ethnic make-up of the force. But his colourful stories suggested other things would always be the same – office politics and the stupidity of ninety per cent of the criminals they encountered.

'You want to talk?' he said. 'Can't guarantee I'll have much insight into either modern policing or modern romance.'

'I'll spare you the gory details on the latter,' she said. 'Stratton's got me on a wild goose chase. A hit and run out near Little Baldon.'

He nodded. 'I know the place.'

'Really?'

'Well, I've driven through it. Used to be a Borstal out that way. Brookhampton. Grim sort of Edwardian place where they send juveniles to learn respect. We had to transport 'em occasionally, or take 'em back when they did a runner. Ruin now. Called it the Buggers' Palace, mostly to scare the kids into behaving.

Funny how things change, eh? Wouldn't get away with that now.'

'Locking up kids or homophobia?'

'Take your pick.' He drained his drink. 'So why's the DCI got you on a hit and run?'

'Same old crap,' said Jo. 'He still thinks I'm likely to go off the rails. Sees me as some sort of paranoid, hormonal harpy.'

'Two out of three ain't bad.'

Jo wagged a finger at him. 'Don't test me. Not today.' They sat a moment in silence. It was one of Harry's specialities, knowing when to keep quiet and when to speak up. One of the reasons she liked his company. At the next table, the old couple rose simultaneously to leave, without any obvious signal or verbal interaction. Maybe at that age, together that long, there was telepathy involved.

'You know what really pisses me off,' she said. 'It's that he'd put me on the hit and run because he thinks it doesn't matter. We've got this other case, a disappearance – looks like a college girl's got herself messed up over drugs. He's got the dad on direct dial, Andy Carrick on a tight leash, uniforms on standby. But the hit and run – some poor girl's dead – and it might as well not matter. It's all about appearances.'

'Welcome to the world,' said Ferman. 'Listen, I need your help.' He fished in his pocket, and pulled out a mobile phone.

'No way!' said Jo.

'I took your advice,' he said. 'Joined the twenty-first century. Problem is, everything looks too small on the screen, and I don't want to be carting the reading glasses around all the time.'

'Let me have a look,' said Jo.

It took a bit of searching through the settings, but she managed to bump up the text display size. She put her number into his phone too, and dialled it.

'Next time I *will* make an appointment,' she said, saving his number to her device. 'Right, I'd better go.'

'Thanks,' said Harry. 'And if you want some advice from me, the best you can do is solve the case. Prove yourself. Stratton won't be your boss forever.'

'You know something I don't?'

He smiled. 'If there's one thing long life gives you, aside from arthritis, it's a sense of perspective. Glass half full and all that.' He held up his, empty. 'Speaking of which . . .'

Chapter 12

FRIDAY

'In my office, please,' said Stratton, beckoning Jo over before she'd even taken off her coat the following morning. Pryce was at his desk, his head down. Was he avoiding her eyes on purpose, because of last night? She'd really need to speak with him, somehow, without making it worse.

Lucas had tried to call, but she'd replied by text that she was in the middle of something and would ring him later. Sometimes the job was a good excuse.

'Close the door,' said Stratton.

'Everything all right, sir?' asked Jo, as she obeyed.

'We've had an official complaint,' he said. 'From Nicholas Cranleigh. He says you've been harassing staff at Oriel college.'

What a pile of shit . . .

She tried to stay calm, externally at least. 'Have you spoken to Andy?' she asked. 'It looks like Malin is mixed up in drug-related crime, and Cranleigh's worried about me asking his pet professor a few questions?'

Stratton held up his hand in a particularly infuriating way. 'I think it's your manner he's objecting to. The Vice Provost is very upset.'

'She manipulated the crime scene, sir,' said Jo. 'Disposing of an unknown quantity of a class A drug and jeopardising our investigation.'

'It's not *your* investigation though, is it?' said Stratton. 'You're supposed to be on this hit and run.'

'And we're following up on those leads,' said Jo, biting the inside of her cheek. 'Pryce and I were out until God knows what hour driving around the county.' She almost added *on a fool's errand*, but caught herself.

'And?' said Stratton.

'Sir, if we could have a few uniforms, it would be much quicker,' said Jo.

'I think I made myself clear on that yesterday,' said the DCI. 'I don't have infinite resources at my disposal.'

There was a knock on the door. It was Pryce. Stratton waved him in.

'What is it?'

'Sir, I couldn't help overhearing.'

'Couldn't you?'

'Sir, respectfully, it was Jo's work on the Sigurdsson case that got us where we are.'

It felt like the air had been sucked out of the room as Stratton turned to him. Jo wished he'd never got involved. She really didn't need a white knight at the moment.

'And where are we, exactly, detective?'

Pryce didn't seem to realise he'd pushed a button. 'Well, we have a fuller understanding of Malin's personal life. The drugs, her relationships. If you ask me—'

'I didn't,' said Stratton. 'Tell me, are we any closer to locating Malin?'

Pryce paused, and Jo said, 'It's all right, Jack. Don't worry about it.'

Stratton shook his head is dismay. 'You know, I took you on because I heard good things from the Met. But if you can't follow simple orders, I might have to re-examine that decision.' He pointed at Pryce, then at Jo. 'Both of you, stick to the hit and run. Work the leads. Got it?'

'Got it, sir,' said Jo.

Pryce nodded, a chastened look on his face. Stratton walked from behind his desk, opened the door himself, and waited for them to leave.

'You didn't have to stick up for me,' muttered Jo, as she sat at her desk.

'I was just stating the facts,' said Pryce. He lowered his voice. 'It's a bit odd, don't you think? He seems very keen to keep us off the case.'

'I think it's me he's worried about,' said Jo. 'Sorry to drag you down with me.'

She tried to stay positive, following Harry's advice. 'Come on, we've got our van-driving cheese merchant to call on . . .'

* * *

Predictably, Tasha Makepeace was a dead end as well. She had an even firmer case than the others, because her van wasn't actually white on the sides, but emblazoned with colour that hadn't shown on the head-on ANPR images – a French flag, and several graphics of famous Gallic landmarks. And though she couldn't swear she'd never taken the road via Little Baldon, her route from her home in South Oxford down to Portsmouth gave her no reason to on the Tuesday in question.

'I can't help thinking we're looking at this wrong,' said Jo, as they drove back towards the city centre. 'We're trying to put drivers on that section of road, but we should be asking why Natalie was there in the first place.'

'Selling sex is the only thing I can think of,' said Pryce. 'Something went wrong. Either the punter kicked her out, or she got scared and ran.'

'I don't buy it,' said Jo. 'She was wearing her work clothes, with her college pass. Hardly hooker attire.' She thought back to the details of the file. 'Hell, even her underwear was what I'd tactfully call functional. We haven't got any evidence that she was a sex worker, there was no sign of sexual activity. We've got the trace of ketamine, but no evidence she was a habitual user.'

'Her mum is.'

'Right,' said Jo. 'But we're not all like our mothers. Trust me.'

'I didn't mean that,' said Pryce.

'We're trying to put Natalie in this box, and she doesn't fit. Look at her bedroom. Neat and tidy, an island of calm in that shithole she shares with her mum. She's holding down a regular job, the sort of place they'd dump her in a second if she gave them a reason. Making her own lunch. Does that sound like any addict you've ever come across?'

'Maybe not,' said Pryce. 'Have you got another theory?'

'Not at the moment,' she replied.

Jo tried to imagine Natalie out walking on that road. The skid marks and blood suggested she was heading away from Oxford, not home. But it was a straight stretch. Though it would have been dark, her coat was pale, and there was enough room at the side to stay safe if she'd wanted to. Suicide was a possibility, throwing herself into the path of a speeding car, but that only raised more questions. Something related to the incident with the man at her college, maybe. And it still didn't explain how she ended up in that spot. She couldn't drive, and there were no buses that went out that way. To all intents and purposes, Natalie had seemed to be getting on with her life, despite the odds stacked against her.

'I think I might go and take another look at the bridge.'

Pryce shrugged. 'If you think it'll help.'

She drove in silence a while, but there was a definite weight in the air between them. If she wanted to talk to him about her ill-advised offer the night before, now would be the time. As it happened, he spoke first.

'I meant what I said to Stratton earlier, about the case. I think he's mad to keep you off it.'

'Thanks,' said Jo. 'He and I have a bit of a history, though.'

'If you want to make a formal complaint about his behaviour, I'd support it.'

'I don't think we're there yet,' she said. 'And you don't need to get on the wrong side of a DCI. Stratton is going to be around for a long time.'

Pryce smiled. 'I didn't request a transfer to St Aldates because I wanted to work with Phil Stratton.'

Jo blushed, remembering what Carrick had said about Pryce looking at her case files. It was almost exactly the same feeling as when Nathan Marshall had sent her a Valentine's card in Year Eleven.

'Well, sorry to shatter illusions.'

'You haven't.'

He was looking at her, she realised, but she kept her eyes on the road, acutely aware that every second she let this go on, she was stringing him along. It would be the easiest thing to stop the car, lean across and make a small mistake into a colossal one. She shook herself mentally. Lucas had lied, but that didn't mean he'd cheated on her.

'Listen, Jack, you're a great . . .'

His phone's ringtone came at just the right moment.

'Hi, Heidi,' he said. 'What's up?'

He listened, nodding, and cast a sideways glance at Jo. 'Ten minutes, or so,' he said, then hung up. 'Stratton wants everyone back.'

'What for?' said Jo, her skin prickling.

'She didn't know. Sounds serious though.'

* * *

When she and Pryce got back to the station, all the other detectives were in the briefing room. And they could barely meet Jo's eye. Stratton, at the front, had an evidence box on the table.

'Good of you to join us,' said Stratton. 'Take a seat please, Jack. Jo, I think you've got some explaining to do.'

What now? 'Sir, I don't understand . . .'

Stratton put his hands on his hips, and Carrick shook his head. 'Jo, I can't believe you didn't tell us. We're supposed to be working *together*.'

'Will someone tell *me* what this is about, because I really have no fucking clue?'

Dimitriou brought a hand to his mouth. Was he actually *laughing*?

Stratton reached into the evidence box, and lifted out a cake. His face broke into a smile. 'Happy birthday, Detective Masters.'

'You absolute fucking arseholes,' said Jo, shaking her head.

Everyone began to laugh, and Dimitriou lit the candles on the cake with his lighter.

'Now make a wish,' said Heidi.

'I'm not seven,' said Jo.

'How old *are* you?' said Dimitriou, grinning. 'No one would tell me.'

Jo blew out the candles. 'I wish I was ten years younger,' she said.

They ate the cake, and while she was eating, Stratton came across. 'Jo, I hope you don't feel I've been unreasonable in the last few days.' His faux sincerity made it hard to swallow, but she managed. 'Of course not, sir. These open cases are tough.'

'I take it you're no closer with the hit and run?'

'I'm afraid not,' said Jo. 'Short of new evidence coming forward, I'm not sure where we go from here.' She almost suggested she get back on the Sigurdsson case, but she didn't want to push his sudden good mood.

He drifted back to his office, and Jo walked up to Heidi, who was wiping cream from the corner of her mouth. 'Was this your idea? I can't imagine the boss keeps track of birthdays.'

'No way,' said Heidi. 'It was Lucas who told us. He's booked a table for lunch at that Lebanese place off the High Street, by the way. Said he'd been trying to get hold of you but you hadn't answered.'

'He told you that?'

'He dropped in first thing,' said Heidi. 'Something up?'

'No,' said Jo. 'I'd better call him.'

'And I'd better eat another slice of that cake,' said Heidi. She looked around surreptitiously, then lowered her voice. 'I know we've not spoken about it much, but I can't imagine what you went through before, with Ben. But you've fallen on your feet with that guy.'

'Lucas? Ha! Thanks. Apart from the dirt under the fingernails.'

'No, I mean it,' said Heidi. 'You can just tell with some people, you know? If anyone deserves a straightforward life, it's you, right?'

Jo thought back to her moment with Pryce in the car. *He's young. Whatever he thinks he wants, it wouldn't be right to take advantage.* She did her best to smile.

★ ★ ★

Lucas was already seated at the table when she arrived. He had dressed in what she recognised as his smartest shirt. The air smelled of spices and grilled meat, making her feel a little sick. She really didn't know how she'd get through the meal without talking to him about the lie. Equally, she knew she couldn't sit across a table from him and ignore it.

He stood up when he saw her, smiling. They kissed, then she took off her coat and hung it over the chair.

'Don't you dare sing "Happy Birthday",' she said, as she sat.

'Wouldn't dream of it. Stratton let you out then?'

'Practically booted me through the door,' said Jo. 'And Bob gave you some time off too?'

'The guy has about two hours' worth of fag breaks a day,' said Lucas.

Jo couldn't help herself. 'He should be careful. All that heavy lifting could finish him off.'

'Huh?'

'Logs.'

'Oh, right, sure.' He handed her a menu. 'Don't know about you, but I'm starving.' They ordered starters and sharing plates, and Jo watched Lucas's face as he ate, looking for any clues she'd missed before. They talked about Christmas, for which Lucas still had a touchingly boyish enthusiasm, and where they would spend it. Paul and Amelia had proffered an invite to both of them, which Jo had accepted, but now she tried to backtrack, suggesting she and Lucas spend it alone. She'd let Ben inveigle his way into her family's affections, and his death had sent tremors through the lives of her nephew and niece. If things were going south with Lucas too, she wanted to nip it in the bud discreetly and avoid collateral emotional damage to those close to her. They'd dealt with plenty already.

She barely touched the food herself, but Lucas seemed not

to notice as he chattered away about this and that, spearing vegetables occasionally across the table.

'You want dessert?' he asked.

'Er . . . no, thanks.'

'You've hardly eaten.' The heating must have been cranked up to the max in the restaurant, because her face felt flushed, sweat threatening to push through the pores. 'Are you okay?'

'Listen, Lucas, sorry about this. I think I need to get back to work.'

'Heidi said it wouldn't be a problem.'

Jo smiled. 'Heidi isn't my boss.'

Lucas looked confused. 'But you said Stratton wanted you out of there.'

'It's not that. There's this case. I feel guilty just sitting here.'

'It's your birthday, Jo. You spend every hour working as it is.' He tried to touch her hand, but she pulled away instinctively. 'Hey. What's up?'

'Nothing's *up.* I told you, I've got to work.'

He stared at her, mystified. 'Have I done something?'

I don't know. Have you?

'Sorry,' said Jo. 'I've just got to go.'

She began to put on her coat. A couple over at the next table were watching them surreptitiously.

'Jo. Please.' Lucas had lowered his voice. 'Tell me what's wrong.'

'Thanks for lunch,' she said. 'See you at yours later.'

The cold air outside was a blessing on her face. She could feel Lucas's eyes still on her as she walked up the street. She told herself the restaurant wasn't the time or place to have a confrontation, but she knew that wasn't really what had stopped her.

It was fear of watching him lie again.

At the station, she got into her car. There might not be any new evidence in or around the Little Baldon bridge, but she was convinced there were answers there nonetheless. Something she, Pryce, and the uniforms had missed.

She got stuck at the first set of lights, then another. It felt like the city was trying to hold her in. Lucas called and she ignored it. She was pulling away again, when the radio crackled with a message from the dispatcher.

'All units. Call to attend. We have a disturbance reported on Burns Close, number 2. I repeat . . .'

2 Burns Close.

Susan Palmer's address.

Jo pressed transmit, to say she was attending, and another patrol car did the same, estimated seven minutes out. Jo switched on her lights, checked her mirrors, and swung her Peugeot in a U-turn.

Chapter 13

She arrived before the marked car, and found a number of kids standing out the back of the house. The lights were on in the surrounding houses, and there was a silver Jeep with a trailer bed parked at an angle outside. She made a mental note of the plate as she blocked it in with her own car.

Jo took her baton from under the seat and went to the front door. She used the butt end to knock. 'Susan? Are you okay?'

There was no answer. Jo went to the front window, but the curtains were drawn apart from a crack. She saw a flash of movement. Someone was lying on the floor, beside the sofa. Bare feet protruded.

The front door burst open to reveal a stocky man in a padded jacket and shorts. He clocked her.

'Police! Stop!' she said.

He ran towards his car, saw it was trapped and doubled back. Jo put herself in his way, but he dropped his shoulder and knocked her aside with ease. She landed on the scrubby grass in time to see him plunging back into the house. Flashing blues told her the uniforms had arrived. She picked herself up as the familiar shapes of Andrea Williams and Olly Pinker came up the path.

'You all right, ma'am?' said the former.

'He's inside. Go!' she replied, then followed them in.

Susan Palmer was curled up on the floor against the edge of the sofa, clutching a bloody cloth to her face. 'He went out the back,' she said.

'Stay with her, Olly,' she said to Pinker.

Jo and Andrea went through the back door and into a tiny garden. The gate hung open, and they came out into the alley running behind the houses and past a row of garages. The suspect had already slowed to an awkward waddle, breathing hard. Andrea sprinted after him, grabbing him by the shoulder, and tripped him. He sprawled on the tarmac, but she went down too. There followed an untidy struggle as Andrea grabbed a wrist, and tried to twist it behind the man's back, but he pulled free and got hold of her dreadlocks, before rolling into a mount position of top of her. He lifted a fist to punch.

Jo swung the baton at the same time as Andrea bucked her hips, and the stick connected with the man's forearm. He roared in pain and fell sideways, clutching his wrist. 'Fucking bitch!' he said. Williams recovered, grabbed the man's other arm, and yanked it around. The suspect toppled on to his face with a thump. Between them, they managed to fasten on a pair of cuffs. 'You broke my fucking arm!' he wailed.

'Sorry about that,' said Jo, fastening the second cuff. 'You okay, constable?' she asked Andrea.

'Yes, ma'am.'

The suspect did a double-take at the height of Williams. 'What the fuck are you?'

'Shut it, tiny,' said Andrea, pulling him to his feet.

'Watch him,' said Jo. Breathing hard herself, she returned to the house, phoning an ambulance as she went. One was already being dispatched, she was told. Back in the house, she found Pinker looking after Susan Palmer, who was now seated on the sofa.

'Are you all right, Susan?'

Palmer nodded. There was still blood all down her chin, and her lip was swelling up.

'Who is that?' she said.

'I don't know his name,' said Susan.

'What did he want?'

'I don't need you here. I'm fine.'

Jo had seen it before. The clamming up. The fear.

'Susan, we think that man threatened your daughter. He might have been involved in her death. You need to tell us what you know.'

Natalie's mother leant down and picked something off the carpet. It was, Jo saw, a tooth. 'I'm sorry,' said Susan. 'I don't know anything.'

* * *

Back at the station, after a doctor had checked him out, they catalogued the man's possessions. The driver's licence and cards in his wallet read Alex Maynard. He had close to a grand in cash. The Jeep, currently seized, contained several small bottles of pills in the glove box, packs of sterile syringes, vials of something called Clenbuterol, which she learned was the proprietary name a popular steroid, a bag of gym kit, and a crate of high-energy sports drinks. Also, and incongruously, a child's car seat. In addition to the smartphone he had in his pocket, there were two others in the car – cheaper pay-as-you-go models. His wrist, luckily, wasn't broken, but had swollen significantly. He held an ice-pack over it.

'So, Alex. Can I call you that?'

'Call me what you want,' he said, slouched in the interview room after they'd taken his prints. Without the jacket, his physique was on full display. His whole body looked like a collection of inflated segments, the veins across his arms like worms as they rested on the table in front of him, his pectorals jutting out under a tight white V-neck T-shirt that read 'MaxGains'. One foot bounced hyperactively on the floor, flexing a bifurcated, diamond-shaped calf muscle. Jo read the tattoos across his knuckles. One side said 'Love' and the other 'Lift'. His face was fleshy, with acne spreading under his neck and across his jawline, although the depth of his tan almost concealed it.

'What were you doing at Susan Palmer's house?'

He shrugged. 'Having a chat.'

Jo smiled at him. 'You can do better than that. You broke her nose, knocked out her tooth.'

'Did she tell you that?' he asked.

'She didn't have to.'

Alex folded his arms, with difficulty, and looked up at the ceiling impatiently. 'This is bullshit,' he said.

'Susan said you were there to collect money.' It was Andrea who'd taken her to the hospital, and got her to open up a bit. But so far she was resisting giving any sort of official statement.

'Is that a crime?' he asked.

'It is if you use force,' said Jo.

He looked right at her. His eyes were slightly bloodshot. 'I didn't,' he said. 'She fell over.'

'Have you got a good explanation for the cash we found in your car?'

'I don't trust banks.'

Jack Pryce came into the room, carrying a few pieces of paper.

'Hello Mr Maynard,' he said.

'When am I going home?' he asked.

Pryce smiled. 'I think we'll be here a while yet, sir. Can you tell us when you last saw Natalie Palmer?'

'I had nothing to do with that,' he said.

'With what?'

'Her mum said she was dead. Good riddance. She was a junkie.'

'A junkie who owed you money?'

Maynard wagged a thick, calloused finger. 'I'm just a collector,' he said.

'So what was the money owed for?'

'Ain't my business.'

'Was it for drugs?'

'Like I said, not my business.'

'So whose business is it?' said Jo. 'Who's your employer?'

Maynard didn't answer.

'So you're a collector? That's your profession?'

'I do security too. Y'know? Door work.'

'How do you know Natalie was a junkie then?' asked Pryce.

Maynard shrugged.

'Ever drive out to Little Baldon?' asked Jo.

'Where's that then?'

'You know where it is.'

Maynard's foot stopped tapping. He spread his hands. 'Help me out.'

'Okay, where were you last Tuesday, after four pm?'

'Tuesday . . . Tuesday . . . I'd have been at the gym.'

'Which gym?'

'Shredded – it's out in Cowley.'

'Until when?'

'I dunno. Eight or nine. Before work.'

'You spend four or five hours in the gym?'

'This sort of body doesn't come easy.'

'Indeed,' said Jo. 'We saw the stuff in your car.'

'All legal,' said Maynard. 'Personal use.'

'And can anyone vouch for your presence there, at Shredded?'

Maynard scratched his eyebrow, where the scar of a ring piercing remained. 'Sure. Loads of guys. There's a camera too.'

Jo studied his body. It could be true, but checking out the alibi would take time, and make them look weak. She needed to find a way past his defences. This wasn't his first time in a police interview room, as the record attested. GBH, possession with intent, drunk and disorderly. He'd served six months for a fight in which another man had lost the sight in one eye. The fact that he hadn't requested any sort of brief suggested he was either stupid or supremely confident.

'Do you have a temper, Alex?'

'Depends what someone does to piss me off. Most people don't try.'

'Steroids can't help,' she said. 'All those chemicals mess with your head.'

'Not if you're a responsible user.'

'Ladies like it, do they? The big look?'

Maynard leered. Under his top, he tensed his pecs. 'Some, yeah.'

Pryce grimaced, but Jo kept a straight face. 'Don't all those steroids . . . y'know, make things shrivel up?' She nodded towards his crotch. 'Downstairs.'

He leant forward, meaty hands entwined. 'Why don't you strip search me and find out, darlin'?'

She heard a knock and saw Olly Pinker at the door. 'One moment, please.'

'That's right, run along,' said Maynard smugly.

Outside, Olly shook his head. 'Susan's still not talking,' he said. 'She says it was a misunderstanding, and she ran into a door.'

'Course she is,' said Jo.

'You want me to get a statement from the neighbour who called us – anything incriminating?' asked Olly.

'I can't see the point. Can you head out to the Shredded gym in Cowley? See if you can get the CCTV for last Tuesday afternoon. We need to check if this lump was there at the time the van was stopped on the Little Baldon bridge.'

'On it, ma'am,' said Olly.

Jo drew a deep breath. They could keep Maynard in, but if Susan didn't want to help, it would be a pointless exercise. She couldn't see how he fit the hit and run – his Jeep could never be mistaken for a white transit, and they'd already run his plates through the ANPR with no hits near the A4074. This whole thing could easily be a side-show. Still, she wasn't ready to let Maynard off the hook just yet. He might easily have access to a white van, or have accomplices who did.

Back inside, she restarted the interview.

'She's not talking, is she?' Maynard asked with a smirk.

He knew the game, all right. He didn't care what the tape recorded, because without Susan's testimony it would never make it to court.

'Let's go back to whom you work for?'

'I told you, it's—'

'. . . none of my fucking business, I know. However, given you assaulted both me, and one of my colleagues, I'd advise you to play nicely.' She turned over one of the sheets of paper. 'You've something of a history of violent behaviour, it seems.'

'I used to have a temper,' said Maynard, muscles twitching involuntarily. 'Time served.'

'Well, yes,' Jo replied, 'but you're still out on licence. This could put you back inside.'

'Doubtful,' said Maynard. 'I was scared. You came at me with a club.'

'A standard issue baton. I identified myself as a police officer.'

'I didn't hear that.' He tapped his ear. 'Years working on sites with no protectors.'

'My colleague, who you tried to punch, is wearing a uniform.'

'Didn't see. She came at me from behind. What is she anyway, a tranny?'

Jo got the impression he was enjoying their little duel. Time to pull out the trump card. 'It's not really you I'm worried about,' said Jo. 'You look like you could handle yourself in prison.' She turned over the pages in front of her until she reached the papers regarding Alex Maynard's complicated visitation arrangements. She ran her finger down the page. 'It's your daughter who concerns me.'

The chair creaked under his bulk as he sat forward, and his eyes glinting.

'What's that supposed to mean?'

'Nia's a pretty name,' she said. 'My little girl is three, too. They're a handful, right?'

Beside her, Pryce shifted uncomfortably in his chair. She resisted looking across.

Maynard just watched her.

'Looks like your rights are limited as it is. One day a fortnight. I suppose it's supervised, given your past?'

He didn't answer, but he looked like he wanted to rip Jo's head off. He probably could too.

'Even if a court won't convict on the assault, there's enough here to give children's services some concern.' She glanced at Pryce. 'What do you think, Jack?'

Pryce looked distinctly ill at ease. 'I suppose so.'

'That's bollocks,' said Maynard.

'I'm afraid it isn't,' said Jo. 'Especially these days. Can't be too careful, right? They'd have to postpone contact while they got the facts straight. That would mean another hearing. The evidential bar is much lower with council busybodies. I could see it being at least a year until you get to see Nia again.'

'Fuck you,' he said, spitting the words.

Jo put on her most sympathetic look. 'I'm trying to help you get out of a hole,' she said. 'If this was just extortion with menaces, I'll be straight, there's a chance you'd get off. But sadly Natalie Palmer is dead, and you were seen threatening her recently.'

'Really?' said Maynard. 'Says who?'

'It's on camera,' said Pryce. 'Right outside the front of Jesus College.'

Jo didn't bat an eyelid, but she was annoyed. There was no footage, and if Maynard called their bluff, he'd know they were grasping at straws.

'My gaffer's got me working the case and he wants results,' she said. 'This isn't going to go away because Susan Palmer won't accuse you.'

'She's right,' said Pryce. 'We've got a witness too – said you were rough with Natalie.'

Just shut up now, thought Jo. *You're trying too hard.*

Maynard was wavering, though – she could see it in the way his fists were curled, like he was trying to hold something in.

'All right, Alex,' she said, standing up. 'I can see you're determined, and that's fine. But I'm not going to sit here and watch you flex. We're going to hold you overnight while we get statements from all the associated parties. Children's services will be contacted in the morning, and we'll provide a narrative report of what happened tonight. You seem like a clever bloke, so—'

'All right, wait,' he said quietly.

'Sorry, time's up,' said Jo. She looked at her watch. 'I can still get home to read a bedtime story.'

'I didn't have nothing to do with that woman's death. The

mum wouldn't pay, so I went to chat to the daughter. Just to see if we could work something out.'

'Between the two of us, I believe you,' said Jo. 'But you can see it doesn't look great. How much did she owe?'

'Two hundred,' said Maynard.

'And who does she owe?' asked Jo.

Maynard laid his hands flat on the table, looking at them. 'If I tell you, they'll know it was me.'

'We'll do our best with that,' said Jo. She sat again.

'I didn't know what the debt was for.'

'Of course not.'

'Sully brothers,' said Maynard. 'Arab blokes. Cad and Mo. Cad's the manager at a place called Lounge Bar on Cowley Road. I work the door there.'

Jo had driven past the place a few times. It had a bit of a bad reputation, changing hands about four months earlier. The name of the manager meant nothing to her.

'Are you supposed to be working tonight?'

Maynard shook his head.

'Good,' said Jo. 'Detective Pryce, can I speak with you outside, please?'

Pryce stood up to leave.

'What about me?' asked Maynard.

Jo told him to sit tight. The last thing they needed was him tipping anyone off.

'Risky move in there,' she said to Pryce at their desks. 'The stuff about the camera footage.'

Pryce looked surprised. 'Really? What about your "kid"?' Jo didn't think the two deceits were comparable, but she didn't need an argument. There was a hint of belligerence in his tone, and it couldn't just be related to the interview tactics.

She ran a check, and 'Cad' was actually Qadir Suleiman. He was clean, but his brother Mohammed, aged thirty-five, previously registered as living in a flat just around the corner from Lounge Bar, had a conviction of possession with intent to supply a class A drug, dating from the previous year. Mohammed Suleiman was currently serving eighteen months at Her Majesty's pleasure. It looked like Qadir might have been running the family business in the meantime.

'Maybe we should visit incognito,' said Pryce. 'Fancy that drink?'

At the end of the corridor, Olly Pinker looked up sharply.

Jo focused on Pryce. She could tell from his open expression, the hint of a smile, that he was trying to make amends, to fix things. And though she wasn't wholly convinced Suleiman was even linked to Natalie's death, if there was a chance of a drugs bust, it would sweeten the pill for Stratton in the event the hit and run remained unsolved.

'All right,' she said. 'But you're paying.'

Chapter 14

Jo wasn't quite the oldest person in the queue for Lounge Bar, she was pleased to see, but she was the most appropriately dressed for the freezing conditions of mid-December. The female clientele weren't students, but scantily clad twenty-somethings in vertiginous heels with plenty of flesh on display; the men, as far as she could see, were a collection of hairstyles that hadn't existed when she grew up. Pryce had returned to his place to change into jeans and a shirt, but he wore his long grey work coat. He just about fitted in, though he definitely looked like he'd come straight out after work. She'd taken longer than she'd intended at her flat, and wore black skinny jeans and kitten heels, and a silver halter-top under a black peacoat Amelia had bought her on her last birthday. It was the sort of thing Paul's wife could carry off effortlessly, but Jo felt self-conscious and poorly insulated. However, all her other, more suitable, outer-garments were at Lucas's. As a gust blew up the street, she hugged herself.

'You want to borrow this?' said Pryce, tugging the lapels of his coat.

'Very chivalrous,' said Jo, 'but I'm okay.'

They were ushered inside by a huge, bored-looking bouncer who gave them little more than a perfunctory once-over. The place was packed with bodies, and pounding electronic music. In Jo's sober state, the smell of sweet alcohol hit her hard, followed closely by the mingled scents of the clientele. It was about fifty-fifty in terms of gender, mostly under thirty years old.

'I'll get drinks,' said Pryce. 'Any preference?'

'You choose,' she replied.

She looked around, but there was nowhere to sit, so she shuffled across to a door reading 'Staff Only' at one end of the bar. Behind was a large fridge, occupied with craft beers at the top, wine bottles at the bottom. The bar staff were both good-looking Asian males. One was mixing cocktails with practised ease, while the other poured shots.

Pryce loomed over most of the other customers, looking out of place. A woman at his elbow spoke to him and he smiled as he replied.

Jo scanned the rest of the room. She had no idea what Suleiman looked like, but there was no one who resembled staff apart from the two barmen and a sulky white girl with a nose-ring collecting glasses. She leant against the 'Staff Only' door, but it was locked. A couple of lone males checked her out, but there was nothing suspicious in their curiosity. Undercover had never been her thing, and she forced herself to move a little to the music.

'This is fun,' shouted Pryce, coming along holding a long cocktail. He handed it over, saying something she couldn't hear. She pointed to her ear, and he leant closer, so she could feel his breath on her hair. 'Any sign of Suleiman?'

She shook her head, then turned her chin up to tell him she was going to check out the back. She sipped the drink first. The fact that it didn't contain alcohol only added to the feeling they were play-acting.

Handing him the glass, she threaded through the other drinkers, then along the corridor to the toilets, passing another door. When she pushed this one, it opened onto another short corridor with two doors off at right angles. The air was immediately cooler. She made sure no one was following, then walked to the first door. It opened into an office, where a man with a shaved head was wearing a suit and holding an espresso cup in his hand.

'You can't come in here,' he said, putting the cup down.

'Looking for the loos,' said Jo. She couldn't be sure, but he looked like a less fleshy version of Mohammed Suleiman in his mugshot.

'Then follow the signs,' he said. 'Get out of here.'

Jo retreated, heart beating fast, and went to the ladies'. The room was painted black, with a large silver-framed mirror, and a single trough sink with faux-antique copper taps. A woman stood drying her hands. She checked out her face in the mirror, then went to the door. One of the two toilet stalls was occupied, so Jo slipped into the other. From the cubicle next to her, she heard the rattle of someone going through a handbag, before the sound of a door unbolting. Jo waited a few seconds before flushing and exiting too.

The woman at the sink was maybe twenty-five, heavily made-up, with a short black asymmetric dress and nails like talons.

'Hi,' said Jo, as she washed her own hands.

'Hiya,' said the woman, smiling.

'You come here often?' asked Jo in the mirror. The last time she'd worn this much make-up was for the photoshoot Thames Valley had forced her into.

'A few times,' said the woman. She looked faintly perplexed at being spoken to.

'My first time in, like, three years,' said Jo. 'It used to be a real dump.'

'Yeah, I heard that,' said the woman. She shook the water from her hands and went to the drier. 'Have a good night.'

'Wait up,' said Jo. 'You know where I can get some blow?'

It was a tactic she'd pre-agreed with Pryce, and the woman laughed nervously. 'Oh, right! No, I'm sorry.' She hurried to the door, before adding, 'Take it easy.'

Shit. That didn't go as planned. The woman would probably tell whoever she was with about the weird old woman in the loos trying to score. Hopefully not a bouncer. And to think *she'd* accused Pryce of messing up earlier.

She couldn't see the other woman when she went back into the bar, but Pryce was engaged in conversation with a different girl, stooped over, holding Jo's drink. He saw Jo and raised the glass, and the girl looked across too, appraising.

She joined them. 'Jo, meet Annabelle. Annabelle, Jo.'

'Hi,' said Jo, making no attempt to be friendly. They needed to get rid of her. 'So Jack says you two are in accounts,' said the girl. 'My dad's an accountant.'

'Good for him,' said Jo. 'Jack, can I speak with you a minute?'

Annabelle's face was close to a snarl, but she touched Pryce's hand. 'See you later, maybe,' she said.

Once she'd gone, Pryce sipped his drink. 'You scared her away.'

'I think Suleiman's in the back,' she said, explaining about the office. 'There's a rear door to his office, so I think we need to take him out that way. Otherwise all hell will break loose in here.'

'We could call for some back-up.'

'I don't know. If there are drugs on the premises, I'd rather do things as quietly as possible.'

'Agreed,' said Pryce.

Jo decided not to tell him about her embarrassing encounter in the ladies. She finished her drink. 'You ready?'

Pryce looked across the bar. 'Dunno. Maybe we should observe some more.'

'I say we move,' said Jo.

'You're the boss.' He put his own drink down.

They both headed towards the back, when the bouncer from the door stepped in front of them.

'Can I help you?'

'We're fine, thanks,' said Jo.

The man mountain raised a hand. 'No, can I *help* you?' he repeated. 'You're looking for something, I think.'

'Yes,' said Jo. 'Coke.'

'You got money?' he asked. Jo reached for her handbag. 'Not here, not here. Follow me.'

He led them back towards the door Jo had gone through previously, but as he opened it and Jo walked through, he put out a hand and stopped Pryce. 'Just her,' he said firmly.

'No way, mate,' said Pryce. 'Come on, babe – let's leave it.'

'Don't worry,' said Jo. 'I'll be back in a minute.'

'I don't like it,' said Pryce, swatting the bouncer's hand aside.

The security guy sized Pryce up and snorted. 'I think you both need to leave,' he said.

'No!' said Jo. 'It's all right, honestly. Seriously, Jack, I'm good. Wait outside.'

She stared hard at Pryce, wondering if his concern was an act or genuine. He backed away, with a bob of the head. The door closed in his face.

'He's just worried,' said Jo.

'Nothing to worry about,' said the bouncer. He led her past the office to the door at the end of the corridor. Inside was a large stockroom, with beer barrels hooked up, and shelves on either side. The girl who'd been collecting glasses was waiting there.

'Thanks, Duke,' she said.

The bouncer waited, hands clasped in front of his waist.

'You've not been here before,' said the girl.

'I've just moved,' said Jo.

'Where from?

'Why is that important?' asked Jo. 'I just want to buy some coke.'

'What makes you think we have anything like that here?'

'I just heard,' said Jo. 'My friend.'

'Who is?'

Keep it vague.

'Her name's Belle,' she said. 'Her ex got some pills here a few weeks ago.'

'Is that right?'

'So she said. Look, if you haven't got what I want, fine.'

'How much do you want?' said the girl.

'I've got fifty quid,' said Jo. She opened her purse and took out the money.

'And you just want coke?'

Jo shrugged. 'What else have you got?'

'We can get you anything.'

Jo feigned hesitation. 'Nah. Just coke. For now.'

The girl took the money and disappeared for a moment through another door. Jo turned and looked nervously at the bouncer, who hadn't moved. If things went south now, she was screwed.

But the girl came back, with a transparent bag of white powder, which she tossed on the table.

Jo reached out, took it, and put it into her handbag.

'You aren't going to test it?' asked the girl.

'Do I need to?' said Jo. 'It's not for me, anyway.'

'That other guy your boyfriend, is he?'

Jo nodded.

The girl gave an appreciative smile. 'Next time, ask for Jenna at the bar.'

Jo followed the bouncer back through into the corridor, feeling a thrill of triumph. As soon as she was outside with Pryce, she'd call a tactical unit.

Before she was back in the bar, the office door opened, and Suleiman came out, talking to someone behind him and laughing. He saw Jo with the bouncer and frowned. Then a second figure emerged, a young woman in a chic belted overcoat. It took Jo a split-second to clock that the face was that of Ross Catskill's receptionist, Selina. When she laid eyes on Jo, her jaw dropped. 'What are you doing here?' she said.

'You know each other?' said Suleiman.

'She's police,' said Selina.

Jo saw Suleiman's eyes deaden like a shark's, and she knew it was game over. She drove her elbow backwards into the jaw of the bouncer, then swung at Suleiman. He ducked underneath, charged forward, and lifted her off the ground. Selina wailed and backed away. Jo was thrown into the wall, then dumped to the ground. Suleiman lifted a fist to punch her, but she got an arm up and raked her nails across the side of his face. Something grabbed her ankle and she screamed as she was yanked across the floor on her back by the bouncer. He clamped his hand over her mouth and nose, and though she kicked and thrashed, there was nothing she could do. Suleiman was clutching the side of his face, and Selina was pressed into a corner. Jo tried to bite, but the bouncer's grip was astonishing. She knew she didn't have long before she blacked out.

Then Pryce came through the door, wielding a fire extinguisher over his head. For a terrible second she thought he was going to hit *her*, but he thrust the butt end into the bouncer's face and Jo was dropped. Suleiman ran through the door into the store room, leaving Catskill's receptionist standing with her hands over her mouth in shock.

The bouncer was squirming on the ground, blood pouring between his fingers. Jo stood up and went after Suleiman, back into the store room, through another door that led down a set of stairs into a cellar lined with more barrels. His feet were just exiting to street level through a hatch up a set of metal steps. She wished she'd worn different footwear, because her heel turned over and pain lanced up her ankle. As she emerged to street level, in a quiet road beside the bar, Suleiman had vanished.

'Fuck!' she shouted.

Gathering herself, she got on the phone and called it in.

Chapter 15

SATURDAY

Jo could've done with a real drink.

Uniforms cleared the place out and set up a cordon, though there were plenty of people still milling around at one am, as the dog unit arrived with a sniffer called Fergie. It took approximately two minutes for him to identify crates in the cellar that were filled with various prohibited substances, and all helpfully stickered with the Calibre logo. Selina claimed she knew nothing about any of it, and that she'd just been discussing business with Suleiman on behalf of Ross Catskill. When she refused to come to the station willingly, Pryce arrested her and she began to cry.

Inside the Lounge Bar, the barmen were detained, along with the girl who'd sold the drugs, and the bouncer who Jo had floored temporarily and whose nose it appeared Pryce had rearranged with the fire extinguisher.

'Officers have been dispatched to the Calibre offices,' Pryce told Jo. 'Stratton's been notified.'

Jo nodded, wondering about the next play. If there was

a chance Catskill was linked to Natalie Palmer as well as Malin Sigurdsson, that changed the complexion of the case considerably. The DCI would probably sideline them at once in favour of Carrick. 'No need for us to stick around,' she said to Pryce.

* * *

Goring was a small town clinging to the banks of the Thames, with nice houses and two pubs, their car parks stuffed with upmarket vehicles. Catskill's house, in one of the quiet residential roads, was a detached thirties place. A swing hung from a tree in the front garden and a security light came on as they approached. A 4x4 and a convertible Porsche Boxster sat under a carport. Inside, a dog barked. It gave Jo little pleasure to think about the peace she was about to shatter.

She rang the bell, long and firm.

A teenage boy opened the door surprisingly quickly given the late hour, over-sized headphones looped over the back of his neck. The striking blue eyes gave him away as Catskill's son. 'Hello?'

Jo held up her badge and hoped her tone was friendly.

'Is your dad in?'

'Mum?' called the boy. 'The police are here.'

An attractive woman of about Jo's age came down the stairs, tying a satin dressing gown. *Emily, wasn't it?*

'We're looking for Ross,' said Jo, showing her badge again.

'What's this about? Have you any idea what time it is?'

'We're sorry about that. It's important we speak to your husband.'

Catskill's wife paused, and in her face Jo caught a hint of comprehension or recalcitrance. Perhaps she wasn't quite the innocent spouse after all. She didn't invite them in, instead nodding to the boy. 'Sam, fetch your dad. He's downstairs in the gym.'

Catskill came to the door sweating and wiping his head with a towel. He wore a T-shirt with dark patches under the armpits and descending his chest, jogging bottoms, and Nikes. When he recognised them, he came outside, pulling the door until it was almost closed behind him. 'What are you playing at?'

'We raided Lounge Bar this evening,' said Jo.

He didn't bat an eyelid. 'And?'

'Come on, Mr Catskill, save us the time.'

'I'm sorry, you'll have to be more specific.'

'Selina March is in custody already, and we'll begin questioning her shortly.'

The wind left Catskill's sails, telling in the sag of his shoulders. 'Right.'

His wife opened the door from within, where she must have been listening. She stepped closer to his side, a look of barely concealed hatred on her face. At the top of the stairs, another boy of six or seven was watching too, dressed in his pyjamas.

'What's going on, Ross?' said his wife.

'You need to come with us and answer some questions,' said Pryce. 'You can come voluntarily, or we can arrest you.'

'It's nothing,' said Catskill. 'Put Harry back to bed.'

'But, darling—'

'I said I'll deal with it.'

He turned to Jo and Pryce.

'Have I got time for a shower?'

'No,' said Jo. 'Time's up.'

* * *

Ross Catskill cut a more shambolic figure in the interview room this time. The heat of the newly working radiators was reacting with his drying sweat and in the confined space, Jo was regretting not letting him wash first. He'd requested a lawyer immediately, saying he wouldn't talk until his representation showed up.

Luckily this gave them time to get a formal statement from Selina March, who, in return for a deal exonerating her, crumbled like a biscuit plunged into a cup of tea. With the duty solicitor's advice, she gave them everything she knew about Catskill's operation, including the various establishments he supplied, which happened to include several gyms. She told them what appeared on the books and what didn't, and how the drug money was cleaned through a string of amusement arcades that Catskill ran. She stuck to logistics mostly, and Jo got the impression quickly that her hands were mostly clean. She insisted she knew nothing about Natalie Palmer or her mother, and suggested that Suleiman may well have been pushing Catskill's products on the street as well as through the bar. Malin she recognised, though – but her statement only clarified what Catskill himself had told them previously. For a while the two had been fucking and Ross had broken it off.

'She was a druggie,' Selina said blithely. 'Ross didn't like it. He wanted her out of his life. They had an argument at some bar and she took a swing at him.'

It wasn't quite the sympathetic story he'd told them at Jukebox, where he'd broken it off gently, but it wasn't so different either.

And it's hardly motive enough to kill her, thought Jo. But maybe it hadn't been premeditated. It sounded like she'd taken the break-up badly, and that would be compounded further if it limited her access to drugs. Maybe she'd invited Catskill over to talk, letting him in through the fire door. They argued about something, and it became physical. She might even have attacked him again, in which case appealing to the self-defence motive would be the best approach.

Selina couldn't tell them much about Alex Maynard either. She'd seen him on the door of various places ('you could hardly miss him, right?'), but he'd never come to the Calibre offices, and she wasn't sure he had a connection to her boss, Catskill.

Stratton arrived in his civilian clothes, straight from the scene at the bar, and Jo filled him in on their findings, especially the new connection between Malin Sigurdsson and Natalie Palmer.

'It's not really much, is it?' he said. 'So Catskill knew Malin personally, and he supplied a bar with a very tenuous link to Natalie Palmer. Doesn't mean he was involved in either Malin's disappearance or the hit and run.'

'The dealer from the Lounge has said all their stuff came through Calibre,' said Jo. 'Alex Maynard was the enforcer. Maybe Malin had a debt too?'

'Without hearing from Suleiman, it's tendentious to say the least,' said Stratton. 'Have you any idea where he is now?'

Jo shook her head. 'We sent officers to his house, but his car has gone.'

Stratton frowned. 'Why didn't you call for back-up earlier?'

'We were just there to observe,' said Jo.

'Did you do a risk assessment?'

'There was no risk. Selina March showing up was completely unforeseeable.'

Stratton didn't reply to that, but the shuck of his eyebrows suggested extreme scepticism.

'Sir, if you ask me, I think DS Masters has got a point,' said Pryce.

Stratton shook his head. 'I didn't ask you, son.' He looked up, just as a red-headed woman in a suit was being shown through. 'Brief's here. Now get in there and do your job.'

* * *

The lawyer, Zara Ripley, greeted Catskill with a kiss on both cheeks, and took an hour to go through things with her client, making studious notes. Jo watched, gritty-eyed with weariness, through the video-feed and saw Catskill alternately standing and pacing and shuffling uncomfortably, sometimes gesticulating with his hands. Ripley had also brought him some fresh clothes, and they allowed him to change in the toilets while Pryce stood outside. When they were all seated again, with the tape rolling, it was Ripley who spoke first.

'My client is willing to admit to the drugs offences and to tell you his supplier in return for bail and being allowed to return to the family home. He's not a danger, and he has no history of—'

Jo held up a hand. 'Slow down. We can get to the drugs in good time. First we need to talk about Malin Sigurdsson.'

'Not this again!' said Catskill. 'I told you, Malin was just a fling.'

'We think there might be more to it than that,' said Jo. 'She was a user, too, wasn't she?'

'So what?' said Catskill. 'I bet half your fucking colleagues are too.'

Zara gave a pinched smile. 'You'll understand my client is simply worried about his family.'

'Did you supply her with drugs?' asked Pryce.

Ripley leaned over and whispered something in Catskill's ear.

'No comment,' he said.

Jo laughed. 'I'll take that as a yes.'

Ripley leant forward. 'Have you any leads on the disappearance of Ms Sigurdsson?'

Jo wasn't in the mood to give much away. 'We're still working on the assumption she was murdered. We know that your client had a public argument with Malin in a bar a few weeks before her death. An argument in which she slapped him. Ring any bells, Mr Catskill, or do you get slapped a lot?'

He scowled. 'She was upset that I was breaking it off.'

'And why was that again? You thought she was getting too attached?'

'I didn't need the hassle.'

'But you must have been worried too. I mean, this unstable young girl knew you were involved in drugs, right? Did she try to blackmail you perhaps?'

'No.'

'Let me put a scenario to you. Malin calls you to talk. You don't want it on your turf – not after last time – so you go to her college.'

'No.'

'She lets you in, but it goes just the same as before. You argue, she gets physical, starts to come at you. You lift your hand to protect yourself and she hits her head. It happens all the time. Doesn't mean you're a bad guy.'

Catskill actually laughed.

'You try to revive her but it's too late. You panic.'

Ripley took a deep breath. 'You have no witnesses. You have no evidence in Malin's room. Come on, detective – this is risible.'

'And Malin wasn't like that,' said Catskill. 'She wouldn't blackmail anyone. She was a good person, despite her issues.'

It was almost exactly what Anna Mull had said.

'You said before that Malin was stubborn. What did you mean?'

'Just that . . . she knew her own mind. She was driven. Wanted to get places.'

'An aspirational smack user?'

Catskill looked introspective. 'I sometimes got the impression she did the drugs because she knew how much it pissed off that MP guy. It was her way of rebelling.'

'But why would she want to piss him off? The way we heard it he took care of her when her dad died.'

'Did the mother tell you that?'

Not exactly, thought Jo. 'What did Malin say?'

'She hated the sight of him. Said he used to walk round in the buff when she was little.'

Jo tried to shake the image away, but couldn't. *This is an interesting development.* 'Are you saying he . . . did something sexual to her? Molested her?'

Catskill shrugged. 'She never said that exactly. She said he used to look at her funny.' Jo let him continue. There was a chance he was just leading them down the garden path, distracting them from himself, and though what he was saying rang a kind of truth, she was wary of letting her prejudices run away with her. 'You've seen pictures of Malin,' said Catskill. 'I think she was about five or six when that old lech came into her life, and he was around while she was growing up. He watched her become a beautiful young woman. He was obviously into Malin's mother. Is it that hard to imagine he might have had a thing for her too?'

Stratton appeared at the door, and crooked his finger.

'Maybe we should take a break,' said Pryce.

* * *

Jo should have known the DCI would be listening in. He shook his head several times in a way that reminded Jo of her nephew Will, when he'd been three years old in his high-chair, refusing mashed cauliflower, even though she'd pretended it was a train and his mouth was a tunnel, complete with chugging sound effects.

'No, no, no. How many times? This is not about Nicholas Cranleigh.'

'Sir, we can't ignore it. We need to talk to him again.'

'Absolutely no chance,' said Stratton. 'On the back of what? The word of a desperate drug dealer? He'll say anything to get out of this fix. And Ripley's a canny piece of work too. They're leading you around by the nose. The depressing thing is, you're letting it happen.'

Jo looked at Pryce, and for once, he didn't seem to know what to say. He was probably beginning to regret supporting her before.

'I'm trying to be open-minded, sir,' said Jo. 'But that means exploring all possibilities. One of which is that Cranleigh might have done something to his step-daughter. Tried to silence her. She was being followed before she disappeared.'

Stratton looked heavenward. 'And pray, remind me, where did that piece of information come from?' Jo sighed. 'Oh, that's right! Ross Catskill.' He softened his stance. 'Jo, please. Don't make this decision for me. I want you to do a good job. For your sake.' He let the threat hang. 'Keep Cranleigh out of it. Focus on what we actually know. We've got this guy. Let's use him wisely.'

'Sir.' Jo turned and strode away.

In the toilets, she splashed water in her face. She knew she was close to the edge, dog-tired and maybe not thinking straight, but still . . .

She considered, for a mad moment, directly contravening Stratton's orders. What would he do? Drag her out of the interview room and suspend her on the spot? Maybe. She might be able to lay a few home truths at his door, but the satisfaction would be short-lived before the reality of professional suicide hit.

There was a soft knock at the door, and Pryce spoke through it. 'You all right, Jo?'

She thought it was the first time he'd called her by her first name, instead of 'ma'am'. It sounded strange in his mouth.

'Just give me a minute,' she replied.

With more water cupped in her hand, she washed off the remains of the mascara, and all her other make-up. Having done so, her real face exposed, she actually felt better. She didn't need war-paint to do her job, and getting hyped up wouldn't help. She remembered what Ferman had said the night before. *Solve the case. Prove yourself.* She dried her face with a paper towel, and smiled at her reflection. They'd brought in about four kilos of cocaine from Lounge Bar, and hopefully taken one of the city's major suppliers off the street. Not bad for an evening's work.

'Glass half full, Josephine,' she muttered. 'Glass half full.'

* * *

'Okay. Let's talk about Natalie Palmer.'

'I don't know who that is,' said Catskill.

'Take a minute to think.'

'Detectives,' said Ripley. 'My client has been as helpful as he can be in relation to the findings at Lounge. And indeed to Malin Sigurdsson. Throwing out random names is wasting everyone's time.'

Jo opened the file in front of her, showing the close-up photo of Natalie's frozen face, and turned it around. 'Jesus!' said Catskill. 'Why are you showing me that?'

'To jog your memory maybe,' said Jo. She revealed the

second photo, one taken from Susan Palmer's house, with Natalie beaming.

'I've never seen that woman before,' he said.

'We think you supplied drugs to her mum through Qadir Suleiman,' said Jo. 'We think she was killed because her mum owed money.'

'Look, I don't tell Suleiman or anyone else how to run his business. I swear I've never seen that woman before.'

'And let me guess, you don't know Alex Maynard?'

He shrugged.

'Detectives, please . . .' said Ripley. 'This is getting silly.'

Jo showed him a picture of Maynard.

'To be honest,' said Catskill, 'I'm glad I don't know him.'

Jo knew instinctively he wasn't lying. The suave and confident playboy they'd first met in Jukebox had gradually been stripped back to this. A slightly smelly, desperate man looking to save his family and freedom. He almost certainly didn't drive a white van, and the idea of him actually getting his hands dirty at all was almost unthinkable. The only people drug dealers cared about were those directly above them, and those directly below by one remove. Those they owed, and those who owed them.

She suspected Stratton, for all his infuriating condescension, knew it too. Trying to tie their open cases through Ross Catskill wasn't getting them any closer to solving either. Drug connections were an invisible web that could link countless people in the city, so maybe it wasn't such a big surprise that one character had a peripheral connection to Malin and Natalie, even though they were coming from two such different places in life.

'I've told you everything,' said Catskill. 'I really don't know anything about Malin or the other girl.'

Jo stood up, gathering her things. 'That's a real shame,' she said, 'because it means I can't help you at all.'

Chapter 16

It was almost half past three in the morning when she let herself into the flat. Lucas was a heavy sleeper, but she crept in quietly anyway, taking a fresh set of clothes from the wardrobe, and her make-up bag from the dressing table. She had a quick shower, but managed to drop the shampoo, which clattered into the tray with an astonishing bang.

Fuck.

She climbed out. Hopefully he hadn't stirred. She was drying herself when the door opened, and Lucas walked through, squinting into the harsh light. He pulled up the toilet seat and started pissing.

'What time is it?' he asked, bleary-eyed.

'Late,' said Jo.

He registered her clothing hanging from the drying rail.

'Are you heading back out?'

'Working a case,' she said.

He finished, and went to the sink. 'Have you slept?'

'Not yet.'

As he was drying his hands, he said, 'Are you going to tell me what's wrong?'

'Nothing's wrong.'

'Really? Not coming over the other night, being weird at lunch. Running off again. It's like you're avoiding me.'

'I can't just drop everything. My job's more important than a lunch.'

'Hey, I know that. But I don't think this is just your job.'

She felt silly being naked while she argued, so put on her bra even though she was still a bit damp. She continued to dress, with him standing there. As she reached for her trousers, he put his hand on them.

'*Talk* to me, for God's sake.'

She snatched the trousers away. 'Fine. I came to the college, Lucas,' she said. 'Two days ago, when we had the leak. Spoke to Bob. He didn't seem to think you'd been there that morning.'

'You were checking up on me?' he said.

'I was trying to *find* you,' she said.

She could barely read his face in the half light. He'd been caught lying, and he wasn't coming up with any excuses. With each second that passed, she felt more detached from the scene unfolding as she shrank into her shell. *Self-preservation, Josephine.*

'It's not what you think,' he said.

'Isn't it? I deal with liars every day. Everyone has their reasons. What's yours?'

When he didn't answer, she left the bathroom. She'd not been planning to walk out, but she found herself grabbing an overnight bag. Stuffing clothes in. *Focus, Jo. Be dignified.*

Lucas entered the room.

'What the hell are you doing?'

'What does it look like?'

He came to her, and moved the bag aside. 'Jo, listen, I'm sorry – I shouldn't have lied, but let me explain.'

'Just leave me alone,' she said.

A fleeting expression she'd never seen before crossed his features. 'At least hear me out.'

'I've really got to get to work,' she said.

'I wasn't at the college, you're right. I was at the travel agent's.'

'Pardon?'

'The specialist winter sports place, out in Summertown. I've used them before.' She let him continue. 'I know you've been wanting to go away, and well, you said you hadn't skied before. I wanted somewhere we could go together. And something flexible, because well . . . your job. I talked to Heidi . . .'

'You what?'

'Sure. I wanted it to be a surprise. And I needed an idea of what time off you could get . . . I didn't want to go to your boss, but I thought Heidi might be able to help me organise things. I guess I should have said rather than trying to do it behind your back. I'm sorry.'

Jo groaned inwardly. So that's what Heidi had been saying, the other day.

. . . you've fallen on your feet with that guy . . .

He looked so contrite she felt even more stupid and unreasonable than before. 'You were booking a *holiday*?'

'Trying. Then all this missing girl stuff kicked off.'

She stared at the bag on the bed, wishing she could crawl inside.

'Jo, what's going on? I mean – and don't take this the wrong way – it's a bit paranoid.'

'Comes with the job,' she said. 'I'm the one who should say sorry. Can we just forget it?'

'Of course.' He tossed the bag off the bed, and put his arm around her. 'Maybe actually getting some sleep would help?'

She smiled coyly. 'Maybe.'

With the light off again, she undressed once more, and lay

on her side with Lucas's body pressed up against hers, his breathing quickly settling into a slow rhythm. For some reason, she felt more awake than ever, with the same questions on a loop in her head. How could she have got it so wrong and misjudged him so harshly? Her history with Ben was one thing, and on the surface it went some way to excusing her trust issues, but that wasn't the thing that really ate away at her. It was the speed and ease with which she'd leapt to her conclusions. She'd gone from thinking everything was fine to full throttle paranoia on the basis of almost nothing. That didn't speak to someone in control.

And if she could go so spectacularly off-piste in her personal life, what did that say about her professional one? Maybe DCI Stratton actually had a point when he'd questioned her judgement. *The depressing thing is, you're letting it happen.*

She was just wondering what Dr Forster would make of it all, when sleep finally overcame her.

* * *

Four short hours later, Jo was back on the road and heading in. This close to the solstice, the sun wouldn't appear until well after eight am, but the sky was finding its colour towards the horizon, a perfect clear azure in which the stars were still visible. She opened the window, letting the frigid air blast away the cobwebs. A skiing trip sounded sort of cool, if a little terrifying. She'd probably end up in a beginner's class. Perhaps it would be good to contact the place herself, and see what was on offer. The last thing she wanted was a holiday where Lucas had to watch her repeatedly fall over with a group of toddlers.

She was driving along the Banbury Road when she noticed flashing blue lights down a side street. And more than one set.

An accident? She pulled over under a streetlight that was flickering on and off, not sure whether to give up for the day, and proceeded on foot. A uniformed officer, fixing tape across the end of an alleyway, recognised Jo.

'Morning, ma'am.'

'What's going on?'

'Not clear, ma'am. Looks like a bike accident of some sort, but Detective Dimitriou wants us to take all precautions.'

Jo continued along the alley, which was partially illuminated by a single working streetlight. It ran behind a churchyard and a tall wall that backed onto the tree-filled gardens belonging to a row of Edwardian three-storey terraced houses. Dimitriou was crouching on the ground, a pen in his hand and turned at the sound of her footsteps. 'Wasn't expecting you.'

'I was just driving by. Saw the lights.' Beyond him on the ground was a mountain bike. Jo could make out the front wheel, which was twisted out of shape. Black spatters a little further on became a trail then a pool. Blood. 'Someone take a fall?'

'We're not sure what happened to her.'

'Her?'

He stood up. 'Come this way.'

He led her to the other end of the alley, where he had parked. Andy Carrick had pulled up too. He and another uniform were speaking to a middle-aged man in running gear, partially wrapped in a space blanket. Laid out on the bonnet of Dimitriou's car was a small rucksack and several other items that Jo guessed were the contents – a purse, a phone, and a water bottle, plus a jumper.

'Jo?' said Carrick, coming over.

She explained the circumstances of her arrival.

'The witness found the bag just up from the bike,' said Carrick. 'No sign of the girl.'

'May I?' said Jo, gesturing to the items.

'Go ahead,' said Andy. He offered her some sterile gloves. She opened the wallet. A student ID card had a picture of a young Asian woman. Rita Prakash. Somerville College.

'Holy shit,' said Jo. 'Another college kid.'

'Undergrad,' said Dimitriou. 'Nineteen.'

'You notified them?'

'Pinker and Williams are over there now, just in case she's shown up. There's been nothing to emergency services, and no admissions at the local hospital.'

Jo looked around at the buildings either side of the alley. It was a dark spot, not overlooked by anything but the church. She couldn't help the quickening of her pulse.

'So she fell off for one reason or another,' said Jo. 'Maybe banged her head. Wandered off in a daze.' It already sounded unlikely. *It would have to be a serious knock to make you leave all your things behind*. 'No idea of the time?'

'Jogger came past at seven-thirty,' said Dimitriou. 'We'll go door to door. See if anyone saw or heard anything. Looks like she might have been going to the gym or something like that.'

'She would have been wearing the bag,' said Carrick. 'Why leave it?'

'Maybe it fell off her back?' said Dimitriou. 'If she was wearing it on one shoulder?'

He didn't sound convinced either.

On the bonnet of the car, the phone began to ring. The caller ID said 'Nabil'. No one else touched it, so Jo picked it up and answered.

'Hello?'

'Who's that?' It was a male voice.

'This is Detective Sergeant Jo Masters, Thames Valley Police.'

'Police? Is Rita okay?'

'Nabil, is it?'

'That's right. What's going on? Is Rita there?'

'Nabil, where are you?'

'Why have you got Rita's phone?'

Jo paused, looking at the blood, then at her colleagues, wondering what exactly to say.

* * *

'I don't understand.'

Nabil Chakarabani had uttered the same form of words several times since he'd met them, alone, at the gates of Somerville College. He was a slight young man with thick-rimmed glasses just the right side of stylish, and a huge mop of side-parted hair that half-fell across his forehead. He studied Physics, he told them, like Rita. At the direction of the college staff – a young female welfare officer – they used the wood-pannelled dining hall for the conversation. They sat at the end of a long table, overlooked by a stained-glass window and the staring eyes of austere college luminaries, all captured in oil paints. The welfare officer sat alongside Nabil, Carrick and Jo opposite, on one of the benches.

'You're a couple?' asked Andy.

'Not officially,' Nabil replied. 'Her parents are strict, you know? Traditional?'

'Religiously?' said Carrick.

'That as well,' said Nabil. 'They wanted her to go to St Hilda's, because it's girls only.'

'But for the record?' insisted Carrick. 'She's your girlfriend.'

'Yes,' said Nabil, nodding definitively.

'And everything's okay between you?' asked Andy. 'No arguments?'

Nabil's tightening features suggested he resented the implication. 'We're in love.'

They'd learned already that Rita was supposed to be attending a weekly army-themed fitness class in the University Parks to the north east of the city at 7.30 am that morning, but that she hadn't shown up. She was due to have breakfast with Nabil back in college at 8.45. She cycled everywhere, Nabil told them, and always wore a helmet. They hadn't mentioned the blood to him yet – though they weren't treating him as a suspect officially, it sometimes paid to control the flow of information and to see if people slipped up and said something incriminating.

'Is there anyone who could verify your whereabouts this morning?' asked Carrick.

'I was speaking with my brother's family in my room from about six-thirty until seven-thirty,' said Nabil.

'Early bird?' said Carrick.

'They live in Mumbai.'

Jo looked up at the large clock on the wall, which read 09.15. There had still been nothing from the hospitals, and the uniforms doing the road had drawn a blank so far. As the minutes passed and the bleak winter sun rose higher, Carrick's theory that Rita was wandering about in a catatonic state was looking increasingly shaky.

Jo had another idea, and tried not to let it run away with her. When you jumped to conclusions, mistakes got made. *But what if . . .*

What if someone had been waiting in that alley, maybe parked at the end? Waiting for the right victim. And they had taken her?

'Did Rita have any enemies?' said Carrick.

The welfare officer's eyes widened in alarm.

'No, of course not,' said Nabil. 'Everyone adored her.'

'So no threats recently?'

Nabil shook his head. 'Her parents are going to be so scared.'

'We've called them,' said the welfare officer. 'They're on their way.'

Mr and Mrs Prakash lived in Moseley, south of Birmingham city centre. Jo guessed they'd arrive within the hour.

'Nabil,' she said. 'We have to ask, was Rita involved with substance abuse or drugs?'

'Don't be silly,' said Nabil. 'She didn't even drink. I've told you, she was from a traditional background.'

'You said her *parents* were traditional. She won't be in trouble – we just want to find her.'

'No, she was sensible. Obeyed the rules all the time.'

'But not her parents' rules?' said Carrick gently. 'You two were . . .'

'That's not the same,' said Nabil, riled. But he quickly calmed down. 'I'm sorry. I just want you to find her too.'

Jo smiled. 'We'll do our best, Nabil. We need to establish what her life looked like. If our questions come across as blunt, it's just because we need to be quick. If there was anything out of the ordinary you can think of . . .'

He nodded at her gratefully, eyes moist, then his irises shifted to one side. 'Wait! I do remember something!'

'What's that?'

'Yes, that's right! About three weeks ago, she said she thought someone was following her.'

Jo's skin prickled. *Like Malin.* 'Go on, Nabil.'

'Actually, it was after the circuit class, I think. She took a different route home because she thought there was a car moving slowly behind her.'

Jo swallowed. 'A car, or a van?'

'A car,' he said. 'A dark one.'

Jo noted it down, though a good sixty per cent of vehicles on the road fell into that category. 'This is very important, Nabil. Did she say anything else about the car? The exact colour? The make? Number plate? Who was driving?'

'A man. That's all she said.' He stared at Carrick, then Jo, beseechingly. 'You think this is the same guy? That someone took her? Why?'

'It's too early to say,' said Carrick, but Jo knew he was feeling exactly the same chills as her.

Chapter 17

While Jo headed back to the station, Andy Carrick decided to wait at Somerville College, to bag any evidence from Rita's room, and to wait for her parents to arrive.

Ross Catskill was still in a cell when Jo arrived at St Aldates. She'd already had her doubts about any real connections to the disappearance of Malin or the fate of Natalie Palmer, and the fact that he was actually in custody for the latest incident confirmed he wasn't directly involved with Rita Prakash. Alex Maynard had been released on conditional bail when the footage at his gym confirmed his presence there on the afternoon of Natalie Palmer's disappearance, and he was kicked out at three in the morning to make his own way home. There seemed no reason to bring him back in following the latest development. Until they found Qadir Suleiman, and established exactly the sort of enterprise he ran, any further link to Natalie was guesswork. Certainly a two hundred quid street-level drug debt with Susan Palmer seemed a petty excuse to kill, or even harm, her daughter.

The mood at the station had changed, and it wasn't just because the central heating was functioning once more. The whole atmosphere was grimly focused. Stratton wanted everyone to drop their work to concentrate on the girls. Despite the chronic lack of sleep, Jo was wide awake.

Heidi had a map up on the board, with two locations marked – 'O' for Oriel, 'S' for Somerville, accompanied by pics of Malin and Rita.

Stratton sat on the corner of her desk. 'Two students, two colleges.'

'Three if we include Natalie,' said Heidi.

'Natalie wasn't a student,' said Stratton.

'Maybe whoever did this didn't know that,' said Heidi.

'Plus, we already have a link between Malin and Natalie,' said Pryce. 'Ross Catskill.'

Stratton shook his head. 'Tenuous at best. Both Malin and Rita went missing from their colleges or nearby. Natalie's a different kettle of fish. God knows what she was doing out there.'

'I don't think we should discount the possible connection,' said Pryce.

'Agreed,' said Stratton, with an icy glare. 'But we can't pursue it as a priority. The colleges are one of the major employers in the city. It could easily be coincidence. The MO is completely different too. Our two girls were taken, violently.'

Our two girls? What did that make Natalie Palmer, Jo wondered – *hers*? She'd kept quiet so far, but a new thought occurred. 'Maybe, sir,' she said, 'but what if the hit and run wasn't an accident? The driver might have deliberately knocked into Natalie with a plan to kidnap her. The road's straight there. The driver would likely have seen her.'

'But he didn't kidnap her, did he?' said Dimitriou. Jo wondered if he was deliberately sucking up to Stratton, or just annoyed that she'd arrived on his crime scene earlier.

'Perhaps she fell in the water before he could,' put in Heidi. 'It would have been a hell of a job to get her out again. Too risky.'

Stratton sighed. 'It's a theory, but I don't buy it. The road's quiet, but it still gets traffic. Only a madman would try to kidnap someone by running them over first.'

Maybe that's what we're dealing with, thought Jo.

'No,' continued the DCI, 'until we find any real evidence linking Natalie to the others, I think we have to follow the most obvious interpretation. Hit and run. Where are we on the Rita Prakash scene?'

'There's no CCTV anywhere nearby,' said Dimitriou, 'and all the house-to-house enquiries haven't turned up a thing. We've got sweet FA.'

'Not quite,' said Jo. She explained what Nabil had told them about the car Rita had said was following her, and wrote 'Dark car?' beneath the victim's blown-up picture.

'That narrows it down,' said Dimitriou.

'It makes sense though,' said Heidi. 'Malin was being followed, too. Whoever took them knew their movements. It looks like he was planning this for weeks at least.'

'Heidi,' said Stratton. 'I want you to get a full staff manifest from the Oriel and Somerville colleges for cross-reffing. All employees, going back three years. Dimi, look into this fitness group, check out the males. Maybe this was someone who knew Rita's routine. Jo and Jack, you can drop Palmer for now. I think it's a dead end, and this is going to draw more heat. Contact other colleges. Try to keep it subtle. We don't want to start a panic. It's quiet this time of year, thankfully, students mostly at home, but it means that the colleges are going to be on a skeleton staff. I want anything suspicious flagged.' Jo had never seen him so fired up. Seeing him actually do some work was novel.

'We are going to have to handle this sensitively,' Stratton continued. 'The press haven't linked Natalie or Malin, but even they can't miss this. I'm going to talk to external comms and work out a plan. We're going to be looking at some silly headlines when it gets out. I don't want anything coming from you guys. Push it all to comms. Got it?'

So that explained his sudden fervour. *Damage limitation.* Made sense after all the cock-ups with the Dylan Jones case.

They all nodded or mumbled agreement, and Stratton headed from the room, no doubt to begin arse-covering.

'Do you think it's worth getting a profile drawn up?' said Dimitriou to rest of the team. 'I mean, if there's some psycho killing students specifically . . .'

'Hey!' said Heidi. 'We don't know they're dead.'

'No?' said Dimitriou.

'We don't know it's a guy, either,' said Pryce.

Dimitriou rolled his eyes. 'I thought you were supposed to be the numbers fella. How many women serial killers are there?'

Pryce smiled. 'Okay, it's probably a male. But Heidi's right – he might not be a murderer.'

'Maybe,' said Dimitriou. 'But if he's not murdering them, and he's not demanding money, then what are we looking at?'

Jo could think of some pretty horrific alternatives. Cases of imprisonment and rape were rare, and she'd been lucky enough never to work on one. All it took though was a psychopath with the right opportunity. When a person was unencumbered by a moral compass, they really were capable of anything.

'Come to think of it, professor,' said Dimitriou. 'You own a dark car. Where were you between the hours of say, seven and eight this morning?'

'In bed,' said Pryce. 'Waiting for your mother to bring me breakfast.'

'Touché!' said Heidi.

Dimitriou looked impressed. 'He's learning! Right, I'm off to see about this fitness group.'

They got back to work, making calls, liaising with uniform patrols, gathering intelligence where they could. Carrick returned just before midday, having logged the evidence from the alley. He'd spoken to Rita's parents, who were understandably in pieces, and completely in the dark about any possible hostility towards their daughter. A search of Rita's room had told them nothing new. She was by all accounts an exemplary student.

At one pm, they heard the first story on the local radio news. The comms team must've worked their magic, because the coverage was muted indeed. Malin Sigurdsson wasn't even mentioned, and Rita was officially a missing person rather than a victim of any sort of assault. Her parents led an appeal for their daughter to get in touch as soon as possible. The Natalie Palmer hit and run didn't make the programme either.

They're trying to hide any connection at all.

And why wouldn't they? Oxford *was* its colleges in many ways. The streets were named after them, visitors flocked to them, half the city's economy was geared to serving them. Jo saw the logic of not spreading panic, based on a theory that was as yet distinctly shaky to say the least. Even if they were dealing with one kidnapper, it might simply be that the colleges had offered him the easiest pickings. And until they spread the word, that would remain the case. There were thirty-eight colleges in all, the majority clumped within a square mile, with a few satellites on the roads out of the city. Far too many to effectively monitor. But each would have staff and students spread out much further afield anyway.

Jo began to make calls – just finding the right person to speak to at the colleges was hard enough, and she hardly knew what to say when she did get through to the right person, partly because it was hard to convince herself of what they were dealing with. Jesus, Oriel and Somerville had nothing in common that she could see, and despite what Stratton had said, there really weren't any clear links in the method involved in taking each girl. Malin's was by far the most audacious, if indeed it was a kidnapping. The perpetrator had actually entered the college. Rita's seemed much less risky – really she could have been any female using the alley in the early hours. But Heidi was right – if they were connected, they were talking significant planning and almost military precision in the crimes themselves. Who knew how many girls their man had been following, looking for the best pickings?

'Do we know the code for Rita's phone?' asked Jo. 'If I was being followed, the first thing I'd do is record evidence.'

'We could get a warrant to serve to the manufacturer,' said Pryce. 'It'll take a few hours.'

While he went to fetch the phone from evidence, Carrick called Nabil and Rita's parents. No one knew the code, but he made a list of any important dates they could think of to try.

It took a couple of lock-outs, but the mother's date of birth proved successful. Jo went to the photos first. There were lots of college life with friends, a couple of chaste shots with Nabil, some Oxford scenery, a series of bored-looking selfies in a library. She tried to stay detached, but the pictures were so full of life, and naïve happiness, that she felt herself welling up. She went back four weeks, but there was nothing that looked helpful. She checked the texts too, which proved slightly more interesting. It looked like Rita had tried to break things off with Nabil during the summer, telling him her parents would never approve. But it appeared they'd picked up their relationship again almost at once in October when the new term began.

Carrick concurred. 'Seems flimsy. Lover's tiff. He was definitely at the college this morning.'

He headed back out again, with Phil Stratton, to liaise with the Chief Constable and the media team. As the office buzzed with activity, and comings and goings, Jo leant across to Heidi's desk.

'Can I ask you something? About Lucas?'

'Er . . . sure.'

'Did he mention booking a holiday to you?' Heidi looked a little flummoxed, mouth flapping. 'It's all right, you can tell me.'

'Yeah, he did. He wanted to know if Stratton would let you have a week off at the end of January.'

'And you said?'

'I told him Stratton would be happy to see the back of you.'

'Thanks.'

'Hey, it was sweet. Last surprise my husband got me was an orthopaedic shoe appointment to help my cankles.'

Jo grinned. 'I'm sure his heart was in the right place.'

'Hey,' said Pryce, 'check this out.'

He had Rita's phone, and flicked it round. It showed Rita at some sort of black tie event. She looked proud, a little shy, and completely innocent, and was standing beside a pink-cheeked man in a dinner jacket, holding a glass of champagne. Jo had to double-take. It was Nicholas Cranleigh.

'No way,' she said.

'Interesting, huh?' said Pryce, in what seemed an understatement.

There were several pictures of the evening, with Rita sitting at some sort of dinner. Cranleigh appeared in only the one. Nabil didn't feature. But another shot, of just Rita and a friend, showed a background with a podium and a panel reading 'Oxford University Young Conservative Association'.

A search on the web showed it had taken place the previous June.

‘We have to speak with him,’ said Jo. ‘He’s a link.’

‘Agreed,’ said Pryce. He looked surreptitiously towards Stratton’s empty office.

‘Look, I get it,’ said Jo. ‘I’ll go on my own.’

‘No,’ said Pryce. ‘You’re right. This is a legitimate lead. We just have to be cautious.’

‘Of course!’ said Jo. ‘He’s not a suspect, he’s just helping us with our enquiries.’

‘And let’s finish calling round the colleges first – cover all bases.’

Jo smiled. Dimitriou was right – Pryce *was* getting the hang of things. It was true that if Stratton were here, there wasn’t a cat in hell’s chance of him letting them talk to Cranleigh. But so far the guy had got a clean pass. True, the thought of him in a white van was pretty much preposterous, and he likely had sound alibis. However, the fact that no one had questioned him officially until now still rankled. If he was involved, in any way, Jo wanted to be the one to bring him in. And even if it was just a case of eliminating him from their enquiries, it would put her mind at rest.

Before they left, she went to the board with a photo of Natalie Palmer. She knew it wasn’t proven, and she knew it would piss off DCI Stratton, but she couldn’t help herself. She circled Jesus College, wrote a J, and pinned Natalie’s picture from her ID beside it.

* * *

They took Pryce’s car – a brand new Honda Civic with all the bells and whistles, and spotlessly clean inside. It seemed to match his personality perfectly. He must be leasing it, Jo thought, then remembered that his father had died early, so perhaps he’d had a windfall. She pondered shamefully what he must have thought of her car, with its scrapes and dents, and stubborn crumbs that even the valet service had failed to dislodge. Did that say something about her character too? she wondered.

Cranleigh's registered address was in Shipton-under-Wychwood on the edge of the Cotswolds and they hopped from one affluent country village to the next, places with one pub, one shop if they were lucky, and a distinct lack of non-white residents.

'Do you think Cranleigh's behaviour has been a bit weird?' she said. 'From the start, he seemed more interested in his own reputation than anything else.'

'Malin's not his kid,' said Pryce. 'It doesn't sound like they had much of a relationship. Can't see why he'd kidnap her, though.'

'Nothing about this case makes sense to me.' After a long pause, she spoke again. 'I never thanked you properly for last night. Coming in to rescue me with a fire extinguisher.'

He shifted in the seat. 'It was pretty crazy, huh?'

'That's one word for it. Selina's March's face though . . .'

He laughed. 'I guess it was all quite tame for DS Masters.'

'Oh, I don't know about that.'

'You've had a few scrapes though, right? Over the years?'

'You're making me sound like a dinosaur! But yeah, I've been lucky at times.'

They reached Shipton, and followed the navigation system up a long driveway towards a resplendent Queen Anne style mansion. A non-operational fountain with a cherub sitting on a sea-serpent's back occupied the centre of the circular driveway.

'How the other half live,' said Jo.

They knocked, and the door was answered by a Korean housekeeper who said that Mr Cranleigh wasn't in, and wasn't expected back for another two hours. When asked where he was, she declined at first to answer until Jo insisted it related to Malin. Reluctantly, she told them.

⋆ ⋆ ⋆

The Nine Elms was a private members' golf course about five miles from the Cranleigh residence, and Jo received several hostile stares from the collection of elderly, well-clad men on the first tee.

'It's like they've never seen a woman before,' she muttered to Pryce.

'You're probably not allowed on the course,' he replied.

They wandered towards the club-house, where an obsequious man at the front desk asked to see their warrant cards and then checked his computer.

'Mr Cranleigh is still out on the course in all likelihood. You're welcome to wait for him in the bar.'

'We'd quite like to speak to him now,' said Jo. 'What time did he tee off?'

'Around noon,' said the receptionist. 'He shouldn't be long.' He addressed himself to Pryce. 'The bar is just through the double-doors to your right.'

'Thank you,' said Jack.

He followed the directions into the bar area which was warmed by a fire, and filled with leather furniture. As Pryce had intimated, the members were all men. A sign above a set of French doors read, 'To the course'. Jo walked through it. Pryce jogged after her.

'Where are you going?'

'I'm not sitting around waiting for him to finish his bloody round.'

As it happened, she saw Cranleigh almost at once, walking down a sculpted slope towards them in the failing light, pushing an automated trolley with his clubs. Another younger man plodded beside him, carrying a set of clubs. Two balls lay on a green shaped like an upturned saucer. When Cranleigh caught sight of them, he said something to his playing partner, broke away, and approached.

'We're sorry to interrupt your game,' said Pryce.

'Have you found her?'

'No, we haven't, sir,' said Pryce. 'We actually just needed to ask you some more questions. Is there somewhere inside we can talk in private?'

'Can I finish my putt? I've got two hundred riding on this par.'

Jo was about to say 'no', but Pryce answered in the affirmative.

So they watched. Whether it was the audience, or just bad play, he took three shots to hole the ball. His playing partner chortled as they shook hands. Cranleigh looked livid.

'Bad luck,' said Jo. 'Drop in the ocean, though, eh?'

'Let's do this in the car park,' said Cranleigh.

They walked beside him as he wheeled his clubs into the car park, drawing out a set of keys. When he pointed them at the boot of a racing green Jaguar, Jo shot a glance at Pryce.

'So what's this all about?' he said, loading in the clubs.

'Do you remember attending an event in the Ashmolean museum, last June?' asked Jo.

'I attend lots of events,' said Cranleigh. 'Be more specific.'

'For the University Association of Young Conservatives?'

'Yes, I suppose I was there.'

'You suppose?'

Cranleigh slammed the boot closed. 'Is this about my step-daughter? Because she wasn't involved in politics at all.'

'It's about a girl called Rita Prakash,' said Jo.

'Who?'

Jo took out an enlarged version of the photo from Rita's phone showing the two of them side by side at the event. 'Rita,' she said.

Cranleigh looked flummoxed. 'I'm sorry, I don't know that girl at all. She probably just wanted a picture with me. I was the main speaker.'

'So you remember it now?' asked Jo.

Cranleigh went to his car door. 'I don't know why you're wasting my time, but it's starting to annoy me.'

Jo couldn't help but ask.

'Where were you this morning, at around half-past seven?'

Cranleigh stopped. 'In bed, like most decent people,' he said. 'I know who you are, Detective Masters. I read the papers. It looked to me like you're the sort of person who goes in all guns blazing, and to hell with anyone who gets caught in the crossfire. Like your boyfriend. Or your family members. Well, I happen to care about my family, and I wonder why you're here asking me questions about some random girl rather than looking for my daughter. If this is another one of your crusades, I'd advise you to tread more carefully. I'm not sure your career can take any more mishaps.'

'Is that a threat?' she said.

He climbed into his car without answering, started the engine, and drove away.

'That went well,' said Jo.

'Do we follow him?' asked Pryce. 'Bring him in?'

'On the basis of a green car and a photo, no,' said Jo. 'Stratton would eat us alive.'

'You think he's clean?'

Jo thought of Lucas.

'I think it's easy to think the worst of someone.'

Chapter 18

Pryce was quiet on the way back to the station, watching the road as a light drizzle began to fall. It was true the encounter had been an anti-climax, but it seemed to have taken the wind out of his sails completely. Or perhaps it was just because the daylight was fading already. The days were passing quickly, and each falling dusk denoted another day in which they had failed to make any real headway with any of the cases they were working.

Jo got a text from her brother as they arrived back on the outskirts of Oxford.

We're home! Come over for Sunday lunch tomorrow and check out my tan.

She replied that she'd do her best, but work might get in the way. She was actually off duty the following day, but something told her she might be pulling overtime.

It was dark as they drove up to the St Aldates station. Inside, the CID room had an air of desperation as the avenues of the investigation dwindled. It began to look, just as with Malin, as though Rita Prakash had disappeared off the face of the earth. Or at least from Oxford. Hana Sigurdsson checked in from the Randolph for an update, and Jo gave her what they had. DNA analysis of the blood had come back from the bathroom in Oriel College. It belonged to a single individual, presumably Malin.

Dimitriou had found out the assistant instructor at SAS Circuit Fitness was neither ex-services nor legally allowed to drive the van bearing the company logo, on account of a previous conviction for driving while intoxicated, but he had an alibi for that morning. There was a brief flicker of excitement when they learned he had also worked on the door of various establishments in the city, and believed he had once met Maynard, but it came to nothing as well.

'A conspiracy of bouncers-cum-kidnappers would have been neat,' said Heidi, 'but I don't think either of them have quite the brains to pull off a double kidnap.'

'You know,' said Dimitriou, from where he stood before the board, 'If I were really into conspiracy theories, I'd say that spells the first three letters of your name.'

Jo wondered who he was talking to.

Dimitriou pointed to each of the colleges in turn. 'J. O. S.' He looked pleased with himself. 'Josephine.'

'Bit of a stretch,' said Heidi.

'And literally the only person to call me that was my mother,' added Jo. 'She's in an old people's home, and hasn't been outside for about eleven months.'

'I'll get a SWAT team ready to bring her in,' said Dimitriou.

Carrick came into the room, looking troubled.

'I've just had Surrey Police on the phone,' he said. 'Anna Mull's parents have reported her missing.'

Things had moved so fast in the previous twenty-four hours, Jo had hardly thought of the timid young student they'd first interviewed at Oriel College.

'I thought she was with friends in London?'

Carrick was frowning. 'Turns out she never checked in with them after all. In fact, they weren't even expecting her.'

'So she was lying to her parents?'

Carrick shrugged. 'I haven't got the foggiest at the moment. Looks like it, though.'

'You want me to get her phone records?' said Pryce.

'Surrey are on it – they're going to share when it comes through,' he said. 'They've got a nationwide alert out on her car too, a mint green Fiat 500. Hopefully it's nothing.'

Jo looked at the other faces in the room. Hope looked to be in short supply.

SUNDAY

The modern semi her brother's family were renting was off the Kennington Road, in the area known as Little London. Jo had wanted to report in for work, but Carrick had insisted, 'as her superior officer', that there was really nothing she could do. She wondered aloud if Stratton had got wind of the latest altercation with Cranleigh. If so, he hadn't said anything directly, which was maybe even worse. Carrick had *said* it was nothing personal; Pryce was off too. It felt as though Thames Valley were caught between two poles trying to deal with the fall-out of the disappearances – not quite sure whether to hit panic stations yet. Jo kept her phone close to her side, checking messages and emails frequently.

As he opened the door, her brother Paul looked the picture of health.

'Hey, sis. No Lucas?'

'It's his five-a-side match,' she said. 'He didn't want to let the team down.'

She handed over the bottle of white wine she'd bought. He examined the label, nodded in approval, and stepped aside. 'You may enter.'

As she passed, he did a little twirl. 'Bronzed Adonis or what?'

'Your bald spot's peeling,' she said.

Paul went to the mirror, fingering his head and trying to see.

Jo walked through to the kitchen, where Amelia was putting a beef joint into the oven. She looked a little tired, which meant she could still pass as the lead actress in an aspirational lifestyle commercial. Just one between takes.

'How are you?' Jo asked. 'Pleased to be back in the land of sub-zero temperatures?'

'To be honest, you can have too much sun,' she said. 'I'm okay. A bit jet-lagged.'

William was sitting on a beanbag by a low table, drawing.

'Wotcha doin'?' Jo said, crouching beside him and kissing the top of his head.

'Drawing,' he said.

Jo looked at the picture. 'Is that a shark eating an apple?'

'It's a spaceship with teeth,' said Will. 'It chews up asteroids.'

'Oh . . . wow! Where's your sister then?'

'Hockey game,' said Amelia. 'She was pretty desperate to catch up with her friends. The wifi at the hotel was patchy, so she was suffering serious gossip withdrawal. Paul's going to pick her up when she calls. Drink?'

'Go on then,' said Jo. 'Whatever you're having.'

* * *

They sat either side of the breakfast bar in the kitchen. Paul regaled Jo with wistful tales of Caribbean luxury; seas as warm as bathwater, unlimited buffets of jerk chicken and melon juicier than anything you could buy at home. Jo indulged her brother. Anything was better than forensic backwaters, number-plate tracking, and door-to-door dead-ends. She drank the first glass of wine quickly, already mentally deciding to take a taxi back later.

'Did you see Mum while we were away?' asked Paul.

'Just the once. She seemed okay. Everyone's happier now the cash is being monitored. Apparently there's a new cook at the home, and she's a "foreigner". Given that all she eats is cheese sandwiches and tinned soup, I told her it probably didn't matter who made it.'

The house phone rang, and Paul left the room.

'Will seems okay,' said Jo quietly. Drawing finished, he was watching cartoons in the living room.

'He does, doesn't he?' Amelia replied. 'We're thinking of stopping the counselling sessions. Paul's not sure what they're good for.'

Jo thought back to her own. It was hard to know if they'd helped or not. She'd not contacted Dr Forster yet, but she really had no intention of continuing. Drinking with Harry Ferman was just as therapeutic.

'I'd go with your instincts,' she said.

'He's stopped having nightmares. No more wetting the bed. The holiday was great, y'know – just spending time as a family.' She was stirring gravy. 'How's work?'

Where would I even start? Almost got choked by a bouncer on a night out? 'Oh, same old.'

'And that new guy? The weird one?'

Jo wished she'd never called Pryce that. It was in his first few weeks, when he was still settling in, trying to please, and when Stratton had been in his full-on adoration phase. 'You know what, I misjudged him. He's actually a really sound copper. Nice guy.'

Amelia looked sideways with the tiniest smile.

'What?' said Jo. *Damnit.* She knew she was blushing.

'Is he handsome too?' said Amelia.

'Hey, I have a boyfriend, remember?'

Amelia's smile broadened. 'You don't have to get defensive.'

'I'm not. I'm—'

Paul came back into the room. Somehow, the tan on his face had faded a few shades.

'It's Em,' he said. 'Something's happened at the hockey pitch.'

'What?' said Amelia, dropping the spoon into the saucepan. 'Is she okay?'

'She is,' said Paul, 'but a girl's been hit by a car.'

'That's awful!' said Amelia. 'How bad?'

'Em's not sure. There's an ambulance there now. I'd better go and get her.'

Jo's own phone vibrated in her pocket. It was Carrick. *It must be about Anna Mull.* She moved out of the room into the hallway.

'Jo, we've got another one. Girl snatched at a school this time.'

It took Jo a moment to make the connection – she could hear Amelia and Paul talking in the kitchen.

'Is this connected to the auto accident?'

'That's right,' he said. 'How do you know?'

'It's my niece's school. She's there now. Okay, I think.'

'That's good. Area's secured. We're still talking to the kids, but looks like a man in a balaclava tried to snatch a girl, and another friend got clipped by the vehicle as he escaped. We've got every available squad car out on the streets. More coming in from Swindon and Reading.'

'It must be the same guy.'

'Looks likely. But these are *kids*, Jo. Sixteen, max.'

Paul was on his way to the front door, hopping as he pulled on a shoe.

'What's happening?' asked Amelia.

'We don't know yet,' Jo said.

As her eyes fell on the wall behind her sister-in-law, sudden sickness churned in her gut. The wine on an empty stomach didn't help, but it wasn't that. She'd noticed the letter when she came in, about an upcoming school trip to Coventry, as part of Emma's World War II syllabus.

'Jo?' said Carrick. 'You still there?'

'Yes.'

Jo moved past Amelia, eyes fixed on the letter.

'Oh fuck,' she said. 'No.'

She felt her brother and his wife staring at her.

Because this wasn't just another missing kid. Myers, Catskill, Cranleigh. None of them mattered. None of them ever had. They'd been chasing shadows. Connections that meant nothing.

She didn't want it to be true, but it was undeniable.

Wasn't it?

She'd told Dimitriou that no one called her 'Josephine' apart from her mother, but plenty of friends and family called her Josie.

'Jo, what's the matter?' said Carrick.

Four girls gone.

Jesus, Oriel, Somerville, and now Emma's school.

The Iffley Road Academy.

J.O.S.I.

'Andy, I think Dimi was right,' she whispered. 'I think the link is me.'

Chapter 19

By the time Jo and Paul reached the playing fields on the edge of the Iffley sports complex, parents had arrived, friends and boyfriends too, and they stood in tearful clumps, with girls wrapped in blankets, the occasional flash of police hi-vis moving between them. There were several police cars; Carrick and Dimitriou were chatting to an adult man in sports gear. An ambulance was parked up beside them, two worried-looking parents peering in.

Emma, standing with her other friends, broke off and ran into her dad's arms. He muttered in her ear.

'It's okay, darling. They'll find her.'

Jo was caught for a moment between being an aunt, and being a police officer. She stroked her niece's arm, then went across to her colleagues.

Carrick introduced her to the coach, Pete Anderson.

'What's the timeline?' asked Jo.

'The girls finished practice at one-twenty,' said Carrick. 'Most of them come to this car park to get picked up, but our victim, Sophie Okafor, lives on Bedford Street, a ten-minute walk south of here. They take a footpath. It looks like he was waiting on one of the cul-de-sacs that back onto the path. About one twenty-five, he jumped Sophie. It happened that her friend Carla had accidentally taken Sophie's phone after practice. She was following Sophie to return it and was about a minute back when she saw the abduction. Tried to stop it.'

'She's in the ambulance?' said Jo.

'Looks like a broken wrist. Brave kid, but she's shaken up. Heidi's in there with her.'

'And Sophie Okafor's parents?'

'It's just the mum,' said Carrick. 'She was at work at the hospital. We've asked Jack to go and get her on his way in. They'll be at her house by now, I think. The boss is there too.'

'You think this is connected to the other girl who went missing?' asked the coach. 'That student?'

Dimitriou and Carrick both looked at Jo, minds obviously still processing what all this meant. Jo felt her cheeks colour. On the way over her thoughts had lurched wildly from one extreme to another: on one hand, this *had* to be related to her. On the other, that was utterly preposterous.

'It's really too soon to tell,' said Carrick. 'But it's one theory we're pursuing. We need you to stay here, if that's all right. To make sure all the girls get home, and just in case there are further questions.'

'Of course,' said the coach.

Jo gazed at the other girls. The lucky ones. *He took the one that strayed from the herd. It didn't matter who it was. An Iffley girl was all he wanted. Four out of five.*

One to go.

She told herself again not to get carried away. Not to miss something. If they threw normal protocol out of the window, they might regret it later. Ask the most pertinent questions. Was there a boyfriend? Where was the dad? Had Sophie reported anything unusual to her friends over the last few days? Was she happy?

Even as her training kicked in, the unstoppable wave of instinct smashed against it. *J.O.S.I.* Four girls she'd never met, four females of different ages, different backgrounds and ethnicities, connected in one outlandish but compelling way.

Me.

She saw Pryce's Honda arrive and it snapped her out of her swirling thoughts. He climbed out and came over to them. He was dressed in casual clothes rather than his usual suit and tie.

'I dropped Mrs Okafor at home with the DCI,' he said. 'What have we got on the perp?'

'Not much,' said Dimitriou. 'He was wearing a balaclava. Chose a spot out of the sight of most of the houses.'

'What about a reg on the van?'

'Heidi's doing what she can with our witness.'

Jo left Carrick and Dimitriou to fill him in, and wandered across to the ambulance. Heidi was climbing out of the back, manoeuvring her unwieldy form. Jo offered a hand to help her down. A girl in hockey kit sat on the gurney, her arm in a sling. Her parents were comforting her.

'She's a tough cookie,' said Heidi. 'Grabbed onto the van door and didn't let go.'

'She give us much?'

'Not really. Our guy is over six foot, medium build, black balaclava. She's pretty sure he was white. The van turned right out of the bottom of Bedford road, so heading away from town.'

'Plates?'

'She's not sure. She thinks it's '09. We've got patrols on all the main roads out to the south of Oxford, stopping anything they can, but if this is as targeted as it looks, he'll be way ahead of us. There was a good twenty minutes between the snatch and us getting word out on the vehicle type.'

'Might be worth checking the road cameras though,' said Jo. 'And CCTV on any shops further out of the Iffley Road.'

'There's only one petrol station with a road-facing camera,' said Heidi. 'I'll get over there. If he went straight out, he'd end up on the 4074.'

'Towards Little Baldon,' said Jo.

Heidi lowered her voice. 'You really think this is connected to you?'

Jo still felt like she was suffering from vertigo. The car park seemed to spin. Something else had occurred to her on the drive over.

'Natalie turned up after Malin,' she said. 'But she was the first to go missing. If it was just the college names, I could just about put it down to coincidence, but it's the order too. J-O-S, now I.'

'It's crazy,' said Heidi. 'I mean, *why*?'

'I've got no idea,' said Jo. And even though she'd racked her brains, it was true. Who the fuck had she wronged this much? The girls had nothing to do with her – they were completely innocent victims, in the wrong place at the wrong time.

'We need to get that profile drawn up,' said Heidi. 'And look back at your collars, see if there's anyone in there capable of something like this.'

Jo nodded, though she'd already thought the same thing and dismissed the idea. Most of her career had been in narcotics. Plenty of low-level burglary in the early days. A task force on people trafficking a couple of years ago. There was no one other than Sally Carruthers who might hold any sort of serious animosity towards her, and she was in the secure wing of a psychiatric hospital. Jo'd put enough people away, and some for several years, but nothing extraordinary, and no cases where she would have been singled out. The sheer level of planning and balls to pull four kidnaps was something else entirely.

And using her familiar name, 'Josie'. Only her closest acquaintances called her that, really. It spoke to something truly psychopathic. A need to punish her. 'Jo' wouldn't have been enough to get the message across. 'Josephine' was even further beyond the realms of possibility. But 'Josie' let her know for certain. It stuck a dagger in her heart and twisted it.

And it begged an obvious question.

Who was 'E'?

Who was next?

* * *

There was a solitary journalist and a cameraman in front of St Aldates when she arrived back just after three pm. She looked ahead stoically as her picture was snapped through the windshield of her car as she pulled in to the car park.

Don't get paranoid. They can't know yet.

The putative connection between the victims was clearly top of Stratton's mind too. 'Under no circumstances is this name crap getting out,' he said. 'We're not even sure it's valid, but until we get clarification, I don't want the press running with conspiracy theories relating to this police force.'

His eyes passed over everyone in the room, but they paused on Jo. It was a look she'd never seen before. Not disapproving, so much as wary. He appeared stunned, as though he were encountering a wild and unpredictable animal for the first time. His look said, *What am I dealing with here?*

Jo wanted to tell him she felt exactly the same way.

'I spoke to Sophie's mother at length,' he continued. 'She said there was a boyfriend sniffing around in the summer holiday. A local scaffolder, Jermaine something. She's not sure what happened, but Sophie was upset afterwards. We're going to question all the friends, and the local firms, see if we can track this guy down. We're also drafting in a couple more detectives from Aylesbury. Detective Tan, get in touch with HR, brief a forensic psych to work up a profile.'

'Yes, sir,' said Heidi.

'I think we should draw up a list of schools and colleges beginning with the letter "E", sir – just in case,' said Pryce. 'He seems to be picking up the pace. Two in two days.'

'Andy's on that.'

'No schools sir,' said Carrick, 'but we've got two colleges. Exeter and St Edmund Hall. Suggest we get at least four officers on each, plain clothes. Two on the street outside the main entrance, and two more inside.'

Stratton looked troubled. 'We can't afford a panic,' he said. 'This is about deterring our man, not public reassurances. Two officers on each, but uniform. Liaise with the college security, but make it clear it's precautionary. It's need-to-know.'

'Andy,' said Jo. 'Anything else on Anna Mull?'

'Negative,' said Carrick. 'I've asked Surrey to call us as soon as they get anything.'

'She's not our problem,' said Stratton. 'Surrey are leading. We've got enough missing girls of our own.'

Jo wasn't quite so sure. The fact she'd vanished off the face of the earth a few days after her friend was troubling, to put it mildly.

Pryce raised a hand timidly. 'As an alternative, sir – we use the press.'

Stratton frowned. 'I hope that's a joke,' he said. 'They'd eat us alive.'

'Sir, there's one outside already. They'll come like flies to shit. I'm not suggesting we mention the connection to Detective Masters, just that we're clear this guy is out there and might strike again. Urge vigilance, set up a line for information. If he takes another girl, it could reflect very badly if we haven't been seen to do all we can to warn people.'

Stratton appeared to mull it over. 'All right. I'll talk to comms. I'd like Dimitriou to monitor the team at Exeter College. Jack, take St Edmund Hall. Let's make it impossible for this bastard. Okay, team?'

Everyone nodded or muttered affirmation.

'What about me, sir?' asked Jo.

'Engage with the profiler, Detective Masters. If your theory is right, you're the key to all of this.'

The tone was accusatory. *He blames me.* Jo felt the urge to make amends, even though she'd committed no wrongdoing.

'And after that?' said Jo. 'I could cover one of the colleges too.'

The other detectives were filing from the room. Stratton waited until they were gone, then closed the door. Jo could already tell what was coming next.

'I don't want you exposed,' said Stratton. 'If this guy really has it in for you, you might be in danger.'

You mean I might embarrass you . . .

'I can't stay behind my desk when the rest of the squad are out there,' said Jo.

'I spoke to the Chief Constable,' said Stratton. 'He's in agreement. Work with the profiler. Don't leave any stone unturned.'

'Sir . . .'

'Dismissed,' said Stratton.

* * *

The forensic psychologist brought in to draw up a profile was a dour, bloodless man of around fifty, rake thin, with a set of rimless, round reading glasses hanging from his neck. His name was Dr Vincent Stein, and he set up his laptop in IR1, coming out occasionally to ask Heidi for particular case files. He also had the board, pinned with the four crime scenes so far, wheeled in. He barely spoke to any one of them, instead choosing to sit quietly and drink from a thermos flask.

After almost an hour, he came to the door, looking into the room.

'Detective Masters,' he said, then went back inside.

'Some people skills,' muttered Heidi.

Jo obeyed the summons, feeling like a naughty schoolchild as she entered the interview room. Or a patient about to get some very bad news.

'Take a seat,' said Stein.

Jo did so. The case folders were set up on the table in a patchwork. For about a minute, Stein's attention was back on his computer as he tapped away periodically.

'I've been over and over in my mind,' she said. 'I can't think of anyone clever or mad enough to carry this out.'

Stein looked up sternly, as if her interruption had broken his chain of thought. 'You've had a stressful few months, I imagine,' he said. 'Since Detective Coombs was murdered.'

Jo had no idea why they were talking about Ben. 'It was hard at first,' she said.

'But you've been seeing a clinical psychologist at the behest of Thames Valley Police.'

He made it sound as though she'd been an unwilling participant. Maybe that was fair.

'It seemed sensible.'

'Indeed.' He made a few notes. 'How was your relationship with Benjamin Coombs at the time of his death?'

His tone rankled.

'What's my personal life got to do with this?' she said. 'It's got to be something related to the job, right? Someone I've put away, or pissed off.'

Stein stuck out his bottom lip lugubriously. 'I wouldn't say that's a given. Indulge me. Tell me about Ben.'

'He's dead,' said Jo coldly. 'Which means he's an unlikely suspect in the current case.'

Stein closed the laptop and peered at her over the top of his glasses. 'I'm not trying to be challenging,' he said. 'I simply want to get an idea of your personality. Whoever is doing this has set themselves up in direct opposition to you. Your nemesis, to use the parlance of archetypes. Your antagonist, in storytelling terms.'

Jo folded her arms. 'There are three missing women. One is fifteen. She has a mother. Why are we talking about *stories* when there's a fucking psycho out there looking for his next victim?'

Stein smiled. 'Good question, Detective. Your antagonist, your nemesis – the *fucking psycho,* as you so clearly put it – sees this as a story, believe me. In fact, he probably sees himself as the protagonist, and you as *his* opposite. It's structured, it's planned; it has inherent drama. It has *suspense.* And he knows it. If I had to guess, I'd say he's been watching it all unfold as well, from closer than you think. Detective Chief Inspector Stratton said you have officers at two potential sites, so if the perpetrator didn't know before that you were onto him, he will now. It's possible, therefore, that he will forgo the final stage of the plan in favour of a twist, something to blindside you.'

'Thanks for the insight,' said Jo. 'Any idea how we catch him?'

'Ah!' said Stein, lifting a finger as though suddenly pleased with his pupil. 'To do that, we have to work out where this story began.'

'Which is what I've been trying to do. Looking over my old cases. There were a couple of gang busts where guys went away for fifteen years plus. I've done six murders, three domestic, two drugs . . .'

'And that would be the most obvious place to search, if this were a simple case of revenge. But in those situations, typically, the perpetrator would have killed you already. It wouldn't be hard, would it? To stab you at your home, to run you down in a car, to pay someone to execute you. He's shown already that he's capable of significant forward planning.'

The way he said it, so matter-of-factly, made Jo uneasy.

'This feels different, does it not?' said Stein. 'The theatricality of it, the drama. He doesn't want simply to kill you, he wants to embarrass you, shame you, make you a viewer of your own suffering. Which isn't to say he won't want to kill you, too, when the time comes.'

'Thanks,' said Jo. 'Is that your professional opinion?'

Stein, for the first time, smiled. 'For what it's worth, my professional opinion is probably not going to tell you anything you can't work out on your own. This individual is a psychopath, you're quite correct. He is highly organised, perhaps a high achiever in whatever field he is in. He knows this area very well, and probably lives in Oxford or the immediate environs. He is not averse to risk – indeed, he might even be a thrill-seeker. He may be independently wealthy, in a powerful position. Probably charming or at least a proven manipulator. And also – I find this compelling – he might be the mind behind this, rather than the actual actor.'

'You mean he's paid someone off?'

'Convinced, importuned, coerced. Perhaps there's money involved, but some psychopaths can be very persuasive. If he wasn't directly involved in the kidnappings, it would give him the opportunity to enjoy the story from a distance.'

'Okay,' said Jo. 'So if these girls mean nothing to him, if they're just disposable characters in a twisted story, what has he done with them?'

Stein looked across at the map, and the four images appended to the locations of their kidnap, or in Natalie's case, the attempted kidnap.

'I don't know for certain,' said the profiler, 'but if I had to hazard a guess, I'd say they may well still be alive. I'd go as far as to say, because of the atypical nature of these crimes, that he might not be disposed to murder.'

'He's murdered Natalie Palmer.'

Stein's brow creased. 'Ah, incorrect, I think.' He sifted through some papers, pushing up his spectacles again. 'Here it is . . . yes. Ms Palmer drowned.'

'Having been run down.'

'Well, yes, but I don't think he *intended* to kill her.' Stein paused. 'And despite his unwillingness to kill outright, I don't have the impression he puts much store in the sanctity of life or the feelings of others. If the rest of these women die, that won't trouble him greatly. After all, he's continued with his plan, despite what happened to Natalie.'

Jo wasn't sure what to make of Stein. He wasn't a particularly comforting presence.

'Don't suppose you have any idea what he'll do next, now that we're onto him?'

'He becomes a lot more dangerous,' said Stein. 'Don't expect him to give up, not this close to his goal. He'll adjust, certainly. And his next step might well take us all by surprise. Our best hope is that he makes a mistake in his desire to finish what he's started.'

The only mistake he made so far ended up with a woman dead, thought Jo.

'So, anyway,' she said, 'you wanted to talk about Ben?'

'Actually,' said the profiler with a rictus smile, 'I think I've got enough for now.'

Chapter 20

Dr Stein spent some time with Stratton while Jo went back to her desk. She wanted desperately to hear what they were saying. Well, specifically what Stratton was saying about her. Probably that she was stubborn, unhinged, had trouble following orders. All of it fair. She thought of all the people she'd interviewed in the same room, how every one of them had been keeping something hidden. Wasn't it only fair they'd assume the same about her?

But I'm not hiding anything. Am I?

She tried to put herself in their shoes – they couldn't see how genuinely confused she was by the situation. They had to think logically, like investigators. If she was linked to these crimes, it was their job to find out how. And all she could do was do the same before she became a pariah.

She called up the ANPR database, planning to go through the images frame by frame. If Sophie Okafor's kidnapper had gone straight out of Oxford by the A4074 route, travelling within or just above the speed limit, she figured there would be a ten-minute window when he'd have passed the cameras mounted over the road. She widened the search to twenty minutes, just to make sure she didn't miss anything.

There wasn't a single white Transit van. Heidi was right – this guy was too clever for that. Looking at the map, there were half a dozen less frequented routes by which he could have left the city. And none were on the camera network. It shouldn't have been a surprise. Going from what the forensic psychologist had said, the kidnapper wouldn't be making any elementary mistakes.

Her phone rang. Paul.

'Hey, sis. Any news?'

'Nothing yet. The parents are going to put out an appeal. How's Em doing?'

'Shaken up. She's known Sophie for years.' He paused. 'Listen, I heard you say something, back at the house.'

'What's that?'

'You said, "I think the link is me."'

Jo looked across at the board in IR1 with the four crime scenes marked so far, spelling out her name.

'I . . . think you must have misheard me,' she said.

'Did Amelia mishear you too?' A beat. 'Jo, I'm your brother. I know we don't speak that much, but I saw your face, too. You looked white as a sheet.'

'It's complicated,' she said.

'Is this connected to Sally Carruthers and what happened before?'

'What? No! Of course not. Sally's incarcerated.'

'Jo, are you mixed up in something?' *Not that I know of. He went to Em's game, but that was only because he needed an 'I' – there was no reason he would have known she was there.*

Even as she tried to reassure herself, she knew it likely wasn't true. The kidnapper was meticulous. Maybe he'd even thought about taking Em herself, but decided there was an easier target. She felt a pang of nausea at the thought.

'Paul, it's fine. Don't worry.'

He sighed. 'If you say so, sis.'

As soon as she was off the phone, she went to Stratton's office. He was writing on a notepad. 'Sir, would it be possible to have someone go to my brother's house? He's there with his kids. If . . .'

'Say no more,' said Stratton, tapping his pen. 'I'll ask Andrea to stay there after she's seen you home.'

'Pardon, sir?'

'I want you out of the picture, Jo. Is there somewhere you can go?'

'I should be here, sir. There are still leads I can follow up.'

'Stein seems to think the next twenty-four hours are crucial. I'm putting you on leave. We need a tight ship.'

'So you're chucking me overboard.'

'A day, Jo. We need to know you're safe.'

'I'm safe here. It's a police station.'

Stratton set the pen down. 'Pryce was right. The press are going to swarm us. They'll want blood.'

'I can handle a few journalists.'

'That's what I'm afraid of,' said Stratton. 'And what happened to the last journalist you got mixed up with?'

It was a cheap shot, and Jo was hit with the freeze-frame of Rebecca Saunders splayed dead and half-naked on the floor of Sally Carruthers' barn. The horror of the memory faded into dull anger. How dare Stratton lay that at her feet?

She was about to challenge him when his phone rang. With his hand over the microphone, he glanced at Jo. 'If you could close the door on your way out, Detective Masters.'

* * *

Andrea Williams followed Jo home, and waited outside until she was in the house, before driving away. Jo thought it was overkill.

Stein was right – if this guy wanted to kill her, there'd have been a dozen chances already. But she was pleased there'd be someone near to her brother's family. She'd asked Andrea to be as discreet as possible.

A bitter wind blew across the car park of Lucas's block, and she was pleased to get indoors.

She found Lucas chopping apricots on a board. The place smelled of cumin and coriander. The washing machine was spinning his football kit, and he was freshly showered, his hair still damp.

'I didn't think you'd be back so soon,' he said.

'Neither did I,' she said. She kissed him on the cheek. 'What are you making?'

'Tagine. You hungry?'

'Starving.'

She took off her coat. 'I'm going to take a bath.'

'Any news on the girl?'

She shook her head. 'It's fucked up.'

'And it's the same guy?'

'That's the current thinking.'

In the bedroom, she prised off her shoes. Lucas's sports bag was sitting on the bed. She grabbed it, ready to sling it into the top of the wardrobe, when something fell out of the side pocket. It was a phone charger. Not for a modern smartphone, but one of the older ones, with a bulky pin connector. She put the bag away, then walked back to the other room.

'Hey, Lucas – what's this?' She dangled the wire.

He was taking a pot from the oven and looked over, then quickly away. Too quickly.

'Old charger,' he said. 'Where'd you find it?'

'It was in your bag.'

He took the lid off the pan and swiped the apricots off the

board. 'Takes you back, doesn't it? Must have been there for years.'

'Want me to sling it?' she said.

'Yeah, sure.'

She went to the bin, about to drop it in. She'd rolled over too many times today already. 'You know, I don't think it was there before . . .'

Lucas, who had his back to her, started waving his hand. 'Ow!'

'You okay?'

'Burned myself.'

He put his hand under the cold tap. He wasn't looking at her.

'I borrowed the bag,' she said. 'About three weeks ago, when I was shifting clothes over here. I'm pretty sure the charger wasn't in there then.'

'It must have been,' he said. 'I haven't seen that thing for donkey's years. Would you mind putting the pot back in the oven?'

She picked up the gloves and did so. 'Lucas, it wasn't,' she said.

He turned off the tap, inspecting his fingers. 'Why are you fixating on a phone charger?'

'I'm not fixating,' said Jo. 'I just don't know why you've still got it. Is there a phone, too?'

'I doubt it,' said Lucas. His gaze was open, innocent, maybe even a little hurt. 'Why would I keep an old phone?'

'I don't know,' said Jo.

He came right up to her, eyes creased in confusion, and took the charger off the counter. 'Jo, you're being paranoid,' he said. 'I'm not lying to you. I'm not Ben.' He dropped the charger in the bin. 'It's an old charger. People have them. Can we just forget about it? It's not often we get to have dinner together, is it? Don't ruin it.' He leant down and kissed her on the mouth. She let him, just to see if she could taste the lies on his lips. 'Have we got any plasters?'

'I've got a first-aid kit in the car,' she said.

Leaving him to douse his hand in more cold water, she put her coat on, and a pair of trainers, then went to the door. On the way, she took his car keys as well as her own. Heading down the stairs, part of her brain was still trying to reason. She had to let this go. What was it that was stopping her believing him? Believing *in* him? What had he ever done to betray her trust?

She walked quickly to his Land Rover. The back was filled with various bits of gardening equipment and other junk, and it would take too long to search through. Instead, she checked the glove box and the central console. Nothing. The door pockets contained crumbs, receipts, and cracked CD boxes.

Why am I doing this?

Then she reached underneath the driver's seat, and her fingers found the plastic casing. She pulled out a Nokia phone. It was switched off.

The feeling of vindication, the pleasure that her instincts were correct, was short-lived. It was followed quickly by a sensation of great weight pressing down on her, squeezing any emotion away. She glanced back towards the windows of the building. No one was watching. She had choices, but the thought of going up there again, confronting him again, watching his lies crumble, made her stomach turn. This wasn't an interview room. For better or worse, it was her life.

Her fingers were already cold. She switched on the phone, but it was locked by a code. She tried the one he had on his smartphone and it didn't work. She tried four zeros, with the same result. There were answers, but the chances of finding them like this were something like one in ten thousand possible permutations.

There were other ways, though. Rules that could be bent.

She sat in Lucas's driver's seat, and dialled '999' from the phone, bypassing its internal security. It rang, and was quickly picked up by the operator.

'Which emergency service do you require?'

She held the phone away from her mouth. 'Billy, is that mine? Give it here!' She brought the phone closer. 'Hello?'

'Do you require an emergency service?'

'I'm so sorry, my little boy got hold of the phone.'

'Happens all the time. Can I take your name and address please, for our records?'

'Jo Masters. I'm a policewoman actually.'

'None of us are immune,' said the operator.

Jo gave her address too, and they ended the call.

She turned the phone off and replaced it under the seat, went to her car and got the plasters. Back in the building, she called Heidi at the station.

'What's going on over there?'

'Fending off the press, but it's a losing battle. I'm knocking off in five. Dimi spoke to Sophie's ex – gave him a bit of a fright. He swore he thought Sophie was sixteen. He's got a leg in a cast at the moment, anyway, which rules him out. Apparently he took a fall at work. Stratton's organising an appeal with Sophie Okafor's mum which should be on the nightly news.'

'All quiet at the colleges?'

'Nothing from Carrick or Pryce. They've briefed the security staff at Exeter and St Edmund Hall, and there'll be a couple of uniforms near each overnight. Whoever this guy is, he'd be mad to try anything.'

'Let's hope he is then,' said Jo, 'because at the moment we've got nothing.'

'Here's to that. For what it's worth, I think Phil's mad to keep you away.'

'Thanks. Listen, Heidi, could you do me a favour before you leave?'

'Sure.'

'It's off the record.'

'Sounds intriguing.'

'I made a phone call to the emergency control centre two minutes ago from Manor Gardens. I need the phone number of the mobile I called from. Can you grab it from them and text it to me?'

'Shouldn't be a problem.'

'Thanks, Heidi. You're a star.'

She hung up, feeling oddly detached from the whole situation. She went back inside to find Lucas stirring couscous in a pan.

'You took a while?'

'Just had to make a call,' she said. She wondered if he'd retrieved the charger from the bin yet, or if he'd wait until a safer moment. 'Let's see that finger.'

He held it out. The skin was blistered and raw, and she placed the plaster over it. Even touching him made her feel sick.

* * *

They ate dinner together, but she had barely any appetite. Heidi sent the number through, which she copied into her phone under 'LB' for 'Lying Bastard', an attempt to bring a wry smile to her day. It failed. Afterwards, she watched the appeal on the national news while she and Lucas cleared up. It was a strange gathering, the participants tightly packed along one side of a long table, that only threw into relief the bizarre nature of the crimes – the sheer number of people involved, and the lack of obvious connection between the victims. They'd managed to locate Sophie's father, and he and his wife sat side by side in the centre, holding hands as they addressed the camera through their tears, begging for the person who'd taken their daughter to bring her back, to contact the police, to leave her somewhere safe, to do any number of things that Jo knew were unlikely. Beside them were Mr and Mrs Prakash, and at the far end, separated from the others by DCI Stratton, Hana Sigurdsson, who looked like she'd wandered in from a 1930s aristocratic dinner party.

Pictures of the three missing girls were displayed on screens behind the parents. Jo recognised Malin's, from her room in Oriel, Rita's looked like it was taken on holiday, and Sophie's was a class photo, in school uniform. All the girls were smiling, perversely, it seemed to Jo. Their happy faces seemed to mock her. *Look at what we were, before you, Josie Masters. Look at the lives we had before we became characters in your story.*

'Do you think they're still alive?' said Lucas, as if he could read her desperate thoughts.

'I really don't know.'

She took a seat on the sofa, to avoid having to look him in the eye. Did he not wonder why she was here, at home, when the rest of Thames Valley were out searching?

She thought back to something Dr Stein had said – that this could all be a game for the perpetrator, not necessarily a murder spree. Most of what he'd conjectured she was happy to forget – the strange little man had clearly loved the sound of his own voice. But this had stuck, or perhaps she was clinging to it. Because games could actually be won.

After Mr and Mrs Prakash had added their appeals to that of Sophie's parents, Stratton spoke next, explaining that the public should be vigilant, but go about their business. He mentioned the potential connection with a white van, and gave a number for information and enquiries. Finally, his tone firmer, he addressed whatever individual or individuals were 'responsible for these horrible crimes'.

'. . . we don't know who you are, but rest assured that all our efforts are focused on returning Sophie and these other young women to their families. There is still time for you to do the right thing, and whatever grievance you have, we encourage you to pick up the phone and talk to us or to someone you trust.'

The news story moved on, but Jo knew that in the press conference room, the questions would be firing. Would anyone, she wondered, make the connection with the hit and run of Natalie Palmer? And if they did, how would Stratton respond? Likely with a simple deflection. There was really no way anyone outside the immediate CID team should make the link with her name.

Lucas rested his hands on her shoulders from behind, massaging firmly. 'You're tense.' His face was reflected in the black window opposite, but she couldn't read his expression.

'I hate just sitting around,' she said.

'I could help you relax if you like?' He bent down and kissed her beneath her ear.

She pulled away. 'Thanks, but I don't think that's going to help tonight.'

He stopped, and straightened up. 'All right. I'm going to crash.'

'I might head back to the office.'

'Now?'

She switched off the TV. 'Sorry. Until this is done, I know I'm not going to sleep.'

It was the perfect excuse. There was no way she could spend the night there, wondering about the phone perched under his driver's seat.

She drove to her old place, head thumping with a hundred confused thoughts. Dealing with Lucas had to wait. In the scheme of things, he wasn't important at all, and neither were their problems. What had it been – six months? Her niece probably had longer relationships. Whoever he was using the phone to ring, whatever secrets he was keeping, didn't matter until they had someone in custody.

Jesus, Oriel, Somerville, Iffley. Natalie, Malin, Rita, Sophie. A white van. A face hidden behind a balaclava. Someone from her past.

But who?

MONDAY

There'd been a time, once, when Mrs Masters had been a formidable cook. When Jo's friends would come to dinner and be treated to an array of exotic dishes lovingly prepared, their ingredients sourced from the early organic markets, the mystifying oriental supermarket, the garden where her father was put to work in all weathers. The kitchen was her mother's domain. At times growing up, Jo had been jealous of her contemporaries enjoying their fast food treats, with parents happy to cook from the freezer, or explore the novelty of ready-made meals. Jo's mother had never owned a microwave, and had treated even tinned food with suspicion. On their early package holidays as a family, she'd often insisted on seeing the kitchens of the restaurants before she agreed to sit down and eat their wares. Some of Jo's earliest memories – the happy ones before she and her mother grew apart – were watching her mother cook. A tablespoon held out for tasting, the cake-mixture to be sampled, vegetables fresh from the ground, almost glossy with life.

So it was somewhat heartbreaking to see her spooning slippery segments of sweetened canned grapefruit into her mouth, a plastic bib fastened to stop her blouse getting spattered.

'I saw Paul on Sunday. He's back from holiday. You should see his tan.'

Jo dabbed her mum's chin with a tissue, and her mother didn't even acknowledge it. 'He never comes to see me.'

Paul, as the visitor log attested, came once a week, normally for about three quarters of an hour.

'Well, he's been away. I'm sure he'll drop in soon.'

'I never see the little ones.'

That much, Jo thought, was true. Not that Jo blamed Paul for not bringing them. The place was hardly a barrel of laughs for a rambunctious six-year-old like Will. And Emma's online social life probably wouldn't withstand the forty-five minute blackout.

'Em's not that little now. She's taller than me.'

'Hm.'

Even with her mind failing, Mrs Masters could still deliver eloquent disapproval in a single syllable.

'And how's Ben?'

Jo had been anticipating the question, because her mum asked it every time she came.

'We're not together anymore, Mum,' she said. 'Remember?'

'Oh, that's right. There's a new one, isn't there? What's his name again?'

'Lucas.' The name caught in Jo's throat.

He'd actually visited on a couple of occasions, despite Jo telling him it wasn't necessary. He'd completely charmed Mrs Deekins in the room next door, and even came along to tidy up the garden one afternoon in October. Jo pushed the fond memories away. That morning she'd requested the call logs relating to Lucas's secret phone number. Strictly, that information was accessible only if there was reasonable suspicion that the phone would yield evidence of a crime, but in practice it was easy to work around. Whatever came back, Jo wasn't sure she wanted to see it. That morning she'd driven to the home through Summertown, and on a whim, taken the side street past Off Piste – the specialist ski travel consultant. The sign on the door was an extra kick in the teeth. It had been closed down for the last two months. So even if he'd spoken to Heidi about a holiday, he'd lied about coming here last Thursday.

The most disappointing thing – besides the deception itself – was how bad he was at it. He couldn't even tighten up his own alibi, and that made her respect him even less.

Jo's phone vibrated in her pocket. It was Carrick.

'Excuse me, Mum,' she said, stepping out into the hall. The door was kept open all the time, in case of emergencies. None of the residents seemed to mind the lack of privacy. To close it would have been like shutting up a tomb. 'What's up?'

'I've had an email from Surrey Police,' said Carrick. 'Just forwarded it to you. They've got the call logs and texts.'

'Sorry?' She was thrown for a moment. How had he found out about her call log request? Then it clicked what he'd said. *Surrey*. 'You're talking about Anna Mull.'

'Of course, and it looks dodgy. The headline is that Anna called a single number several times between the hours of ten pm and one am the night Malin disappeared. That directly contradicts her story that she went to bed after the news. The last call that night, at 12.36, came from inside or close to the Oriel college grounds, not the house she shared on Longwall Street.'

'Bloody hell. So she was close to the crime scene.'

'She rang the number again the following day, three times, after you and Pryce interviewed her at the college.'

'Let me guess, it's an unregistered phone.'

'Afraid so. I've tried the number, but it's not working anymore.'

'So where's Anna's phone now?'

'We don't know. It's stopped pinging. But the last time it connected was to the same number, and we have that location. Bernwood Forest.'

'I know it.' It was a small place, less than three miles from where she grew up in Horton, north-east of Oxford.

'I'm going to head there shortly, but the DCI wants me here when Nick Cranleigh comes in. Every available uniform is out in town. Are you busy?'

Jo looked at the clock over her mother's dresser. She'd been there less than twenty minutes. Her mum was chasing the final segment of grapefruit around the bottom of the bowl. Her grasp of time passing was limited, but that wasn't the point.

'Give me another ten minutes.'

Chapter 21

Carrick texted her the GPS co-ordinates, and she plugged them into the car's SatNav, then drove out of Oxford. As the time to her destination shrank, she felt her nerves sharpen. There'd been something about Malin's friend from the start, now she thought about it. A current of shrewd intelligence lurking underneath the scared expression and shy glances. What had Myers called her? *That little minx*. At the time she'd written it off as sour grapes, but maybe he'd spotted it too. Anna had come across as the most straightforward witness when they'd first met her. Out of the watchful eye of her Vice Provost, she had proved the point, detailed in her responses, completely credible. But since then, most of what she'd told them appeared to be unravelling.

Then there was the plagiarism accusation Pryce had mentioned – it hadn't really registered, because it had seemed insignificant at the time. But now, from somewhere deep in her memory banks, a thought surfaced for the first time in decades. There'd been a cottage industry of essay-flogging that had gone on when she was at uni too. In fact, after an ill-advised long weekend of getting hammered with mates, she herself had panicked and purchased a two-thousand-word piece on the Russian Revolution from a student four years above her. In the end, she'd bottled out of submitting it, coming clean with her tutor about missing her deadline. But it had been cowardice and the fear of getting caught rather than any moral rectitude that had stopped her. If Anna Mull was the sort of person who would go through with that type of deception, perhaps she wasn't as risk-averse and upstanding as she'd appeared. How that possibly connected to Malin's disappearance was another question entirely.

She reached the edge of Bernwood Forest in no time at all, and soon was passing trees to her right, a plantation of established conifers. She drove past a couple of narrow tracks blocked by metal-barred gates. As she neared the location of the phone's last signal, she considered parking up at the side of the road to proceed on foot, then saw there was an entrance sign for a car park. She turned in, under a height-restriction to which a sign was attached, saying that the woodland was managed by the Forestry Commission and that visitors were welcome, but should stick to the marked paths. She slowed her car to a fifteen miles per hour crawl on the pot-holed track. She thought she might once have come here as a girl, perhaps even with a boy, but it was a vague feeling of recognition with no emotion, good or bad, attached. Neither the occasion, nor the young man, could have been that memorable.

As soon as she reached the car park, she saw the green Fiat registered to Anna. It was the only other vehicle about. There was no one nearby that she could see, but she pulled over fifty yards away, switched off the engine and climbed out. The air was still in the clearing between the trees. Mid-morning on a Monday in December was never going to be a busy time for dog-walkers or ramblers.

Her chest felt light as she leant back into the car and took out her baton. She hefted it in her right hand. Couldn't be too careful.

Her footsteps crunched across the car park towards the Fiat. In her left hand she thumbed through her phone to Andy's number.

'Anna?' she called.

Her voice was swallowed by the trees.

As she got nearer, she could see the seats were empty, and the doors were locked. She tried the tiny boot, and was almost glad to find it locked too. She checked around the car, looking for obvious footprints, or any other markings. Nothing.

She called Carrick and told him what she'd found.

'Doesn't sound good,' he said. 'I'm about to leave. I'll order forensics.'

'Better get a dog unit out here as well, Andy.'

After he'd hung up, Jo stared into the dark spaces between the trees. Maybe it was because the forest was artificially planted, or the air was so still, but it seemed oddly devoid of life under the wintry sky.

'Where've you got to, Anna?' she muttered.

* * *

While she waited, she checked on her own device the phone files that Surrey had sent through. Carrick had annotated a few – Anna's parents, Malin, the mystery burner Anna had called so many times around the time of her friend's disappearance. What Jo noticed immediately was that Anna hadn't actually called Malin the morning she came to her room, claiming to be worried about her friend. So she'd been lying to them about that too. What explanation could there be for not making that call, other than the most obvious – that she'd known all along that Malin had gone, and coming to Oriel College, then subsequently alerting Belinda Frampton-Keys, was all a cover?

But there was no way she had carried her friend out wrapped in a shower curtain. Not alone, anyway. Anna Mull couldn't have been five-four in heels. Maybe Stein was right about the accomplice. But if Anna was the assistant – the person who'd opened that fire door or the security pass entrance, who had she admitted? The owner of the unregistered burner was untraceable.

There were a few texts – mostly to her parents. Nothing to Malin or the other phone, which was not that much of a shock. SMS was almost obsolete among Anna's generation.

Forensics and Carrick arrived in convoy, the dog unit a few minutes later. Jo was glad of the company in such a lonely place. Carrick himself broke into the Fiat quickly with a specialist rod slipped down the door seal, and the boot proved to be empty. He and Jo donned protective gloves and began to catalogue the contents of the car, but none of it looked promising – a takeaway coffee cup growing mould, a month-old magazine, a college sweater, rubbish. They let the German Shepherd get a good sniff of the clothing and the handler set off into the forest.

'How d'you think she's connected with all this?' asked Jo.

'I've stopped hazarding guesses a long time ago with this case,' said Carrick.

Jo reached into the seat-back pocket. A road atlas. She almost smiled. Her dad had given her one, when she'd got her first car, and she'd never even used it. She wondered if Anna's had come to her that way too. She was about to put it back when she saw the corner of an envelope sticking out from the middle pages. She pulled it out. It was unsealed, but the front had a typed label reading 'Hana Sigurdsson, Randolph Hotel'.

Holy shit.

'Andy . . .'

'Got something?'

Inside, there was a single sheet of paper, which she unfolded. A thick lock of blonde hair fell out onto her lap. Carrick looked over her shoulder. In printed, courier font, the note was just a few lines.

IF YOU WANT TO SEE YOUR DAUGHTER AGAIN, DO NOT INVOLVE THE POLICE. DELIVER £50,000 IN CASH, WRAPPED IN A PLASTIC BAG, TO THE WASTE BIN IN THE BERNWOOD FOREST MAIN CAR PARK. YOU HAVE UNTIL MIDNIGHT ON 14TH DECEMBER, OR THE NEXT PIECES WE TAKE WILL BE MORE PAINFUL.

* * *

Forty minutes later, the ransom note lay on the table in IR2 at St Aldates, sealed in plastic. Hana Sigurdsson seemed afraid to touch it. DCI Stratton had his arms folded, leaning against the wall. Carrick and Jo sat opposite Malin's mother.

'You think this girl, Anna, wrote it?' asked Hana.

'There's a printer in her bedroom,' said Jo. 'We can test the ink if we need to, but the note was found in her car, and we've uncovered a pattern of lies which suggests she knows a lot more than she was letting on about Malin's disappearance.'

'So where is she now?' asked Hana.

The dog had found her phone, about twenty yards into the treeline, spread over a two metre square area. It looked like someone had driven over it then tossed the pieces into the bushes. After that, they'd expected the worst, but the search for a body had come up empty. It looked like Anna had abandoned her car for one reason or another.

'We don't know,' said Jo.

'We're curious though,' said Carrick, 'why this note's addressed to you, rather than to your ex-husband Nicholas?'

'Presumably they thought I was more likely to pay. I'm not sure Nicholas has fifty thousand pounds lying around.'

'But you do?' said Jo.

Hana looked at her sharply, like a bird of prey. 'I would be able to get my hands on the funds fairly quickly, yes.'

Jo moved on. 'We think it's likely Anna was working with someone,' she said. 'There's a possibility she let them into the college through the fire door in Malin's corridor.'

'What confuses me is that the note wasn't delivered,' said Hana. 'Why kidnap someone and then not extract the ransom?'

Jo and Carrick had discussed the same thing most of the way back to the station. Even if Malin was dead, there was nothing preventing the kidnappers continuing with their ruse.

'It might be that Anna and her accomplice had a difference of opinion on the way to proceed,' said Jo. 'He and Anna stopped communicating by phone three days after Malin disappeared, and we haven't received ransom notes for any of the other missing girls.'

Hana Sigurdsson touched the note. 'It rather looks like Anna might have paid the price, doesn't it?'

* * *

Dr Stein was in agreement.

'The note seems amateur to me. I mean, the hair? Whoever took Malin from her room must have knocked her unconscious, and clearly isn't afraid to spill blood. In real cases of kidnap of such violence, I'd expect them to send a finger, perhaps an ear. It would deliver the message a lot more convincingly.'

Stratton nodded, though he looked a little alarmed.

'And bearing in mind the growing body of information on Anna Mull,' Stein continued, 'I'd say she shows signs of classic sociopathic behaviour. The cheating at university, the thefts from her youth. She takes short cuts and she's willing to use others to get there.'

It was Surrey Police who'd dug up Anna's juvenile misdemeanours. An expulsion for stealing from a teacher, a suspension for vandalism and bullying a younger child into taking the blame. It was a wonder she'd managed to keep it all under wraps in her application to Oriel College.

'So the friendship with Malin was a sham?' asked Carrick. 'She said they'd known each other since they started uni.'

'Typically, sociopaths don't have real friends,' said Stein. 'They might have had the appearance of a friendship, and indeed Malin could well have been very fond of Anna, but the feeling wasn't reciprocated. Anna might have attached herself to Malin for the status the friendship conferred, but when she saw her chance to use it to make money, she probably didn't hesitate.'

'Even if it meant physically harming Malin?'

'I admit, that's the part that vexes me. The note, the hair – it shows a certain reticence to do harm. Whether that's some residual core of moral conscience, or fear, I don't know. But I don't think Anna is the arch manipulator here. I think she's the one who was being manipulated. Used by someone who was a step ahead. The profile I drew up initially still stands. He's not interested in ransoms. His motives are . . . *purer* than that.'

'But he killed Anna?' said Jo.

Stein nodded. 'Almost definitely.'

'You said before he wasn't a murderer.'

'Not by *nature*,' said Stein. 'He probably killed Anna as a logical act. A necessity. Psychopaths have a very *weak* moral compass – they have trouble applying the same hierarchical value systems to crimes as neurotypical people. She may have pushed him to it. I think she was part of his grand scheme, but ultimately an expendable pawn.'

A hand rapped on the door, and it opened. It was Heidi, her face flushed, and Jo's first thought was that she was going into labour.

'Something's happened,' she said. Her voice was an octave higher than normal. 'At St Edmund Hall. Jack's in trouble.'

Chapter 22

Carrick drove them both, speeding down the High Street with the blues on. The ambulance was already parked outside the modest entrance to the college. Jo climbed out of the car before Carrick had applied the handbrake and ran to the front doors. Two paramedics carried a stretcher through, with Pryce lying on top. Blood saturated the front of his shirt, but his eyes were open.

Jo rushed to his side as they reached the open doors of the ambulance. 'Jack?'

'Can you move please?' said a paramedic, practically barging her aside. 'We need to get him in.'

Jo stepped back. Pryce's skin was ghostly. 'I'm sorry, boss,' he said. 'What happened?'

'I think I killed him,' said Pryce weakly as they loaded him in. 'He came at me . . . I didn't mean to.'

Jo watched as the ambulance doors closed, and before she could even gather her thoughts, it was driving off, sirens screaming. She stood in shock for a moment, then headed through the college doors with Carrick, where a porter in uniform stood on the edge of a small quad. His hands were covered in blood she assumed was Pryce's.

'He's that way,' he said, pointing to a stone passage. 'It was some sort of fight.' The man didn't seem keen to move, so Jo and Carrick went alone, through the passage to a small paved area lined with bare flowerbeds filled with muddy footprints, and copious streaks of coagulating blood. A large bowie-knife lay in the middle of it. A man in a balaclava was slumped against a wall, lying in the dirt. Blood – a hell of a lot of blood – was pooled beneath him. After the shock faded Jo felt a flood of dull relief. The balaclava suggested this was their man, the one behind the kidnaps. And he was definitely dead. It was over.

But in the back of her mind, she knew immediately why Pryce had been apologetic. Dead men couldn't tell you anything.

She had no gloves, but she made the judgement call. She had to know. She stepped into the flowerbed, gripped the bottom of the balaclava, and prised it off his head. She flinched back at the sight of the man's face.

'Mary, mother of God,' said Carrick, crossing himself.

The man had undergone extensive plastic surgery – patches on his skin even looked slightly different shades, and there were several deep scars, tinged in a shiny pink. It gave his face the appearance of a patchwork, a modern Frankenstein's monster. One of his lips was non-existent, drawn back to show more of his upper teeth than was natural, and his nose reminded Jo of a boxer's, crushed in at the top. The eyebrow over his left eye twisted sharply downwards, growing into a puckered scar at the top of his nose. The whole effect reminded Jo of a strange contorted fruit. The sort of thing she would have turned her nose up at as a girl, but which her dad would have forced her to eat, with a phrase like *Don't be a fusspot, love. It's just grown a bit funny.*

But it wasn't his appearance that shocked Jo. It was the past, coming right back to haunt her.

'I know him, Andy.'

He blinked, coming to his senses. 'You do?'

Jo nodded. She'd last seen him, not in the flesh, but in a courtroom sketch. He'd worn a protective face covering the whole time he stood in the dock, and the police barrister told her later that he'd been taking regular hits of morphine from a portable tank. The press had relished the speculation about what lay behind the mask. Ben had said it served the fucker right, and he was a good advert for seatbelts.

'His name's Frank Tyndle,' she told Carrick.

* * *

For the second time in less than a week, she told the story of the pursuit almost ten years earlier, when Tyndle had jumped a red light and paid a terrible price. She left out the part about the ambulance – it didn't seem relevant. They searched his pockets, and found only a phone, which they bagged straight away. They sealed off the college completely and waited for the crime scene officers. Carrick called the ID back to the station, where Heidi set about finding out everything she could about Tyndle's recent movements, acquaintances, address. The phone would go to the analysts for any call and location data. If the girls were still alive, time was running out.

Jo and Carrick went to speak with the porter, passing Mel Cropper and his CSO team coming the other way. Cropper had a sausage roll in his hand. 'You might want to finish that before you go through,' said Andy.

The porter told them Pryce had come to the college around eleven, just to check in. About ten minutes later he heard a commotion, and came running. The fight was over already, with Pryce crawling on the ground, the other man dying. He couldn't tell them how the balaclava'd man had got in, but it wasn't through the front entrance.

Once they were gloved up, boots on as well, Jo and Carrick stood back and watched the crime scene officers photographing the aftermath of the carnage.

'I'm guessing he didn't have much luck on Tinder,' said Cropper. The team worked professionally. One lifted the dripping knife into a transparent plastic evidence bag. They placed a sheet over Tyndle, concealing his face, but the mess of it stayed with Jo. All the time, as they processed the scene, she thought about Pryce. If he died, because of Tyndle, because of *her* . . .

She called the hospital, but they couldn't give her any news other than that he'd been rushed to trauma. If she wasn't a family member, they couldn't give out information.

'I'm his colleague,' said Jo. 'Detective Sergeant Masters. I just need to know how he's doing.'

'I'm sorry, Detective. You know the protocol. If you want to put an official request for information through the proper channels—'

Jo hung up. 'Fuck.'

'This isn't your fault, Jo,' said Carrick.

'Isn't it?' She pointed to Tyndle's covered corpse. 'Because that ugly bastard begged to differ.' A couple of the CSOs turned to look, then Cropper spoke.

'Are we okay to move him?'

'Go for it,' said Carrick. 'We'll need his prints and a DNA sample as soon as possible for cross-referencing.'

They watched as the body was laid out, almost reverentially. From the gash up Tyndle's inner thigh and the volume of blood loss, she guessed that the blade must have gone through his femoral artery. The CSO zipped up the bag.

'He was in for nine years,' said Jo. 'He must have been released quite recently.'

'Don't beat yourself up.'

Jo couldn't help it. She looked around, trying to read the scene. 'So what was he planning to do? Drag someone away?'

'Given the blade he was carrying, I think he might have had other things on his mind,' Carrick replied.

Just like the profiler had said. *He becomes a lot more dangerous.* If he came there to kill, what did that mean for the girls?

Heidi called back, and Carrick listened, asked a few questions, then related the info to Jo.

Tyndle had been released from HMP Nottingham approximately five months ago, having served eight and a half years. His liaison officer had an address in Corby, and officers were on their way there as a matter of urgency. Next of kin was listed as a daughter, who they were trying to reach. He had no registered vehicle, but a clean licence after his historic ban had been lifted.

'I want to get back to the station,' Jo said. 'You think Stratton will be okay with it?'

'I suspect it might be all hands on deck now,' said Carrick with a sombre look.

* * *

There were two more detectives in the squad room back at St Aldates. One she recognised as DC Kevin Carter, her old colleague from Bath. The last six months clearly hadn't brought great improvements in his personal hygiene, because she smelled him from the corridor. The other she didn't know, but she learned was Nina Creasey, who'd replaced her when she transferred to Oxford officially. Jo wondered why they'd been allocated Avon and Somerset personnel rather than other Thames Valley detectives.

'Can't keep out of trouble,' muttered Carter as she stripped off her coat.

'Good to see you too, Kev,' she said, smiling as frostily as she could.

Stratton barely batted an eyelid at Jo's presence.

'Corby's a dead end,' he said. 'Tyndle spent a couple of nights there when he first got out, but he's not been seen since. The daughter is estranged, lives in Canada. At the moment we have no idea what that fucker's been doing for approximately three months.'

'Planning,' said Stein. He was sitting slightly apart from everyone else. 'He didn't want anything getting in the way of his singular vision.'

Jo felt a surge of impatience. Pryce was lying in hospital, going through goodness knew what, and the profiler seemed to be enjoying it. The commentary *really* wasn't helpful. For all his philosophising about narratives and antagonists, Tyndle had turned out to be a simple case of a man with a grudge. A pretty severe one – the loss of his face – but a grudge nonetheless.

'Nina,' said Stratton to Detective Creasey, 'Rob Bridges tells me you're something of an expert in mobile comms. I want you to be the contact for Tyndle's phone.'

Jo understood now the reason for the Avon and Somerset secondment. Rob Bridges, her old DCI, was friends with Stratton. There was less chance of embarrassing info getting out. And Rob would be only too happy to take some of the credit for a good outcome.

'Any insights on where he might have taken the girls?' she asked Stein.

'None at all,' said Stein. 'It may have started with an element of gamesmanship, but circumstances might have forced his hand to more desperate measures.'

Across the room, shoulders visibly sagged. Stratton lifted his gaze as if in prayer. 'That doesn't get out of the building,' he said. 'As far as the public are concerned, we're still looking to find these young women alive.'

Jo let her head drop, closing her eyes. She needed a moment to digest, and to chart back how the disappearance of one college girl a week ago had descended into this current hell. If she had done something different at any stage, might things have turned out otherwise? Why hadn't Frank Tyndle been the first person in her mind when they realised this was connected to her? Maybe because she'd never truly thought she was connected to him, or in any way responsible for what happened. It could have been any uniform in pursuit that day. And he was the one who had skipped the red light, causing the accident that disfigured him. He was the idiot who hadn't bothered with a seatbelt.

But more than that, it really didn't logically make sense. How could he have known she was in the vehicle on his tail? Her name had never been connected to the broader investigation. In the tribunal that followed the crash, which was prompted by the miscarriage in the ambulance, Jo was never called on to testify in person in the courtroom. And in any document, she was named simply as P2, to protect her identity. Tyndle would have needed friends in high places to track her down.

Not that any of the nuance would matter to DCI Stratton. If he needed a reason to throw her under the bus, this was it.

The phone on Heidi's desk rang, and she listened, then replaced the receiver. 'That was the hospital. Jack's stable and conscious.'

'Thank God,' said Jo, and she meant it.

'We need to interview him,' said the DCI. 'If Tyndle said anything, anything at all . . .'

'I'm on it, sir,' said Jo.

Carter had folded his arms, shifting his bulk slightly to block the way to the door. 'We'll clean up the mess here, Sarge. I can have a chat with Detective Pryce.'

'No, let her go,' said Carrick. 'She and Jack have been working together. A friendly face will do him good, I'm sure.'

Jo was grateful for the support. When Carter didn't move quick enough, she shoved past, harder than necessary.

She was crossing to her car when she was approached by a middle-aged man in a suit and a long coat. 'Detective Masters?' he called.

She backed away. 'Can I help you?'

'Tim Lester, Associated Press. Is it true these crimes are all related to you personally?'

She smiled. 'I'm afraid I don't know what you're talking about.'

'A source has told us the locations of the crimes are linked to your name.'

'I really can't comment,' said Jo, turning away.

'They're calling his victims the "Josie Girls",' said the journalist. He had a Dictaphone in his hand now. Jo opened her car door.

'Was the death at St Edmund Hall this morning connected in some way?'

Jo slammed the door. Her hand was shaking as she started the engine. The journalist stood outside, coat flapping in the wind. She pulled away.

So much for keeping things in the building. Who the fuck had leaked it? Carter was an obvious choice, but an easy conclusion to jump to. It could just as easily be one of the civilian staff who'd got wind. She phoned Heidi on the way and told her.

'Better pass it on to Stratton,' Jo said.

'He *will* be happy,' said Heidi. 'Say hi to Jack for me.'

* * *

Pryce was still in intensive care, sickly pale, lying half-propped up in bed with a drip in his arm. One hand was heavily bandaged, the other in a sling.

'Christ, how much blood did you lose?' said Jo with the best smile she could muster. She hoped the forced bonhomie might make him feel better. But when he looked across at her, head rolling on the pillow, she could see he was in a lot of pain. His eyes were sunken, his forehead damp with sweat.

'About two pints, apparently,' he said. 'My hands got the worst. The one to the gut is pretty shallow.'

'I feel bad now. I didn't even bring you any grapes.'

He laughed, and then winced. 'No joking, please.' He pressed a button to deliver a kick of painkillers, then rested his head back on the pillow. 'He's dead, isn't he?'

Jo nodded. 'We've got a lead, though. His name's Frank Tyndle.'

'History?'

'Interesting,' said Jo after a pause. She gave him the abbreviated version.

'It makes sense,' he said when she'd finished. 'You ruined his life, so he's ruining yours. Quid pro quo.'

'I guess so,' said Jo.

'You don't buy it?'

'I don't . . . I don't know. When you put it like that, it seems a bit too easy. He doesn't really match the profile that Stein came up with. I mean, he didn't, anyway. Stein's ideas seem malleable to say the least.'

'I've never put much faith in them,' said Pryce. 'Seem to state the obvious most of the time.'

A nurse came in to check Pryce, taking his pulse and blood pressure. Jo waited until they were alone again.

'The Tyndle we knew back then was good at one thing –

keeping people in line through intimidation. I wouldn't say he was particularly bright, or forward-planning. If someone pissed him off, he broke their legs, or burned down their house. This is so much more elaborate.'

'Sounds like you took a lot more from him than nine years though,' said Pryce. 'With a face like that, the psychological effects alone would be devastating.'

'Perhaps,' said Jo. *Maybe I just don't want to believe it myself.* 'But I can't see the connection to Anna Mull. I mean, if she's the accomplice. How the hell does she come into contact with Frank Tyndle?'

'It's a good point. You say he wasn't carrying any ID? No wallet or keys?'

'Just a phone and that fuck-off knife he stabbed you with.'

'The phone's the thing then,' said Pryce. 'If we link Mull and Tyndle, the case is solved. I guess there's a chance it will give us the location of the girls too.'

Their corpses, anyway, thought Jo.

Pryce swallowed and hit the pain-relief button again. After the wave had passed, he licked his lips. 'Can you get me some water please?'

Jo went into the hall, found a disposable cup, and lifted it to his lips. He drank gratefully, and a little spilled down his chest. She waited for his head to settle back on the pillow before speaking again.

'I'm here on official business, I'm afraid.'

'I guessed as much. You want to know what happened?'

'And if he said anything before he died.'

Pryce sighed. 'I think it's been a wasted trip then,' he said. 'I'd just got there, relieved the uniforms outside. I spoke to the old duffer in the lodge, did a circuit. I remember thinking it was unlikely he'd come there. The place isn't big, is it? Then I saw someone coming over the wall – there's another college over the back. Maybe I should've shouted, but in the back of my mind I knew he'd scarper. So I let him come over. He saw me pretty much straight away.'

'Did you tell him you were police?'

'Damn right I did. He . . . he came at me with . . . well, it looked like a kitchen knife. It all happened pretty quick, but we ended up on the ground. My hands were bleeding all over both of us. I . . . the knife must've slipped, because suddenly there was so much blood. I thought it was mine, but he stood up, I think, holding his leg. He wasn't worried about me anymore. I knew I had to try and keep him alive, but I couldn't stand up at all. I couldn't even get to my phone. He bled out pretty quick, but he was talking.'

'And what did he say?'

'He called me a cunt, I think.'

Jo grinned. 'Figures.'

'Yeah.'

Pryce looked subdued. 'Look, I know I fucked up.'

'Don't be stupid. You're a hero.'

'Will I get one of those medals like you keep in your drawer?' Jo chuckled. 'I'm serious,' continued Pryce. 'Those girls . . . they're out there somewhere . . .'

But not necessarily alive, thought Jo. 'Whatever happened to the others, you saved a life, Jack.'

His eyes were glassy, as if the gravity of what had happened was finally sinking in.

'I'd better go,' said Jo. 'You need to rest.'

He nodded. 'Keep me informed, won't you? I want to help. I feel useless here.'

'Just focus on getting better,' said Jo.

'They said I might be able to get out tonight.'

'That isn't the same as being better, you silly sod.'

Chapter 23

Her phone rang on the way out of the hospital. An Oxford number she didn't know. But the voice on the other end was instantly recognisable. Hana Sigurdsson.

'Detective, I think you owe me an explanation.'

'Pardon?'

'A man called Lester in a horrible suit has just accosted me in the lobby of my hotel. He tells me that Malin's disappearance is related to a personal vendetta against you.'

Jo tried to gather her thoughts. 'Ms Sigurdsson, that's one possible explanation.'

'One you and your colleagues didn't think it necessary to share earlier this morning?'

'We're pursuing several avenues of enquiry.' She knew as she was speaking that she sounded almost exactly like DCI Stratton, but didn't know what else to say. 'It would be premature for us—'

'A man was killed this morning at a college. Was he trying to kidnap another girl?'

'I really can't share that information with you.'

'I thought I could trust you,' said Malin's mother. 'When

you first came to my hotel, I was open with you, and I asked you to be the same. You assured me that you would.'

'I am being as open as I can,' said Jo.

'Then tell me what is *happening*!' For the first time since Jo had met her, Hana Sigurdsson sounded scared, her voice tremulous.

But what could she say? 'I'm sorry, Ms Sigurdsson. We're doing everything we can.'

The line went dead.

* * *

Carrick's call came through on the way back to the station.

'How's Jack?'

'On the mend,' she said. 'He said Tyndle came over the wall – it's New College on the other side. They've got a lot of open ground, so it would be the easiest way in. I've been thinking – Tyndle must have a base in or near Oxford. If Stein was right, and he was watching me all this time, making plans, he had to have been staying somewhere close, but somewhere he couldn't be seen coming and going. Not looking like that. Maybe he has connections locally. Someone who'd be willing to put him up. Might be worth checking the visitor log where he was serving time.'

'We're on it,' said Carrick. 'Listen, Jo, Stratton doesn't want you back here.' He sounded defeated. 'The press are all over it. They'll try to find you. Is there somewhere you can go, just to lie low while we figure this out?'

'Fuck. Will they try my brother?'

'It's safe to assume that,' said Carrick. 'Your flat too.'

Jo's hands clenched on the wheel. 'Any idea who leaked it?'

'Not at the moment. Stratton's trying to control the story, but it's like bailing out a sinking ship.'

'I could go to Lucas's,' she said, reluctantly. He wouldn't be there, and it would give her a chance to pack a few things.

'Do that,' said Carrick. 'I'll share anything that comes up.'

Jo turned around, and headed out towards Abingdon. To think, a week ago, she'd thought she was putting her past behind her, but now she was mired in it once more. *Got to give credit to whoever came up with 'The Josie Girls*', she thought bitterly. It had a ring to it, for sure. If it ever became 'The Josie Murders', more so. No doubt that's what Tyndle had wanted. She called Lucas at work, on the way back to his apartment. She couldn't see how he'd get dragged into this, but it couldn't hurt to warn him. He didn't answer, and she left a message, just saying not to speak to the press if approached. It would worry him, but she didn't really care anymore. That ship had sailed.

Heading back towards Lucas's block, she felt like it was *her* on the run from the police. She called Paul, and left a rambling message on his answerphone about the possibility of press questions, then wished she could go back and delete it. This was the last thing he and his family needed. She was supposed to be an adult, not a little sister who needed looking after.

Deidre Plumley was coming out of the elevator as she entered Lucas's apartment building.

'Hello, Jo!' she said cheerfully. 'How are you?'

Jo pressed the button for the second floor. 'Been better, to be honest.'

'Yes, I saw that awful story on the news last night.' The doors began to close, and Jo didn't stop them. 'I hope you—' The lift climbed.

In the flat, Jo opened her laptop on the dining table. Her inbox was piling up as the new investigation gathered pace, and the other ongoing enquiries continued in tandem. More crime scene reports, statements, photos. Qadir Suleiman, the owner of the Lounge nightclub, had been picked up in

Glasgow and was being driven back down south. That night, and those arrests, seemed a lifetime ago already. Even if they put Suleiman and Catskill behind bars, it wasn't going to save the girls.

As she reached the most recent correspondence, one email caught her eye. The log for Lucas's secret phone had come through. She paused a moment, cursor hovering over the link. Had this been the problem all along? Getting distracted by her personal life, and missing things on the case? Deep down, she knew that wasn't a fair assessment, but that didn't mean Stratton would see it the same way if he found out.

And now – what else was she supposed to do? They'd shut her out completely.

She clicked through the records, and saw the phone had been used to call a single number, a landline in Oxford.

Which made sense, if Lucas was fucking another woman behind her back. She logged onto the directory and found the address: 12 Orion Close in Temple Cowley. A check with the land registry confirmed the current owner since March that year was Carly Granger. The name meant nothing. Jo searched through the DVLA next for a driving licence. The woman in the photo was a redhead, twenty-nine years old. Pretty. She didn't look like she sold winter holidays.

Jo sat back, feeling vindicated and nauseous at the same time. She knew she was supposed to stay put, but the thought of being here when Lucas got back from work was plainly ridiculous. She'd taken enough shit. Maybe it was time to take control, of this at least. She grabbed her computer, her purse, and her coat. Someone – not Paul – could come later on her behalf and get her things and hand back the key to Lucas. She left the apartment, knowing she'd never set foot in the place again.

* * *

Orion Close was in the middle of a modern estate of identical semis built in the nineties. Her heartbeat galloped as she saw Lucas's Land Rover actually parked in the driveway of number 12, beside a black Audi. *Fancy that . . .*

For once fate seemed to have conspired *with* her. She'd only been planning to gather intelligence, but this whole sorry mess could come to a head much quicker than anticipated. She didn't even think about leaving. It struck her, as she slowed, that this was almost exactly the same time of day she'd gone to the college a few days before. It was a regular thing, then. A mid-afternoon quickie.

She pulled over up the street, took out her phone, and dialled Lucas's number. It rang several times, and she was just wondering whether to leave a sarcastic message about imaginary skiing trips, when he picked up.

'Hey, babe.'

'Where are you?'

'I'm just dumping some waste at the tip. Everything all right?'

She hung up, then drove further along the road. She parked over the end of the drive, on the pavement, and climbed out. A woman with a pushchair coming along the pavement tutted as she squeezed past. Jo ignored her and marched to the front door. She rang the bell – a long, insistent blast. No one came. They were probably upstairs. She slammed a fist on the door, then opened the letter box. 'Lucas?'

Through the small, distorted glass pane a shape appeared. A woman.

'Who are you?' came a fearful voice.

She banged the door with her fist.

The least you can do is look me in the fucking eye.

'I'm here to see Lucas,' she said. 'Open this door. Now.'

The shape retreated quickly down the corridor.

Oh no you don't . . .

Jo went to the side gate, and tried to open it. It was latched. Without thinking too hard, she hoisted herself over, and landed on the other side, then walked along the side-passage. There was a trampoline in the back garden, covered in dead leaves. *Kids?*

Through a set of French doors she saw a girl, maybe thirteen, in school uniform, and immediately regretted her rash actions. The girl was on the phone, watching her.

Jo pulled out her badge, and laid it against the glass.

'I'm police,' she said. 'It's okay.'

The girl rushed the other way.

Fuck . . .

Jo jogged back to the side-gate, opened it from the inside, and ran into the drive.

A family of three were walking along the road towards her. A girl of eight or nine wore school uniform. The woman was Carly Granger, wearing a bobble hat with a few strands of red hair poking from the bottom.

The man holding the girl's hand was Lucas.

The schoolgirl spotted Jo first and said something to her mother, who looked across. A second later Lucas saw her and stopped. Carly glanced at him, and said something. Then the front door opened and the older girl came running out, crying 'Mum! Dad!'

Lucas let go of the girl's hand and rushed over, wrapping the older one in his embrace.

Jo couldn't move from the spot. *Dad?*

'What are you doing here, Jo?' said Lucas over the girl's shoulder.

Jo was reeling, eyes snapping to the woman and kid then back to Lucas. Carly was speaking to the younger girl.

'I think I should be asking the questions, don't you?' she said.

'She was trying to get in,' said the girl he was hugging. 'Who is she, Dad?' Lucas kissed the top of her head. 'Go to your mum a sec, Jen. It's all right. I know her.'

He said it like she was his work colleague or something.

Lucas's older daughter fixed Jo with a suspicious glare as she retreated to Carly's side.

Lucas came forward in small, uncertain steps. 'Babe, I know I've messed up, but please, hear me out . . .'

'They're both yours?' asked Jo.

'Yes,' said Lucas quietly. He stopped, about two metres away from her.

Jo's mind was trying to process, trying to catalogue their time together and work out how, over the last six months together, she hadn't seen this. Hadn't had a fucking *clue*.

'Does Carly know about me?'

Lucas's eyes registered surprise. 'You know her name.'

'I'm a detective,' said Jo.

'Then you know we're not a couple,' said Lucas. Jo shrugged, buying time to process the information overload. 'Maybe we could go somewhere else,' Lucas added. 'Talk.'

'What is there to talk about?'

'It's complicated,' said Lucas.

'It *really* isn't,' said Jo. 'You've got a family you never told me about.'

'I was going to. I wanted to. I only found out they were moving here recently. I hadn't seen them for years. Jo, it's . . . there's a lot I haven't told you.'

'That's an understatement.'

'Jo, I used to have a problem. A drink problem. A really fucking bad one. It messed my life up for a long time. Theirs too.' He was speaking quickly, eyes filling with pleading tears. 'Jo, I didn't see my kids for *three* years. I *couldn't* see them until I'd cleaned myself up. Then they were here – in Oxford – but

I'd already met you. I should have told you, but it was going so well. I didn't want to lose you, scare you away . . .'

Jo heard the words coming out of his mouth, saw his face twisted up with emotion, and a part of her even then wanted to comfort him. But it was a tiny part. And not nearly enough. Because the rest of her was a ball of rage and shame and disappointment. 'Goodbye, Lucas,' she said, and walked past him towards her car.

She climbed in, started the engine and pulled away, just as a squad car drove into Orion Close with the blues flashing.

Chapter 24

The embarrassment and anger came in waves. First, it was Pinker and Williams who'd answered the call from the dispatcher, responding to 'a possible break-in attempt'.

Lucas tried to diffuse the situation but that only complicated matters, as he wasn't the registered homeowner. So then Carly had to step up and explain. *She* had to defend *Jo*, the crazy bitch who'd just jumped her garden fence and terrified her poor daughter. Jo was asked to wait in the back of the police car, the doors locked. Despite the fact that she outranked them both, there was still procedure to follow.

As Carly led the girls into their house and Lucas lingered, Pinker questioned Jo, who did her best to convince him it was just a mix-up. The look of pity on his face was almost too much to bear. Andrea Williams, she could have coped with, but Pinker . . . the chance of him keeping this to himself was tiny.

Then there was the fact that most of the neighbours, many on the school run themselves, seemed to think it was a spectator sport. Every one of them another witness to her abject humiliation. The other woman. The blind, foolish female. The fucking *cliché*.

In the end, they let her go, though Pinker apologised with fist-chewing levels of condescension that he'd have to write it up. No crime had been committed, he said, so it wouldn't be logged on her official record. It could have been much worse, she thought – the fact that a girl had called it in might easily have caused more alarm in the current climate. They could have sent detectives too. *Small mercies.*

Jo managed to hold it together until she was back in her car and well away from Orion Close. Then she pulled over in a bus stop and burst into tears, wrenched up from deep in her gut.

Her phone's chimes brought her round. If it was Lucas, she already knew she wouldn't answer. But the number was Andy's. She wiped her eyes, gathered her wits. Told herself there was no way he could have heard about what had just happened. Not yet.

'Jo, we found an address for Tyndle through his benefit claims. In Newbury. Local police are there now.'

'Don't keep me in suspense. They find anything?'

'You could say that, yes.'

'The girls?'

'Not exactly. I think you should get down there. I'm bringing Stein too.'

'What about Stratton? I thought he wanted me out of this.'

'I think he'd understand,' said Andy, cryptically. 'Just meet me there, okay?'

★ ★ ★

Getting out of the city felt like a release, and as Jo left Oxford behind, her eyes were dry again. She'd never been one for self-pity – it was one of the traits she'd shared with her dad. When he'd collapsed, quite suddenly in the garden at just sixty-two years old, only to be told he had an advanced brain tumour, his first response was to worry about the upkeep of his veg patch.

The address was actually in Thatcham, east of Newbury itself, on a rundown estate of tower blocks and poorly maintained low-rise social housing. It was the sort of place Jo knew well from her early days in uniform. Domestic violence, anti-social kids, joyriding. The estate where they sent rookies, because the day-in, day-out taught you more about the people skills you'd need to be an effective police officer than just about anything else. The kind of neighbourhood where neighbours slashed each other's tyres or got into fist-fights. Where suspects always ran, even though they knew they'd be caught, because having a criminal record did nothing detrimental to their life prospects – they didn't have any in the first place.

She stopped at a row of grim sixties pebbledashed terraces where a squad car was parked up, plus Andy's Toyota. As she approached, she showed her ID to a young female officer.

'They're already upstairs,' she said. The slightly awed look she gave Jo wasn't reassuring. She was pretty sure she'd cleaned any evidence of tears away, so it could only relate to what was inside.

Carrick was actually at the back door, on the phone, and he ended the call. 'Still trying to get the landlord,' he said. 'Looks like this place is being let to Eastern European workers for the most part but Tyndle had the bedroom at the front for the last eight weeks or so. We are struggling to get much out of the other occupants, but the local police have got a translator they can call. Go up and have a gander. It's really something.'

She walked into a small kitchenette, dirty crockery piled around the sink and the bin overflowing. There was a lounge, but it had two double mattresses on the floor, and a second uniformed officer – a young man – was watching two surly-looking Slavic males. The stairs were bare wood with a few scraps of carpet still clinging on to the grippers in places. On the upper floor was a bathroom, clean enough, but completely bare apart from a bar of soap on the sink and a single towel. There were two further bedrooms. Stein stood just inside the one at the end of the short landing. The door lock had been smashed off, splintering the jamb.

'Here cometh the lady of the hour,' he said.

Jo walked in. She'd known what to expect when Carrick had filled her in on the way, but she still wasn't prepared for the reality. Apart from a plastic garden chair and a single bed with a sleeping bag and no sheet, the room was unfurnished, three walls scuffed and stained. The fourth was entirely covered with photos, all of them of her. She moved nearer, lips parted. Here she was, leaving St Aldates. Here out running along the towpath. Entering the supermarket. Picking up William at school, the day she'd taken him to see a movie at the cinema. There were pictures of Lucas too – chatting with Bob outside Gloucester College. But by far the majority were of her. In her car, drinking a coffee before one of her sessions with Dr Forster. On the phone, walking through the town centre, entering The Three Crowns for a drink with Ferman. There was even one outside the Bright Futures Fertility Clinic in Bath, smiling in a summer dress, taken, it seemed, from the small railed-off park opposite. Jo did a mental calculation. They must have all been taken over a six-month period. Each photo had something else in common too – her face had been shredded with a sharp object, sometimes leaving nothing but a ragged hole.

'I imagine this is rather sobering,' said Stein.

'It's reassuring, in a way,' she said. 'That he's dead, I mean.'

There were newspaper clippings too – from the spate that had appeared in the press after the Sally Carruthers case. *The Clown Killer. Hero Detective Closes 30-year-old Case. The Evil That Lurked in the Oxford Suburbs.*

Jo went to the wardrobe where a few items of clothing were

hanging. In the bottom was an old suitcase. She opened it. Inside were several plastic medication pots, tabs of pills, a pair of wellington boots. Also a framed photo of Tyndle as a much younger man, his face unmarked and happy-go-lucky, with a girl on his shoulders. She wondered if the daughter who'd emigrated to Canada had ever visited him when he was inside, and what she would have thought if she had. His face had had nine years to get better, but it was still hard to stomach now. She'd no idea how a kid would have coped seeing it.

There was a long, leather case leaning up against the inside of the wardrobe. Her first thought was a rifle, but it was too lightweight. Unzipping the side, she saw it contained a fishing rod.

'Even psychopaths have hobbies,' Stein said.

Jo heard footsteps. It was Carrick entering the room.

'Translator's arrived,' he said. 'You want to lead the questioning?'

Jo went back down, where a young woman in jeans and a thick coat was waiting with the uniform. They shook hands and the woman introduced herself as Julietta. 'They're scared,' she said. 'They don't have all the correct papers.'

'Tell them that doesn't matter now,' said Jo. 'It's the man who lived upstairs we're interested in.'

Julietta spoke to them. One shook his head, but the other seemed more willing to talk. He gestured at one point to his face with a grimace and a twist of his hand.

'He says the man kept himself to himself,' said Carrick. 'Some of the local kids used to freak out when they saw him around. He used to wear a hoodie a lot.'

'When did they last see him?' asked Jo.

The men talked to each other after Julietta had relayed the question.

'They think perhaps five days ago, but they're rarely here in the daytime.'

'And what about a vehicle? Did they see one?'

Again, they conferred before answering.

'A white van,' said Julietta. 'Really old. It broke down a couple of weeks ago, and they helped him to jump-start it.'

'Don't suppose they have the reg?' she asked.

The answer, predictably, was no.

One of the men whispered to the other, who shook his head.

'What are they saying?' asked Jo.

Julietta spoke to them both and after some mutterings back and forth, Julietta's tone became impatient. She scolded them both, and the quieter of the two men spoke in several mumbled phrases.

'He says the man upstairs had a visitor a couple of times, maybe a fortnight ago.'

Jo wondered if they were talking about Anna Mull. 'A woman?'

'No,' said Julietta. 'They think it was a man, from the voices.'

'But they didn't hear what was said?'

Julietta responded in the negative.

'Okay, thanks,' said Jo.

Outside the room, she spoke to Carrick. 'Thoughts?'

'The other man could be anyone,' he replied. 'I think if we find that van, we find the girls.'

'I'm not sure,' said Jo. 'The van must be in Oxford somewhere, given that's where he ran into Pryce. I can't see him keeping three dead women in the back. Not for this long.'

'You have another theory?'

'Looks like he was a keen angler,' she said. 'I don't know the fishing spots around here, but if there was somewhere remote . . . Remember Natalie, dumped in the river. What if that wasn't an accident after all? Might be his preferred method of disposal.'

'Let me do a search.' He took out his phone. 'Stein still upstairs?'

Jo went to check. She found the psychologist holding the photo of Tyndle and his daughter. 'You finished up here?' she asked.

He faced her, frowning. For the first time, he seemed less than sure of himself. 'Does this feel right to you?'

'What's that?'

'Tyndle,' said Stein. 'I get the impression you're not entirely convinced by the validity of my profession, which is a prejudice I'm used to dealing with. But you can be open with me if you have doubts about my analysis in this particular case.'

Jo pointed to the wall. 'I'm no expert, but the fact he's ripped my face to bits seems a strong indicator that he didn't like me.'

'Yes, it does, doesn't it?'

'So why the umming and aahing?'

Stein held up the photo. 'This man doesn't look like a psychopath to me.'

'That was before his unfortunate meeting with a car windscreen.'

'Indeed. It might be that he was mentally impaired during or after the accident. But I find it odd that he kept this photo. It speaks to a man of complex emotional investment, of hope. That isn't the typical profile of a psychopath. And this room – it isn't what I expected. It all feels rather desperate. Barely a life at all. There's no egotism, no narcissism that seems to match the nature of the crimes.'

Carrick called up. 'Jo, I might have something.'

She left Stein again. Andy was on the stairs.

'There's an old flooded sand quarry, four miles from here. Popular in the summer with the angling crowd. I imagine there's not much going on there in the winter months. Could be worth a look.'

'It's all we've got,' said Jo.

* * *

Chiltern Aggregates had once owned the quarry, according to the ancient sign illuminated by Jo's headlights. It also warned that trespassers would be prosecuted, and that swimming was strictly prohibited.

But the fence that had once stood blocking the entrance lay to one side, twisted out of shape, so they drove off the main road and up a track. The ground was slick with mud and Jo's wheels spun a couple of times. It would be the cherry on her day if she had to get towed out. She shifted to a low gear, following Carrick until the track ran out at an old Portakabin, its windows smashed and its door hanging open.

A cloudy starless sky was the only witness to their arrival, and Jo left her engine running, headlights on as she pulled alongside the Toyota. As she popped open her door, the freezing evening air seeped quickly into the car's interior. Carrick shone his torch towards the Portakabin, approached the front step and pushed open the door. She saw the flash of the light coming through the shattered panes, then he turned back, shook his head, and descended.

They moved side by side, two metres or so apart. Outside the arcs of their torches, there was pitch black, and Jo rolled her beam back and forth over stubby, thistle-pricked ground, picking out scraps of rubbish, but nothing more.

Then Carrick's snagged on what was clearly a vehicle track through the glistening mud, leading on from where they'd parked their cars.

'Looks recent,' he said.

They focused both beams on the tyre marks and continued. The ruts led off over uneven grassland that sloped gently downwards. The ground was boggy, and cold water quickly seeped through to Jo's toes. She was in danger of losing a shoe. Carrick slipped, his torch jerking, and landed with a splat.

'Flippin' heck!' he said. One half of his coat was covered in mud as he clambered to his feet.

Jo would normally have grinned at his pre-watershed exclamations, but there was something about the atmosphere tonight that repressed humour, however wry or black. Her torch picked out a fence of barbed wire ahead, with more warning signs about a steep drop and unstable ground. The tyre marks led through the thistles and scrub to a section of the fence that was missing, the wire lying in twisted coils, still attached to unearthed wooden posts.

'Careful,' said Carrick.

Jo had to see. The ground was drier here anyway, and she crept to the edge. She couldn't see any sign of the van, but the tyre marks led right over the drop. Either someone had *Thelma-and-Louise*'d it over the side, or they'd pushed a vehicle over. The water was only fifteen feet below and as still as a millpond, reflecting the yellow of her torch and her own spectral face.

Something told her that real ghosts lurked just beneath that calm surface.

'I think we might have found them.'

Chapter 25

TUESDAY

By the time the Marine Unit arrived at first light, under command of a sergeant called Howe, Jo was exhausted. It hadn't been worth returning to Oxford, so they retreated to a 24-hour truckers' cafe a couple of miles away on the edge of an industrial estate, drinking mug after mug of strong tea through the early hours. Apart from the waitress, Jo had been the only female in there. She'd surprised herself by finishing something called a mega breakfast that she was still struggling to digest, while Carrick had stuck to fluids. He retreated at 7 am into Newbury itself, returning with a fresh smoked salmon bagel.

In the grey drizzle of the morning, the scale of the quarry became clear. It was at least two hundred feet across, with a kidney-shaped pool of water. There were more signs suggesting swimming might not be the best idea, though there were four small rescue buoyancy aids at regular intervals around the perimeter just in case someone was stupid enough to try. Through the long drag of the night-time hours, Carrick had found out that Chiltern Aggregates had ceased trading over a decade ago, and technically the local council was responsible for the site now. The man they'd sent out to liaise and monitor looked rather annoyed to be there, and sat in his car back by the abandoned cabin.

A lone fisherman appeared from the mist at around half eight, setting up a chair further along the bank. If he saw them, he showed no interest in Sergeant Howe and his team assembling their gear. Carrick wandered over to speak with him.

Jo spoke with Howe as he stripped to thermals and began to pull on his dry suit. Most of the work they did now was terrorism-related, he explained – patrolling the various culverts and inlets of the Thames. He'd been a regular uniform in London for most of his career, but made the switch a few years ago after first falling in love with scuba diving on holiday in the Caribbean.

'This must be a tad less glamorous,' she said, casting her eyes over the quarry.

'You're not wrong.'

She'd told him what they were dealing with already. The fire service hadn't been keen to send a winching unit until they knew what was down there, but Stratton had gone straight to the Chief Constable who oversaw the whole of Thames Valley. They'd bashed heads, figuratively at least, and the upshot was that a specialist rig was on its way.

Howe and one other diver were heading down, while the remaining guy stayed on the cameras in the van. Jo guessed the water could only be a fraction above freezing and wondered if they'd drawn straws for the honour.

Carrick came back from his interview.

'Chap's not all there,' he said, tapping his temple. 'He comes here a couple of times a week, but never speaks to the other anglers. He thinks he remembers seeing Tyndle once or twice, but not a van.'

'We're ready,' said Sergeant Howe, tightening the straps on his partner's breathing apparatus. They both had waterproof headtorches attached to their masks, and utility belts at their waists. He and his colleague walked awkwardly in their flippers, following the contour of the slope down to the lake's edge.

Jo watched them wade into the water until it was chest deep. Then they slipped the mouthpieces in, and with a couple of hand gestures, dived in. She followed their progress by the bubbles that disturbed the surface.

After less than a minute, the third member of the team called from the van. 'This what you're looking for?'

On his monitor was a split-feed, showing the chest-mounted camera footage from his colleagues labelled D1 and D2. Jo saw the white bodywork of a vehicle from different angles, a tyre, a door handle.

D1 headed towards the window at the front, his headtorch rotating onto the glass.

Suddenly he jerked backwards, and the image spun dizzyingly.

'What is it?' asked Carrick.

The image stabilised, and the diver approached the front of the van. Jo saw at once through the windshield that there was someone in the passenger's seat. Brown hair fanned out in the water around pale skin.

'Closer . . .' Jo whispered.

The other diver came into shot at the passenger window, so the split-screen showed the corpse head on and in profile. Her eyes were open, staring right at them. Elfin features. Completely unafraid.

'God rest her soul,' mumbled Carrick.

'You know her?' asked the marine cop.

'It's Anna Mull,' said Jo. The initial shock faded fast. 'Tell them to try the rear doors.'

Both D1 and D2 drifted through the water to the back of

the van, and Jo saw a hand reach out to open the doors, close to the blue oval of a Ford badge. She was holding her breath. Both guys knew what to expect, but she wasn't sure she was ready to see it herself. The doors were evidently locked. D2 waved a finger in front of his camera.

'Can they break a window?' said Carrick.

'Not easily. And if there's evidence inside, you're better waiting until we can get the vehicle out in one piece.'

Carrick folded his arms. 'Let's get the plate while they're down there,' he said.

Jo went to tell the site manager from the council what they'd discovered. It looked like Tyndle would be keeping his secrets a while longer yet.

And if she was right about what was inside, she could happily wait a lifetime.

* * *

The growing commotion was too much for the lone fisherman, or maybe he figured any potential catch would be disturbed. Along the bank, he gathered his things, and plodded away. They'd checked on the van's plates – it was almost twenty years old, and registered to a Matthew Maguire in Slough. They called him straight away, and he told them he'd sold the van to a scrap merchant almost a year ago when it failed its MOT for the third year running and the repairs were exorbitant. Clearly someone had decided it deserved a second lease of life and it had ended up in Tyndle's hands. Carrick, meanwhile, put in a long call to Surrey Police, asking them to notify Anna Mull's parents of the upsetting find.

The scene had been populated considerably, with a squad car, a fire engine, and a winching rig supported by a substantial truck-mounted crane. A crime scene team stood by, with one member video-taping the whole enterprise. Further back, in recognition of their very much supporting role, two ambulances waited in anticipation of the bodies to be transported. Maybe twenty-five or thirty people, all unwilling participants to Tyndle's atrocities. The ground that had been boggy before was a quagmire and Jo was sure her shoes were beyond salvation. Her patience had reached breaking point as the hours passed, but now at last as the divers emerged from tethering the van, the signal was given for the winching to begin. With a squeal and shriek of mechanical energy, the coil of metal cord began to rotate, hauling the van upwards. It rose, pale, like the corpse of a dead, bleached creature from the depths, before it emerged from the water.

The crane lifted the van clear of the quarry edge by its rear axle, water streaming through the door seals. Anna Mull wasn't belted in and the dead weight of her body flopped against the inside of the windshield, face pressed into the glass, limbs at awkward, ungainly angles. The crane rotated until the van hovered over dry land, then the crew stepped forward. Wearing thick steel-mesh protective gauntlets, they guided its progress downward carefully until it was lowered onto its four wheels. Anna slipped back into the seats, one hand jammed up against the steering wheel.

Attention turned to the back of the vehicle and everyone congregated in a loose semi-circle around the van's rear end. A fireman brandished a crowbar to Carrick. 'You want to do the honours, detective?'

For once Jo was glad she didn't outrank him. Carrick took the crowbar, walked decisively to the rear doors and jammed in the lever just above the lock. It took a couple of flexes, bending back the bodywork and inching it further in. Then the lock broke with a crack. Carrick jumped back as gallons of water rushed out over his feet and ankles.

No one moved, so Jo stepped up alongside him, and gripped the edge of the door. *So this is it. This is what he wanted me to see all along, the final macabre act in his theatre of death. The Josie Girls.*

The door creaked open.

The back of the van was completely empty.

Chapter 26

The crowds dispersed like hyenas from a scavenged corpse, peeling away with little ceremony. Once the front doors were levered open too, the CSOs removed Anna from the seats and laid her on a stretcher. The man from the council threw up noisily. Jo had seen much worse before. Water slowed down any putrefaction considerably, so Anna Mull looked like she might have been killed anywhere between two hours and two days ago. There was no guile in her face now though, no hidden layers of artifice. Death did that to the features – it stripped it all away. Showed the world what you really were.

Jo couldn't get a fix on her emotions. Whatever Anna had become mixed up in, whatever frankly stupid decisions she had made, she'd paid too high a price. But at the same time, Jo had little mental space for her at all. Mull was dead, and the van that should have been the tomb of three others was empty. Malin, Rita, and Sophie had been given a reprieve. Tyndle hadn't killed them, at least not here. The divers went back down a final time – it couldn't hurt to be sure.

'Looks like we've got something,' said the lead CSO. He pointed to bruising that looped around the front of Anna's throat. 'We'll have a peek in her lungs back at the morgue, but it appears she may have been strangled. From the lack of tissue abrasions and the bruising pattern, I'd guess manually.'

Jo went to the front of the van to check the seats and glovebox, in the vain hope that she could find anything which might be an obvious lead to the other girls. There was nothing at all, but that was hardly unexpected. Something else troubled her, and she found Andy speaking with the CSOs.

'How did he get to Oxford from here?'

'I wondered the same thing,' said Carrick. 'I can't see him on public transport, somehow. He must have ditched the van because of all the heat it was getting. Perhaps he had another vehicle.'

'And no keys on him?' Andy didn't have an answer to that. 'Let's get back to Oxford. If we can run these plates through the ANPR, there has to be a match somewhere. If we can work out where he's been, there's a chance we find the others.'

'You think they're still alive, don't you?'

Jo found it hard to consider the case objectively. She wanted them to be alive, for sure, and the reasons weren't entirely selfless. 'Stein said originally he wasn't a killer by nature. I don't think he meant to kill Natalie. And I think he killed Anna because she was a liability. The Tyndle I knew was practical. Vicious, brutal, direct, a piece of shit. But I don't think he got off on killing girls.'

They walked back to their cars, and Jo plugged her dead phone into the charger as she started the engine. There were lots of missed calls. Four from Lucas. Three from Paul. One from Evergreen Lodge. Jo's throat felt tight.

Evergreen.

E.

Calm down, Jo. He's gone. He's dead.

She called the home straight away. Mum had never got on with the mobile Paul had bought her.

It rang and rang and rang.

Another call came through, from Dimitriou.

Jo switched over. 'Dimi, hi. Listen, can you get over to a care home called—'

'Evergreen Lodge? I'm here now, Jo. Your family were trying to reach you.'

'Is my mum okay?'

'Everyone's fine. But there's been a development. Jo . . . it looks like the girls might still be alive.'

★ ★ ★

She filtered through her voicemails as she sped back towards Oxford, with Carrick behind her. Evergreen had called her first, confused at a curious item Mrs Masters had received in the mail. Then her brother Paul, bemused in the first message, progressively freaked out in later ones. Lucas, the evening before, had only said he wanted to talk, but today said he was calling about something to do with her mum; that he'd spoken to Paul, and people were trying to get hold of her. Something about photos that had come to the home.

She and Carrick arrived at Evergreen Lodge. Paul was still there, along with Dimitriou. He was handling three Polaroids, wearing gloves.

Malin Sigurdsson, Rita Prakash, and Sophie Okafor. All photographed close-up in seated positions, and from the lighting, presumably in the same location. There was almost no background in shot, but it looked to be indoors, because Jo saw the corner of a window in one photo, and in another, what appeared to be metal pipework. The camera's flash highlighted the girls' tormented faces in stark detail; the whites of their terrified eyes, their faces grubby and streaked with tears. Malin looked the worst, with a gaunt face, eyes sunken and hair matted, a bruise and deep cut around her cheekbone. One of her wrists appeared to be cuffed, the skin raw and streaked with dried blood.

Paul emerged from their mother's room. 'Jo! What's going on? No one will tell me anything.'

Dimitriou looked sheepish. 'Stratton's orders.'

'Is Mum all right?' asked Jo.

'She's confused,' said Paul.

Jo went past them both and into the room. 'Hey, Mum,' she said.

'Have you brought the kids?' she asked.

'Not today,' said Jo. She kissed her mother's cheek. On the bedspread was a torn envelope, addressed to 'Jo Masters, c/o Mrs B Masters' at the home's address. First class stamp. It was postmarked in Oxford. She picked it up at the very corner.

'I'll be back in a mo.'

In the corridor, she handed it to Dimitriou. 'Get this processed.'

'Jo . . .' said Paul. 'I saw the news. They're saying someone is targeting you.'

'Not now,' said Jo.

'Talk to me, sis. Please.'

Dimitriou looked uncomfortable standing between them.

'What are you waiting for?' asked Jo.

'What are you expecting to find?' asked Dimitriou. 'Tyndle must have sent it. Sunday night or Monday morning. Before . . . well, you know?'

'Who's Tyndle?' asked Paul.

'It doesn't matter now,' said Jo. 'Stay with Mum.'

'Jo . . .'

'I promise I'll explain, but later, okay?'

She hated leaving him the dark, but there really wasn't a second to spare.

In her car, as Carrick drove, she stared at the photos. There was no indication when they were taken, but she assumed at the same time. Given Sophie's presence, that meant some time after Sunday, when she'd been snatched returning home from hockey. Malin would have been gone for nearly four and half days by that stage. No wonder she looked so bad.

Jo found herself trying to read their expressions, because it wasn't just fear and bewilderment in their eyes. What had he said to them when he took the photos? Perhaps they knew about what he was doing, and why. Maybe he had told them about *her*. She couldn't help thinking they were looking through the lens at this very moment, when the woman at the root of their torture, the only one who could perhaps release them, would bear witness. That was it. That was what lurked in their gaze.

Hope.

⋆ ⋆ ⋆

Carrick led the way back to the station and parked in front deliberately badly. The gaggle of press took the bait, and headed over in a mob. It allowed Jo to sneak into the car park unnoticed.

Heidi was the only person in the CID room.

'Jack's called a couple of times. I've filled him in. Your mum okay?'

'I think she'll have forgotten by lunchtime,' said Jo, and felt bad for saying it. None of her family deserved any of this.

'Lucas called by too – in person. He seemed concerned.'

'You don't need to worry about that.'

Heidi looked like she was about to say something else, when DCI Stratton entered with Carrick. He saw Jo, did a double-take, and glanced at Carrick with disapproval.

'Masters,' he said. 'You shouldn't be here.'

'Respectfully, sir, I think you need me.'

'It's not my call,' said Stratton. 'The Chief Constable doesn't want you involved.'

Jo sat at her desk, and fixed him with a glare she normally kept for the most recalcitrant suspects in the interview room. *And who's been keeping the Chief Constable abreast of the situation? Santa Claus?* 'Well, the Chief Constable can come here and move me then. Because until she does, I'm going to do my job.'

Stratton's mouth was still flapping when Nina Creasey, the detective from Bath, came in. 'We've got partial data from Tyndle's phone,' she said. 'Still waiting on the location services, but it looks like he only ever received calls from one number, which was unrecorded. He never dialled out – the phone has no credit.'

'Anna Mull?' said Stratton.

'We can't tell,' said Creasey. 'We've got the times of the incoming calls, but that's it. I've saved the call log to the case file.'

Jo brought it up on screen to crosscheck with Anna's phone.

There were several calls over the last few days, but the one that stood out had been made on Monday at 11.30 am and lasted just over a minute. Prior to that there were two or three calls on each of the preceding days, with five late on Saturday night, and two in the day before Malin disappeared. Before that, nothing at all. And none corresponded to Anna Mull's call log.

'The phone was only registered last Saturday,' said Creasey.

'So if it's not Mull he's talking to, who is it?' said Stratton.

Jo felt a heat over the back of her neck as she recalled her conversation with Vincent Stein in Tyndle's bedroom. 'Perhaps the profiler was right.'

'Right about what?' said Stratton.

'What if Tyndle wasn't the manipulator at all? What if he was being used, just like Anna?'

'We all need to slow down,' said Stratton. 'We've got motive, we've got the means – the van. We've got opportunity – a loner with no job or connections.'

'But he didn't match Dr Stein's profile,' said Jo. 'He's not in a position of power. He's not a narcissist. Hell, I don't even think he's a psychopath. And now we've got this phone record. He was talking to *someone*, right? The downstairs neighbours said he had a male visitor. We need a list of all his known contacts. Anyone he was inside with. This took serious planning.'

'Makes sense,' said Carrick. 'He came to Oxford with someone else, in a different vehicle. What if this third individual was waiting near St Edmund Hall somewhere? Maybe they heard the sirens coming and fled.'

'This is wild speculation,' said Stratton, but he was beginning to sound desperate. 'I saw Tyndle's choice of wall art. He *hated* you, Jo.'

'No doubt about that,' she replied, 'but that doesn't mean he's behind all this.'

'It makes him the perfect tool,' said Carrick. 'A man who will do almost anything.'

Something else Stratton had said lodged in Jo's mind. 'Heidi, what was Tyndle's exact release date?'

She tapped away. At the same time, Jo brought up the images taken from the Thatcham house of Tyndle's pictures.

'Looks like September 2nd,' said Heidi.

Jo zoomed into the right side, then again onto a particular photo, the one at the Bright Futures clinic. Only Heidi even knew about her egg-freezing treatments, and she felt no need to share those details now. It wasn't the point, anyway. 'That one was taken in Bath,' she said.

'He must have followed you there,' said Stratton.

'It was also taken in the middle of August,' she said.

Stratton breathed a heavy sigh. 'Are you sure, detective?'

They'd been monitoring her ovulation cycles via thrice-daily temperature readings. She knew exactly the date. In fact, she'd met Constable Rhani Aziz for lunch immediately afterwards, a colleague from the station in Bath. Rhani been really cut up still about Ben, and kept bursting into tears.

'Perfectly. I was on my way to see a friend. Tyndle couldn't have taken that photograph.'

Phil Stratton was silenced at last. Jo stared at the photo. She'd been happy that day that she was finally getting on with her life. It had felt like a fresh start, the beginning of a new story.

Now it looked like it was just the start of someone else's.

Chapter 27

Jo kept expecting Stratton to put his foot down and kick her out. She suspected Andy had something to do with her continued presence – he was one of the few people Stratton could be guaranteed to listen to. Or it might simply be that the DCI was as busy floundering as the rest of them.

The list of Tyndle's connections began to emerge slowly, in two broad groups. Those from his life with a face, and those from afterwards. The prison acquaintances were the hardest to identify. He'd attached himself to a neo-Nazi gang in the early years of his sentence, but the various welfare assessments indicated he'd later drifted apart from their group. He'd taken a course in automotive repair, which he'd passed with good marks. Of his pre-incarceration contacts, several were dead or inside currently. One that stood out was his former tenant, Tommy Somers, believed to have fled abroad while on bail for armed robbery, and also linked with an attempt on the life of an Essex businessman. His file was still open, a warrant out for his arrest. When Heidi spoke to the investigating officer in charge of his case, he couldn't help at all. Somers was by all accounts off the grid, probably gorging on rubbery paella, with second stage skin cancer somewhere in the south of Spain.

Heidi stretched her back after she got off the phone to Somers' ex-wife.

'She said she hadn't seen or heard from the "stupid prick" for two years. He didn't even send his kid a birthday card.'

'You should go home,' Jo said. 'You look like shit.'

'Thanks.'

'I'm serious,' said Jo.

'Thanks again.'

'About leaving, I mean. I bet you've been in since seven.'

'Five, actually.'

'You're eight and a half months pregnant. We can cope here. Phil's hardly going to say anything.'

Heidi rolled back her chair and levered herself up. 'All right. But if you need me, I'm on the phone.'

'Go away before I squeeze you through the door myself.'

'Once again, thanks.' Heidi began to put on her coat. 'Er . . . should you be here?'

Jo thought at first she was speaking to her, but a shadow moved past her desk. It was Jack Pryce, walking stiffly and wearing a tracksuit. His hair was a mess, he hadn't shaved, and one of his hands was bandaged in a sling. 'Couldn't stay away,' he muttered.

'Jack? What the fuck? Did you drive here?'

'Oh, this?' he said, wiggling the sling. 'It's just for decoration. Got to keep it elevated as much as possible apparently.'

He sat awkwardly. 'What have we got then? Anything from the phone?'

'It's what we haven't got that's interesting – no direct connection between Anna Mull and Frank Tyndle.' She told him the latest theory about a third suspect.

'The plot thickens, huh? Want me to check the ANPRs again, now you've got a plate?'

'You need to go *home*,' said Heidi. 'If you die at your desk, it's going to look *really* bad.'

'Dimi is looking at the road cameras,' said Jo.

Stratton returned, clocked Pryce, and came over. 'I was going to come to the hospital.'

'Saved you the trip,' said Pryce.

'You can't be here, Jack,' he said.

'I keep telling everyone, I'm fine. Might not be chasing down suspects any time soon, but—'

'It's not that,' said Stratton, with a fleeting expression of concern. 'Do you want to come into my office a moment?'

Pryce's face hardened. 'Come on, boss. Please. You need me here.'

'I'm sorry, Jack. It's out of my hands. Standard procedure in the case of a death by officer.'

'It was self-defence!' said Pryce. He held up his bandaged hands. 'Scars to prove it.'

'That's immaterial, and you know it,' said Stratton. 'It's a mandatory suspension, without prejudice.' He came over and laid a hand on Jack's good arm. 'I promise, we'll get it processed asap. You'll be back in a few days. But we really can't afford any more procedural fuck-ups.' He glanced at Jo. 'Not after all the others.'

Pryce looked to Jo too, as if she could help. She didn't know what to say, but her heart went out to him.

'I'm sorry, Jack,' said Stratton. 'I really am.'

* * *

More calls from Lucas. Jo ignored them and deleted the messages without listening to them.

Creasey managed to get the locations of the Tyndle's calls. His phone was mostly pinging at the address in Thatcham, or in that vicinity. Once at the quarry. Once at a service station just off the A34, the main road between Oxford and Newbury. And twice in Oxford itself, the day before Malin Sigurdsson's disappearance. They dispatched a team and a dog unit to the service station, just in case there was any trace of the girls. It was just as likely he'd stopped to make a call or to get petrol though. Dimitriou, back from Evergreen too, began to cross-check the information and times into the ANPR network.

'The building in the Malin polaroid looks industrial to me,' said Carrick.

'Hardly narrows it down,' said Carter. They were gathered around the board, on which the three images had been blown-up and attached.

A text came through, and Jo peered at her phone. Lucas again, but this one was different.

Jo, I know you don't want to talk right now, but there's a journalist pestering me. There's a video online. Of what happened at the house. I'm sending a link.

Jo looked up – Carter was staring at her suspiciously.

The link came through a few seconds later in another text. Her heartbeat felt laboured in her chest. 'Excuse me a second.'

She took herself off to the corridor, checked she was alone, then clicked through to the YouTube link. The video window was entitled 'Police arrest "crazy" woman in Oxford street.'

What the fuck . . .

The clip loaded. A woman – her – stood right up against Carly Granger's front door, shouting, 'I'm here to see Lucas. Open this door. Now!'

She lowered the volume and watched, gripped and horrified at once, as she scrambled over the fence.

The video looked like it had been taken from across the street.

The woman with the pushchair . . .

She reappeared, through the gate, at speed, then Carly's daughter ran from the front door in her slippers, up the drive and into the road, where she threw herself into the arms of Lucas. She looked terrified. It looked like Jo was chasing her. Thankfully the audio didn't pick up any of the conversation that followed, but from the body language the argument between her and Lucas was clear. And then Jo left, clearly in a fury, screeching from the kerb only to be cut off by the police car driven by Olly Pinker.

Jo willed the clip to end, but she could see from the time-bar at the bottom that it ran for another ten minutes. They'd captured every second of the mortifying episode. She hit pause, took a deep breath, and bit her lip to stop herself crying again. She needed to get the woman's number, get the video taken down, but she had no idea how to do that. Heidi would know, but she'd left. Dimitriou was concentrating on his computer.

Looking at the screen once more, she saw the video had only had seventeen views. There was still a chance to keep it contained.

She refreshed. 30 views.

She returned to her desk, trying to lie low. As the minutes wore on, and the team worked in silence, Jo sank deeper into the private nightmare, seated at her desk. Every time she checked, the number of views grew. One hundred. Four hundred. In less than half an hour, it had topped a thousand. The comments began to flow.

AWKWARD!!!!

Where is this?

What did they arrest her for?

And then, inevitably:

I think that's the policewoman who solved a missing child case. Masters or something.

The next commenter had copied a link to the *Oxford Times* profile Thames Valley had insisted she do in July.

Yep – it's definitely her!

Jo's desk-phone rang and she picked it up.

'Detective Masters?'

'Hi, we spoke earlier. Tim Lester.'

'No comment,' said Jo. And put the phone down.

A few seconds later, it rang again. She let it. *How had he got her personal number?*

'You going to answer that?' said Dimitriou.

Jo snatched it up.

'Detective, I know you don't want to talk. There's a video that's surfaced online . . .'

'I've seen it. It relates to my private life, and has nothing to do with the current case.'

Dimitriou looked over. Carter too.

'I suspected that was the case,' said the journalist. 'But you see why I'm calling. People might jump to the wrong conclusion.'

'People?'

'I'm not your enemy here,' said Lester.

'You're sure as hell not my friend,' said Jo.

'Perhaps you could help us put the record straight. The public are worried about the missing girls.'

'As am I,' said Jo. 'And I'm wasting time talking to you when I could be looking for them. I'm sorry, I can't help you.'

She hung up once more.

Almost at once, her mobile rang. It was Heidi.

'Jo, something's been shared to the Thames Valley Twitter feed. I think you need to see it.'

That was it, then. *So much for containment.*

* * *

Just when she thought it couldn't get any worse, Stratton arrived back with the Chief Constable in tow. They both decamped to his office, and the inevitable summons came shortly after.

'Is this about the video, sir?' she said pre-emptively.

'This is about a lot more than the video,' said the Chief Constable. 'Though it looks bad. We're fielding press enquiries left and right. Whether you like it or not, these disappearances, these deaths, they're becoming synonymous with your name.'

'The Josie Girls,' Stratton added helpfully. He reminded her of the little kid hiding behind the school bully, though in fact the Chief Constable was a diminutive woman in her mid-fifties with the demeanour of a small, but particularly vicious, cat.

'So surely I'm the best person to look into it,' said Jo.

'Maybe you should have thought of that before you decided to partake in . . . in whatever soap opera we just watched,' said the Chief Constable. Jo didn't have much to say to that. 'You're toxic, Detective Masters.'

'At least let me help,' she said.

The Chief Constable looked to Stratton.

'We think you'd be better elsewhere,' he said.

Jo stood her ground. 'You're making a mistake.'

The Chief Constable walked past her and opened the door. 'Detective Masters, do we need to have you escorted from the building?'

* * *

She drove away from the station, past a clutch of reporters, and headed out of town before she realised she was blindly following the route to Lucas's place. She took a right at the next T-junction.

'Fuck! Fuck! Fuck!' She hammered the steering wheel with every exclamation, hard enough to make her regret it.

There was no way back now. She wouldn't even be allowed to cross the threshold at St Aldates. Out of the loop, there was nothing she could do or say to help those three scared young women. He – whoever *he* was – had won. She wondered whether, if she called Rob Bridges, her old DCI, he might be able to talk to Stratton, convince him to let her back . . .

She took out her phone, but didn't dial. Rob might talk Stratton round, but not the Chief Constable. She drove on, aimlessly. Was it just her imagination, or were more people looking at their phones than normal? It seemed like every other person on the streets was inspecting their screen. She told herself they couldn't *all* be watching her humiliation unfolding, and resisted checking the number of views the video had reached now. If it had entered the Twittersphere, there would be no stopping it. Ex-colleagues, friends, everyone connected to the case . . . She felt like a fish in an aquarium, the whole world looking in. *Christ*, her niece Emma would surely have seen it by now too. Would she show her mum and dad?

She parked up a couple of streets over from Canterbury Road, proceeding on foot to The Three Crowns. Walking through the door, she felt the tiniest salve of relief. Guaranteed, in here, no one had a bloody clue who she was apart from Harry. Ferman wasn't there, but a few of the other regulars were in, and she very much doubted any of them had a Twitter handle. She ordered a double vodka at the bar, paid, and drank it before Connie had even brought her change.

'Tough day?' said the barmaid.

'Tough week,' said Jo. 'Can I have another please?'

The TV was showing a highlight reel of speedcross crashes, bikers losing control and slewing into the barriers or one another. It seemed an apt metaphor for her recent career trajectory. She watched anyway, and tried to take the second drink more slowly.

Her phone rang. Lucas. She switched it to silent. Fuck them all.

She was on her third, maybe fourth drink, when Ferman shambled in.

'Hello, Ms Masters,' he said. 'This is becoming a habit. Usual, Connie, when you've got a moment.'

Jo kissed his cheek, not their normal greeting. He frowned. 'You all right?'

'Fucking dandy, Harry.'

'How many have you had?'

'Not enough,' said Jo. 'Connie, I'll get these.'

* * *

She didn't go into details. Something told her the world of YouTube upvotes and social media shares would go over Ferman's head. She filled him in on the other bits of the case – Tyndle's van, Anna Mull, the photo that Tyndle couldn't have taken – but she was aware as she related it all that she might not be making complete sense, because it still didn't make complete sense to her. Harry drank at his usual pace, rum and chaser, steady, and they fell into sync. Her phone rang every few minutes. Paul, Lucas, Jack Pryce. She thought about answering the latter, but she knew she'd probably be slurring by now. She finished her latest drink while Ferman still had three quarters of a pint.

'You want another?'

'You sure you're not done?'

'You're not my bloody dad, Harry.'

He took a long pull. 'Same again then, if you're buying.'

A couple of people came and went. Jo put some Sam Cooke

on the juke box. 'A Change Is Gonna Come'. The TV started showing European football.

'I need a piss,' she said.

Her feet were unsteady, but she made it to the loos in pretty much a straight line. Did her business. In the mirror she thought she actually looked okay.

As she got back to the table, she saw Pryce had called again.

'You're in demand,' said Ferman.

She went to the bar. 'Another vodka, Connie.'

'Sorry, love. Last orders have been and gone.'

Jo blinked up at the clock. It was twenty past eleven. *How did that happen?*

'Go on. No one's watching. I'm a copper, you know?'

Connie looked over towards Ferman, who shuffled across. 'We'll call you a taxi,' he said.

Jo leant on the bar. 'I'm parked around the corner.'

He looked at her and shook his head. 'Let's not make today any worse, eh?'

'I'll walk,' she said.

'Your place is four miles away,' he said. 'From what you've been saying, Lucas is off the cards.'

'Did I tell you about that shit?'

'Once or twice,' said Connie. 'You told the whole pub.'

Jo groaned. 'I think I need to lie down.'

On the bar, her phone rang again. Pryce. She wasn't sure what exactly made her answer this time. 'Hey, Jack.'

'I spoke to Carrick. He told me what happened. Are you okay?'

'Can I crash at yours?' she asked. A split-second after she'd made the request, the other, more sensible Josephine Masters, sat up somewhere in the back of her mind, suddenly taking notice, and said, *Are you really sure about this?* 'I think there might be journalists at my place.'

'What about Lucas?' said Pryce.

'Look, if it's a problem, I can get a hotel.'

'No, no – it's fine. Do you even know where I live?'

'Text me your address. I'll be there in a bit.'

* * *

Pryce lived right in the town centre, not far from the train station, in a modern block of flats with a gated entrance. Jo wound down the window of the taxi all the way to try to sober up, and by the time she arrived, she thought it might have worked a little. Enough, anyway, for Josephine to again protest that this might all be a bad idea.

She rang the bell for number 34, and he buzzed her in. Having briefly considered the stairs, she took the lift instead. The place felt like a hotel – identical doors lining a long corridor. It swayed a little as she walked.

His flat was pristine, and she felt suddenly a pang of the old inferiority complex that had plagued her as a girl, a mental shortcut to a teenage Josie who felt she was never good enough. How had he got his existence into this much order?

The books on his up-lit shelves were neatly arranged, the subtle tones of the room and the furnishings combined perfectly. The mugs hanging on the pegs over the kitchen counters all matched, hanging at exactly the same angles. He walked across and took one now.

'You want a coffee?'

He was dressed in the same tracksuit bottoms as earlier, but he'd stripped the hooded top and wore only a vest. It was strange seeing his naked arms, and the hint of his chest. She'd always thought he carried himself with a slightly odd gait, stiff and reticent, but he had the body of an athlete, lithe and in control of his environment.

'You got anything stronger?'

He opened a cupboard. 'Whisky?'

In the back of her mind, the last vestiges of sensible Jo tried to offer wise counsel, but she was ignored. 'I wouldn't say no.'

He poured a tumbler for each of them, adding ice from a dispenser in the front of his fridge. He pushed one across to her with his bandaged hand, then raised a toast. 'To DCI Stratton contracting a terminal illness?'

'I'll drink to that,' she replied, laughing.

'The futon pulls out,' he said.

'I really appreciate it.'

'No worries.' He sipped. 'Things not good with Lucas?'

'Don't pretend you haven't seen the video. My last shred of dignity can't take it.'

'It looked painful,' he said. 'I'll go and grab some bedding.'

He set his glass down then padded over to what she guessed was his bedroom.

She walked across the room. Above the TV was a large triptych of photos showing rock faces and a climber perched in precarious positions, bare-chested, the cords of his muscles taut and perfectly balanced, his long hair hanging down. She realised, as she stepped nearer, that it was Pryce.

'Holy shit!' she said. 'You some sort of daredevil?'

'Used to be,' he said, coming back in with a pile of sheets and blankets that he deposited on the futon. 'That was Yosemite. I did a semester at UCLA. There's quite a climbing scene there. You must think I love myself.'

'If I could do that, I'd put up the evidence too,' she said. She gestured at the room. 'Nice place by the way.'

'Thanks.' He started to make the bed.

'Leave that. I'll sort it.'

He nodded. 'There's a spare toothbrush in the bathroom cabinet. Help yourself to anything you need.'

'I might have a shower if that's okay? Been in these clothes since yesterday.'

'You want a T-shirt or something?'

'If you've got one.'

'Sure – I'll leave one out. Goodnight.' He left his whisky glass on the counter, and retreated into his bedroom.

Jo went into the bathroom. It was just as pristine as the rest of the flat. Towels neatly stacked. Even the few items in the bathroom cabinet sat at right angles. She switched on the shower and stripped as steam filled the room and misted the mirror. She closed her eyes as she washed, turning the heat up as high as she could bear in an effort to drive all the other thoughts from her head. She almost succeeded, but she couldn't help wondering what might be happening in the CID room that very moment, at the Randolph Hotel, in Sophie Okafor's house, at the guest rooms in Somerville College. So many people relying on her, and she couldn't help them at all.

She finished washing and towelled herself dry, then brushed her teeth. She realised she'd made a rookie error – what were the chances Pryce had a hairdryer, even if he once had long hair? She checked the cabinets, with no luck.

As she left the bathroom, towel wrapped around her, the cooler air of the living room brought the skin of her arms up in goose pimples. Under Pryce's bedroom door, a faint light still glowed. She padded over and knocked gently. 'Jack, sorry, have you got a hairdryer?'

'Yeah, sure. Just a sec.'

She heard a bit of clattering, then the door opened, and he stood there in just his jogging bottoms, a bandage taped around his midriff, holding the hairdryer, the contours of his lean physique caught in light and shadow. 'Did you find the T-shirt I left out?'

She'd made so many mistakes already, that one more hardly seemed to matter. And really, both stupid drunken Jo and Catholic-school Josephine had been skirting around the issue since the moment she'd answered his call in The Three Crowns. She reached up and slid a hand around the back of his neck, tipping up her mouth to meet his. For a moment, she felt him resist. His eyes met hers, a hint of confusion. She let her hand drop. 'You're my boss,' he said.

'Not for much longer, I expect,' she said. 'Listen, sorry. I misunder—'

His lips came down quickly onto hers, and the hairdryer dropped to the carpet as both his hands reached around her, pressing her body into his. They stumbled backwards, and he landed on the bed, wincing.

'Are you all right?' she said.

He nodded, laughing. 'Just be gentle with me. Stitches, remember.'

Lucas's face came briefly to her thoughts, then vanished. She reached under her arm to loosen her towel. 'I'm not making any promises.'

Chapter 28

WEDNESDAY

She woke to a pounding head, and the faint tang of peatiness on her tongue . . . had she drunk whisky? She hated whisky. She rolled over, momentarily confused at her surroundings. Then it all came back, and with it, a terrible, yawning feeling of regret. She raised her head off the pillow, but Pryce wasn't in bed beside her.

Well, that was fucking stupid, Jo . . .

Had they even used protection?

She looked around for something to wear, and saw a dressing gown hanging on the back of his door. Hurrying over, she put it on. Through the fog, her mind tried to steer a critical path. What was the quickest way she could get out, with the least embarrassment and awkwardness? Her clothes would still be in the bathroom.

She opened the bedroom door and smelled rich coffee. Pryce was wearing shorts, over in the kitchen. He seemed fresh as a daisy.

'Hey,' he said, sheepishly.

'Morning,' she replied.

'You want breakfast?'

The very thought threatened to turn her stomach. 'Just fluids,' she said. She pointed to the bathroom. 'I'm going to . . .'

'Go for it. You know your way around.'

Don't I just? Another wave of shame. She'd practically forced herself on him.

She was relieved to get through the door. She found her clothes, neatly stacked, even – cringingly – her underwear. Forget the coffee. How could she even look him in the eye? She threw cold water over her face, tied back her hair, and dressed. Her slightly crumpled work clothes still carried the geriatric scents of The Three Crowns. In the mirror, she could've been the poster for a movie called *Walk of Shame*.

'You really are old enough to know better,' she told the face looking back at her.

She had a couple of items of make-up in her bag, and did her best with them. Her phone was low on charge again. There was a message from Harry, just before 1 am: *Did you get home all right?*

She texted back quickly, *Yes. Thx 4 chat x*, before considering he probably wouldn't approve of the shorthand.

Embarrassment stole over her again. What must he have thought, watching her demolish most of a bottle of vodka? She'd even said she could *drive*. The private mortification deepened at the memory. Harry's nineteen-year-old daughter had been killed by a drunk driver. What a fucking dreadful thing to say. How could she? She sent another message.

I'm really sorry. I was way out of line.

Jo emerged from the bathroom, and Pryce walked over with a mug.

'Maybe I should just go,' she said.

'Don't be silly.' He held the cup towards her. 'We can be grown-ups.'

She took it, and sipped. It was strong, working its magic almost instantly. Another two and she might feel half-human.

A pity coffee can't turn back time.

'You feel all right?' she asked.

'Sure,' he said. 'I only had one drink.'

As soon as he'd said it, she wished he hadn't. The implication hovered between them. *She* had an excuse for what had happened. She could write it off as the sort of dumb thing people did when they were smashed off their faces. If he was sober, that meant something else.

'It shouldn't have happened, Jack.' He turned away. 'This case . . .' she said, feeling the need to explain. 'It's messed me up. I like you, you're a great cop, and you've had my back from the start . . .'

'Don't worry,' he said. 'It's okay.'

'It's not,' she said. 'I just needed someone, and I took advantage of my position.'

'I said, it's *okay*. Let's forget it happened.'

Jo could see he was protesting too much, but what was the point of pushing it any further? She told herself that things might be difficult for a while, but these sorts of fuck-ups happened all the time between colleagues. If they *were* still colleagues. Stratton and the Chief Constable might indeed have other plans for her.

She drank the coffee and he poured her another from a filter machine. 'Sure you won't eat?'

'No, thanks. The coffee's doing wonders.' He took out a pan and placed it on the induction hob. 'You heard anything from the station?' she asked.

He shook his head. 'I can't help thinking they're chasing shadows.'

'How do you mean?'

'This third suspect.' He'd missed most of the conversation the day before, she realised.

'The phone records suggest there's someone else.'

'Or just another phone,' said Pryce. 'Maybe Anna had two.'

He seemed slightly annoyed with her, as if he'd suddenly had enough of the case and the evolving theories. Maybe things weren't going to be okay between them after all, but she could hardly blame him for lingering resentment. 'Why would she have two?'

He shrugged, his face still wearing the same exasperated expression. 'Look, I get that it would be great if there was another person involved, because it might mean the other girls are alive somewhere. But the fact is Tyndle killed Anna Mull . . .'

'We don't really know that,' said Jo. 'It might have been someone else.'

'She was in his van. The same van which hit Natalie.'

He was right on that point. *Still* . . . 'How do you explain the photo then? One of his pictures was taken before Tyndle was released.'

'Maybe he just had contacts on the outside. This whole thing took serious planning. He might have paid someone to tail you, establish your movements. You never saw him. Could be because it wasn't him at all, but someone more inconspicuous. I mean, come on, look at his face. It's enough to send kids screaming.'

Jo paused with her coffee. He'd said something similar back in the hospital bed about Tyndle's appearance. It had bothered her then, but now she knew why.

'Jack . . . when did you see his face?'

He cracked an egg into the pan. 'Sorry?'

'Back at St Edmund Hall, when you encountered Tyndle, he was still wearing his balaclava. When did you see his face?'

He dropped in a second egg.

'The photos from the crime scene,' he said. 'You sure you don't want some omelette? Bit of paprika? I swear by it for a bad stomach.'

Jo put down her mug. 'I'm fine. Sorry to push, but you said it in the hospital too. That was before you could've accessed the crime scene photos.'

Pryce put his arms above his head, one hand clutching a wooden spoon. 'Steady on, detective. Heidi called me, when I came out of theatre. She told me.'

Heidi hadn't seen his face either, but Jo recalled Carrick had filled her in on the grim details. It was plausible, then.

'Remind me never to get stuck on the wrong side of an interview with you!' said Pryce nervously.

He stirred the pan.

'Go on then, I will have some,' said Jo. 'Don't be offended if I can't keep it down.'

* * *

As she ate, Pryce went to take a shower. Perhaps she was obsessing, but she couldn't let it go. She searched her hungover mind for what exactly he had said in his hospital bed. She was pretty sure . . . no, certain – that his exact words were 'With a face like that . . .'

Like *that*.

Is that the word he'd have used, if Heidi had told him, over the phone, about Tyndle's disfigurement? It sounded a lot like he was picturing it, in his mind's eye. In his *memory*.

Or maybe she was reading too much into it. Because there really seemed no way Pryce could ever have known about Tyndle before, even if he'd searched through her case files. It wasn't an incident she liked to shout about and her name hadn't been connected with Tyndle afterwards, during the enquiry.

The shower was still running. There was another way to check his story. She called Heidi.

It was Dimitriou who picked up. 'Oh, hi, Jo,' he said. 'I heard about yesterday. It sucks.'

'Is Heidi there?'

'Just nipped out for her billionth bathroom visit of the morning.'

'You try being thirty-eight weeks pregnant. It's not pleasant.'

'A year off sounds all right though.' He chuckled, then lowered his voice. 'Listen, Jo, I wanted to talk to you about something. It's a bit sensitive.'

'I'm listening.'

'Well, I've been going over the ANPRs. The good news – we've got Tyndle's van using the A34 between Thatcham and Oxford repeatedly. But we've also pinged on the A4074 that runs past the road to Little Baldon.'

'That's good too.'

'Yes, but here's the thing. The cameras picked it up on the night our witness spotted the van parked up by the bridge,' said Dimitriou. 'During the window you specifically searched. I went back in the files, and it looks like Jack somehow missed it when he did his search. You went out and interviewed five drivers.' He paused, and Jo imagined him looking around the CID room surreptitiously. 'But there were six vans.'

Jo glanced towards the bathroom door. The shower had stopped.

'Are you sure?' she said.

'Completely. I didn't want to go to Carrick or Stratton yet, but it made me think. We'd have tagged the van as suspicious a lot earlier, and it passed loads more cameras after that. We'd have picked him up sooner, wouldn't we?'

Jo's throat was dry, and she gulped her coffee. 'Yes, we would. Can you identify the driver?'

'Light's not good enough and he's wearing a hoodie,' said Dimitriou. 'Obviously wanted to stay hidden. Okay if I leave it with you? Pryce is a great guy, despite me always taking the piss. I'm sure it was just an oversight, but in the scheme of things, it's a real fuck-up.'

The bathroom door opened and Jack came out with a towel around his waist. The stitched up wound across his abdomen looked angry and sore.

'All right, Dimi,' said Jo. 'Thanks.'

She hung up.

'Everything all right?' asked Pryce.

I don't think it is. Not at all. Her stomach was recoiling, and she thought she might be sick.

'Uh-huh. I was checking in on the investigation. All dead-ends so far. They'll be bringing us back in no time.'

Pryce smiled. 'Make 'em beg, I say.'

He went into the bedroom.

Jo stood up – her heart felt like a panicking bird in her chest. It made no sense at all. None.

At the window, she turned the blinds that opened into the courtyard below. Pryce's dark grey Honda Civic was parked near the gate. Dimitriou had even said it . . .

Come to think of it, professor. You own a dark car . . .

She told herself to slow down, but her mind had other ideas, throwing Stein's words back at her.

Highly organised.

You bet.

Probably lives in Oxford.

Check.

Thrill-seeker.

The pictures of him climbing stared back at her from the wall.

One thing stopped her brain going into freefall panic. She

didn't *know* Jack Pryce. Never had, until he transferred. She'd met him for the first time less than six months ago. He was a fucking police officer. A good one. The son of another. There was no reason on God's green earth why Jack Pryce should be involved.

She'd *slept* with him.

I'd say he's been watching it all unfold as well, from closer than you think.

'Penny for your thoughts?'

She spun around to find him standing a couple of feet away, fully dressed and smiling. He was wearing a hoodie.

'I've got to go,' she said, standing up quickly enough to tip over her chair. She caught it.

'I can give you a lift if you want. Your car's back at the pub, right?'

'Oh . . . it's okay, I'll take a cab.'

'Well, stay here. I'll call one.'

'I can do it outside.'

He was blocking her way. 'It's freezing out there, Josie.'

The way he spoke her name chilled her.

She side-stepped, banging onto the table and sloshing coffee over the rim of her cup. She grabbed her bag.

'What's wrong?' said Pryce. He was actually smiling.

'I just need some fresh air.'

She hurried to the door, which was chained. Her hand was shaking as she unhooked it. She heard him crossing the floor towards her. She turned the handle.

It was locked.

She twisted around. 'Where's the key, Jack?'

'Will you tell me what's wrong?' he asked. 'You're scaring me. Did I do something?'

He spread his hands, and every long finger made her think of the bruises on Anna Mull's neck.

'Just let me out,' she said. 'And stay away from me!'

'Okay, chill out,' he said. He lifted his palms towards her, and backed off.

She watched him walk over to the kitchen, and open the top drawer. He pulled out a bunch of keys and threw them across the room. They skidded over the floorboards and fetched up against the bottom of the bookshelf. With her eyes still on Pryce, Jo stepped forwards, scooped them up, and turned back to the door. If she'd got all this wrong, then she'd answer for her behaviour later. Right now, she needed to get out.

She pushed the first key in, but it didn't turn.

'You know, I didn't force you last night,' said Pryce. 'You wanted me.'

Jo tried the second key. It didn't fit at all. She tried the first again.

'These are the wrong fucking keys, Jack,' she said.

His hand went around her middle, and the other came up over her face, holding some sort of material against her nose and mouth. He dragged her backwards, trailing her scrabbling feet, until he fell into the sofa. With her legs extended in front, he held most of her weight. She reached for his hand, trying to prise his fingers from her mouth.

'Easy does it,' he said. 'Easy . . .'

Whatever chemical he'd doused the cloth with was working. She couldn't breathe at all and with each second the room became more muted and her limbs became heavier. It felt like she was falling into a hole.

With a final push, she raked her nails into his face, towards his eyes. She felt his head turn away but she found his socket and drove her finger into the soft tissue as far as she could, hooking the top of his nose. Pryce screamed and flung her off him. She rolled over the coffee table and her foot smashed into the front of the TV. Pryce was bent over with his hand over his face.

Jo stood up, but her left leg was completely paralysed, and she had to drag herself towards the bathroom door. Pryce came after her, eye leaking blood, but she got in first and slammed the door behind her, crushing his bandaged hand as it reached through. He howled in pain and withdrew it. Jo locked the door.

'Let me in, Josie,' he said.

He threw himself against the other side, but the lock held. Jo pressed her back into the door. 'Fuck you!' she shouted.

The door shook under another impact. Jo didn't have her phone. She scanned the room, searching for a weapon. A set of electronic scales. A shower curtain pole. A chair. In the mirror, she looked petrified.

There was silence on the other side of the door, and she waited, struggling to find a regular rhythm to her breaths. Her head was slowly clearing, feeling returning to her leg. She'd no idea what he'd soaked the cloth in. *Chloroform?* Did people even do that outside of spy films?

The seconds passed.

But still she waited, pinned by fear. She pressed her ear to the door, listening for any sound, for at least two minutes. She was almost sure he'd gone.

Either he'd given up, or he'd gone to get something to break down the door. *Was he waiting outside?* She thought about screaming, but her voice wouldn't come. Even now her reasonable self was clinging to the idea that this wasn't really happening. Couldn't be. Detective Jack Pryce couldn't be a killer. Not after last night.

Her insides revolted at the thought, and she rushed towards the toilet as her diaphragm went into spasm. She made it just in time, dropping to her knees and spewing a noxious flood of vomit. It wasn't just the booze, she was sure. It was wanting to somehow eject everything that had happened the night before. A second evacuation followed, and she gripped the seat as her body took over, then rolled back so she was sitting against the edge of the bathtub. She wiped her mouth. Her forehead was clammy.

I can't stay here. I've got to get a message to the others.

She picked up the bathroom scales, went to the mirror, and brought the corner down hard on to the glass. The pane splintered. Another whack scattered several jagged pieces into the sink. She selected one about nine inches long, wrapped one end in a flannel, and brandished it as she returned to the door. Silently, she slid the bolt open and put her hand on the handle, listening again and hearing nothing from the room on the other side.

Now or never . . .

She flung the door open. Pryce wasn't there. Edging out, she scanned the living area and the mess their brief fight had caused. The coffee pot was still on in the kitchen. She checked the bedroom too, and the sight of the crumpled sheets almost made her throw up again. Last of all she went to her bag for her phone, but it had gone.

He took it.

She looked around for a landline, but couldn't see one. At the window, she saw that his car was no longer parked below. There was a man in a fluorescent tabard, crouching and checking what might have been a fuse junction. She opened the window.

'Hey! You!' she called down.

He stood, looked round, then up. 'Me?'

Jo held out her badge. 'I'm a police officer. Don't go anywhere. I need to use your phone!'

Chapter 29

A police car arrived in four minutes, and she met it at the gates. In ten minutes she was back at St Aldates.

Stratton gave her the floor in the briefing room, and the eyes of all the bewildered detectives and uniforms were on her as she laid out the case against Pryce, starting with the ANPR anomaly first, then the evidence for his prior connection with Tyndle. She didn't go into the profiling similarities. 'And when I confronted him, he attacked me, then fled the scene.'

Everyone was speechless, and she wondered if she hadn't been convincing.

'Any questions?' said Stratton.

'Yeah, what were you doing at his accommodation?' asked Carter. 'Are you two . . . you know . . .?'

'No,' said Jo. 'I misplaced my house keys last night and needed a place to stay.' Carter looked unconvinced. She wondered if they could still smell the booze on her.

Stratton moved alongside Jo. 'We have a team turning his place upside down now,' he said. 'There's a nationwide bulletin issued for his car. Our priority is to find him first, then press him for the location of the other girls. We'll be putting out a national appeal for information too. He can't get far.'

'Do we know why he's doing this?' asked Dimitriou. For once, he didn't have a quip ready.

'Not at the moment,' said Jo. 'As far as I'm aware, I met Pryce for the first time the same day you did. We've had a good working relationship until now.'

'Move it, all of you,' said Carrick.

The team dispersed, and Stratton caught Jo by the elbow. 'Masters, I think you should go to the hospital – get checked out.'

'No chance. I'm fine.'

'With all due respect, you don't look it. There may be side effects to whatever he incapacitated you with.'

'I think I know what it was already,' said Jo. 'I need to speak with Vera Coyne.'

* * *

She opened the files on Natalie Palmer. Cropper and his team had drawn a sketch of the scene, including the bridge, the skid marks and the blood spatter on the road. From the measurements, it looked like the blood spread over a distance of some thirty-six feet. It had struck her as odd before, because for Natalie to have travelled that far suggested a significant impact not borne out by her injuries. The skid mark itself was over seventy feet long, and didn't start until about twenty feet beyond the bridge. She'd thought that meant he'd put the brakes on after the impact, but now she had another thought entirely.

She called the pathologist.

'What can I do for you, detective?' asked Coyne.

She explained. 'I've been looking at the files on the Natalie Palmer hit and run, and wanted to run a couple of things by you.'

'Please do.'

'The auto forensics team have said that the vehicle skid marks indicate braking from a speed of approximately forty to fifty miles per hour. Does that speed tally with the injuries Natalie sustained?'

'Almost certainly not,' said Coyne, 'but we don't know at what stage of braking the collision happened. The vehicle could have been travelling much slower at the moment of impact.'

'Here's the thing, though,' said Jo. 'I don't think the blood spatter indicates that.' She looked at the diagram as she spoke. 'The first blood on the road occurs *before* the rubber marks even appear.'

'You mean earlier in the vehicle's progress?'

'Indeed. So that means it hit her at forty miles per hour at least, maybe faster. You said you'd expect more leg trauma.'

'At that speed, I'd expect multiple fractures,' said Coyne, 'and severe internal and external bleeding. But there's another possibility.'

'Oh?'

'It might not have been the van that hit her at all,' said Coyne. 'The van could have been an innocent passer-by, who saw something and braked hard.'

'That doesn't fit our current intelligence,' said Jo. 'There's another thing though. You said Natalie had traces of ketamine hydrochloride in her lungs.'

'That's right.'

'Is it possible to knock someone out with that, say if it was ingested in liquid form?'

'I wouldn't advise drinking it,' said Coyne. 'Even a small dose could be fatal.'

'What if it was soaked in a rag?'

'You mean like chloroform, in the movies?'

'Exactly.'

Coyne paused. 'I'm probably not best qualified to answer. You should ask an anaesthetist.'

'But in your opinion?'

'Yes, I expect it would have a soporific, numbing effect, and in a large enough dose, or prolonged exposure, it would render a person unconscious.'

'Thank you, Dr Coyne. You've been very helpful.'

She got off the phone, and turned to Carrick. 'I don't think Natalie was a hit and run,' she said.

'No?'

'I think Pryce snatched her from somewhere between Jesus College and her home, incapacitated her with the same ketamine he used on me, then put her in his van.'

'So how did she end up in the river?'

'I think she woke up and panicked. I think she jumped from the moving vehicle. They have a door release from inside, right?'

He nodded.

Jo pointed at the diagram. 'She jumps here, where the first blood stain appears. He realises, brakes, and she comes to a stop around here, where the last blood was found. He's stopped further up, gets out and rushes back. She's trying to get away. She's suffering the come down of the ketamine, and a head injury. One way or another, she falls in.'

'Okay, it's a good theory.'

'But you know what it means if I'm right?' asked Jo. 'She wasn't there at random. He was taking her *somewhere*.'

Understanding dawned on Carrick's face. 'Somewhere that required him to use that road.'

Jo's eyes went immediately to the images of the girls sent to her mum's home, and specifically the iron pipework Carrick had thought was industrial. Only now she looked at it again, she knew at once it wasn't the case.

'Fuck,' said Jo. 'I think I know where.'

* * *

Carrick's speedometer touched one hundred and ten. With the head-start Pryce had got, it wouldn't be quick enough. An armed unit was coming too, and two squad cars, but they hadn't wanted to wait. They easily cut through the traffic on the A4074, and Jo caught glimpses of the drivers' astonished faces as they streaked past.

Not industrial pipework, but a radiator. One with a hefty, cast-iron column design. Maybe nineteenth century. Hard to imagine where it could be, except in a really old building. And that had been the clue. An old building that made sense of using the Little Baldon route.

It was a small clutch of buildings, not marked on her GPS, but clear on the map. Less than a kilometre from the Little Baldon bridge, shielded by trees on two sides, and gently sloping farmland on the others, labelled 'Prison (derelict)'.

Brookhampton Borstal, aka 'Buggers' Palace', where Harry Ferman had transported juvenile prisoners in the early years of his service.

They drove through the sleepy village of Little Baldon, slowing to eighty, then accelerated out the other side. Jo saw the column of smoke in the distance. Something that way was on fire.

'Oh no . . .'

* * *

She'd done everything she could. The fire engine was still eleven minutes out. AR unit six. Ambulances, she didn't know.

The road up to the former prison was a single track of tarmac, and when the austere building swung into view through the trees, there were flames coming through the ground floor windows right of the door. Brookhampton looked like a manor house designed with the intention of punishment; a symmetrical block of brown stone, with a neo-classical façade and two jutting wings. All of the tall windows were cracked or missing, and the outer walls had been redecorated with patches of graffiti. There was an old guard tower, and fence posts around the perimeter, circling a yard, but the fencing itself had been removed. Jo could almost imagine boys being marched outside by a drill-sergeant type – hair cropped close to their skulls, stripped of any innocence by the treatment they'd received in juvenile detention. The Borstal system had been abolished in the eighties, when politicians had finally accepted that the Victorian ethos of harsh discipline and borderline imprisonment and brutalisation of young offenders had no obvious benefit to them or to society.

Carrick pulled up twenty yards from the front of the building and they climbed out, rushing towards the scallop-shaped front steps. There was no sign of Pryce's car. Jo heard screams coming from inside at once.

'Bolt-cutters,' she said to Carrick, then she ran up steps, through the open door, onto bare floorboards. Apart from a few scattered chairs, there was no furniture. The walls were scarred with more spray-can daubings. Frayed electrical wiring hung from the ceiling where the light fittings had once been.

'Malin? Rita?' she called. Smoke hung in the air, not dense where she stood, but thickening. She could smell petrol. She moved from the vestibule along a wide corridor towards the threatening glow of the fire. 'Hello?'

'Upstairs!' called a voice. 'Please!'

Jo felt the temperature rising now, and turning a corner, saw flames licking up a wall and along the balustrade. She'd never been so close to a fire like this before, so fierce and chaotic. Her feet stopped of their own accord, as if every fibre of her being rejected her will to move forwards. Plastic was burning somewhere, rolling blacker, acrid smoke along the ceiling. She took off her coat and held it over her nose. The stairs were completely smoke-filled. It was impossible to see what was at the top. The heat prickled her skin. She'd seen the aftermath of house-fires before. Recovered the bodies of those caught unawares. They'd had a day's training with the fire service. The smoke could overcome you quicker than you'd think possible, confusing and disorientating as it diminished the oxygen in the blood and brain. She could feel it messing with her head already.

Carrick came along towards her, brandishing the cutters.

Suddenly part of the ceiling burst inwards, showering plaster and ash down onto the stairs. Jo shielded herself with her arms, and most of the pieces slid off. She smelled burning hair and brushed the cinders from her head. The next breath she took seemed to contain no oxygen at all and her windpipe tightened in reflexive protest. She pushed on up the stairs, finding a cleaner spot, and took a deep, instinctual breath. Mistake. It only made her cough even more. Carrick grabbed her and pushed her head down so that they were crawling. Jo had no idea if they'd be able to get down the same way they'd come up.

'Where are you?' she called.

She thought she heard a voice, but it was almost impossible to work out exactly where the sound was coming from. The smoke boiled, and the carpet had already burned away in patches. The heat felt like a hot shower on sunburn. Then Jo saw movement to the right, through a door. A person.

'Andy! In here!'

It looked like an old classroom, with tiers of roll-top desks. There was no fire, but plenty of smoke. Malin Sigurdsson lay on her side, completely still, arms trailing limply to the radiator. Rita Prakash was curled in a ball, her top pulled up to cover her face, but she lowered it to say. 'I think she's dead.'

No Sophie Okafor.

Carrick went to Malin first, and cut through the link in the cuffs. Malin's arms flopped.

'Get her out,' said Jo. She took the cutters and freed Rita, who jumped at her and clung on. 'It's okay. We're police. Where's Sophie?'

Rita wouldn't let go. 'He took her,' she said.

Carrick hoisted Malin into his arms and rushed out of the room.

'Are you sure?' asked Jo.

'I think so. He said he needed her.'

Jo had no time to process it. 'All right, let's get you out.'

She supported Rita from the room and blindly back towards the stairs. The smoke was making her feel dizzy, stinging her eyes so she could only open them briefly. She couldn't see Carrick at all. For the first time, she felt not just afraid, but in fear for her life.

A tremendous rumbling sound seemed to come from below, and the floor under their feet shook. Rita whimpered in her arms. Then Jo saw that the stairs had gone, collapsing into a twisted pile of flaming timbers. The heat and smoke that rose up was so great she stumbled back from the inferno.

'Is there another way out?' she asked.

'I don't know,' said Rita.

They hurried along the corridor, past the room where they'd been imprisoned, but it was a dead end. Jo had no sense of direction anymore. It didn't seem like a building at all, set out with any sort of logic. It seemed a labyrinth of fire. A hell.

In the distance, she heard the faintest sounds of sirens. Fire engines.

Hungry tongues of flames lapped along the ceiling towards them. There was a door to her left, but it seemed locked when she tried it. 'Let go of me a sec,' she said.

Rita didn't want to, but Jo forcefully detached her clinging fingers. Jo put her shoulder into the door, and it didn't budge. She slammed as hard as she could, and the pain almost made her knees crumple.

The smoke was thickening all the time, and she knew they didn't have long. 'Help, dammit!' she said. Rita threw her weight at the door too, with a similar result. 'We go at the same time,' Jo shouted. 'One . . . two . . . *three!*'

This time something crunched in Jo's shoulder, ligaments tearing or a bone slipping some way it shouldn't. For a few seconds she was completely frozen, the shoulder throbbing, before a choking cough racked her body and doubled her over. She could almost feel the smoke, coarse and deadly, flooding her airways like black cotton wool. Clogging her lungs. Rita, crying, slid down the door. 'We're going to die.'

'Not on my fucking watch,' Jo said. 'Out of the way.'

Rita stayed where she was, so Jo grabbed her arm and pulled her roughly aside. She took a step back and aimed a foot at the lock, cradling her injured shoulder. Basic training, years ago. The key was momentum, a good run up, using all your weight, your hips. And not to aim at the door, but to visualise a point eighteen inches on the other side. She remembered the tactical instructor well – muscles on muscles. He looked like he could have kicked over a tank, Ben had said.

She lifted her foot and drove every ounce of power through the heel, right beside the keyhole.

She barely felt any resistance at all and the door flew open. Rita looked amazed, whimpering as she hurried through. There was an office on the other side, with empty shelves, grey filing cabinets, a sink in the corner and a rather grand desk under a single, intact sash window. Jo went straight to the window, tried to hoist it up, but it was painted shut. Of course it was. But single-pane. She bent her arm, told Rita to stand back, and drove her elbow into the centre. It shattered into large segments. Jo stood on the desk and kicked out the rest with her feet. Looking down, she saw they were right over the steps leading to the front entrance. She could see Malin, lying on an ambulance stretcher, Carrick looking up. The other units were there too.

Smoke flooded out behind her. The ground looked a long way down.

'Get the van underneath,' shouted Carrick to the ARU.

The van manoeuvred into position, but it could only get so close to the front of the building because of the steps. She couldn't lower Rita down. 'We'll have to jump,' she said. It looked like twenty feet plus.

'I can't,' said Rita. 'It's too far.'

The fire was coming through the door like a living thing, searching for them. Carrick and the AR team spread out around the van. 'We'll go together,' said Jo, taking Rita's hand.

'No . . .' She pulled back.

'Trust me,' said Jo. 'I've not gone through the last few days to die in here.'

Rita looked momentarily confused, and the resistance in her grip vanished. Jo took the chance and pulled the girl with her, leaping out. Rita screamed, and the pull of gravity was sickening.

It *was* too far, and as their feet slammed down on the roof of the van, pain shot through Jo's knee. Rita went forwards, Jo to the side. She slid off the back of the van, lifting her hands to break her fall. But she fell into bodies, and they caught her before she hit the paving stones. As she found her feet, Rita was sobbing in the arms of one of the armed squad.

Jo staggered, then limped, reeling back from Carrick. 'Malin?'

'They're trying to stabilise her,' he said.

'He's still got Sophie.'

She hobbled towards the car. Her knee kept buckling.

'Jo, stop!' said Carrick. 'We need to regroup.'

'He'll kill her.'

'Wait, are you Josie Masters?' said Rita quietly. She pulled away from the officer, her cheeks streaked with ash, and reached into her pocket. 'He said, if you made it, to give you this.' She pulled out a phone. 'He made me memorise the code – it's one two zero three.'

Jo took it, and entered the numbers. She went through to the contacts, but there were no numbers stored. Nothing in the call logs or messages either.

Come on, you sick fuck. What are you waiting for?

Chapter 30

Malin Sigurdsson was taken away in the ambulance, breathing but unconscious. From what Rita told them while the paramedics checked her over, it sounded like the girl from Oriel was suffering severe dehydration and starvation. Pryce hadn't fed either of them, and the only moisture they'd managed to get was from licking condensation where it collected on the windowsill.

The fire service was still struggling to get control of the conflagration, even with three engines, and didn't want to enter the building because of the obvious structural risk. Their shouted communication and the thump of jetted water on masonry soon receded into the background. Jo had written off finding anything of use inside anyway. The paramedics wanted to check her over, but Jo told them it could wait until after she'd spoken to Rita.

'It's really important, Rita,' she said. 'Did he say anything at all about where he might be taking Sophie?'

'I'm sorry, he didn't. He barely spoke to us at all.'

She told them everything she could, but there wasn't much they didn't know or Jo hadn't guessed. Pryce had pushed her off her bike in the alleyway before her army fitness class, and used something to knock her out. She'd woken in the van, watched over by some guy in a balaclava, and screamed her head off until he pointed a gun at her. When Pryce had let her out, it was at the Borstal, and he'd secured her next to Malin, then left, returning the next day with Sophie. She had a similar story too – snatched by the man with the balaclava, with Pryce the driver. A two-man job.

The three girls had no idea why they were there – all the psycho had told them was that his name was Jack, and it was all for Josie. Only Sophie had seen the other man without his balaclava and she said he was horribly deformed.

'We tried to keep each other's spirits up,' said Rita. 'We talked about trying to escape. Malin thought she could get the cuffs off if she dislocated her thumb, but she passed out with the pain. Then we tried to wrench the radiator off the wall.'

Later, they wondered if they could tempt Jack close enough and incapacitate him, but by then Malin was too weak, and Sophie too scared. They'd offered Pryce money, given him the numbers of their parents, but he wasn't interested. Malin started sleeping for long periods and even when she was awake she'd stopped making much sense. When she got delirious she kept talking about a girl called Anna.

'She was worried that something had happened to her,' said Rita.

When Pryce had returned today, she could tell something had happened. He'd seemed more animated. Rita had thought he might actually let them go, even when he started spreading petrol. It was only when he took Sophie and she heard the engine of his van that it really sank in that he was going to kill them.

She broke down in sobs again, and threw her arms around Jo. 'Thank you,' she said, over and over again.

Carrick held out his phone to her. 'I've got your parents, Rita. They know you're safe.'

As the young woman took the phone, Jo turned away to give her some privacy.

'How's the shoulder?' asked Carrick.

Jo pulled aside her top with her good hand. The joint was swollen, already bruising, and she couldn't lift her arm above neck height. 'Pretty fucked,' she said.

'I'll drop you at the hospital if you want?'

The phone rang. *Unknown*. They could still trace it later, even if they couldn't call back.

'Hello, Josie,' said Pryce.

His voice was the same, but not. He sounded like a different person entirely. 'Where's Sophie?'

'She's with me,' he said.

'What do you want?'

'You still don't understand, do you? I shouldn't be surprised, but I'll admit it's a tad disappointing.'

'I have no fucking clue why you're doing this.'

'You will,' he said. 'We'll speak soon, Josie.'

'No, wait—'

The line went dead.

Chapter 31

Rita Prakash was reunited with her mother and father at St Aldates. There were floods of tears. Nabil arrived shortly after, too. After a tense stand-off, a family liaison officer ushered them into one of the interview rooms. Jo let the paramedics look at her injuries in the CID room. They reckoned the knee was a torn ligament. They strapped it heavily as she sat at her desk. Her left shoulder they put in a sling. The phone from Pryce didn't leave her hand the whole time.

Heidi was sorting the trace on the unknown number, but even with the best will in the world, it looked like it would be twelve hours until they could get a result. And if Pryce had been willing to leave Malin and Rita in a burning building, Sophie Okafor might not have that long. The Armed Unit remained on standby.

Dimitriou continued to monitor the ANPR network, in case Pryce's car appeared, though no one at St Aldates held great hopes that it would. Thc TV was on, showing aerial footage of the smoking school in Little Baldon. The press were fully briefed on the current state of play. Two girls rescued, one still missing. Pryce's picture was circulating. DCI Stratton hadn't come off the phone for more than a few seconds at a time. There was a continuous comms link open with Thames Valley Central Command in Kidlington.

Word came from the hospital in the early afternoon that Malin Sigurdsson was conscious and talking, with her mother Hana at her side. Nicholas Cranleigh gave an interview on the news, thanking the police, but calling already for an investigation. Heidi wondered aloud if he'd still be on Stratton's Christmas list after all this was said and done.

As the world swirled around her, Jo stared at the phone. Creasey, the Bath detective, had it wired up to a console, ready to track any incoming call. Jo willed it to ring. Pryce held all the cards, because he had the only thing that mattered now – a terrified teenage girl.

Stein drifted in, drinking a cup of tea, and holding another, which he placed on the corner of her desk.

'Why isn't he calling?' Jo asked.

'This whole enterprise has been about bringing you pain,' said the profiler. 'I wouldn't expect him to stop now.'

Jo had to ask. 'Do you think he'll kill her?'

Stein slurped. 'I think the only thing that's stopping him is that it will mean an end to your suffering.'

Jo shook her head. 'I just don't understand. Jack's been in the force for seven years. His father was police too. He's put criminals away. We've looked at his career records and there's no hint of corruption. Nothing iffy at all.'

Carrick came past holding a folder. 'We have found something, though. Those prison visitor records came through for Tyndle. Guess who went to see him twice in the lead-up to his release?'

'Jack?'

'That's right.'

'So did they know each other?'

'That's not clear. But we spoke to a former boss of Jack's,

who wrote his principal reference before he enrolled with the Met's fast-track recruitment programme. He told us Pryce suffered a really bad period, a couple of years into his employment. Took three months off work for bereavement. His partner killed herself.'

Jo felt light-headed. 'So, nine years ago?'

'Indeed,' said Carrick.

The truth hit her like a sudden, unexpected gust on a calm day, throwing her bearings into disarray.

One two zero three.

The 12th March.

'You okay, Jo?' said Carrick. 'You've gone white as a sheet.'

The moment of dizziness passed, and she was steady again. But the outlook had completely changed.

'I know why all of this is happening,' she whispered.

* * *

The leaflets she'd been given, when she'd lost her own child the Christmas before, said it was common to blame yourself at first. Mistakes of diet, strenuous activity, even mental health, were all explanations grieving mothers reached for to explain the inexplicable. But there was no compelling evidence that any of those things could harm a foetus in the womb. The fact was, around a third of conceived embryos were simply unviable, and the human body was a finely tuned machine. It wasn't Mother Nature being ruthless; there was no moral component – it was inexorable biological imperative.

But in Jack Pryce's case, the violent death of his unborn baby on the 12th March, ten years earlier, had been eminently avoidable. The course of action leading to it had been painstakingly recorded in a coroner's narrative verdict, a set of decisions by other characters that day: Frank Tyndle, P1 and P2, aka

Benjamin Coombs and Josephine Masters. And what had been officially deemed a tragedy in the final act for those individuals – the end of a police chase in which a foetus had died in utero, for Jack Pryce it was just the first shocking scene, the inciting incident of a horror story that had claimed his fiancée as well.

Jo wondered how he'd persuaded Tyndle to help. Had he even told him that he was the partner of the woman in the ambulance that had overturned? Lizzie was her name, Carrick told them after searching out the files. Lizzie Mackintosh, soon to be Lizzie Pryce. When Jo and Ben's lives had moved on, Jack and Lizzie's hadn't. They'd remained trapped in a hell of grief that Lizzie had seen only one way to escape. A hell partly of Jo's making. Or at least that's what Pryce clearly believed. Cause and effect. Sin, and punishment to be exacted. He, the one to exact it.

A quick check of his record confirmed it. He'd joined the police around a year after his fiancée killed herself. Had he joined the police for that purpose, to get at her, and for that purpose alone? It was almost unfathomable. Maybe at first he'd actually wanted to do good, as he'd claimed in the car to her. But it couldn't be a coincidence that he'd asked to transfer just after the Dylan Jones case. Seeing her name in the paper – seeing her celebrated as a child's *saviour* – it must have been too much. She wondered who it was who'd scratched her face out in all those images. Maybe Stein was right, and the real psychopath wasn't Tyndle at all. It might have been Jack Pryce who couldn't bear to look at her.

The phone was ringing, and the other detectives gathered round, with the Chief Constable too. Jo answered it on speaker.

Pryce's voice filled the room. 'Hello, Josie. Worked it all out yet?'

'Yes,' she said, her own voice hoarse. 'I understand now, Jack. You don't have to hurt Sophie.'

'Are you telling me what to do, Josie?'

'I'm just saying, she's done nothing wrong.'

He laughed. 'Neither had my fiancée.'

'Jack, it's me you want, isn't it? Let Sophie go, and you can have me.'

'How did I know you'd say that?'

'It's the only way this ends,' said Jo. 'They'll lock you up, but at least you'll have killed me.'

They hadn't had time to rehearse any of it, but no one interrupted.

For a long time, Pryce was quiet. 'Perhaps you're right,' he said at last. 'I assume you're tracing the call?'

Stratton shook his head.

'Yes,' she said. The DCI scowled.

'Come alone, Josie,' said Pryce. 'I mean that. You'll understand, I'm not planning much after today, so if I have to kill Sophie, I'll do it in a second.'

'I'll come alone, I promise. Can I speak to Sophie please?'

'Be here in an hour. I'll be waiting.'

He hung up.

Everyone was looking at her.

'Why did you tell him about the trace?' asked the DCI.

'Because he's not a fucking idiot,' said Jo.

'Looks like he's in the village of Little Pelham,' said Nina Creasey. 'Tiny place. It's about five miles away.'

'Get the armed response team out there,' said the Chief Constable.

'No,' said Jo. 'He'll kill her.'

'She could be dead already,' said Stratton.

'And if you send in the AR, she'll be dead for certain.'

'You can't go in alone,' said Carrick. 'He's got a gun.'

'There's no other way,' said Jo. And really, there wasn't.

* * *

People crowded back into the briefing room. Twenty minutes had passed already. It would take fifteen to get to Little Pelham. As well as Stratton and the CID team, plus the two detectives from Bath, there were five armed response officers and their sergeant, Menzies, plus the Chief Constable, and six uniformed officers. The windows were misted with the heat from all the bodies.

Carrick displayed the satellite map on the screen, and pointed to a small clutch of buildings on the west bank of the Thames. 'Little Pelham.'

'Why there?' said Stratton.

'The call's been traced to the church,' said Heidi. 'It's unmanned in the week – the local vicar is based in Dorchester, so it's a chaplain who takes the Sunday service. We can get a key.'

'It's quiet,' said Carrick. 'It might be one of the places he scouted when he was looking for somewhere to keep the girls. The good news is there's no way he can get away. One road in, one out.'

Sergeant Menzies spoke up. 'What about civilians, local residents?'

Carrick pointed to what looked like a manor house beside the church. 'This whole complex is the office of an environmental charity, Oxford Green. We've put in a call, and told them to get staff to a safe location. All fourteen are accounted for, and are currently in the cellars. The next nearest house is three hundred yards away. We couldn't ask for a better location.'

'We could get a couple of men into the upper floors of the house,' said Menzies. 'And maybe approach the graveyard from the north. It looks like there's decent tree cover.'

Jo spoke up. 'If he sees you, he'll kill her.'

'He won't see us,' said Menzies, grim-faced.

'You can't be sure about that. He's been a step ahead from

the start. He knows our procedures. And he's a triple murderer now. One more body won't give him much pause.'

'I'm inclined to agree with Detective Masters,' said Stein. 'He may have selected a graveyard for poetic reasons.'

'Poetic reasons?' said Menzies, with a barely concealed sneer.

'I mean he might not be planning to leave at all,' said the profiler.

'Respectfully,' said Menzies. 'If this guy's as crazy as it seems, the only way to stop him is a bullet in the head.'

'You're not going to have to face Sophie Okafor's mum,' said Jo. 'Sometimes it's more complicated than kicking down doors and spraying bullets.'

The Chief Constable stood up. 'All right. Enough. Menzies, keep your men away from the church-side of the building. We've no idea where exactly Pryce will be when we get there. And without seeing what's on the ground, we don't know what the line of sight will be like between the house and the church. Jo, we'll put a wire on you. Any chance you get, let us know the geography, and any safe ways to approach.'

'If he sees an earpiece . . .'

'We'll keep comms one-way. You won't be able to hear us, but we'll hear you through a mic.'

'He'll shoot her as soon as she's in sight,' said Carrick.

'I suggest we put her in a vest,' said Menzies. 'If he shoots and misses, or shoots non-lethally, we might have time to swoop in and end it.'

'Agreed,' said the Chief Constable. 'Are you sure about this, Jo? We can't force you.'

Jo felt the eyes of the room on her. She owed it to them. She owed it to Natalie Palmer. Maybe she even owed it to Pryce himself.

'I made a promise,' she said.

As the room broke up, she went back to her desk. Lucas had texted again.

Please. Let's talk. I don't want to lose you, Jo.

She wasn't going to reply, but as her eyes fell over the open files littering the CID work station, they fell on the coroner's report on Pryce's fiancée, Lizzie – she'd cut her wrists in the bath. Jo wondered if she'd actually said goodbye, and if it had been Jack who found her.

She texted back. *I'll call later.*

Menzies brought her a bulky vest similar to the ones his team wore. She'd worn one before, on raids, but this seemed very different. In those cases she'd never believed there was an actual bullet with her name on it.

Stein was hovering. 'You know, I admire you for what you're doing.'

'Tell me, honestly, do you think he'll let her go?'

'The endgame's approaching. We've only got pawns. Our position is weak.'

Menzies clipped the straps of the vest, and tightened the straps. As he did so, Jo had an idea. 'Not if we cheat.'

Stein smiled. 'It's hard to cheat at chess.'

Jo looked at Menzies' side-arm. 'What if I'm not a pawn?'

* * *

Jo drove slowly into the sleepy village of Little Pelham, between the denuded and tangled hedgerows iced with frost. If it weren't for the occasion, it would have been picture-perfect. Her knee was throbbing, despite the painkillers, and she'd ditched the sling to give herself a fraction more mobility. The vest she wore was level II body armour – it would stop a low-calibre round, and from what Rita had said, Pryce only had a handgun.

'No sign of anything so far,' she said.

'I'm one hundred metres from the house with the AR team,' said Carrick through the car's speakers. 'Awaiting confirmation that we can approach.'

The armed unit had parked a mile outside the village, proceeding on foot via the bridleway. Jo passed the entrance to Oxford Green, and could see the spire of the church. Between the two was a small copse of bare trees.

'You should be able to come into the house from the rear,' she said. They'd pick up her voice through the phone on the passenger seat, and the microphone she wore just under her collar. 'But I'm not sure you'll get a view on the church.'

'Understood,' said Carrick. 'I'll tell Menzies to get men in position on the upper floors.'

Jo pulled up about fifty metres from the church.

'Getting out now,' she said.

'Good luck, Jo,' said Carrick. 'Remember, we're not far away.'

But not close enough, thought Jo. *I'm on my own from here.*

She left her phone on the seat, took the one from Pryce and shoved it in her back pocket. Despite the cold, she was sweating as she walked with a limp towards the lychgate, eyes scanning the trees and the graveyard beyond for any sign of movement. She had no idea if Pryce was a good shot or not. His file didn't indicate any firearms training at all, but hitting anything with a handgun at more than twenty yards was unlikely without serious skills. If he was waiting, close by and with a very good aim, she might not feel anything at all. Might not even hear the gun go off. It was a fucked-up thought, and doubly fucked-up that it might be her last.

The church was Anglo-Saxon – a squat, square tower at one end. The iron-strapped wooden doors that filled the archway were closed. The graves were mostly a collection of stubby headstones, many at angles and mottled with age, their inscriptions illegible. But around the far side of the church, hidden from the windows of the manor house, stood some more ornate sarcophagi which she guessed were Victorian from their elaborate statuary – weeping angels and ornate floral carvings. Poetic, indeed.

The stained-glass windows were dull and completely opaque under the wintry sky. If he was watching her from inside, she'd never be able to tell.

'I'm here!' she called. 'Jack?'

A light breeze carried the vapour from her breath up into the spindly branches of a beech tree. The cold swallowed her words without echo. The seconds passed. Nothing moved in the churchyard. The adrenalin seeped slowly, unlocking her limbs and leaving her shivering.

'Jack?' she called again. 'Sophie?'

Still nothing.

'I don't think he's here,' she muttered. With the relief came profound, almost painful disappointment. Maybe he'd had second thoughts, or something had gone wrong. Maybe he was still playing the game. If he wasn't here, for whatever reason, that only augured badly for Sophie.

In her back pocket, the phone vibrated. She took it out.

'In the church,' said Pryce. 'Side door.'

'Is Sophie—?'

He hung up.

'He wants me to enter the church,' she whispered for the mic. 'I'll confirm if he's inside.'

She walked around the curved wall of the chancel, following a gravel path. She found the wooden door ajar. It was barely five and half feet high, and she had to stoop to enter. It opened straight into the nave.

Sophie Okafor was sitting in the front pew, perfectly erect, trembling in her school hockey kit. One knee was covered in dried blood, and a tight gag cut into the sides of her mouth.

In the gloom of the unlit interior, the whites of her terrified eyes were the brightest thing. Pryce sat directly behind her. His right hand held a gun at the base of her neck, but he was looking Jo up and down.

She was caught for a moment in the memory of kissing him, and had to swallow back a retch.

'It's going to be all right, Sophie,' said Jo. 'My name is Jo Masters, and I'm a detective with Thames Valley—'

'She knows who you are,' said Pryce. 'I've told her all about you.' He pulled out the gag. 'Tell her, Soph.'

'Please . . .' said Sophie. 'Please let me go.'

'Why don't we send Sophie outside?' said Jo. Even if the team hadn't heard Pryce's voice, they'd know he was present now. 'I've come, just like you asked.'

'Alone?' said Pryce. 'Or is that big old building opposite full of armed police? I don't think the DCI would let his most celebrated detective come all the way out here on her own.'

'Notorious might be a better description,' said Jo. 'I really don't think Stratton gave a fuck. I'm on my own.'

If she ran at him now, he'd have to turn the gun on her. He'd get one shot off for sure. If it missed, she could reach him. If Sophie had it in her, she could get out.

A lot of *ifs*.

She took a step forward, and the barrel was on her in a fraction of a second.

'Don't be silly, Jo,' he said. 'That vest might stop one bullet, but you won't be running anywhere afterwards.'

She couldn't move. Fear made her legs like jelly. Jo was fairly certain the gun was a Glock. Ten rounds, if fully loaded. Plenty to kill both of them several times over.

'Enough people have died,' she said.

He laughed suddenly. 'That's rich, considering. Enough for whom?'

'Enough to prove your point,' said Jo. 'You've won. You're better than me. I'm finished.'

'Move away from the door. Towards the altar.' He waved the gun.

Jo did as he said. 'Jack, you don't need to hurt her. You're not a child-killer.'

Pryce grabbed Sophie's hair, yanking her to her feet. She wailed, twisting painfully in his grip. He put the gun into her back. Jo worried the AR team would hear and decide to move.

'It's okay,' she said, to them as much as Sophie. 'We'll get you out of here.'

'It won't be me that's killed her,' said Pryce. He kept Sophie close to him, gun tight into her ribs, as he dragged her towards the door.

'Don't . . . please,' said the girl. She stumbled and tripped, almost falling but he caught her and hauled her with him. He kept his eyes on Jo as they reached the door. 'Outside,' he said to Jo, then he went through the door. She followed, teeth gritted against the pain in her knee. Back in the open air, they moved around the chancel. 'Keep your fucking distance,' he said.

Sophie's eyes were pleading as he marched her across the graveyard, past the weeping stone angels. Jo cast a glance back to the manor house. Too many trees. No clear line of sight for Menzies' snipers, even if they were in position. Still she prayed for the crack of a shot.

Pryce pushed Sophie to the ground. She was sobbing. 'You can't. You can't. I need to see my mum. You can't . . .'

Jo ran to her side, putting her body in between the gun and the girl.

The veins on Pryce's head were unnatural. Demonic. The man she'd worked with – cool, collected, in control – was gone completely.

‘Turn around, Jo. Take a look.’

She did as he said, and saw a modest, newer headstone, made of speckled white marble.

Elizabeth Mackintosh, 1986-2010. Taken from us too soon.

‘Jack, I’m sorry,’ she said, turning back to him.

‘Look at it!’ he shouted. ‘Look at it or I’ll shoot you in the fucking face!’

She turned her head.

‘Jack, I didn’t know about Lizzie. I never knew.’

He moved quickly, rushing towards her, and grabbing her hair. The gun was pressed into the side of her head so hard she thought it might crack her skull. Sophie was whimpering.

Run! thought Jo. *Just run, you stupid girl.* Pryce’s voice hissed in her ear. ‘Of course you didn’t know, you fucking bitch. You and that corrupt fuck of a boyfriend walked off into the fucking sunset, didn’t you?’ He thrust her forward onto the ground, and spat a gobbet of warm spit into her hair. ‘Didn’t you?’ he yelled. He lifted the gun to hit her with the butt end, but then backed off towards Sophie once more.

Jo let the spit run down her neck.

‘I did my best afterwards,’ said Pryce, talking almost to himself. ‘I read books, so many fucking *books*. We went to grief counselling. There are plenty of *resources* you can access, you know? Groups where people talk about their miscarriages and their dead children. But we were a bit too hardcore for them. I mean, come *on*, we had the best fucking sob story of the lot. Our kid wasn’t ill, wasn’t some clump of fucking cells.’ He winced, pressing the gun’s hilt to his temple as if to still the raging thoughts inside his skull. ‘She was ready. She was *beautiful*. I was at the hospital waiting for the ambulance. An hour later, I’d have *held* her. Do you have any fucking idea how that feels, to think you’re an hour from holding your baby and then they hand her to you and she’s fucking dead?’

Jo could only shake her head. 'Jack, I'm sorry,' she said.

The horror fell from his face, and his eyes were cold in an instant. 'You know, that's exactly what Tyndle said. He had no clue either. He was so happy to help. So happy to get his own back on the woman who left him looking like that. Thought it was just a fun game. Take a few girls, demand the ransom. Thought we were going to get rich, the thick bastard.' He smiled, nodding. 'But I let him know, right as I cut him. I let him fucking know.'

Sophie was watching, eyes agog. As Pryce talked, Jo went over the possibilities. If she could get to him now – get him on the ground – she'd have a chance. She just had to distract him for long enough.

'What was her name, Jack?'

'*What?*' he said.

'Your little girl? We called ours Madeleine.'

Pryce's face twisted and he lifted his arms to his face, looking like he might throw up. Jo launched herself at him, eyes only on the gun, and her hands closed over his wrist.

'Run!' she shouted to Sophie.

Jack wrenched her backwards with him, twisting the gun, and she lost her grip. With a flailing arm, he caught her across the side of the head. She heard a bang and at the same time her whole body spun around.

She found herself lying on her back. Sophie hadn't moved and was pressing herself against another headstone, hyperventilating. Jo's vest was hitched up to her neck, and she saw smoke rising from the front. Pryce stared at her, a look of utter amazement on his face, then lifted the gun and fired again. For a moment, Jo thought he'd missed, but then there was pain unlike anything she'd thought possible, ripping through her stomach – sharp, like a lance of red-hot metal. Which seemed strange, because there was nothing sticking into her. There was a weight on her stomach, spreading through her hips and thighs like someone was sitting on her middle. And it seeped up under the vest too, making it hard to breathe. She reached down to her lower abdomen as Pryce walked over to her.

Her fingers came away bloody.

He shot me. I've been shot.

She knew she didn't have long at all – each breath was harder than the last. Her fingers slipped over the clasps of the vest, unhooking the bottom ones.

'You're dying, Jo,' said Pryce, coming closer, eyes fixed on hers. 'Look at me, Jo. There's a bullet in your guts. You're dying.'

I know I'm fucking dying.

God! Why couldn't she breathe? The pain was going, but she felt like someone had driven a lance through her belly and skewered her into the ground.

'Tell me how it feels,' said Pryce.

Jo had pins and needles in her fingers as she scrabbled with the second set of catches. She had to get the vest off.

Pryce leant closer. 'Please tell me. Does it hurt?'

The catches came loose. As they did, the gun she'd secreted underneath fell to the ground at her hip. Pryce saw it as she grabbed it. The hilt was warm from her body. She brought it around, and for a second his eyes flared with fear, followed by a sort of admiration. She pulled the trigger and the kick-back was astonishing, jolting the gun from her hand. Pryce staggered backwards, clutching the right side of his chest, as blood, thick and tinged almost black, bubbled over his fingers.

'I'm sorry,' said Jo, almost by instinct.

Pryce, still standing, lifted the Glock to point at Sophie's head. 'Go fuck yourself,' he replied.

'No . . .' said Jo, reaching out. She heard a soft *pop*, and the side of Pryce's face blew apart, spattering the gravestones beside him with lumps of pale meat. He stood upright for what seemed an age before falling sideways. Sophie's mouth opened wide.

Jo heard male voices, shouting, and a screaming that didn't stop. She lay back, sapped of strength, a dead weight. The sky above was darker than it should be, unless she'd got the hours all wrong and night was falling already. It darkened further as she watched, closing in from the sides, until there was just a small circle of white, crisscrossed with black branches. Then it was a face. Andy Carrick's face.

'Keep your eyes open,' he said. 'Stay awake.'

She knew what he was saying, but she really didn't want to. After the day she'd had, going to sleep felt like just the right thing to do.

Epilogue

It was Carly who'd persuaded her to give Lucas another shot, and they were taking it slowly. Moving back in seemed a way off, for sure, but the few meetings they'd had on neutral turf had been amicable, even fond. Harry Ferman had tentatively said he thought it was a good idea too – that she'd always seemed happiest when talking about Lucas. And even when Jo had told him the full story of how Lucas's marriage had failed, he'd still refused to condemn. 'Everyone deserves a second chance,' he'd said.

As for Lucas himself, he poured it all out. How his drinking had been heavy before the kids even came along, but had only got worse, as had the lengths he had gone to, to conceal it from his family and colleagues. It had come to a head when he'd pulled out at a junction after picking the kids up from school following a few pints in the pub. He'd managed to give his details to the other driver at the scene, but Carly had known straight away. She could smell it on him. She'd given him an ultimatum to stop, or she'd take the kids away. He'd promised he would, and then broken that promise almost at once, totalling the car a week later near their house. This time, thankfully, the kids hadn't been in it. Carly had taken the blame for the crash, but thrown Lucas out. From that point he'd got worse, until eventually a hospital admission after a three-day bender, and a referral to an abstinence clinic had helped him turn a corner. Six months later, he'd re-established contact with his family, and begun the long, slow process of proving himself to them by working and staying sober. By then, Carly had understandably moved on.

Jo still wasn't sure why he'd never told her. She *thought* she'd have understood and given him a chance. After all, there were plenty of coppers with similar substance problems. She wasn't naïve. Lucas said he'd thought about telling her lots of times. Bob Whittaker, the head gardener, was an addict too – they'd met at AA – and he'd often urged Lucas to come clean. But he'd just been so scared it would mess things up. He figured that Jo had probably had to deal with drunks so often in her line of work that knowing she had a potential one for a boyfriend would be too much. Especially after Ben, and *his* demons.

At their last meeting, a winter walk along the canal, they made a pact. A fresh start. No more lies.

As Jo parked up in the hospital car park, she told herself the story she was spinning down the phone now didn't count.

'It's just a check-up,' she said. 'I don't need hand-holding.'

'Okay,' replied Lucas, 'but call me afterwards.'

Jo grimaced as she climbed out of the car, and a groan escaped her lips. Even now, six weeks after the shooting, it still felt like she'd been kicked in the chest by a mule. Though the second bullet had potentially been lethal, it was the first bullet, the one stopped by the vest, that had given her the most pain. There wasn't much they could do for a cracked sternum, except advise bed-rest. And she'd had quite enough of that.

The automatic doors swished open, delivering a blast of heat from above. At the reception desk, the partner of a heavily pregnant woman was filling in a form. Jo waited for her turn, then gave her details.

'Waiting room 2b,' said the receptionist. 'Go to the end of the corridor, turn right, and there are some chairs.'

Jo followed the receptionist's instructions, past various consultation suites, blood rooms, and offices. She sipped the water bottle nervously, though her bladder was close to bursting already. There was one other woman sitting waiting, with a toddler on his hands and knees, pushing a toy car around on the floor.

Jo smiled at her as she took her seat.

She'd had about enough of hospitals. They'd kept her in for four days after the shooting, three in intensive care, then moved her to another ward for monitoring and convalescence. The first few hours were a complete blur as they pumped her full of morphine. Paul and Amelia said they'd visited, but Jo couldn't remember it at all. The second bullet had passed straight through the soft tissue of her insides, narrowly missing her spine. They'd had to remove a length of her small intestine in emergency surgery and stem the internal bleeding, but by all accounts, as the doctor had said, she had been lucky. Very lucky indeed.

When the team had come to visit on the second day, Dimitriou had asked afterwards if they'd let her keep the bullet.

'Why the fuck would she want that?' Heidi had said. She'd come to visit two days shy of her due date. 'To put under her pillow for the bullet fairy?'

'For posterity,' said Dimitriou. 'I would.'

Jo assumed they'd taken it for evidence, along with the one embedded in the vest. The internal inquiry into Pryce's death would be long and drawn out, no doubt. Putting together the chain of events by which he managed to kidnap four young women while employed by Thames Valley Police, deceiving a team of presumably seasoned detectives, would be embarrassing. Questions would be asked about how his personal history had been overlooked in the recruitment process, or deemed to be non-relevant. Carrick had taken Jo over the initial findings already. At the stage Pryce had applied to join the police, his academic record was exemplary. He seemed to be just what the police force needed – young, passionate, driven. He'd been on anti-anxiety medicine for several years though, in increasing doses, and it looked likely that he was self-medicating too. The scariest thing for Jo was that he'd applied to move to Avon and Somerset a year ago, when Jo was still based there, but there hadn't been a vacancy. If he *had* transferred then, she wondered how things might have panned out. The thought was sobering. Perhaps Ben would still be alive, and she would be dead.

A petite, very young nurse in a pristine white uniform came along the corridor.

'Josephine Masters?'

Jo stood up and followed her into a small room, with a semi-reclined medical couch in the centre, a spotlight on an articulated stand, and a bulky monitor and console.

'My name is Yolanda, and I'm going to be carrying out your sonogram,' said the woman. She went through Jo's details, then asked her to hop onto the bed. Jo took off her coat and hung it over the single chair, presumably for partners, then got on.

'Swing your legs up for me,' said the sonographer, 'and pull up your top.'

Jo did so, revealing the lower tide-mark of green bruising from her breastbone, and the two scars, almost healed, across her belly. The nurse raised her eyebrows.

'Would you believe, someone shot me?' said Jo. 'They missed the important parts, though.'

The nurse frowned, clearly struggling to work out if Jo was

attempting a joke. 'I thought your name rang a bell. You're the detective with Thames Valley Police.'

Jo smiled.

'Gosh.' She picked up a tube. 'Well, normally I warn people this is going to be cold, but you're probably tough enough. Can you pull your underwear down a tad too, please?' Jo obeyed. The sonographer squeezed out clear cool gel across Jo's stomach, then used the end of the ultrasound scanner to smear it across Jo's skin.

'When was your last period?'

Jo told her the date, roughly seven and a half weeks ago. It was early for a scan, but they were taking extra precautions given what Jo had endured.

On the screen, black shapes flitted about, speckled with static. Jo had no idea what she was looking at, but the sonographer watched intently, moving the scanner back and forth. She focused on a small, shapeless patch of white.

She smiled. 'There you are!'

Jo craned her neck. She'd done more pregnancy tests than she could count, but she needed someone else to see it too – to prove it to herself. 'Is everything okay?'

'Looks absolutely fine. I just need to take some measurements.'

Jo kept her eyes on the screen as the sonographer moved a cursor over the screen, snapping free-frames, and making notes by hand. 'Your baby is in the normal range we'd expect for that gestation.'

The tears came from nowhere, fast and heavy. 'I'm sorry.'

'Don't be.' The sonographer handed her a tissue. 'Everyone cries the first time.'

Jo didn't correct her. Madeleine must have been buried in the records somewhere. In fact, the last time she'd been in a room like this would have been almost exactly a year ago, holding Ben's hand as a different sonographer told them the bad news – that despite all the positive tests they'd done at home, their child had stopped growing at around nine weeks and showed no signs of life.

'Is it really okay? No problems at all?'

'Absolutely. Because of your age, we'll want to bring you in for regular scans.'

'Of course.'

'Would you like to hear the heartbeat?'

'Can I?'

'It's not normally something we do at this stage, but given everything this little one's been through, it only seems right. Just lie back and relax.'

Jo lay her head down and looked at the ceiling. In a few seconds a soft, rapid, rhythmic squishing sound came through the speakers.

'It's fast!'

'Quite normal,' said the sonographer.

Jo wiped her belly clean with another cloth, pulled down her top and put her coat back on. The sonographer gave her a piece of folded card with the sonograph image inside.

'Thank you,' said Jo. 'For everything.'

She left the consulting room feeling like a different person entirely from the one who had gone in. She went to the toilet to empty her full bladder. At the reception, she handed over the form, making another appointment for the twelve-week scan.

'Congratulations, Ms Masters,' said the receptionist. She looked at the screen. 'We only have one contact number here. Is there another – just in case? The baby's father, perhaps?'

Jo smiled. 'I'll give you my brother, if that's all right.'

Back in the car park, she looked at the black and white image.

She'd read up as soon as she first suspected she might be pregnant on paternity testing in utero, worried that the only methods were invasive and risky. But there were other ways. Bright Futures would do it, though she would need samples of the potential father's DNA.

Or only Lucas's, she surmised. Because if his didn't match, there was only one other possibility.

She made the decision then and there not to find out. She touched her stomach with her fingertips.

'The two of us have survived enough already, don't you think?'

Love Josie Masters? Then why not go back to where it all began?

Available in all good bookshops now.